THE DEAD
SHALL NOT REST

Books by Tessa Harris

THE ANATOMIST'S APPRENTICE

THE DEAD SHALL NOT REST

Published by Kensington Publishing Corporation

THE DEAD SHALL NOT REST

A DR. THOMAS SILKSTONE MYSTERY

TESSA HARRIS

KENSINGTON BOOKS
www.kensingtonbooks.com

KENSINGTON BOOKS are published by

Kensington Publishing Corp.
119 West 40th Street
New York, NY 10018

All Kensington titles, imprints, and distributed lines are available at special quantity discounts for bulk purchases for sales promotion, premiums, fund-raising, educational, or institutional use.

Special book excerpts or customized printings can also be created to fit specific needs. For details, write or phone the office of the Kensington Special Sales Manager: Kensington Publishing Corp., 119 West 40th Street, New York, NY 10018. Attn. Special Sales Department. Phone: 1-800-221-2647.

Kensington and the K logo Reg. U.S. Pat. & TM Off.

ISBN-13: 978-0-7582-6699-6
ISBN-10: 0-7582-6699-5

First Kensington Trade Paperback Printing: January 2013
10 9 8 7 6 5 4 3 2 1

Printed in the United States of America

To Philip and Reinhilde

Author's Notes and Acknowledgments

I first encountered Charles Byrne in 1998 at Tate Britain art gallery, in London. His image, or rather a silhouette of a clay model of his skeleton, formed part of an installation by Christine Borland, whose work was nominated for the prestigious Turner Prize that year. To the side was a small, leather-bound volume, open at a page that gave a tantalizing glimpse into the extraordinary story of Charles Byrne, known as the Irish Giant, and his tormentor, the aptly named Dr. John Hunter.

For almost fifteen years I have wanted to tell Charles's story, first in the form of a screenplay. Hilary Mantel's excellent but totally different novel, *The Giant, O'Brien,* was published after I had written my film script, and for another five years my own version of the story remained in limbo until it was optioned by a production company. The project was shelved after a year.

Now, however, I am so thankful to have the opportunity to bring Charles Byrne's story to a wider audience with this, the second in the series of the Dr. Thomas Silkstone Mysteries. While *The Dead Shall Not Rest* is essentially a novel, I have not changed the names of the three main protagonists because their stories and characters are so extraordinary, I did not want to detract from them. Charles Byrne, Dr. John Hunter, and Count Josef Boruwlaski were all real, and to a great extent I have remained, as far as is possible, faithful to their recorded characters, appearances, and actions. There is one important exception, however. There is no evidence to suggest that the count betrayed Charles Byrne and was instrumental in the treatment of his corpse. Boruwlaski went to live in Durham, in the north of England, and died at the age of ninety-seven. The very unsavory characters of Howison, Crouch, and Hartnett were also real.

For the purposes of dramatic unity I have compressed the action that occurred over the course of fourteen months, from April 1782 to Charles Byrne's death in 1783. For unity of place, I have confined the action to Hunter's home in Leicester Square, although he did not move there until 1783. Charles Byrne did not lodge with the count (who had lodgings in Jermyn Street, opposite John Hunter, for a time) but in Cockspur Street.

For readers whose interest in this period has been awakened, I can recommend no finer book on Dr. John Hunter than Wendy Moore's *The Knife Man.*

As ever, I am grateful to Dr. Kate Dyerson for the benefit of her medical knowledge. My thanks also go to Patsy Pennell, Katy Eachus, and Beverley Vine for their help. Finally, my gratitude goes to my agent, Melissa Jeglinski, and to my editor, John Scognamiglio, and the team at Kensington Books, for their belief in me.

—England, 2012

If I have seen further it is by standing on the shoulders of giants.

—Sir Isaac Newton,
from a letter to Robert Hooke, 1675

Chapter 1

London, England,
in the Year of Our Lord 1782

Death was not sleeping in St. Bride's churchyard that night. She was wide awake and watching, in readiness. She knew her peace was about to be disturbed. She had only claimed what was rightfully hers. Dust to dust, was it not written? But there were those who wished to rob her of her precious new treasure. Fresh flowers had been laid on one of her graves, snowdrops and primroses, and she understood the prospect of new flesh was too much of a temptation for some. So she watched and she waited.

Dr. Thomas Silkstone had been there only a few hours before. The child they had laid to rest was one of his patients. Just eight years old, Evelina had suffered corruption of the flesh. A bad fall meant that a surgeon had no choice but to amputate her leg, but infection had already crept in and invaded her whole body when her distraught parents had brought their rag of a daughter to him. In life her pretty face had been twisted with pain and her flaxen hair soaked with sweat. But now that the peace of death had descended on her, it seemed as though she was merely asleep. She looked just as his own dear sister had looked when she passed at a similar age all those years ago in his native Philadelphia.

Evelina's parents, Mary and Peter Chepp, were good, honest

citizens. Evelina was their third daughter, and their second child to die before the age of ten. They had brought her to him when her blood was already poisoned. All he could do was dress the bloodied stump, clean it with oil of thyme and alum, and keep down the girl's fever. But to no avail. The passing of any of his patients always affected Thomas, even though he knew it should not. It was all part of the circle, the endless round of birth and death that physicians dealt with daily. But when it was a child called before its time, it was all the more heartrending.

As Thomas watched the couple, standing forlornly together, overseeing the gravediggers lower the little coffin into the earth, his thoughts turned to another funeral. He recalled Lady Lydia Farrell at her mother's interment. It had been a long and lonely winter without his beloved, with only her letters for comfort. Now that the weather was turning and spring was on its way, the coaches from London to Oxford would soon be running their daily service and he would return to Boughton to see her. He was just waiting for her word and he would be with her. Both of them agreed that it was best, out of respect for the dead and for the sake of their reputations, to keep their plans secret for the time being. If they were to announce their betrothal so soon after her late husband's death, vicious tongues would wag once again. Thomas did not want Lydia to suffer more than she already had.

"We have paid both the undertaker and the sexton well," Mr. and Mrs. Chepp told Thomas as the gravediggers smoothed over shovelfuls of soil, patting them into a mound. The doctor smiled and nodded reassuringly. He hoped that their monetary incentives were enough to keep the grave robbers at bay. All the same, he feared for their daughter's safety even more than his own that night.

Now that winter had loosened its icy grip on the earth, the sack 'em up men could work with impunity. No corpse was safe. The dissecting rooms of London needed cadavers, and the anatomists did not care how they came by them or who they were. Feeding this insatiable appetite for the dead was a lucrative business for those with low enough morals and strong stomachs—and there were plenty of those—as Thomas knew only too well. He had been approached many times by such scoundrels, but had always sent them away. Once you did business with them, it was hard to break free. He had even heard of a surgeon who refused to play by their rules and woke to a rotting corpse on his doorstep the next day.

"Our Evelina will be safe," repeated Mr. and Mrs. Chepp to Thomas as they left the graveside. "No one will steal our child."

Now it was a late hour. The spring-guns were set around the churchyard wall, or so the sexton said. The night was moonless. A dog barked and the men appeared. There were four of them and they knuckled down to work as if they were smithies in a forge or infantrymen loading their rifles. Each knew his task and performed it efficiently. Two dug a hole down to the coffin where the head lay while the other two stretched out a canvas sheet to receive the displaced earth. They dug with short, flat, dagger-shaped pieces of wood so that the sound of iron striking stone did not alert anyone.

Within half an hour they had reached the small coffin. The lid came off effortlessly—the undertaker had seen to that—and they pulled out the girl's body with ease. And there she was, pure and delicate, dressed in a flowing white shroud and with a garland of fresh flowers wreathed around her pretty head. Still they stripped her. Their own lives were worth more than a few grave-clothes and faded petals. They would not swing for stealing a shroud. So they bundled her, naked, into a sack. Carefully they reburied her grave-clothes and lowered the coffin back down, taking great care to smooth the surface all around. No one must know that the earth had already given up one of its newest and sweetest secrets.

The sexton, who had been watching proceedings, keeping lookout by the spring-guns which he had previously disarmed, nodded at the men. He saw them slip the sack over the wall and he knew his work was done.

All that remained was to take the booty—there were two other corpses on the cart—to Castle Street in Leicester Fields. The moon that had been so obligingly absent earlier now reappeared from behind a blanket of cloud, so that the road was easier to trace.

The cart pulled up in front of a large town house and one of the men alighted by a wooden gate. He tapped on it and a few moments later there came the sound of locks being unbolted before it creaked open. A swarthy guard appeared, lantern in hand, and nodded to the men, who were clearly expected. He returned inside and a few seconds later a drawbridge was lowered into the street and the cart was driven through. Once it was inside, the guard climbed on board. Bending down, he took a tape from around his neck and measured the length of each sack from top to bottom before opening all three of them, one after the other. Seemingly satisfied with their contents, he counted out a number of coins and handed them to the man, who signaled to the others to begin lugging the cargo off the cart and through the gate.

A few minutes later, their transaction complete, the men drove off. The guard looked up and down the street once more, making sure that no one had been privy to these unconventional business dealings, then cranked up the drawbridge once more.

Chapter 2

The annual spring fair at Boughton, in the county of Oxford-shire, was in full swing and it did not take long for the crowd to swallow the little man. At first they must have taken him for a child. Measuring barely three feet tall, he was the height of a six-year-old, but this was no grubby urchin out on a thieving mission. Abandoning his usual dapper French-cut redingote, Count Josef Boruwlaski sported a drab dung-colored frockcoat to blend in with the unwashed horde and headed, virtually unremarked, into the bowels of the throng.

Each April, beginning on the first Thursday of the month, the fair was held on the estate, near the village of Brandwick, and had been for the last three hundred years. The world and his wife rubbed shoulders with each other as all manner of entertainments, contests, and sports were laid on for the general delectation of the public. There were soothsayers, who would give you good fortune if you crossed their palms with silver and curse you if you did not, and mountebanks who sold miracle cures for a variety of agues and malignant effluvia that, most often, did more harm than good. There were prizefighters and wire walkers, fire-eaters and ropedancers, jugglers and acrobats. There were pigs that could fire a cannon and horses as small as dogs. There was a man who could lick his nose with his tongue like a cow and a hermaphrodite with both breasts and male genitalia clearly visible under its breeches. But as blasé to such spectacles as the good people of Brandwick had become over the years, even they were intrigued by what was billed to appear on a raised dais at the far edge of the fairground.

As the drum rolled in the shadowy twilight, the gypsy violins and tabors fell silent, the dancing troupe was stilled, and the costermongers and quacks stopped hawking. The servant girls in their Sunday best hushed their swains, and even the painted women shut their scarlet lips as the showman's voice rose hard and loud above the throng. All were drawn toward a makeshift stage that was flanked by two flaming torches.

"Come and see the tallest man in the world," he cried, dressed in yellow pantaloons and wearing a curly-brimmed green hat. His face was set in a wide, almost demonic grin. "He is not six foot, not seven foot, but eight foot high," he called into the chill air.

All eyes now focused on the stage. They did not notice the little man edging his way toward the front. Weaving past starched skirts and coarse smocks, he huffed and puffed. Buttons and brocade scratched his cheeks and boots bludgeoned his toes, but he remained steadfast in his purpose.

Now and again he would jab his elbow into a man's buttock or tug at a lady's skirt so that he could pass. One woman screamed when she looked down, believing him to be a cut-purse, but he managed to duck under a bridge of thighs and scurried off too quickly to be caught.

A few seconds later he reached the edge of the stage, out of breath and with his graying hair quite disheveled, but, he told himself, the excellent view was well worth the discomfort.

The drum roll grew louder and the excited murmurings from the crowd receded to a hush.

"And now, ladies and gentlemen, the moment you have all been waiting for," called the showman, his eyes wild with excitement. "I give you, all the way from the Emerald Isle, the truly amazing Irish Giant." He flung his arm toward the tall drapes that hung behind him from taut ropes at the back of the stage as the drum thundered. Nothing happened.

Some apprentice boys had clambered up on hay bales stacked

by the stage for a better view and, emboldened by strong liquor, began to heckle.

"Where is he, then?" one called.

"Buggered off back to Ireland," shouted another.

The showman smiled nervously and repeated himself, only this time even louder, making another sweeping gesture with his arm. "The truly amazing Giant Byrne."

Still nothing, and a rotten cabbage landed on the stage. "Get on with it," called a gruff voice, and the crowd started to murmur. The showman began to move backward, his face still set in a wide grin, when suddenly the drapes were drawn apart and a figure appeared in the amber glow of the torchlight.

A collective gasp of amazement rose as all eight feet of Charles Byrne, the Amazing Irish Giant, lumbered forward, causing the flimsy stage to creak and groan under his weight. He was, indeed, like a storybook ogre, with flowing black hair and arms as fat as ham hocks. Around his massive shoulders was draped a cloak, which dropped to the floor to reveal his naked torso and tight breeches. But his expression was vacant rather than vicious, and he looked more bewildered than belligerent.

Nevertheless, the showman's expression changed instantly from one of nervous anticipation to exalted relief. "Such a giant as never was before seen on these shores," he shouted out, barely able to contain himself, as the audience cheered and whooped.

When the cries had settled down to a murmur, the showman leaned forward. "Ladies and gentlemen," he said. "Let me take you back through the mists of time. A time when this man's ancestors roamed the land. The dark days." He motioned to the giant, who began to stride purposefully from one side of the stage to the other as directed. To gasps of alarm, he then stopped to look out over the audience, shielding his eyes from the torchlight in an exaggerated pantomime gesture.

The showman continued his patter as the giant hunched his shoulders menacingly and obligingly mimed gestures to match the speech. "These evil ogres strode over the hills and dales, terrorizing our towns and villages. They slew the menfolk. They carried off our women and used them for their own gratification. They even ate our babes."

There were more squeals from the female members of the audience. "Ladies and gentlemen, this giant, this Goliath that stands before you here today, is their descendant," cried the showman, delighting at the ensuing alarums of amazement. "Yet be not afraid, for this colossus is made of altogether gentler stuff." The showman looked at the giant, who was still grimacing. "Gentler stuff," he repeated, and the giant duly forced a smile. "Yet he still has the strength of a hundred men, as you will now see with your own eyes."

The showman danced over to a large object on the center of the stage that was covered with a crimson cloth. Bending low, he removed it with a flourish to reveal a ship's anchor.

"This anchor, ladies and gentlemen, comes from the thirty-ton lugger, the *Phoenix*, that was shipwrecked off the shores of Cornwall last year. It weighs half a ton, and Giant Byrne will now lift it and raise it above his head in a show of his extreme power."

There was another sharp intake of breath from the crowd as the drum rolled and the giant, his enormous chest muscles gleaming in the torchlight, proceeded to put a leather halter around his neck. The halter was attached to a short, thick chain at the end of which was the anchor. Crouching down, with his head low, but never taking his eyes from the audience, the giant took a deep breath and began to rise slowly. As he straightened his torso, the chains began to move, too, like metal snakes uncoiling. And finally, as his legs began to straighten, so did the anchor begin to shift. It came slowly at first. Beads of sweat started to appear on the giant's brow and some began to doubt, but then the movement hastened as he steadily lifted his arms above his head. Straining every fiber in his being, he straightened his back until, at last, the anchor left the ground and was clearly suspended from the halter around his neck.

The crowd erupted into loud applause. "Bravo, bravo," they called. The showman grinned and gestured to the giant to take a bow. Looking bewildered by all the noise, he simply nodded and let the anchor drop slowly down onto the stage. Ignoring the crowd's adulation, he then turned toward the drapes and would have disappeared again from view had the showman not lunged after him. He took him by the arm and pulled him back to face his admiring audience once more.

"Bow again, you dolt," he said through clenched teeth, his face still holding a grin. "Bow."

The giant did bow, from the waist this time. But there was no satisfied smile, only a pained look. As a crookbacked youth passed around a hat to collect a few paltry coins, the showman led him off the stage through the drapes and down wooden steps to a tent that was pitched nearby.

The crowd now dispersed as quickly as it had formed, tempted by the many other delights of the fair, leaving the little man at the front of the stage. For the past ten minutes he had been pinioned to the wooden fascia board, having to force his head back to watch the show that played out above him. His neck was now exceedingly stiff, but he was glad that he had witnessed the spectacle firsthand.

Lady Lydia Farrell was also glad to have seen the show. Her carriage was parked on a ridge above the natural amphitheater of the fairground. She remembered visiting the fair as a small child and still loved the sights and sounds of it, albeit from a distance these days. Her father had always been happy to allow the didicoys and dancing troupes to park their wagons on the edge of the Boughton estate for the duration of the fair, and she was glad to continue the tradition.

On this particular occasion she observed proceedings through a pair of opera glasses from the comfort of her carriage. Her view had not been completely satisfactory, but it had sufficed for her purposes. It would not have been seemly for her to mix among the vulgar people, especially as she had been widowed only a few months before. Nor did she wish to be seen in her carriage, so she wore a hooded cape that she pulled down low, covering the top half of her face.

As the crowd dwindled she watched her envoy approach.

"So, Count," said Lydia as the little man was helped into her carriage. "What do you think?"

"I think there is much to discuss, your ladyship," he replied. Lydia nodded. They would talk about what they had just seen over dinner at Boughton Hall and then decide whether or not to proceed with their course of action the following day.

Chapter 3

"God's truth, but it cannot be!" Thomas Silkstone stared incredulously at the *Daily Gazetteer*. He was sitting by a spluttering fire in the study of his London home, which he shared with his mentor and friend, Dr. William Carruthers.

"What is it, young fellow?" asked the old man, who sat opposite him, cradling a brandy in his arthritic hands. It was the custom every evening, after dinner, for the young anatomist to read out the latest obituaries. Dr. Carruthers may have lost his sight a few years back, but his wit and intellect remained razor sharp.

"Sir Tobias Charlesworth is dead."

"Charlesworth, from St. George's?"

"Yes." The young doctor ran an agitated hand through his hair in a state of bewilderment. "I was speaking with him only last week. He asked me if I would look at some specimens he had recently acquired."

Dr. Carruthers looked shocked. "When? How?"

"On Tuesday. It does not say how," replied Thomas, frowning.

"He was a fine surgeon," reflected the old man. "And a good card player!"

Thomas sighed. Such a loss. He had the utmost respect for Sir Tobias, who had always shown him the greatest of courtesies when others did not because he came from the Colonies. As the chief surgeon at St. George's Hospital he had also kept a firm grasp on the professional conduct of other surgeons and physicians. Thomas knew them to be a pompous, priggish band of men, more concerned with their reputations than the welfare of their patients. They closed their eyes to the squalor around them in the hospital wards and their minds to any advances in surgery.

"Yes, he will be sorely missed," he said.

"I pity the poor devil who takes his place," reflected Dr. Carruthers. "Those surgeons would sooner be at each other's throats than their patients'."

Thomas knew what he said to be true. There was so much infighting for power and reputation at the hospital that he was glad not to be part of it.

"Gunning, Keate, and Walker: I'd sooner show my neck to a hangman than trust it to any of those mealy-mouthed sycophants," chuntered his mentor.

"The funeral is tomorrow, sir," said Thomas, ignoring the old doctor's ranting.

"What? Oh, yes, funeral, you say?" he replied, suddenly aware that he was letting his temper get the better of him. "Then we must go and pay our respects."

It seemed as if the entire London medical fraternity was gathered at St. James's Church in Jermyn Street to pay tribute to Sir Tobias. From the chief physician to the king down to the lowliest apprentice at St. George's, they bowed their heads in remembrance of a respected colossus among their ranks. Hymns were sung, psalms read, and eulogies delivered in an air of reverence and gratitude for a life lived in the service of medicine.

Afterward, when they emerged from the gloom of the church into the sunlight of a spring day, Thomas found himself shepherding Dr. Carruthers between old acquaintances eager to see their friend, who so rarely ventured out in public these days. They greeted him fondly, patted him on the back, and inquired after his health, seemingly oblivious to the earnest-looking young man standing self-consciously by his side.

"Well, if it isn't Carruthers!"

"Carruthers, my dear fellow!"

"How are you faring, dear chap?"

"Terrible shame about Charlesworth."

The chorus of genial salutations and commiserations went on for some time, making Thomas feel slightly awkward. Even though this was his sixth year in this great city, he remained very much an outsider. He was still dismissed among his profession as simply "that colonist." Ever since his evidence at the trial of Lydia's husband, Captain Michael Farrell, had catapulted him to fame in the newssheets, his peers had regarded him with suspicion. "A self-publicist," they said. "Too clever for his own good! An upstart, a parvenu!"

Added to this the British Prime Minister, Lord North, had just resigned over the war with America, making his position even more awkward among those, and there were many in his circle, who would rather cut off their own limbs than give his homeland its independence. All he could do was look solemn and nod until, after what seemed like an age, he became aware of someone standing close behind him.

"Is it Dr. Silkstone?" came an unfamiliar voice.

Thomas turned to see a young man, in his early twenties, he guessed, with a pleasing smile and a confident manner.

"Yes, I am he," he said, relieved that at last someone was acknowledging his presence.

"I am a great admirer of your work, sir," said the young man, bowing politely.

Thomas was flattered. "Thank you, Mr. . . ."

"Giles Carrington is my name. I am a student at St. George's."

"Then you will be mourning the loss of your master," said Thomas.

"Indeed, we all are," he agreed.

"I was speaking with him only the other day. He seemed well enough then. His death must have come as a great shock," ventured Thomas.

Carrington looked grave. "Yes. He was struck down with a sudden apoplexy and was dead when they found him in his office."

"Terrible shame."

"Yes. Dr. Hunter says 'twill be hard to find a man who cares more for the hospital," replied the young man.

"Dr. Hunter," repeated Thomas.

Carrington shrugged. "Forgive me. Dr. John Hunter is my mentor."

Thomas had heard of this Dr. Hunter. His antics were the talk of the coffeehouses and cockpits. It was said that he would pickle anything that moved and dissect anything that died. It was said he kept strange and exotic animals that roamed around in his gardens. It was said that he carried out all sorts of experiments on these creatures. There was even a rumor he had grafted a human tooth onto a cock's comb and slit open a dog's belly while it was alive. If he carried out such abominations on animals, then perhaps he would do such a thing to humans, too!

"I am told his methods are slightly," he searched for a diplomatic term, "unorthodox," he said.

Carrington laughed. "You could say that, I suppose, sir."

Just then, the object of their conversation appeared in person, although had they not been introduced. Thomas would have taken the surgeon for an artisan or a shopkeeper. Instead of sporting a wig, customary for a man of his years, Dr. John Hunter wore his tawny-colored hair in a ponytail, and a stubbly beard sprouted from his chin. His topcoat was stained and frayed around the cuffs and his manner was bluff and discourteous.

"Stop ya prattlin', Carrington. There's work to be done," he barked, ignoring Thomas altogether. To the young doctor's ear, he did not sound like a gentleman at all, and his accent was thick and unfamiliar.

Carrington looked sheepish. "I must go, Dr. Silkstone, but it was good to meet you."

Realizing he was interrupting a conversation the anatomist turned to Thomas.

"Silkstone, eh? Yes, I've heard of you," he growled in a low burr before walking off again, his student following obediently behind.

*   *   *

"John Hunter. There's a rare one," chortled Carruthers. Thomas and his mentor were talking over dinner later that evening after returning to their home in Hollen Street. They had been a little later than planned, and pinch-faced Mistress Fine-silver, both their housekeeper and cook, and a woman neither liked to trifle with, had burned the venison pie.

"Now, there are two brothers who could not be less alike, or close. William and he are as chalk and cheese," continued the old doctor.

Of course Thomas knew of both the Hunter brothers. The elder, William, lived in a very grand house nearby and had attended at the births of several of the royal children. But of John he knew less, and the many rumors he had heard were all scurrilous.

"How so?" pressed Thomas, his appetite whetted by his mentor's enigmatic choice of words rather than the burnt offering on the plate before him.

"John is a maverick," mused Carruthers. "But a brilliant one, nevertheless. It has taken time for his light to shine." He chuckled again. "He told me once that when no one turned up for a lecture he dragged a skeleton into the room, seated it, and addressed his talk to him!"

Thomas raised an eyebrow. "But now, I trust, he attracts a good-sized audience."

Carruthers gulped his claret and tilted his head to one side in thought. "He has his followers, Athenians around their Socrates. But I wouldn't recommend you adopt *all* of his methods, young fellow. By Jove, I would not."

Thomas was bemused. "Why is that, sir?"

The old doctor huffed. "Let's just say he strays onto the wrong side of the law on occasions. There's nothing he won't do for a good corpse."

Thomas nodded knowingly. He could tell by Hunter's very appearance and manner that he would feel more at home in a spit-and-sawdust tavern than a genteel London salon. He was about to say as much when a knock at the door interrupted the conversation. Mistress Finesilver stood on the threshold looking even more out of sorts than usual. He wondered why she seemed so agitated. Had he not given her the nightly dose of laudanum she so enjoyed?

"Begging pardon, sirs, but a messenger has just brought this letter from Boughton Hall. He said it was urgent."

Thomas nodded and took the folded paper from the housekeeper.

"Urgent, eh?" queried the old doctor, wiping his chin with his napkin.

"Yes," replied Thomas. "It seems Lady Lydia needs me as soon as I am able to be there."

Chapter 4

On the second day of the fair the showman sat on the steps of his painted wagon after the evening's performance, swigging beer from a pot. His large hat was planted on the back of his head. The heavy kohl makeup that lined his eyes was smudged and his rouged lips had bled at the edges. He let out a loud belch and wiped his mouth with his sleeve.

As he drew closer, Count Boruwlaski could make out the faded letters painted in gold on the side panel of the wagon. THE GREATEST WONDERS OF THE WORLD, they proclaimed. A few feet away a large red and yellow tent was pitched. Inside, lights had been lit, and he knew the giant was inside because he could see his silhouette on the canvas. It made him appear even more enormous, but the dwarf was not fazed. Without hesitating he grasped hold of the tent flap and drew it aside. The giant did not notice him at first. Nor did the crookbacked youth. They were both sitting on the floor, eating hunks of bread like ravenous dogs.

The little man glanced around the tent. In the far corner he could make out a large wooden crate. He could hear a low growl, and from the stench of it, he guessed it held an animal. He did not wish to alarm the giant, nor the youth, but neither had noticed him, so he cleared his throat as loudly as he could.

The giant, who was sitting cross-legged, swiveled 'round on his rear and looked up toward the tent opening. At first he did not spot the little man in the shadows. "Who's th-there?" he spluttered through a mouthful of bread.

The dwarf was fearful he would alert the showman. The crookback turned awkwardly and also looked toward the opening. Straining his eyes, he could make out the small form of the count.

"Who's there?" he repeated, rising and limping toward him.

The count drew himself up to his full three feet three inches, puffing up his chest and sticking out his chin. "I wish to speak with Mr. Byrne," he said in a strange accent that marked him as a foreigner.

The giant frowned, looked at the crookback, and then peered down at the dapper dwarf. His eyes filled with wonderment, like a child seeing its first flakes of snow fall.

"Come closer where we can see you," ordered the youth.

The little man held his nerve and stepped forward so that the light from the rush lamps clothed him in a soft glow. He, too, could see more clearly. There was a large carpet on the ground, such as he believed came from old Araby, and in the far corner the crate did, indeed, hold an animal—a black cat the size of a wolf. He had seen something similar at the court of the Holy Roman Empress Maria Theresa in the Hofburg in Vienna, but it had broken loose and killed several peacocks. The creature fixed a stare on him and growled, louder this time, probably anticipating its next meal, thought the little man.

"What do you want with me, dwarf?" boomed the giant. His voice was as deep as a rumble of thunder but he spoke slowly and deliberately, as if each word needed to be shaped with the utmost care. He did not mean to be frightening, but the sound he made was so great that the dwarf jumped and put his tiny finger up to his lips in the hope that the giant would speak more softly. He looked over his shoulder to see if the boom had alerted the showman, but satisfied it had not, he continued. "Permit me to introduce myself, sir. I am Count Josef Boruwlaski from Poland," he said in a hoarse whisper.

The crookback let out a shrill laugh and pointed a mocking finger. "You, a nobleman?"

"Indeed I am," he replied haughtily. "And I am come to make you an offer, sir," he said, addressing the giant. He tugged hard at his brindle waistcoat, which had risen above his plump midriff.

"And what might th-that be?" asked Byrne.

"I, too, am blessed with"—he gave a self-conscious little cough—"with unusual physical attributes. But I have used them to my very great advantage."

"You have?" mocked the crookback.

"You have?" echoed the giant. The count nodded, puffing out his chest.

"Yes, but I am pleased to say I have confined my activities to polite society: ladies and gentlemen of considerable breeding, who are indeed curious, but never crude; patronizing, but never plebian."

The giant shook his head. "There's naught to choose 'twixt a rich man's stare and a poor man's," he said, adding ruefully, "They can both wound."

"True, but surely the pain is more bearable if it is paid for handsomely?" countered the little man.

The crookback nodded. "You could eat proper. Not just the scraps he gives you," he suggested to the giant.

"Indeed so," replied the count. "Whole capons and mutton pies could be yours."

The idea of a plentiful supply of food was clearly appealing to the colossus.

"And just where might I f-find these ladies and gentlemen?" he asked, shifting on his haunches.

"Why, in London, sir!" cried the count.

The giant's eyes widened, but he remained silent, as if trying to grasp the prospect of traveling to the capital city of England. Thinking he might need a little more persuading, the count went on: "Just think of the fine clothes and the soft bed and . . ."

"That matters not," spat Byrne, spraying the dwarf with his saliva.

The little man was taken aback. "Forgive me, sir."

The giant shook his head. " 'Tis not wealth I am wanting," he moaned.

The crookback limped forward and put a hand on his shoulder. " 'Tis justice he is after, sir," said the boy.

"Justice?" repeated the count. "How so?"

Charles Byrne took a deep breath and motioned to the little man to sit beside him in a gesture of friendship. "I seek a royal pardon for my da."

The dwarf raised an eyebrow. "Is that so?" The count frowned, looking at Charles.

"He says he does," chimed in the crookback. "Says he needs to speak with King George himself."

Boruwlaski nodded sympathetically and then smiled. "You see this ring?" He held up his hand and pointed to a large diamond twinkling in the torchlight. "It was given me by the daughter of the great Empress Maria Theresa, Marie Antoinette. She is the Queen of France now."

The crookback lunged forward, grabbed the dwarf's digit, and bit the diamond hard. " 'Tis real," he cried gleefully.

The count rubbed his hand. "I do not lie," he retorted, darting a contemptuous look at the ruffian who had yanked at his ring finger. "I enjoyed great favor in the courts of Europe." Then, turning back to Charles, he said: "There are ways of gaining an audience with His Majesty King George."

The giant's usually vacant face broke into a broad smile. "Then, sir, I will come with you," he said, and he proffered his hand to the little man, whose own hand would have fitted inside at least a dozen times.

"You're not going anywhere," came a voice from the entrance. All eyes turned to see the showman, dark circles of kohl under his eyes, standing, glaring at them. There was no trace of the broad grin he had worn on the stage and in his right hand he held a long cane. "Well, well, well: a giant and a dwarf. What a pretty pair you make," he cried, his voice tinged with menace.

Charles Byrne's shoulders slumped and his head bowed instantly, as if he had become a child again as his master drew nearer. The showman rested his gaze on the count and looked him up and down mockingly.

"So, dwarf, you would steal my giant for your own troupe, would you?" he sneered, stroking the count's head condescendingly, as if he were a cat.

Boruwlaski swallowed hard. "I did not know that you owned Mr. Byrne, sir."

The showman narrowed his eyes. "Indeed I do," he said, circling the little man and throwing the cane from one hand to the other like a baton. But the count refused to be intimidated.

"Then you must tell me your price," he said, looking upward to meet the showman's gaze.

"So you would bargain with me, dwarf?"

"Indeed I would, sir."

"But you are in a very weak position."

"How so?" asked the count disingenuously. The showman let out a cruel laugh and bent down so that his face leveled with the dwarf's.

"Can't you count, Count?" he sneered. "There are three of us and," he sniggered, "only half of you. We could feed you to that cat over there and it would still be hungry." He pointed to the crate with his cane. The creature growled and the dwarf began to feel decidedly uneasy.

"I have money, sir," he blurted as the bully continued to circle.

"I am sure you do," the showman agreed, gesturing to the crookback, who limped forward and rifled through the count's coat pockets. He pulled out a drawstring purse and held it aloft before handing it to his master. The showman tossed it in the air and caught it.

"A goodly weight." He smiled.

"Twenty guineas," informed the count.

"Twenty guineas," repeated his tormentor. "So you would buy my giant for twenty guineas?"

At these words, Byrne, who had sat passively on the carpet until this point, looked up. "I am n-not *your* giant," he said slowly, and with that he began to rise, uncrossing his legs and kneeling up, so that he was now the same height as the showman.

"What did you say?" the showman asked incredulously.

"I am not *your* giant," he repeated, only this time more assuredly. "My ancestors were kings in Ireland, great leaders of men. I'll be doing your bidding no more."

The showman sneered once again. "We'll see who's the master," he cried, raising his cane above his head to strike. The giant, however, was too quick for him and stayed his hand. Then, taking the cane, he snapped it in two in front of his shocked master's eyes.

"You do not *own* me," repeated the giant. "And Charles Byrne cannot be bought. I will go with the dwarf to L-London." With those words he eased himself up, still bending forward so that his head did not touch the canvas of the tent, and began to walk toward the entrance.

"Not so fast," cried the showman, darting in his way. "Crookback, the cat!" he shouted, pointing at the crate.

"Are you mad?" exclaimed the count.

The boy, too, simply looked at his master as if he had lost his senses.

"The cat!" he screamed. "Open the cage." The animal let out a roar as if it scented blood, but the urchin remained transfixed. "Then I will do it myself," shouted the showman above the creature's tumult, and he strode toward the crate.

He grasped the lever and was just about to pull up the hatch when suddenly there came a woman's voice at the entrance of the tent.

"I would not do that if you value your life, sir," cried Lydia above the din.

The showman stopped dead in his tracks and turned to see the gentlewoman, standing perfectly poised a few feet away.

"And who might you be?" he asked, looking askance at the diminutive figure draped in a long, black, hooded cloak.

"I, sir, am Lady Lydia Farrell, and I own the land on which you stand," she replied.

The showman began to walk toward her, smirking. "You do, do you?" he chided.

"Indeed I do, and unless you go immediately, leaving the giant here, I will have you arrested for the theft of twenty guineas."

The showman unclenched the hand that held the purse and looked at it for a moment. He then leered at her before throwing it down hard to the ground. "Curse you," he muttered under his breath.

"Now leave, before I call the peace constables," she ordered in a voice that belied her size. "Men have hanged for much less."

The showman began to mouth oaths. "A curse on you and your seed," he said as he charged past Lydia, cuffing the count on the head as he went.

"I want you off the Boughton estate within the hour, otherwise I will add assault to the charges," she called after him as he stormed off to his wagon.

The crookback began to follow sheepishly, but just as he was at the entrance to the tent, the count caught hold of him by the waist of his breeches.

"Here's two guineas, boy," he said, shoving the coins into his dirty palm. "Use them wisely."

The startled servant smiled, showing a mouthful of yellow tombstone teeth, and limped off in the opposite direction to his master, leaving Lydia and the count with the giant standing in shocked silence, none of them quite believing what had just passed.

Feeling a sudden shiver, Lydia drew her cloak around her.

"You are cold, my lady," remarked Boruwlaski.

"Yes, a little," replied Lydia, knowing that she was shaking with fear and anger rather than the chill. She looked up at the giant. He was, indeed, so amazingly tall and yet she could see in his eyes that he was so very vulnerable at the same time. "You are in good hands now, Mr. Byrne," she assured him. "On the morrow, God willing, Dr. Silkstone will arrive and all will be well."

*   *   *

Wrapped in a shawl against the nip of an easterly wind, Emily O'Shea braved the labyrinth of narrow lanes of St. Giles. She ducked and dived her way under the dripping carcasses of meat strung across the alleyways of the butchers' shambles and dodged around the gaping hatches that opened up in the ground by alehouses. Overhead the signs of makers and shopkeepers were caught now and again by a brisk gust and creaked plaintively on their hinges. She was anxious to reach her home before nightfall. The messenger boy had said she was needed urgently and the housekeeper, Mistress Goodbody, had given her leave for the night, but she was to be back at work by first light.

She reached her destination shortly before six o'clock and paused for a moment outside a dilapidated gate as if composing her thoughts before climbing a flight of rickety stairs into the rookeries. The walls were green with moss and the last vestiges of daylight could be seen through a hole in the roof. At the top of the landing she reached a doorway. Children were running hither and thither, one almost sending her flying. Yet above the general din she could still hear a baby's cries from within. She knocked.

" 'Tis Emily," she called, hoping her voice would be heard over the noise. A moment later a woman answered, the screaming baby firmly planted on her hip.

"I came as soon as I could. What is it, Ma?" she asked anxiously.

Her mother's face was drawn and gaunt and her breastbone protruded from the top of her bodice. " 'Tis your gran. She's been calling for you these past few nights," she shouted above the baby's bawl. She opened the door wide onto a cramped, unlit room. Soiled rushes were scattered thinly across the floor. Another child, a boy of no more than six, played with a bone.

"She's been talking shite, she 'as," mumbled a man, who sprawled in a chair in the corner, swigging liquor. When Mad Sam O'Shea wasn't addled by strong drink he would hawk anything he could get his grubby hands on. He'd even have sold his own daughter if the price had been right, but thankfully for Emily she had found service before that could happen.

"Rambling on and on," said her mother, leading Emily over to a cot in the corner. The girl looked at the old crone. The woman lay on her back with her eyes shut and sunken into her skull. Her emaciated body was covered by a filthy sack. Emily stretched out a reluctant hand to touch her. Her skin felt like cold parchment.

" 'Tis me, Gran," she said softly.

At the sound of her voice, Grandmother Tooley's eyes opened in an instant, startling the girl.

"Thank the Lord you're here, child," she croaked, taking her granddaughter's hand. "You need to know."

"Know what?" Emily frowned.

The old woman tugged her hand so that Emily bent down low. Her grandmother reeked of piss.

"He's coming soon," she whispered.

"Who, Gran? Who?"

"The tall man," said Grandmother Tooley, lifting herself up on twig-thin arms.

Emily's mother now joined her daughter, the babe still screaming on her hip.

"She makes no sense," she said, shaking her head.

"Who, Gran? Who's coming?" repeated Emily.

"The tall man from across the water," said the old woman, looking at the young girl intently before dropping back into the cot and closing her eyes once more.

Chapter 5

Thomas arrived at Boughton Hall just as the last rays of the April sun were setting on the Chiltern Hills, turning them burnished gold. He had taken the coach from London to Oxford at first light, then been met by Lydia's head groom, Jacob Lovelock, in a chaise. He was tired and sore from being jounced about in the carriage and anxious as to what he might find on his arrival. Lydia had not specified why she wanted to see him urgently, only that she had a special visitor who needed his help.

The carriage turned into the imposing wrought-iron gates that marked the boundary of the estate and started up the long drive toward the hall. The long shadows of the trees began to mingle and dissipate into twilight. A week of dry weather had followed on from heavy spring rains, and the ruts in the driveway were deep and hard as clay, making Thomas's ride even more uncomfortable. But the surroundings were reassuringly familiar to him and he relished the silhouette of the family chapel as it came into view, knowing that Boughton itself lay just over the brim of the hill beyond.

He had just reached for his hat on the opposite seat in preparation for alighting when one of the horses let out a terrible whinny and reared up. He felt the carriage lurch and heard Lovelock try to calm the other three mares. But it was too late. The chaise veered off the drive and Thomas felt its back wheel drop into the ditch, knocking him sideways.

Scrambling to his feet, he managed to haul himself up and

look out of the window. Lovelock, who had been riding postilion, had jumped out of the saddle and was holding the bridle of the lead horse, trying to calm it. It still appeared uneasy, its eyes full of fear, and Thomas looked up the track to see what might have caused it to rear. He did not have to search long. Standing in the middle of the drive, a few yards away, was a huge figure of a man. He guessed he must have been at least eight feet tall and was as wide as a sedan. As he walked up to Lovelock, Thomas was amazed to see that this stranger's hips were level with the groom's head. He had never seen anyone like him before, not even in his medical books, and for a moment he abandoned all his professional training and allowed his jaw to drop open in amazement.

"Calm yourself now, girl," Lovelock urged the mare. He did not seem shocked or disconcerted by the giant apparition that stood a few feet away. "Perhaps you could give us a hand, Mr. Byrne," he called.

The figure approached slowly. "I-I am s-sorry," he stuttered in a voice as deep as thunder. The mare champed at the bit once more.

"Can ye get 'round the back? The wheel's stuck," called Lovelock, still holding on to the mare's bridle as she sauntered and sallied on the spot.

Thomas looked out of the carriage window in wonderment as he watched the man position his shoulder under the wheel arch and lift up the entire carriage out of the rut and back onto the driveway without so much as breaking into a sweat.

"Will ye need a ride?" enquired Lovelock of the giant.

"No. I'll walk, so I will," he replied, waving a large hand dismissively in the air.

"All's well, sir?" the groom called back to a bemused Thomas.

"Yes. Yes indeed." He nodded, leaning out of the window.

Lovelock climbed back onto the lead mare, and with a gentle nudge the horses started off up the drive once more, leaving Charles Byrne alone in the encroaching dusk to make his own way back to the hall.

* * *

Lydia had been watching for Thomas's carriage from an up-stairs room and saw it crest the hill, its shape silhouetted against an orange sky. She was seated in the drawing room, her skirts arranged in a fan around her, when Howard the butler ushered the young doctor in. She waited until he had left the room to fetch refreshments before rising and rushing forward to greet Thomas.

"My love, it is so good to see you," she blurted, burying her face in Thomas's coat.

"And you, my beloved," he replied, holding her tightly, breathing in her scent. It had been almost five months since they had last held each other, and for a few snatched moments they simply found each other's lips until Howard's footsteps could be heard once more.

Decorum quickly reestablished itself as tea was poured, but Howard was dismissed as soon as possible, leaving them alone to talk.

"But is all well?" asked Thomas, remembering Lydia's urgent note. "You have a visitor?" Her garbled message had simply told Thomas that she knew of someone who urgently needed his help.

She nodded, as if suddenly recalling the reason for his arrival, which had been lost in the excitement of his presence. "A visitor. Yes. Indeed. I am most anxious for you to meet him."

"I think I may have seen him already," said Thomas.

"Mr. Byrne?"

"He must be one of the tallest men in the world."

"Indeed so," replied Lydia. "And cruelly abused."

"How so?"

"By a showman at the fair."

Thomas knew of such cases where nonconformity to nature's norm meant curiosities would be exhibited. In inns and hostel-ries in his own homeland he had seen a dead whale caught in the Delaware River and a strange beast from Russia that was part bear, part camel. These were harmless distractions and amuse-ments, but soon they had taken on a more sinister mantle. A Negro slave with a rare skin condition that turned him from black to white or a woman without arms or legs who could paint holding a brush in her mouth drew in much bigger crowds.

"And you have freed him?" he asked her.

Lydia smiled. "Mr. Byrne will be a guest here for as long as he wishes."

At that moment the door opened. "And here is another of my guests," said Lydia. Thomas looked down in amazement to see a small figure approaching him confidently despite his bandied gait. He was dressed for dinner in a fine brocade jacket and a lace cravat all tailored in perfect proportion to his tiny frame.

"Count Josef Boruwlaski, I would like you to meet Dr. Thomas Silkstone," said Lydia.

The little man stopped in front of Thomas, who was trying to hide his surprise. "Lady Lydia has told me much about you and your skills, Dr. Silkstone," he greeted him cheerily, bowing low.

"My late father and the count met in Warsaw many years ago and became firm friends," explained Lydia.

"I have decided to make England my home, and her ladyship kindly invited me to stay," added the dwarf.

"And I know her ladyship will do everything to ensure you are made to feel welcome," replied the young doctor.

Lydia could see that Thomas was still bemused by his extraordinary encounters all within the space of the last few minutes. "But you must be exhausted, Dr. Silkstone," she said cheerfully. "Howard will show you to your room and then we can talk further over dinner."

Thomas smiled graciously. He hoped that after he had washed and changed his clothes he would be able to make more sense of the situation than he could at the present. There was obviously some good reason for Lydia to be playing host to these, the tallest and smallest of men, at Boughton Hall, and he was eager to find out more. He said simply: "Thank you, your ladyship," and took his leave.

An hour later the doctor returned to the drawing room feeling refreshed. Lydia was now dressed for dinner, too, and he found her speaking to a mutual old acquaintance.

"Sir Theodisius," greeted Thomas, outstretching his hand. The portly Oxford coroner had helped him solve the mystery of Lydia's husband's death the year before. He had since been a great comfort to her in her widowhood. On this occasion he was accompanied by his wife, Lady Harriet, whom he called Hetty; a nervous woman, as thin as her husband was wide.

"Good to see you again, Silkstone," said Sir Theodisius, giving Thomas a firm handshake.

"And you, sir," replied the young anatomist, smiling broadly.

"So, her ladyship wishes you to meet her mystery guest, I believe," said the coroner.

"Indeed," said Thomas, still unsure of the role Lydia wanted him to play.

At that moment Howard opened the door and in walked the count, this time accompanied by the giant. For a moment the two men stood side by side, framed by the doorway, and the extraordinary sight caused Sir Theodisius to choke on his glass of sack.

"Gentlemen, I am delighted to introduce Mr. Charles Byrne." Lydia beamed.

This time Thomas was able to check his own fascination. He willed his eyes not to stray over the giant's frame and his expression not to betray his utter amazement. It would not be seemly at such a gathering. Any professional interest he showed must be confined to a medical examination, he told himself.

Mr. Byrne, however, looked decidedly ill at ease.

"And where is your home, sir?" ventured Thomas, trying to make polite conversation.

"I c-come from Ireland, sir, that I do, sir," replied Byrne, his gaze firmly fixed to the floor.

"It is a great pleasure to meet you," said the doctor, trying to ease the giant's awkwardness. Even so, he could not help noting with his physician's eye that his tongue appeared far too big for his mouth as a thread of spittle dribbled down his chin.

"And you are come to show yourself?" enquired Sir Theodisius, taking up the conversation.

Before the giant could formulate a reply, however, Lydia cut in.

"Dinner is served, I believe," she told her guests, and Thomas duly offered her his arm to accompany her into the dining room.

Lydia had ordered Mistress Claddingbowl, the cook, to prepare at least twice as much food as she would normally for a dinner party of this size.

"We have some hearty appetites to feed," she had told her prior to her marketing.

The company feasted on roast mutton and stewed carp, and no one turned a hair when Mr. Byrne helped himself to a whole pheasant. Indeed, Sir Theodisius deemed it politic to follow suit.

The count appeared, thought Thomas, to be as witty and erudite as Mr. Byrne was morose and his conversation flowed as freely as the wine, although the little man declined to drink anything strong himself.

"I have drunk only water since 1760," he declared, raising his glass in a toast. "I believe it keeps the intellects sharper and the body healthier."

"Then we shall drink to your continued good health." Sir Theodisius smiled.

"And to yours, Mr. Byrne," added Thomas, even though he doubted his health was, indeed, good.

Throughout the meal the giant remained quiet, concentrating on his food rather than the conversation. Lydia smiled as the servants cleared away the plates.

"Lady Pettigrew and I shall withdraw now and leave you gentlemen to your port," she said, rising from the table. As she did so, she turned to Thomas and whispered: "The count will explain everything."

While the others imbibed glasses of port and, to Sir Theodisius's delight, a whole Stilton cheese, the count did embark on an explanation for Mr. Byrne's presence, but he started with his own story.

Thomas found himself listening intently as the little man began to tell them of his upbringing in his native Polish Russia. "My parents were of middle size," he began. "They had six children, five sons and one daughter. Three of these children grew to above the middle stature, whilst the two others, like myself, reached only that of children in general at the age of four or five." When his father died, when he was aged just nine, his mother was persuaded to let her son live with a noblewoman, and from then on fortune shone upon the boy. His wit and good manners, which had clearly not deserted him, thought Thomas, endeared him to aristocratic women and opened the door to the courts of Europe. "I have enjoyed great patronage and the love of many beautiful women," proclaimed the little man with a twinkle in his eye.

"You have indeed been fortunate, sir," remarked Thomas. He could easily recall his first—and only—visit to St. Bartholomew's Fair in London. With his own eyes he had witnessed a bearded lady and twins joined at the head. They had all been exhibited by a showman, who no doubt took the lion's share of what little money was made from their disabilities. It had galled him greatly to see such exploitation, and from then on he had vowed never to go to an English fair again.

"Of course not all of us with," he paused, searching for the right word, "with unusual physical assets are treated well," he said, his demeanor suddenly changing.

Thomas and Sir Theodisius nodded sympathetically in unison. Boruwlaski looked over the table at Charles Byrne, who had been downing wine for much of the evening. Thomas noted the giant's complexion was rather pallid and now and again he coughed, but he remained sitting impassively as the count turned his attentions to his predicament.

Boruwlaski continued: "I had been staying with her ladyship for a few days and was aware of his reputation: The tallest man in all Christendom, they said. His reputation clearly went before him, but having also been aware that gentlemen with such attributes can be ill-treated, I decided to find out for myself if I could be of assistance."

The count suddenly became even more serious. "I knew that he would be at the fair at Boughton. Lady Lydia was most obliging in this matter and, being a woman of great compassion herself, offered to assist me in helping Mr. Byrne, should it be required."

Thomas nodded. It was so like Lydia to involve herself in a good cause if she felt an injustice was being committed.

The little man went on: "We encountered a few problems, but managed to persuade the showman to let Mr. Byrne go freely."

"You are to be congratulated, Count," said Thomas.

"Hear, hear!" echoed Sir Theodisius through a mouthful of cheese.

"Ah, but that is only the beginning, gentlemen," said the count, his little finger jabbing the air.

"The beginning?" echoed Thomas.

The dwarf, who was seated on silk cushions on his chair, leaned forward over the table. "There are certain goals that Mr. Byrne wishes to achieve."

Thomas looked at the giant, who remained hunched over his plate. He seemed a little worse the wear for drink, but he glanced up at the mention of his name.

"Will you tell them, or shall I, Mr. Byrne?" asked the count gently.

The giant nodded slowly and lifted his gaze to meet the company's. His eyes moved languidly from face to face before he took a deep breath. "My da was h-hanged last year," he said. His words were slurred and Thomas was not sure if his congenital condition or the strong liquor was responsible, but his statement still came as a shock. He darted a glance at Sir Theodisius. There was more. The giant went on: "S-strung him up, they did. Said he killed a girl. Only he n-never. He were innocent."

There was a stunned silence before the coroner, thinking out loud, said, "There's many a man goes to the gallows protesting his innocence, Mr. Byrne."

"Aye, but there were proof he didn't do it," retorted the giant, this time raising his voice and losing all trace of his stammer.

The count intervened to calm the situation. "A boy confessed and has been convicted of the crime," he explained.

Sir Theodisius showed uncustomary humility. "I see." He nodded, wiping his mouth on a napkin.

" 'Tis why I want a royal pardon, to clear my da's name," boomed the giant indignantly.

"We all understand," said the count, patting Charles Byrne's large hand, which had been brought down to bear in a fist on the table. "And I am sure that these gentlemen will assist if they can."

Thomas smiled sympathetically. *This man is a victim,* he thought. He had seen so many of his kind, vulnerable and wronged, during his years of practice and he would certainly volunteer his support.

Sir Theodisius, however, was less understanding. "A royal pardon costs money," he barked.

Unfazed, the count nodded. "Mr. Byrne shall stay at my lodgings in Cockspur Street and will have money when he exhibits himself in front of London's *polite* society." He smiled. "He shall show himself in Spring Gardens."

Thomas was familiar with what occurred in the public rooms in this fashionable area and found the goings-on thoroughly distasteful. Dukes, duchesses, and even royalty would pay their pennies to gawp at boys with unsightly skin conditions and children born with congenital deformities. *So this is why Lydia called for me,* thought Thomas. She wanted him to examine the giant to ensure he was well enough to embark on showing himself to the public. "Perhaps you would allow me to see that you are in a fit enough state of health for such an undertaking, Mr. Byrne," he said.

The giant did not reply, but simply glanced nervously at the count. "I am sure that would be helpful. Thank you, Dr. Silkstone," acknowledged the count courteously.

Sir Theodisius, however, had other things on his mind. Helping himself to another spoonful of ripe Stilton, he said: "Pardons are never easy to come by. But I have a nephew at Lincoln's Inn, my sister's boy. He's an ambitious fellow, and sharp, too. I can ask him to look into the case."

The count's face broke into a broad smile. "You are most

generous with your time and expertise, gentlemen," he said. "We are most grateful, are we not, Mr. Byrne?" He looked at the giant, who was still glaring across the table.

"Y-yes," he stammered reluctantly before a bout of coughing stopped short any further gratitude he may have wished to express.

Later that night, when all the guests and servants were in bed and the house dogs were asleep, Lydia came to Thomas. He breathed in her sweet scent once more and thrilled at the touch of her skin as she settled beside him naked under the coverlet. The months of absence had only heightened their mutual desire. So lost did they become in each other that only the light of the breaking dawn brought them back to their earthly senses.

"I must go to my room now before we are found," whispered Lydia, reluctantly leaving the warmth of Thomas's body. He took her hand as she rose naked from the bed and pulled her to face him so that he could catch one last glimpse of her milk-white beauty before it disappeared under her nightgown.

"We cannot be married a moment too soon," he told her gently. She smiled, freeing her long chestnut hair, which had become caught down her back from under her dressing robe. "I love you, too," was all she said in response. Thomas had hoped for more. He wanted to hear her say that she could not wait to be his wife, but he let the moment pass and watched in silence as she closed the door behind her just as the first rays of sun hit the bedchamber floor.

Chapter 6

Dr. John Hunter stared death in the face every day and embraced it. He stored it in jars on his shelves and he displayed it in glass cases in his laboratory. He distilled its essence and put it in phials and he plunged it in a spirit of wine mixed with acid to preserve it. In his sinewy hands, which bore the scars of so many little nicks from scalpels and knives during dissection and surgery, he held a jar containing a fetus. One of his patients had miscarried and he had spared her the agony of burying her five-month-old, womb-dead son. Instead he would be preserved for posterity and join all the others in his army of unborn, suspended for all time in yellowed embalming fluid, their mysteries waiting to be unlocked.

One day, not in his lifetime, perhaps not in the next century, but maybe in the next millennium, man might be able to reach the unreachable, fathom the unfathomable, control nature itself. In his own small way, he liked to think he was laying the foundations for those who would follow. Those specimens in the jars were the building bricks of knowledge. He hoped men would thank him one day, speak his name in a hushed reverence. But he had no time for pomp and priggishness.

He did not care for his profession, or rather those at the top of it. Their backbiting and infighting bored him, and their irksome rantings frustrated him to the point of exhaustion. Too lazy to give lectures, too full of their own self-importance to impart their knowledge to students, they were only interested in their titles and their stipends. "We all have vermin that live on us," he would say.

There was only one whom he might rate since the days of old Carruthers, the stalwart whom he had met when he first came to London from Scotland all those years ago, and that was his student, Thomas Silkstone, who, like himself, was an outsider. Up until their first meeting at Charlesworth's funeral he had only known of him by reputation. He had made quite a name for himself at Farrell's trial, ruffled a few feathers among the old guard. He was every bit as good-looking as they said he was, as well. Too handsome for his own good, he mused. Too easily distracted by women? Perhaps. Next time they met he would engage him properly. He always welcomed a good debate and all too often at St. George's had to brook fools. Yes, Silkstone was one to watch, but for now he had work to do, and he worked alone.

When he looked at his jars his thoughts were concentrated on his purpose. When he gazed on a worm-riddled codfish, a decayed molar, a two-headed fetus, or a six-fingered hand, he would contemplate the wonders of nature and medicine and see beyond to a world without disease and deformity. And when he dared to look even further into such a future, he also foresaw a world where those with the ability to control such demons would wield great power. They would not be men of medicine, whose true purpose was to relieve pain and to cure, but men like those who now conspired against him; men who put their own personal gain before that of mankind's suffering and well-being. He thought of them, gathered even now somewhere, whispering against him, and he pitied them, just as he pitied himself.

Reaching down, he opened a drawer in his desk and took out a key. In the half light of a lamp that cast eerie shadows, he walked over to a door in the wall and unlocked it. Stepping inside a small alcove, he held his lamp aloft to inspect the shelves. There they were, his very special preparations; priceless beyond imagination, but only in the right hands. And there, taking pride of place on the middle shelf, right in his eyeline, was his latest specimen: the beautifully preserved heart of Sir Tobias Charlesworth.

It was Mrs. Adam, his housekeeper, who brought him back to reality when she knocked on the laboratory door.

"There is a Lady Charlesworth here to see you, sir," she called. She knew better than to open the door for fear of walking in on a scene that might scar her mentally for years to come.

Hunter frowned and glanced back at the heart floating serenely in the jar. What would the widow of a surgeon at St. George's want with him? She could not know, she must not know about her husband's heart. As luck would have it, he had been with Charlesworth when the fatal attack came on. He recalled how he had just risen from his desk to show him the door when the surgeon, a man who enjoyed his port, was suddenly overcome by a great seizure. He had put his hand to his chest and gasped for air before falling like a stone to the floor.

"Show her into the drawing room," he instructed. His laboratory was no place for a lady. Hurriedly he secured the door to his secret stash, then washed his hands with particular zeal, as if sloughing off some decidedly unpleasant substance.

Hunter found Sir Tobias Charlesworth's widow waiting for him a few minutes later. She wore a simple dress of dark gray and a veil that covered her hair and face as befitted a woman of her rank who had lost her husband only the week before.

"Lady Charlesworth, good day to you," greeted Hunter, although such courtesies sounded strange, even to him, in his rough Scottish guttural.

The woman, in her middle years, was dignified in her mourning. She lifted back her veil to reveal eyes that were red from crying.

"My condolences once again," he said.

She allowed a flicker of a smile to settle momentarily on her lips. "You have been most kind, Dr. Hunter. Everyone has, and I know that no more could have been done to save my husband. I am so thankful that you happened to be with him at the time."

"The Lord works in mysterious ways," said the doctor. It was one of the useful platitudes he wheeled out on occasions such as these.

"I am so thankful for all your assistance. You were most diligent in making the arrangements afterward. I was in such a state, I do not know what I would have done without your help," she told him, dabbing a tear from the corner of her eye.

The doctor felt a little uncomfortable talking about such matters, but his expression remained sympathetic and his manner self-deprecating. "Och! I am a practical man," he said, waving his hand nonchalantly.

"You did more than your duty asked of you, calling the undertaker yourself, liaising with him," insisted the widow. "And, of course," she added, "seeing to it that my husband was spared the knife."

Hunter nodded sympathetically. His associate, a Mr. Pertwee, could always be relied upon in such situations where great delicacy and discretion were required. He was wondering where all these appreciative remarks were leading when Lady Charlesworth pulled a small box out of a drawstring bag and handed it to him.

"I hope you will accept this as a token of my appreciation," she said. "This is for all you did for my husband in his last hours and afterward."

The anatomist opened the box. It was a mourning ring: a plain gold band onto which was mounted a small glass receptacle containing a lock of Sir Tobias's hair.

Hunter smiled graciously. "You are most kind."

The woman shook her head. "You are a master of your profession, Dr. Hunter. No other physician would have handled matters more discreetly. 'Twas a real blessing you were with him when he was taken from us."

John Hunter merely nodded sympathetically. "As I said, dear lady, the Lord works in mysterious ways." He wondered if she would be so generous if she knew that he had so much more than a mere lock of her late husband's hair in his possession.

The widow rose slowly. "Yes, my husband will be sorely missed," she reflected. "But I am sure Sir Oliver will do an excellent job."

"Sir Oliver?" repeated Hunter.

Lady Charlesworth looked at him quizzically. "Oh, I have spoken out of turn," she upbraided herself. "There is to be a formal announcement tomorrow. Forgive me."

The anatomist forced a smile. "Sir Oliver De Vere will make an excellent head of the surgical staff, your ladyship," he said. "But in the meantime, I'll not say a word," he assured her.

He waited until Mrs. Adam had closed the front door behind Lady Charlesworth to venture out of his study. In the hallway he could hear music, pleasing fortepiano music accompanied by a sweet soprano tone. He did not recognize it as his wife's. While her voice was perfectly agreeable, this one had a cadence and a quality he had not heard before. He moved nearer to the salon door as if drawn by some strange melodic power. Outside the room he listened for a moment until the last note sounded, and he was just about to open the door when he heard men's voices join with his wife's tinkling laughter.

Anne was so very different from him, he thought; sociable, witty, and accomplished in the arts. She would often hold gatherings, but she had not mentioned any visitors on that particular afternoon. Feeling indisposed to wait any longer, he put his head around the door. He saw his wife standing by the fortepiano while a gentleman was at the keys. Anne was pointing to something on the score, leaning over his shoulder with a familiar ease that did not please him. Franz Joseph Haydn had been a regular visitor for the last few days, working with Anne on some librettos. Women, he had heard, found this Austrian charming and warm and he attracted them like bees to a honeypot, despite his pockmarked face and enormous eagle's nose. Hunter, on the other hand, did not care for him.

There were two other men in the room; from the color of their skin he guessed them to be southern Europeans. One was about his own age and the other much younger, barely a man.

"Ah, John dear," greeted his wife warmly, holding out her

arms. "We were just putting the finishing touches to the can-zonettas for the concert."

Hunter did not return his wife's conviviality. He looked be-yond her to Haydn, who now rose from the keyboard and bowed stiffly.

"Sir," he greeted him, a smile on his face. "Your wife's poetry is an inspiration to us all."

"I am glad to hear it," Hunter replied grudgingly.

Ignoring her husband's curmudgeonly manner, Anne took him by the arm and drew him into the room. "Let me introduce Signor Leonardo Moreno and his protégé Signor Carlo Cappelli from Tuscany. Did you hear him sing? Does he not have the voice of an angel?" There was a girlish enthusiasm in her tone as she tugged at her husband's arm as if trying to cajole him into some sort of positive response.

Hunter eyed the two Tuscans carefully. They were both taller than average, and rather rotund, with their chests broad out of proportion to the rest of their bodies. Their fingers, too, he noted, were extraordinarily long. And that soprano voice he had just heard and could not quite fathom at first; now he could make sense of it, but to them he said nothing. Instead he simply turned to his wife.

"I look forward to hearing your libretto, my dear," he said sullenly, darting a parting glance at Haydn. And he left the four of them to return to his work in the laboratory.

Chapter 7

Thomas found the giant in his room after breakfast as arranged. Charles Byrne sat on a chair looking blankly out of the window. His shoulders were rounded and his head was slightly sunken into his neck. Last night the young doctor had regarded him as an acquaintance at a social gathering. A curious one, granted, but no more than that. Now, in the cold light of day, that relationship was very different. The distance between them seemed to have shifted.

The giant turned his head slowly to acknowledge Thomas. His eyes were dull and listless. Had last night's wine left him with a throbbing head, wondered the young anatomist, or was it that he was permanently in a state of melancholy brought about by some underlying condition or disorder? He noted, too, his patient's skin: "The canvas upon which the state of the other organs is painted," as Dr. Carruthers put it. If the liver is at fault, then the skin will turn yellow as bile seeps across it. If the heart labors hard to pump the blood around the body, then the skin becomes gray and mottled with purple. If the blood lacks nutrients, then the skin will be as white as paper. But there were other reasons to fear a pallid complexion, too.

This man's skin is as pale as a full moon, thought Thomas. The white death sprang to mind. He smiled warmly at his patient, but received no response. He then set down his bag and carried a chair from beside the bed, positioning it opposite. Still no flicker of civility, but was that suspicion he detected in the giant's look as he took out a notepad and pencil?

"I am here to help you, Mr. Byrne," he began. The man's large, square jaw remained set. "Do you feel generally well?"

The giant, who had remained staring ahead with glassy eyes, turned his head, his arms crossed defensively. "You are a s-surgeon?" he said slowly, a thread of saliva appearing on his chin.

Thomas nodded. "Yes. I am."

A look of dawning disgust spread across the giant's face. His brows knitted in a frown and his lips set in a scowl. "I do not speak to surgeons," he hissed.

Thomas remained calm. He was not altogether shocked. He had encountered enmity toward his profession many times before.

"May I ask why?" he ventured.

The giant was looking beyond him and out of the window again. "I do not l-like your sort," he replied.

The young doctor wanted to agree. He had not been at all impressed with his fellow surgeons in England, particularly after that shameful episode when two of them refused to conduct a postmortem on Lydia's dead brother. Nor had they covered themselves in glory at the subsequent murder trial. No, he did not like many of the anatomists he had encountered, either, but he would not allow himself to be defeated.

"I am not only an anatomist, but a physician, too. I heal the sick."

"You think I am s-sick?" asked Byrne.

"I do not know. I need to examine you first," replied Thomas.

There was a silence. The young doctor would change tack. A patient would always open up to him if he spoke to them about what mattered most in their lives.

"Tell me about your home in Ireland," he said, momentarily allowing his own thoughts to cross the thousands of miles of ocean that lay between him and his beloved Philadelphia.

The giant turned to face him. At last, a breakthrough, thought Thomas.

"I l-live on a lough," he said slowly. " 'Tis in the north of Ireland, and when the sun rises on the purple heather there's no place on earth more fair."

Thomas knew just how his patient was feeling. "You must miss it very much." He nodded, a pang of homesickness stabbing his own guts.

"That I do," replied Byrne, nodding slowly.

"I miss my home, too," sighed Thomas.

His patient turned to him, suddenly showing interest. "And where might that be, sir?" he asked.

Thomas smiled. Had he made a breakthrough? "In America . . . what the English call the Colonies."

Charles Byrne looked at him. Suddenly he seemed interested. Thomas persevered. "It seems as though we might have won our war." He had recently read that the British Parliament had called for the end of hostilities and the recognition of the Colonies' independence. He also knew that the Irish had good enough reason to hate their English masters, too.

"Aha, you showed 'em," cried the giant. His pallid face broke into a grin and he clapped his large hands together in delight. It was the first time that Thomas had seen him smile, but his physical exertion carried a penalty and he began to cough once more, this time bringing up sputum. He pulled out a brown-stained handkerchief from his breeches and held it to his mouth.

"There is b-blood," he told the doctor. His voice was resigned.

Thomas nodded, as if there was no need to tell him. "How long have you had this cough?"

The giant paused for a moment. "Since last Candlemas," he said.

Thomas stood up and held the heel of his hand to his patient's forehead. "You feel unwell, feverish?"

"I am well enough to go to London, sir," he replied.

The young doctor looked at him. His dull eyes seemed to twinkle at the prospect. "Then you shall go."

*   *   *

Emily left the rookeries just as dawn broke, stopping only briefly on her way back to scrape the cow shit from her boots. She made it to Cockspur Street just as the bell of St. Martin's struck six o'clock. The handsome house, flanked by trees, had been leased by the count a few months before. It was less than two miles away from where her family lived in St. Giles, but it may as well have been a different world.

" 'Tis a good job you're here, girl. We have work to do," Mistress Goodbody, the housekeeper, scolded. "The count and his guests will be here by nightfall."

Emily curtsied and went to fetch her apron. She had been tasked to make up the bed in the green bedroom on the first floor, but when she arrived she saw that two bed frames had been laid together side by side.

"I don't understand," she told Mistress Goodbody, who had come upstairs to check on her progress.

"You're to put the sheets and coverlets on loose," instructed the housekeeper.

"But please, I still don't . . . ," protested Emily, a pitcher and ewer in her hand.

Mistress Goodbody looked heavenward, as if asking for divine strength. "I suppose I may as well tell you now," she said, rolling her eyes. "Save you making a fool of yourself, gawping. The count is bringing back a special guest to stay: The gentleman is from Ireland and he's a—well, he's a giant."

Instead of preparing Emily for a shock, however, the housekeeper's words had the opposite effect on her.

"A tall man from across the water," the girl whispered breathlessly, her eyes wide with disbelief, and she dropped the pitcher of water on the floor, smashing it to pieces.

Chapter 8

They arrived at Cockspur Street in the early evening. Thomas was grateful that the surrounding streets were not busier. He did not wish the giant's arrival to cause a sensation. He could imagine him triggering panic, or even a crowd gathering outside the house hoping to catch a glimpse of him. Hence they waited until Lovelock signaled the all clear and Charles Byrne was quickly dispatched, without incident, into the safety of the count's lodgings.

At dinner the difficult journey did not seem to have dulled the little man's wits and he regaled his guests with more tales of his antics in the courts of Europe. Once again Charles Byrne remained taciturn, coughing into his balled kerchief now and again. It was not until it was time to leave for his own lodgings that Thomas managed to steal a few moments with Lydia alone.

"My love, I need to tell you something," he said, clasping her hands in the drawing room as he waited for the butler to bring his coat. "Mr. Byrne is ill."

She sighed deeply. "I feared as much. That is why I asked you to examine him, so that you can treat him. You will be able to cure him of any ailment."

Thomas shook his head and wondered at her blind faith in him. "I suspect he is *very* ill."

Lydia frowned.

"I need to examine him properly in my laboratory," he told her. "But I am not hopeful of the prognosis."

She shook her head. "What are you saying, Thomas?"

The young doctor took a deep breath. "I am saying our giant may not be long for this world."

A look of disbelief flitted across Lydia's face, but she composed herself. There it was again, he thought, that look of a supplicant at an altar, convinced her prayers would be answered. She told him softly, "I know you will do all you can."

Sleep had not come easily to Emily that night. When she closed her eyes all she could see was her aged grandmother calling out, and her ears were full of her ranting. And now she knew them to be more than mere blatherings, the insane ramblings of an old crone. They were prophecies. In the olden days they would have called her a witch and ducked her in the Thames to see if she floated. Nowadays, Emily told herself, people had more sense and took her soothsaying for what it was— true, for the most part. Had she not told her to look out for a "tall man from across the water"? What more proof did anyone need that her grandmother was a prophetess? But now that the giant from Ireland had come into her life, what next? Her grandmother had not told her if he was an ill omen or if he brought with him good fortune. She had heard tell it was bad luck for a woman with child to look at a dwarf for fear she might miscarry, but she knew nothing of giants.

She rose from her bed as dawn broke and dressed hurriedly, shivering with both cold and fear. She fetched the bucket of kindling, the tinderbox, and the tapers from the kitchen and climbed the stairs to the giant's room.

Putting her ear to the door, she listened. There was no sound, so she gently turned the handle and entered. The room was still dim, although she could make out a pair of enormous feet sticking out of the side of one of the mattresses that had been laid together.

She walked over to the fireplace, trying not to make a noise, and knelt down by the grate. Just as she had begun laying the kindle, the giant coughed. She looked over to the bed. He was still asleep. She carried on laying the fire. He coughed again, only this time it was louder.

In his bed the giant stirred. "Ma," he called out. "Ma, is that you?"

Emily stood up. "No, sir. 'Tis Emily, the maid, come to light the fire, sir," she told him awkwardly.

Shocked, Charles Byrne sat bolt upright in bed, the covers falling away. His torso was naked and Emily looked away modestly, feeling her face flush.

"Begging pardon, sir," she said.

Realizing his own nakedness, the giant, too, became embarrassed and drew the bedclothes up under his chin. He could show his bare torso to crowds of spectators, but it was not seemly to be seen by a lone young woman, and a fair one at that, he told himself.

"Would you like me to carry on with the fire, sir?" Her gaze settled on the floor.

"No. No, th-thank you," he replied.

Emily retrieved her bucket from the hearth and gave a small curtsy.

"If there's anything you need, sir, just ring," she said, looking at the pull cord by the bed.

"Thank you." Charles nodded. "I will."

Only the destitute or the devilish ventured out onto the streets of St. Giles late at night. Not even the linkmen with their lamps would guide the unfortunate stranger around the potholes and steaming dunghills of the district. God-fearing residents would fasten their shutters and bolt their doors against the cattle drovers, cutpurses, and footpads who became masters of this domain at dark.

Ben Crouch did not appear destitute. Dressed in a fine velvet topcoat and a beaver felt hat and carrying a silver-topped cane, he seemed every inch the English gentleman. Until, that is, one beheld his face. His large nose had been broken in several places and now veered sharply toward his right cheek, while above his left eye was a five-inch-long scar—a memento from a knife attack. For Crouch had once been a prizefighter, and this was his territory. As he roamed the streets that evening, his companion Jack Hartnett at his side to hold the lantern, he knew exactly who, or what, he was looking for.

The bell of St. Martin-in-the-Fields struck one as the pair rounded into Coal Alley and passed the Queen's Head tavern. From inside came the sound of fiddle music, mingled with bawdy laughter. A large, round figure leaned against the wall by the entrance. As Crouch drew nearer, he could see it was a woman. Spying the two men, she pulled out one of her pendulous breasts from her bodice.

"Fancy a feel of me bubbies?" she called. Crouch simply ignored her, but Hartnett, a sickly youth of no more than eighteen, put his hand out to touch before his master smacked him soundly about the head.

"We've work to do, remember?" he barked.

Hearing the voices, a blind beggar who had been sleeping in the lee of a wall nearby awoke. "Spare a penny, kind sirs. A penny for the blind man," he called, waving his cup. Hartnett spat on him.

On the other side of the lane, in a doorway of a hovel, Grandmother Tooley sat watching, a thick shawl wrapped around her hunched shoulders.

"Beware those that walk in the shadows," she called out loudly.

"Shut your mouth, you old witch," came a man's voice from a window above.

A moment later her daughter appeared at the doorway. "Come now, Mother. Back to bed with you," she urged, gently leading the old woman inside and closing the door on the night.

Undeterred, the pair carried on till the lane narrowed.

"So, 'e was somewhere here, you say?" Crouch muttered to himself as much as to Hartnett, and he began tapping the ground and the walls with his cane, edging his way through the shadows.

"Yes. A bit farther yonder," said the boy nervously.

"More light here," Crouch instructed.

The glow from the lantern fell on what seemed to be a large bundle of rags propped up in a corner. Hartnett let out a triumphant whoop. "Yes," he shouted as he kicked the pile with his boot. The bundle fell sideways and a man's emaciated hand flopped out of the dirty folds.

"I knew he were a gonna," cried the youth.

Crouch bent down and lifted the material. "Not much meat on him, but he's fresh enough," he concluded.

Hartnett smiled, feeling pleased with himself.

"Now get him up quick, or the others'll be turning before we get shut o' them."

The young man unfolded a hessian sack that he'd brought out of his topcoat and began stuffing the bundle into it as if it were straw while his master held the lantern aloft, all the time looking around him.

Between them they carried the sack back the way they had come, down to the end of the lane and around the corner once more to where a hay cart was waiting. They then heaved the cargo on board, where it joined three other sacks of a similar size, extinguished the lantern, and drove off down the road by the light of the moon.

Half an hour later they arrived at Leicester Fields and were met by the swarthy servant.

"Another lot for the doctor, Howison," growled Crouch, jumping down from the cart. Once inside the gates, Hartnett heaved the sacks into the cold store one by one, dumping them without ceremony on the stone slabs. A dull thud sounded each time a head hit the ground. Outside, Crouch held out his hand to Howison for payment, and a few guineas were deposited in his palm. Seemingly satisfied, he had just turned to leave when the servant called him back.

"Wait up," he said, beckoning. "Not so fast, fella. There's a special job for ye."

Chapter 9

Lady Charlesworth received Thomas in the darkened drawing room of her spacious town house. A small dog sat at her feet.

"How kind of you to call, Dr. Silkstone," she said softly. He was surprised at how young she looked, despite the puffiness around her eyes from shedding so many tears.

"I am so sorry for your loss," he said, clasping the widow's cold hand to kiss it. He had been meaning to call on her sooner, but his unexpected visit to Boughton Hall meant that almost a week had elapsed since the funeral.

"My husband's death took us all by surprise," she sighed.

Thomas nodded. "I was speaking with him only the week before. He seemed well enough then," he ventured. There were no physical signs of any illness that he could recall. "In fact, he had asked me to meet with him. I felt there was something he wanted to discuss," said Thomas. "Perhaps he had concerns about his own health," he suggested.

"That may well have been, Dr. Silkstone. He had complained to me about pains in his chest, but he was under much strain at the hospital," she told him; then, leaning forward in a confidential manner, she said, "I think there was some infighting."

Thomas had heard as much and knew firsthand how cruel and bitter his own profession could be, especially if prestigious hospital posts were at stake.

"I had begged him to take to his bed that day. He had one of his headaches, but he insisted on seeing Dr. Hunter in his study," said the widow.

"Dr. Hunter?" echoed Thomas.

"Yes, the two of them were in the study when Sir Tobias was taken ill."

"I see," said Thomas. "That was fortunate indeed that the doctor should have been on hand."

The widow bent down and picked up the small dog that was pawing at her skirts. She placed it on her knee and stroked it. It looked up at her with guileless eyes. "My husband was going to discuss some changes he was going to make at the hospital with Dr. Hunter."

"Changes?" repeated Thomas. "Do you know what sort of changes, your ladyship?"

She stroked the dog. "I was not privy to my husband's plans for St. George's, Dr. Silkstone."

Thomas felt duly chastised for asking too many questions.

"Poor Pixie here was most upset at the time," she continued. "She came barking to fetch me, didn't you, darling? But it was too late. The master was gone."

Thomas nodded sympathetically. He had to respect the widow's unquestioning acceptance of her husband's untimely death. To him, however, it seemed a strange coincidence that Sir Tobias died so suddenly on the eve of bringing in major reforms at St. George's. To add to these nagging suspicions, from what he had heard, he doubted very much that even Sir Tobias's corpse had escaped John Hunter's scalpel, with or without his prior consent.

With this in mind, instead of returning directly to his rooms, Thomas decided to go via St. James's Church in nearby Jermyn Street. It was here that Sir Tobias's death would have been recorded. The young doctor was a familiar face to the parish clerk. He was all too often called to register a death of a patient himself.

Looking down the pages of the ledger in the silence of the vestry, Thomas soon found what he was looking for: the entry relating to Sir Tobias. It was just as he anticipated. There was his name, the place of his death, his date of birth, and his occupation. As expected, the name of the doctor who attended was given as Dr. John Hunter, and in the sixth column, under the cause of death, was written "angina." This was certainly consistent with Lady Charlesworth's version of events, Thomas told himself. Nor did the entry in the final column come to him as any surprise. The death was "uncertified." John Hunter had seen to it that there was no official postmortem.

Thomas returned to Hollen Street just in time to prepare for a thorough examination of Charles Byrne. At Boughton Hall he felt he had managed to win the giant's trust, but now, surrounded by his instruments and textbooks, he knew he would be able to undertake a reasoned and informed investigation.

At the duly appointed time, Mistress Finesilver arrived at the door with his new patient. He was accompanied by the count.

"I shall wait outside, Dr. Silkstone," assured the little man. Thomas was relieved. What he feared he might have to tell the giant was in the utmost confidence, and it was clear to him that he remained ill at ease, surrounded by the paraphernalia of medicine. His patient's eyes flashed from one specimen jar to another with a growing sense of panic.

"I think we will be more comfortable in here," suggested Thomas, motioning him into a small room that he sometimes used for his female patients. There was a sofa, a dressing screen, a rug on the floor, and a high window that was inaccessible to prying eyes.

Anticipating the giant's unease, Thomas had already transferred all the instruments he would need into the room.

"It is good of you to come, Mr. Byrne," he said, motioning to a chair. "I understand your dislike of my profession, but I can assure you I am only here to help you."

The giant nodded his large head and sat on the sofa, which creaked under his weight. Thomas took out of the table drawer a notebook and pencil and proceeded to write.

"I shall ask you a few questions first, before I examine you. How old are you, Mr. Byrne?"

"I be twenty-one years," he replied.

"And where do you live in Ireland?"

"In a place called Littlebridge, near Derry."

"And do you have family?"

"I have a mother, sir, and was robbed of my father."

Thomas saw grief crumple his pale face.

"Do you know of anyone else in your neighborhood who is as tall?"

The giant paused to think. "I do that." He nodded. "Not five miles away. The Knipe brothers."

Thomas noted the fact. "And are you related?"

The giant shook his head slowly, then said helpfully: "No, but 'tis said we was all begat on top of a haystack."

Thomas smiled and nodded. It did not surprise him that such superstitions existed. "I will need to take measurements and weigh you. Is this acceptable to you?" he asked.

Byrne looked apprehensive. "It will not hurt," Thomas assured him. "But I would ask you to slip off your coat and your shoes so that I can be more accurate."

Standing on a stool, Thomas, using a tape measure, recorded the giant's height at eight feet two inches. His hands were eighteen inches long from the wrist to the middle finger.

"And now, Mr. Byrne, I need to examine you in little more detail," he said. Again, standing on a chair, he looked into the giant's mouth. He saw that his teeth were in a poor state and that several were missing, presumably because they had been extracted. His tonsils were also very large and pustulated, indicating to Thomas some form of infection.

It was an examination of the thoracic cavity, however, that Thomas was most eager to undertake. He had recently devised a form of ear trumpet that enabled him to listen to the beat of a man's heart and the sound of his lungs as they inflated and deflated. The idea had come to him when his father had given him a large knobbed whelk shell acquired on his travels along the New Jersey shore. He had been only ten years old at the time, but already he knew he wanted to follow in his father's footsteps and study medicine. Like all children he had put the shell to his ear to listen for the sound of the ocean. He heard it, of course, or imagined he did, but he wanted to hear more, and as

he grew into manhood, so, too, grew the notion of being able
to listen to the inner machinations of the human oceans that lie
within the body. His wooden ear horn enabled him to listen
past the gurglings of the trachea and the rumblings of the stomach and journey into the inner cavern of the rib cage that
housed the lungs. This would be the perfect occasion for its
first real trial.

The giant looked at him suspiciously as he held the strange
contraption in his hand. "Could you open your shirt, Mr.
Byrne?" asked Thomas. "I hope to listen to your lungs."

His reluctant patient obliged and Thomas set to work.
Putting the widest part of the cone onto the bare chest, he closed
his eyes. He could hear the sound of the ocean, of waves washing against a shore, but beyond that there was more. There was
the sound of a rhythmical rattle, a telltale rasp coming from the
lungs that to him cried out just one word—tuberculosis.

That night six men met in an upper room at St. George's. Sir
Oliver De Vere, the new chief surgeon, a cunning politician who
would always play one man off against another for his own
gain, sat at the head of a long table. Now that Sir Tobias was
gone they could formulate a plan. John Hunter was too arro-
gant. John Hunter was too powerful. John Hunter was bringing
their profession into disrepute, embracing newfangled instruments and unproven hypotheses, expostulating absurd theories,
and even consorting with known criminals. Their list of griev-
ances against him was endless.

To start, this John Hunter dared to challenge the great Galen.
Thomas Keate spoke out: "Surely, it is a universally held truth
that all illnesses stem from an imbalance of bodily humors? He
would challenge that, sir!" he told Sir Oliver.

"What cheek, what audacity!" cried John Gunning.

But there was more. This philistine, this Scotchman, eschewed the time-honored tradition of bloodletting, that most
versatile means of both prevention and cure of almost every
imaginable ill. "He would deny this most basic principle,"
wailed William Walker, his head in his hands.

"And instead of inducing a healing pus, he would allow wounds to scab over," added Gunning indignantly once more.

Worse still, Hunter was pressing for free lectures to be delivered to students, allowing them to practice their craft on real corpses. Sir Tobias had fallen into his trap and had been about to grant his wish when he so conveniently gave up the ghost. As if the practice of dissection could ever further the art of anatomy. "He grows too big for his boots!" exclaimed Everard Home, Hunter's son-in-law, and they all shouted "Aye!" in agreement.

Apart from their professional differences of opinion, there was, of course, the matter of the Scotchman's upbringing and origins. He was not one of them. He had not attended a good school, nor even been educated in the classics. He had shunned elocution lessons and spoke in his coarse Scottish Lowland burr. How could a surgeon take the Hippocratic Oath when, in all probability, he did not have an inkling as to the character or background of the great Hippocrates himself, they asked. He was terse in manner and sharp of tongue. He did not hold back in his criticism of them and spoke his mind far too freely. A soft humor and a winning smile were not his way. His conceited insolence and insufferable vanity, they said, were out of hand. Yet his physical appearance, disheveled and unkempt, with no notion of fashion or flair, showed him to be of a base and vulgar disposition.

There were rumors, too. Rumors they found very easy to believe; that he consorted with the lowest sort in taverns and did deals with resurrectionists to procure his corpses. "We've all been known to do that when times are hard," admitted Walker, "but these footpads, coves, and cutpurses he treats almost as his equals."

Keate agreed, banging his fist on the table. "He is nothing more than a cozening mountebank and a dilettante quack, and his 'work,' such as it is, is damaging our reputation and tarnishing our profession."

Sir Oliver, who had been listening attentively in silence, now held their attention. "You are right, gentlemen. Something must be done," he concurred, nodding his elegant head emphatically. "But what?"

Chapter 10

At first only a handful gathered 'round to look. Then, as those who could read saw the notices pinned on trees and affixed to doors, the news began to travel from Covent Garden, out to Holborn, Ludgate Hill, and beyond.

"Mr. Byrne, the surprising Irish Giant, the tallest man in the world . . . ," proclaimed the posters. This extraordinary spectacle, the reader was told, was to present himself at the cane shop next to Cox's Museum in Spring Gardens for the delectation of the nobility and gentry for the princely sum of half a crown each person.

" 'Tis said the giant has to take a walk when 'tis dark so as not to affright anyone," confided one of the motley onlookers to her neighbor.

Another woman trumped that. " 'Tis nothing," she chimed. "I've heard night watchmen have see'd him take the tops off street lamps and light his pipe by the flame."

A third smiled and said: "Well, I've heard he's hung like a donkey," and all of them cackled like a gaggle of fishwives.

Talk of the giant's physical attributes had also traveled to the Temple of Venus, a pleasure palace run by a libidinous fraudster, James Graham.

"You have an invitation to try out his famous celestial bed!" cried the count, flourishing a large card in front of Charles's nose on the morning of his first public exhibition. He was standing with Thomas in the drawing room of his Cockspur

Street lodgings. The giant, however, remained less than enthusiastic.

"I am not versed in the ways of Venus, sir," he replied languidly.

"Come, come, Mr. Byrne. I have heard great reports of Mr. Graham's temple. Delights that are out of this world." The little man nudged his friend suggestively, but he remained unmoved.

While Thomas did not share the count's enthusiasm for such bawdy pleasures, he still had his misgivings as to the giant's health. Charles sat looking morose in the corner. Yet still he refused to entertain Thomas's suggestion that he rest for a few days. He appeared determined to go ahead with his plans, and no amount of persuasion seemed to be able to divert him from his purpose.

Boruwlaski looked at the timepiece on the wall. "Three hours to go. Just time for a good shave," he declared. "I shall take you to my barber in St. James's. He will make you look like a veritable Adonis," he told Charles.

The giant, however, was less than eager. "I don't want no b-barber shaving me, sir," he muttered. The count looked at the uneven growth on his broad face and frowned. "But we must have you looking your best, dear friend," he exclaimed.

"I'll not go to a barber's, sir," said Charles Byrne, clearly brooking no argument. There was a hint of aggression in his voice that Thomas had not heard before.

Unhappy at this rebuff, Boruwlaski tugged indignantly at his waistcoat. "Well, I shall certainly go. There is nothing like a good shave to make a man feel civilized," he said, his tiny chin jutting out in defiance. He turned to Thomas. "Will you join me, Dr. Silkstone?"

The young doctor was slightly taken aback by the invitation. He had not intended to go for a shave, but after a short pause, he agreed. "I should like that." He smiled, feeling the light growth on his own chin.

The count nodded. "Then we shall take ourselves to see Monsieur Dubois this very instant," he concluded, and with that he left the room.

Thomas looked at his patient half apologetically as he remained in his seat. "We shall return before noon," he assured him. The giant nodded.

The red and white striped pole outside a bow-fronted shop in St. James's signified that Monsieur Francois Dubois was a practitioner of the art of barbering. It also signified blood and bandages. Thomas recalled hearing tales from the days of the barber-surgeons from his father, who was also a surgeon. Just before he was born, these men with no education or training would perform the duties of a physician: bloodletting, pulling teeth, and giving clysters. In Thomas's opinion, the Act of Parliament that separated the two companies had not come before time. Nowadays barbers brandished razor blades instead of scalpels and applied pomades instead of poultices. It was a great advancement, he told himself as he stepped into the small salon with the count by his side.

The first thing that struck him was the smell, the sickly-sweet perfume that wafted about the place, pungent, yet pleasant. He detected notes of sandalwood, musk, and exotic spices. Large flacons and apothecary jars were ranged on shelves around the salon. They reminded him of his own laboratory. There were even weighing scales so that Monsieur Dubois could, no doubt, concoct the olfactory sensations for which he was so renowned, the voluptuous scents of civet and ambergris that masked a multitude of malodors. His mastery of his art and its accoutrements had made him the talk first of Paris and now of London. Accordingly the more savvy gentlemen about town would bring their stubbly faces and their bulging purses to this most trusted and deft barber and emerge feeling smooth, scented, and sensuous.

Thomas and Boruwlaski found Monsieur Dubois, a lean-looking man in his later years with weasel eyes and a prominent chin, concluding a transaction with a customer. *"Au revoir, Monsieur Haydn,"* he said to the distinguished-looking gentleman who had just been shaved.

The count looked at the man. "Ah, Herr Haydn," he greeted

him familiarly, his little arms outstretched. The famous composer was an old acquaintance. "I trust you are well."

Haydn would regularly patronize Dubois's establishment during his stays in London. He bent down low to greet Boruwlaski. "It is good to see you, Count," he said in a heavy, guttural accent.

"May I present Dr. Thomas Silkstone?" said the little man.

Thomas bowed politely. Haydn's reputation as being popular with the female sex was known to him and he was, indeed, striking, although not conventionally handsome, thought Thomas, with his pitted complexion and strong features. What his physician's eye did note, however, was an inflammation and swelling around his nose. At first sight Thomas's instinct told him he could be suffering from severe nasal polyps. He said nothing and switched his gaze quickly from the composer's nose to his eyes when he smiled at him.

"Vot a pleasure," said Haydn as Dubois helped him on with his coat, but he was clearly in a hurry. He made toward the door that the barber held open, but walking out of the shop he called back: "We must dine togezer soon."

"Indeed, sir," the count called after him.

Boruwlaski, Thomas, and Dubois all watched the composer hail a sedan before returning to the business in hand. The barber's eyes momentarily emerged from under their sagging lids. "I am at your service, sir."

"Dubois, this is my good friend Dr. Silkstone. I have told him that you give the best shave in all London," announced the little man.

The barber's lips twitched. "Then we must see that we live up to your recommendation, sir." He turned and clapped his hands together loudly twice in the direction of a door at the back of the salon. "Jean-Paul," he called.

A heavy-framed youth appeared with dark, simian features and the same jutting chin possessed by Dubois, only this one sprouted scant black whiskers. *If this is Dubois's son,* thought Thomas, *it's a wonder that the barber has not dispatched that unsightly growth.*

The barber gestured to Boruwlaski. "The count," he said, and without further instruction the boy, who Thomas estimated was no more than sixteen or seventeen, lifted the little man up as if he were a sack of eider feathers and deposited him effortlessly on the pile of silk cushions the barber had arranged on a high chair.

"That will be all," the barber told his son, who, without ceremony of any kind, returned to the door from whence he had come.

Now that his task had been facilitated, Dubois proceeded to wrap a scented napkin around the count's tiny throat as Thomas watched from a seat nearby.

Silence was not a natural state for Boruwlaski, and as soon as his mouth was free again he began to jabber once more. "Herr Haydn is in London to work on his librettos with Anne Hunter," he said, recalling their recent encounter as Monsieur Dubois lathered his tiny face with scented soap. "He is giving a series of concerts this week," he informed Thomas.

"Anne Hunter, you say?" queried the young doctor.

"Indeed," replied the count. "She is John Hunter's wife and, I am told, Herr Haydn's muse." Thomas detected a certain tone in the count's voice that implied their relationship went beyond the professional.

"They are a strangely matched couple, the Hunters," remarked the little man as Dubois prepared his blade. "But happy in each other's company," he added reassuringly.

There was a slight lull in conversation as Dubois began his work. Thomas watched him with a strange fascination. Here was a man, he thought, who took his art very seriously, stroking the count's face with light sweeps of his razor; his hands, both of which, Thomas noted with interest, he used with equal alacrity, were steady and confident. The look of concentration on his face carried the same focus as that of Thomas's fellow surgeons. And why should it not, Thomas asked himself. After all, one careless slip of the blade and a man could be dead. The barber's face remained earnest throughout until at last, after a few moments, he flourished the blade away from the count's slightly nervous-looking face.

"Bravo," said the little man, feeling relieved to have emerged without a nick.

Now it was Thomas's turn to feel the barber's blade. His face lathered with a pleasantly scented soap, the young doctor concentrated on his own image in the large looking glass before him. With an almost hypnotic fascination he watched Dubois, razor in hand, execute his strokes with consummate skill. From out of the corner of his eye he could see the count was watching the process with equal fascination. He also noted, from his mirror view, that another man, an artisan from his attire, had entered the shop quietly and had walked directly into the back room.

Thankfully for Charles Byrne, the ladies and gentlemen who attended him on his first day exhibiting himself in the cane shop in Spring Gardens were not as lewd as the common throng, who could ill afford to pay a day's wages to view him.

Dressed in an elegant cutaway coat and knee breeches made in the choicest materials and wearing a fine tricorn, the giant's demeanor and appearance did not look out of place in these altogether more genteel surroundings. The count had seen to it that his waxy complexion and his lips were lightly rouged to mask his pallor, and he wore an elegant wig.

When the doors opened at noon sharp there was already a sizeable, but orderly queue waiting in a high state of eager anticipation. Charles Byrne stood in the main reception area on a slightly raised dais, but there was a chair for his own comfort should the weight on his legs become too much to bear. The count had instructed him to smile as much as he could and dribble as little as possible. He provided him with a large lace kerchief to assist him should his spittle become a hindrance.

The count himself had chosen to be in attendance at least on the first day to offer assistance, should some be required, and to field any abusive visitors, although he was sure good manners would prevail. And, of course, there was the added attraction of seeing the tallest man in the world standing beside one of the smallest men in the world at no extra charge. Who could resist such a memorable tableau?

Thomas and Lydia were also present. After Thomas's prognosis, the doctor was keen to see that his patient was not taxed too much.

From the sidelines they watched as the great, the good, and the downright curious filed past the increasingly famous giant, gawping and gasping at the sight. Thomas found the whole scene very distasteful and so was glad to see a familiar face in the crowd.

"Sir Theodisius," he called out. He and Lydia had been anticipating a visit from the Oxfordshire coroner during the week.

The portly gentleman waved a chubby hand above the melee and made his way toward the pair.

"Dr. Silkstone, Lady Lydia," he greeted them cheerfully. "What a show, eh?"

"You came alone, sir?" asked Lydia.

Sir Theodisius turned to face the crowd. "No. No. Lady Pettigrew is in there somewhere, with my sister and her son. He's the lawyer I spoke of. I will introduce him to you." He gestured to his wife and her companions, who were making their way toward him.

"Lady Lydia Farrell, Dr. Thomas Silkstone, I would like you to meet my sister Lady Marchant and the Right Honorable Mr. Rupert Marchant." He smiled as mother and son arrived. "Of course you know my wife."

Lady Marchant looked considerably older than her brother, but she had tried to compensate for the fact that her lined face gave her age away by painting it. Her skin, thought Thomas, had been liberally layered with white lead powder. Had she been his patient he would have advised against the use of such a cosmetic, which he believed to be toxic. Her elaborate wig was piled high with silk peacocks and ribbons.

She was fanning herself in an agitated fashion. "That giant is most disagreeable," she huffed, ignoring Thomas and Lydia. "He asked me why I should want to put birds in my hair."

Thomas stifled a smile.

"Have no care for him, Mama. He is just an ignorant ogre," chimed in her son. He, too, was dressed à la mode, bewigged and carrying a cane.

"He is but of lowly birth, my dear," comforted Lady Pettigrew, "and ignorant of good manners."

Lydia felt she could not stand idly by and see the giant's character attacked in such a way. "I can assure you, Mr. Byrne had no intention to offend you, your ladyship. He is from Ireland, where fashions are different," she said, eagerly jumping to his defense.

At these words, Rupert Marchant gave Lydia a curious look. "So you are familiar with this Goliath, my lady?" he sneered.

Thomas did not like his tone. "Her ladyship was instrumental in bringing Mr. Byrne to London, sir. She hopes to help him obtain a posthumous royal pardon for his father."

"Indeed so," chimed in Sir Theodisius, trying to lighten the ill-tempered exchange. "I suggested you might be able to offer your services in drawing up a petition, Marchant."

The lawyer paused, as if considering the suggestion, his eyes playing on Lydia's face as he did so. "That does sound an interesting proposition," he said slowly. "I am sure I could be of great assistance to her ladyship. Here is my card."

His manner made Thomas bridle, yet Lydia smiled graciously.

"That is most kind, sir," she replied, taking the card in her gloved hand.

"I look forward to receiving you in my chambers very shortly," concluded Marchant, bowing his head.

Meanwhile, over at the dais, the count had also spotted an old acquaintance.

"It cannot be," he cried, unable to contain his excitement as a handsome figure stood in front of him. "Leonardo Moreno, my dear, dear friend."

Tall, heavily built, yet elegant, the man, in his later years, bent down to embrace the count. "*Amico!* It is good to see you.

You haven't changed a jot," he greeted him in his native Tuscan tongue.

"No. I have grown neither outward nor upward!" The count laughed. The men had met at least forty years before at the Holy Roman Emperor's Court in Vienna and had remained firm friends, often coming across each other as they both toured Europe.

In those early days Moreno was in his prime as a soprano singer, famed for the exquisite tenor of his voice and the refinements of his style. His trills, roulades, and cadenzas were unrivaled among all his peers.

"So what brings you to London?" quizzed the count.

"I want to introduce the great cities of Europe to my protégé, Carlo Cappelli."

"So you are no longer singing?" asked the little man.

Moreno shook his head slowly. "I gave that up a while ago, my friend. No, now I am keen for Carlo to assume my mantle. He has exceptional talent." He paused for a moment. "In fact, he is performing a new libretto by Haydn the day after tomorrow at the Hanover Square Rooms. Would you do me the honor of being my guest?" He handed his friend his card. "I shall see that you are given a good seat. Please invite your own guests, too."

Boruwlaski studied the card with gold-embossed lettering. "I would not miss such an occasion for the world." He smiled.

Chapter 11

The sign that hung drunkenly on the door told all and sundry that Monsieur Dubois's salon *pour les messieurs* was closed for the day. Those more discerning clients, however, knew otherwise. Each Tuesday and Wednesday evening, the oil lamps in the back room of the barber's shop—and there were necessarily many of them—burned late into the night. Monsieur Dubois, the gentlemen's groomer and purveyor of pomades, wielded his blade in a far more exacting role. For on those two nights each week he was also a surgeon. Or so he fancied.

There were those of good means who would visit him regularly for bloodletting. Relieved of a few ounces, they would leave his premises either with a spring in their step or feeling rather light-headed, but they always returned for more. Just as some men would play cards or place wagers on cocks, so did a few hold out their arms for a spot of recreational venesection. It cleared their heads, sharpened their wits, and made them better between the sheets, they told him. But there was so much more to his talent. While clysters and tooth pulling were his bread and *beurre,* his many and varied chirurgical skills were also applied to corrupted tonsils, unsightly moles, and ingrowing toenails. He had even attempted an amputation once, although the outcome of that was less than satisfactory. However, all surgeons had their mishaps, he comforted himself, and yet because he could not frame a piece of parchment on his wall, he was denied the kudos and respect, let alone the income, that was due to him.

Tonight, however, was his chance to prove beyond all doubt that he was worthy to join the ranks of the real surgeons, the ones who had cast off his fraternity with such disdain almost forty years ago at the start of his career.

The patient, a carter by trade, had arrived not half an hour ago. Monsieur Dubois guessed he was roughly the same age as himself, but his wife and child had died a decade before. His complaint, he said, had been troubling him for more than two years and was worsening each day, so that now the pain was excruciating. A salty pearl was growing inside the oyster of his bladder. Its crusted spikes pressed like spurs on its lining, making the passing of a few bloodied drops of urine as eye-wateringly painful as pokes from Satan's pitchfork.

This carter was not, however, a man of means, and his continuing agony had meant that work was becoming increasingly difficult for him.

"*Ça ne fait de rien,*" Monsieur Dubois had told him. "No matter. I will remove the stone and not charge you." This would be his proof. If he could perform such an operation and his patient defied the odds and lived, then surely he would be welcomed into the surgeons' ranks with open arms.

Pain was written on the carter's face as plainly as if it were ink on parchment. Pain and apprehension. After all, this could be one of his last moments. As he sat nervously on a chair, the heel of his hand pressed hard against his lower abdomen in a vain effort to quell the sharp stabs, Dubois offered him a stoop of ale mixed with laudanum. He drank long and hard, so that by the time the two gentlemen entered the room he was barely conscious.

They arrived at the appointed hour. Jean-Paul opened the door to them and was quickly joined by his father, wearing a large apron with a capacious pocket at the front.

"Gentlemen, I am honored," Dubois addressed them, bowing low.

They followed him into the back room where the oil lamps were now lit. Ideally he would have operated in the daylight, near his window, but he would have to make do.

The carter was now asleep and Jean-Paul had deposited him unceremoniously face up on the long table in the center of the room. His buttocks rested on folded towels so that they were higher than his head. Dubois had removed the man's wig to expose a haze of white stubble over his crown, and his breeches lay folded on a nearby chair. A soft gag had been inserted in his mouth, so that if he awoke and cried out, the noise would be muffled.

"S'il vous plaît," said the barber, pointing to two chairs, one on either side of the table. The gentlemen seated themselves as if they were at the theater or about to play a game of cards.

From out of his apron pocket Dubois produced two strips of linen and motioned to his son to approach the table. Pushing both the carter's legs up brusquely so that his knees were bent, the boy then grasped both the patient's ankles in his great hands and thrust them back to meet his wrists.

The carter let out a befuddled yelp. *"Doucement.* Take care, Jean-Paul," chastised his father. He glanced at his silent audience and said apologetically: "He does not know his own strength." They remained expressionless.

Next he secured the ankles to the wrists with the linen strips. "The knees, Jean-Paul. Hold them apart," instructed the barber.

Now he took his place on the stool at the end of the table. The carter's perineum was presenting itself to him. He clasped his hands in silent prayer: "Oh Lord, guide my hands to do thy will," he intoned. At times like these he was so grateful to be ambidextrous.

From out of his pocket he produced a long, hollow tube and dipped it in oil from a vessel on a small table at his side. The first beads of sweat oozed onto his forehead as he inserted the lubricated catheter up the urethra. The carter winced.

"Hold him still." Jean-Paul clasped the knees tighter.

Now, with the tip of the tube, he probed for the stone with his right hand. Delving into his pocket with his left he found his scalpel. Had they seen him shake? It was now or never. He must work fast. He took a deep breath and cut the perineum, straight and clean. No sudden jerk from the carter. Good. Next he probed the incision with his forefinger. It felt warm and sticky. And there was the catheter above. Now a cut into the bladder. This time a wince and a stifled cry. At least the man was still alive. With his other hand he plunged into his pocket once more for a grooved rod; this he inserted into the bladder to capture the stone. It was there, craggy and malevolent, but it did not wish to budge. He moved the gorget inside with a circular motion. The stone seemed fixed. It would not drop into the groove. He prayed. "Oh, God, roll away this stone as you did at the tomb of your Son." But it refused to dislodge itself.

The carter tried to sit up. Jean-Paul knocked him back down with a blow to his jaw. The two gentlemen flinched, but said nothing. Dubois retracted the gorget, but there was no stone. He inserted it again, twisted it, jiggled it, retracted it once more. Still empty. Now came the blood, a trickle at first that soon turned into a stream. He reached for a towel and pressed it against the wound. He rose to check on the carter. His pulse was faint. He took the gag out of his mouth. His breathing was shallow. He rushed to the wound once more; the white towel now turned crimson. Sutures. He must stitch the wound. He jabbed the threaded needle in and out, but still the blood came, until it was impossible to see what he was doing. He floundered, his hands flapping in the bright, thickening blood.

Jean-Paul stood watching, transfixed by the scarlet ribbon that coiled on the floor below. The men rose.

"Sirs," pleaded Dubois. "What should I do?"

"You have done enough," said one.

The carter let out a strange gurgling sound, shuddered a little, then relaxed.

The barber's bottom lip jutted out. *"Pour l'amour de Dieu!* But you cannot leave me. I beg you!"

The other man remained unmoved. "We can give you a good price for the body," he said. The barber's eyes opened wide in disbelief. "Someone will call later tonight." And with that they left the shop and Monsieur Dubois alone with his bloodied hands, his silent son, and the still-warm corpse of the carter.

Chapter 12

That evening Charles Byrne slumped into an armchair with such force that it groaned under his weight. Emily had been making the room ready for the party's return, lighting the fire and plumping cushions. She turned to see the giant close his tired eyes.

"You are exhausted," said the count, handing him a glass of gin.

"Aye," he replied wearily. "Rich folks seem to stare h-harder than poor ones."

"But they pay well for the privilege," countered the little man cheerfully. "You made nearly twenty guineas today."

Charles Byrne nodded and took a swig of his gin, but just as he did so, he began to cough. In his ensuing struggle for breath, he let go of the glass tumbler, sending it smashing to the floor. The count hurried over to him as the ghost reached for the kerchief the count had given him earlier and held it to his mouth. His shoulders heaved up and down in great waves as he gasped and spluttered.

Emily looked on anxiously, feeling helpless.

"Shall I fetch her ladyship?" she asked, but just as she did so, Lydia, alerted by the coughing, rushed into the room.

"Call for Dr. Silkstone," she instructed.

The butler, the liveryman, and the footman were all summoned to help Charles Byrne upstairs to bed. He was able to walk slowly, but needed support and had to crawl on all fours up the stairs. They laid him down gently, and Lydia told Emily to fetch some water and a sponge.

"Today was obviously too taxing for you, Mr. Byrne," said Lydia.

Charles frowned. "I am tired, your ladyship," he acknowledged.

Emily returned carrying a pitcher just as Mistress Goodbody announced Thomas's arrival.

"Sponge Mr. Byrne's forehead," instructed Lydia as she left the room.

The young servant set down the ewer and poured water into it. She then soaked the sponge, wrung it out, and placed it softly on the giant's forehead, dabbing the beads of sweat off his brow. Her touch was tender and brought a smile to his face. Their eyes met and she returned his smile.

"Thank you," he said, staying her hand in his. He held it for a moment, then, much to Emily's shock, kissed it lightly. She shocked herself even more by not withdrawing from his grasp immediately, allowing her hand to linger in his for a little while longer.

A few minutes later Thomas had given his patient some soothing linctus for his cough and a draft to help him sleep.

"He must rest tomorrow," he told Lydia afterward in the drawing room.

"Of course," she replied, pouring Thomas a glass of sack from a decanter. "I shall see Mr. Marchant in the meantime."

"The lawyer?" he said quickly, recalling their ill-tempered exchange at Spring Gardens. "Then I shall come with you."

"That is kind, but I think not."

Thomas felt himself tense. He feared she would say as much. Jealousy was an emotion that he had never experienced before he met Lydia, and he disliked himself for giving way to it, but he felt an overwhelming need to protect her. She had experienced so much harm and hurt over the past few months. The last thing he wanted for her was to be the victim of yet more deception and cruelty at the hands of another unscrupulous braggart.

"That man cannot be trusted," he blurted.

Lydia simply smiled at him and brushed his arm lightly. "I do believe you are jealous."

Her observation piqued him, but he told himself to remain calm. "My dearest, do not forget what happened with another lawyer we both knew." He realized it was a cruel blow to deal. Her husband had been murdered by his own attorney, James Lavington, but as soon as Thomas had uttered the words he regretted them.

Lydia's expression changed instantly. She looked deeply hurt, and the young doctor rose and walked over to the sofa where she sat.

"I am sorry," he said, putting his arms around her, but she pulled away. Undeterred, he protested: "My love, I am merely warning you that the man has designs on you. It was patently obvious the way he looked at you."

Lydia shook her head. "That is precisely why he will do all in his power to help us," she replied. "I know what I am doing."

There was an awkward silence as they both realized that those were the first cross words that had passed between them. Thomas returned to his seat.

"Tomorrow evening should be enjoyable," he ventured, trying to lighten the mood.

"The concert?"

"Yes. It was kind of the count to invite us." He was going out of his way to be civil.

"I am looking forward to it," she replied, her voice softening.

"So am I," said Thomas, and, compelled to touch her, he rose once more and took her hand to kiss it tenderly.

"I will always love you, Lydia," he said, any resentment he had felt toward her quickly melting away.

She clasped his hand and placed her cheek on it, closing her eyes. "I do hope so," she whispered.

In his laboratory not two miles away, Dr. John Hunter was working late into the night, as he so often did. On his dissecting table lay one of the hessian sacks that Howison had acquired two nights before. It had been deposited in the cold store. He went over to the door to check that it was locked before returning to the table to inspect the contents. Loosening the drawstring, he pulled down the hessian to reveal the face of a young man in his prime.

Despite the sickly-sweet stench of death that emanated, he smiled to himself. The body had been well dressed for the grave, he thought to himself. Spices and herbs had been used, marjoram and musk and pulverized lemon, but of his grave-clothes and personal effects there was no trace. The sack 'em up men had been careful to strip him bare for fear of being tried for theft and therefore liable to swing.

His relatives would, no doubt, be praying that this man's soul would now be in heaven with the angels, but John Hunter knew differently. He had proof that this young cove had not led a blameless and pure life. His facial expression might have appeared calm, but it belied a darker side. Had he lain with a child virgin in the vain hope he might be cured? Had he infected his own wife, and if so, did his children now bear the scars of his licentious legacy?

He did not judge. So many came to him, even of his own kind, knowing the consequences of a moment of lust in a back alley or a stolen burst of pleasure in Covent Garden or Haymarket. Even prelates were prone to stray now and again. Man was a slave to his loins, no matter the consequences.

He was just about to resume his task when a sudden noise distracted him. He heard a clunk, the sound of something falling in a cupboard perhaps, or a sudden breeze from the high, half-opened window rattling a box. He looked about him. No one was there. His own nerves were getting the better of him.

With a scalpel he cut through the hessian, working his way down to the groin area. There was the telltale scabby rash on the torso, the copper-colored blotches on the skin, and, yes, there were the genitals, the penis now shriveled and limp. Despite its sad appearance, it spoke volumes to him. He picked up a magnifying glass and peered at the flaccid organ. A look of delight swept across his face at the sight of it: a pus-filled volcanic crater the size of a half crown, a magnificent chancre—the indisputable sign of venereal infection.

It was a disease that had blighted mankind even before Columbus's sailors brought it back from the natives of Hispaniola, he told himself. A plague sent by the Almighty as a curse on all profligates and their innocent offspring. It treated its prey without mercy, corroding the flesh, the bones, the vital organs. Worse still, it affected the mind, driving men demented and leaving their offspring a legacy of torment. It left thousands, no, millions, of men—and women—dead in its path. But he, John Hunter, would find a cure. There would be no more need to treat the disease with mercury, which poisoned the blood. No more need for the slow harbinger of death to gnaw away at the body. One day men would bless his name and women would sing his praises. He would be hailed as the healer of the scourge, the savior of mankind. But before that he needed to study the disease in depth. He needed to monitor its progress, notate every stage. He needed in-depth knowledge of every facet of its grotesque existence. And to do that, there was only one option.

Lancet in hand, he pierced the chancre with the needle and drew off the yellow fluid. He held it up to the candlelight. Liquid gold, he told himself, holding within it so many secrets and so many answers to mankind's problems.

Carefully laying the pus-laden lancet down on his table so that none of the precious cargo escaped, he unbuckled his belt and took down his breeches. He felt the beads of sweat on his brow start to run down his face, but he must not shy away from his task. He had to go through with this, he told himself, for the sake of humanity. He shuddered, swallowed hard, and took a deep breath, puncturing first his foreskin, then the head of his penis, before passing out in a dead faint on the floor.

Chapter 13

Lydia's carriage swept through Lincoln's Inn Archway and deposited her in New Square. The sky was heavy with gray clouds. She felt apprehensive, a feeling that was compounded by the fact that she appeared to be the only woman within the huge courtyard.

As she alighted the first rain began to fall, sending the lawyers in their black gowns scudding hither and thither like crows after a pistol shot. She wished now that she had accepted Thomas's offer to accompany her.

Standing at the bottom of a small flight of steps, she read the gold lettering on a wooden tablet: THE RT. HON. RUPERT MARCHANT. A somber-looking clerk answered the door and asked if she was expected. She was then led through to a room lined from floor to ceiling with hefty tomes. Not only that, but the floor, too, was covered with leather-bound volumes of all shapes and sizes, and seated at a desk in amongst them sat the elegantly dressed figure of Rupert Marchant. His wig was perfectly coiffed and the scent of sandalwood enveloped him. He rose as soon as he saw Lydia and walked over to greet her, bowing low and kissing her gloved hand.

"My dear Lady Lydia, it is so kind of you to grace me with your presence." He gestured to a seat.

She did not like his pretentious manner, but smiled and sat down. "It is good of you to see me, Mr. Marchant."

"I always have time for a charming lady," he replied, catching her eye. She felt the color rise in her cheeks and wished that Thomas was sitting beside her. But she would not allow herself to be distracted from her mission.

"As you know, I am here on behalf of Mr. Byrne," she began.

"Ah, yes, the famous Irish Giant," he said almost mockingly, sitting back in his chair and clasping his manicured hands on his lap. "I hear there is even talk of a pantomime in his honor at the Haymarket."

Lydia had heard the rumor, too, but continued undeterred. "His father, sir, was executed last year for the murder of a young woman in a village near Derry. He died protesting his innocence."

Marchant let out a dismissive laugh and threw his hands in the air. "Don't they all? I wish I had a guinea for every felon who told me he was not guilty."

Lydia felt indignant at his insult but, ignoring the slight, she placed a small leather satchel on the desk. "The real perpetrator of the crime has been arrested and convicted. You will find all the documentation here, sir," she told him in a very businesslike fashion that wiped the smirk from his face.

He leaned forward and opened the satchel, taking the documents out and scanning them briefly. His face hardened.

"And you wish a posthumous royal pardon for this"—he looked at one of the documents—"Patrick Byrne." His voice dripped with contempt.

Lydia nodded. "I do, indeed, sir."

He paused and looked at her. His gaze was intense, and if his aim was to make Lydia feel uncomfortable, he certainly succeeded.

"My services do not come cheap," he snapped eventually.

"Mr. Byrne will be able to pay you, sir."

"There will be a petition at the King's Bench. It will need to be brought by the *right* people, of course. There is the paperwork, the court fees . . ."

He was now gazing down at his desk, mentally calculating the monetary gain that he could make on the pages of some imaginary ledger, thought Lydia.

"I am sure, sir, that I can attract much support for the cause," she told him, her back stiffening in anger.

He looked at her with an unsettling glint in his eye. "Your giant is an Irish peasant, your ladyship."

Lydia bristled at his harsh words. "If that is how you see him, then I shall need to find another lawyer who is more sympathetic," she retorted, rising to leave.

"Please, please, my lady." Marchant rose, too. "Do not be so hasty, I pray you. Please." He motioned to her to sit down. "I may be a lawyer, but on this occasion I speak plain. You will not find many who want to take up this man's case."

Lydia frowned. "Why would that be?"

"Your giant is Irish and the king, as you well know, has no love of his sort. God knows they have caused us enough troubles over the years."

Lydia paused for a moment. "But is not justice a right to be enjoyed equally by all of His Majesty's subjects?"

Marchant snorted. "Now you are sounding like a colonist!" he mocked.

Lydia rose. "I see I had better take my business elsewhere."

Again Marchant relented. This time the sneer on his lips was nowhere to be seen. "I deal with realities, your ladyship." His tone seemed to soften. "If you are to succeed in your task, you must know the obstacles you have to overcome. Please," he said, motioning to the chair once more. She looked at him warily, but did as he bade.

"Mr. Byrne will need to enlist the support of as many of high rank as he is able," he told her earnestly.

Lydia nodded. "Indeed," she said, feeling that perhaps she was beginning to make some progress.

"But such support can cost."

Lydia was unsure as to his meaning. "Are you saying, sir, that we will need to *bribe* officials?"

He fell back in his chair, snorting once more. "Oh, oh, we do not use that word within these hallowed precincts," he chided her. "All I am saying is that certain hospitality may need to be offered in return for the signatures of eminent supporters."

"Hospitality?" Lydia felt the color in her cheeks rise again.

"Tokens of appreciation, favors . . ." His voice trailed off, but he held her gaze.

"As I said, Mr. Byrne will pay you, and pay you and any," she searched for an appropriate word, "associates handsomely. He is attracting many paying spectators."

"Indeed, and that is all to the good." A smile flickered on his lips. "If these documents stand up to scrutiny," he said, pointing to the satchel, "and there is enough support from those of high rank, then there is every possibility of success."

Lydia suddenly felt reassured. "So, you will act on behalf of Mr. Byrne?"

"I shall draw up a contract, if it is your wish, my lady," he said, leaning forward in an intimate manner.

"Yes, yes, it is." Lydia nodded, allowing herself to smile.

"Then I shall make ready the necessary paperwork and we shall arrange to meet again next week so that Mr. Byrne can sign the relevant documents of engagement."

"Thank you, Mr. Marchant," she said, and she rose to leave the office. She only hoped she had just taken a decision that she would not come to regret.

Chapter 14

Charles Byrne lay on his bed, thinking of home. Closing his eyes, he could see the sun shimmering on the glassy lough and the green-clad hills beyond. He could hear the gulls as they swooped and called over the water and he could smell the heather on the breeze and he wondered if he would ever return.

A timid knock broke his rest. Emily put her head around the door.

"Mistress Goodbody said I was to check on you, sir." She walked toward the bed. "Can I fetch you some water, or food, perhaps? Cook has made some broth."

Charles opened his eyes to see her face, fresh and youthful, looking down on him. He saw tendrils of pale blond hair peeking out from underneath her cap and the cherry red of her full lips.

"Will you sit with m-me?" he asked slowly.

Emily was straightening the bedcovers and stopped still at his words. She dared not look at him.

"Mistress Goodbody would scold me for that, sir. She would tell me I ought to be scrubbing or cleaning the brasses."

Charles Byrne's gaze remained fixed on her face. "And what would you say, Emily?" He said her name slowly and deliberately.

She allowed herself to look at him, his black hair spread out, his eyes tired and sad, and his skin so white that it was almost the same color as his pillow.

"I would say I would, sir."

His face broke into a grin. "Then I would say I was a lucky man."

They smiled at each other, and their smiles dissolved any barrier there had been between them before. Charles raised himself on his elbows and Emily plumped up his pillows. "In that case," he said, "I shall ask you to bring me a bowl of broth."

"Very good, sir," she said, curtsying.

He shook his head. "I am Charles."

"Very good, Charles."

She turned to go, but just before she went out of the door, he called her back.

"Tell Mistress Goodbody that my h-hands are very shaky," he said, holding up his right hand and waving it loosely in jest. "I shall need you to feed me."

Thomas had spent much of the afternoon lecturing on the physiology of the liver and was collecting up his papers as two or three dozen students were filing out of the theater when he spied a familiar face approaching.

"Ah, Carrington," he said. The student smiled briefly, but seemed unusually earnest. Gone was the affable ease that had so impressed Thomas before. "Is something wrong?" he asked.

"May we talk in private?"

The doctor ushered him into an adjoining consulting room and bade him sit. "What is it?"

The young man looked apprehensive and wrung his hands nervously in front of him on his lap. "It concerns Dr. Hunter, sir," he began. "I felt you were the only person I could turn to."

"Go on," urged Thomas.

"Last week I went to his laboratory late to continue some work for him, but I was overcome with sleep. I went into the small room that lies just off the laboratory for a quick nap. I must have been asleep for about half an hour when I heard Dr. Hunter return. I did not want to be chastised, not again. I knew it could mean an end to my career with him, so I hid in the room. There was a knothole near the bottom of the door, so I

crouched down to see what he was doing." The young man reddened.

"And?" pressed Thomas.

"I wish in God's name, sir, that I had not seen what I did."

Thomas frowned. "What did you see, Carrington?"

The student swallowed hard. His mouth was dry, as if the
words he needed to say were withering on his parched tongue.
Staring ahead of him he said: "He infected his own genitals with
pus from a venereal chancre."

For a second or two Thomas remained silent, computing
what he had just heard. "By God!" he exclaimed a moment
later. "Who in their right mind would do such a thing?" But he
could tell from the student's face there was more.

"It was a great sacrifice in the name of medical research, sir,"
he said solemnly.

Thomas nodded, but the shock was still shackling his tongue.

Carrington continued, twisting his hands as he spoke. "I
am afraid one of the prices Dr. Hunter might be paying is his
sanity."

"What do you mean?"

"I fear he is becoming irrational," said Carrington. His voice
was more measured.

"In what way?"

"The other night he was with Mr. Haydn in his study."

"Haydn, the composer?" Thomas recalled his encounter with
the Austrian in the barber's shop.

"Yes, sir. I was in the room next door and could hear them
talking when suddenly their discussion became very heated."

"Yes, and then?"

"Mr. Haydn suffers from nasal polyps."

"I am aware." Thomas nodded.

"I'd heard Dr. Hunter say that they should be removed before, and I assumed this is what they were discussing, but soon
there was a commotion. It sounded like a chair was being
knocked over and then the door burst open. I looked to see Mr.
Haydn being chased by Dr. Hunter. He shouted for Howison
and together they grabbed the poor gentleman and dragged him

back into his chair. I rushed in to see a pair of forceps poised over him, but he kicked out and managed to free himself."

"Then what happened?" urged Thomas, picturing the episode in his mind's eye.

"Mr. Haydn persuaded him to put away his instruments and he left."

"How extraordinary!"

"Yes, sir, and the strange thing was it seemed that Dr. Hunter pitied Mr. Haydn for not wanting to undergo the happy experience of enjoying his skill."

"Strange indeed," agreed Thomas.

Carrington nodded. "And I fear there will be more like that to follow, Dr. Silkstone," he said.

"More?"

The student turned his head, making sure that no one was eavesdropping on their conversation. "I fear that the infection is turning Dr. Hunter mad, and there will be no end to what he will do."

That evening Thomas called at Cockspur Street to check on his patient before accompanying Lydia and Count Boruwlaski to the Hanover Square Rooms.

"Mr. Byrne seems in remarkably good spirits," he said, settling himself next to Lydia in the carriage after examining the giant.

"Yes, he is much restored," she said, adding: "He says he will be strong enough to return to the cane shop tomorrow."

"Whatever you gave him, it seems to have fortified him," chimed in the count.

Having seen the way that his patient looked at Emily, who had been in attendance in the room at the time, Thomas was not sure that his sudden improvement could be attributed to any medicine he had administered, but he said nothing. Nor did he broach the subject of Lydia's appointment at Lincoln's Inn that morning. He did not want to stir up trouble. It was the count who raised the matter.

"Her ladyship's meeting with Mr. Marchant earlier today was most fruitful," said the little man.

"I am glad to hear it," said Thomas coolly, looking at Lydia.

Dressed in all her finery for the concert, she appeared even more beautiful to him. He knew she could sense his desire and tauntingly she held his gaze.

"We are to engage his services officially next week," she told him. He nodded but did not respond further, knowing that his own feelings of jealousy might surface once more.

For the rest of the journey, the count regaled them of tales of his friendship with Moreno and of how they used to entertain the crowned heads of Europe.

"But my dear angel no longer sings," he bemoaned. "We are to see his protégé tonight." Thomas had already read of this young singer in the newssheets. From all the talk of his "angelic" voice, he surmised he was a castrato. He knew from his research that in certain Italian states parents sometimes offered up their sons for castration to enhance their singing voices. The castrato's voice was prized for its combination of pitch and power. The operation, usually performed when the boy was around eight years of age, meant that his voice would never break, enabling him to reach the highest notes, delivered by the powerful lungs of a fully grown man.

When he had first read of the custom, Thomas was shocked, but while the Roman Church also officially frowned on such practices, it was one way a poor household could make money, as such boys were much in demand in church choirs. He wondered at the irony of it; how ugly it was to pervert the power of surgery in order to replicate the beauty of angels' voices. As a physician he could in no way condone such operations, yet he remained curious about the physical effect on the male body. Would its physiology be different? Would the chest be larger, the throat wider, he mused.

"I have heard this Cappelli can sing two hundred notes in one breath," said the count excitedly.

Thomas had heard, too, that he could sustain a note for a whole minute, but he remained silent.

Lydia smiled and looked directly at the doctor. "I am sure it will be an evening to remember," she said.

Chapter 15

The lords and ladies who spilled out of their carriages and up the steps of the Hanover Square Rooms that evening reminded Thomas of the exotic stuffed parakeets he had seen at the menagerie at the Tower of London. Bedecked in a dazzling array of colors—silks of crimson and blue, brocades in gold and green, and plumes of yellow and black—they squawked and preened themselves as they entered the lofty room where Carlo Cappelli was about to perform.

The count, himself looking resplendent in Polish military dress, complete with sword, waved Moreno's card at a liveried attendant and was led immediately to the front row of seats, followed by Thomas and Lydia.

There were greetings from acquaintances and stares from onlookers as they made their way through the throng. Moreno himself stood near the fortepiano at the front and went to greet his guests as soon as he saw them.

"All of London society is here, my friend," said the count, surveying the audience behind them.

The Tuscan smiled. "The whole world loves to hear the voice of an angel."

Thomas took his seat next to Lydia.

"I must tell you how beautiful you look tonight," he whispered. She turned to him and gave him a smile that told him all was well between them.

Thomas looked about him. The room was bathed in a magical glow from hundreds of candles. This was only the second concert he had ever attended. Or was it the third? He preferred the theater, the visual spectacle, but just watching these knots of colorful gowns and frock coats was a show in itself. At the other concerts, they had all milled about chatting, or eating chicken legs and swigging wine, only stopping their promenade when a particular oratorio or soloist took their fancy. This was altogether more civilized.

From the back of the auditorium he saw a couple walking toward the stage. As they drew nearer he recognized Joseph Haydn and, on his arm, a tall woman of obvious refinement. They both acknowledged the cheers that rose from the audience as they progressed down the aisle. This lady, this handsome, talented, bright-eyed woman, must be Anne Hunter. For a moment he watched her and he pitied her. Had she already been infected by her husband, he wondered.

From the stage before him, he could hear movement. He turned to see Leonardo Moreno striding into view. Now, as the Tuscan stood in front of the orchestra and choir to address the audience, a reverential hush descended, just as it did among Thomas's own students at the anatomy school as soon as he took to the floor.

The handsome former soprano smiled broadly. "My lords, ladies and gentlemen, it gives me sie greatest of pleasures to introduce a new work by si esteemed composer Herr Joseph Haydn." There was a burst of applause. "The libretto for sis new piece was written by Mrs. John Hunter." Another pause for applause. "And for the first time in sis great city of London, it gives me great pleasure to introduce to you a voice sat is so out of sis world that you will sink it is that of an angel. I give you Signor Carlo Cappelli."

More enthusiastic clapping greeted the young singer as he appeared on the stage and bowed low. Thomas estimated he was no more than eighteen or nineteen years of age and was possessed of very fine features. His eyes were large and fringed by long, dark lashes and his nose was aquiline. He was also extremely tall, he noted, and his chest was very broad. He strode purposefully toward the fortepiano, confidently surveying his audience just before the orchestra struck up under the guidance of Haydn himself.

From the first note to the last chord, the music was, indeed, ethereal. Cappelli's voice certainly surpassed anything that Thomas had heard before. Although he was no expert on the aria, it seemed to him that every trill, every roulade, and every cadenza was truly astonishing in its execution. The end of the first half of the concert was greeted with tumultuous applause.

"Is he not wonderful?" enthused Moreno, seeking out the count's party immediately.

"Indeed so, sir," agreed Lydia.

"Truly amazing," said Thomas.

"Bravo. Bravo," chimed in the count.

While the count and Moreno were engaged in singing Cappelli's praises, Thomas caught Lydia's gaze. He wished he could spend time with her alone, but their commitments in London had been so great that stolen moments were all they seemed to manage. He longed for the peace and quiet of Boughton Hall. But as he watched her, half-listening to the conversation of his male companions, he could see she found their talk tedious. She was scanning the room herself, looking for someone, anyone, she knew who might give her an excuse to break away. He would rescue her. He was about to suggest that they take a turn around the room together when something strange and inexplicable happened. He saw her expression change in an instant. Suddenly all the blood seemed to drain from her complexion and her eyes widened in terror. She turned hastily toward Thomas.

"What is it, Lydia?"

"I-I need some fresh air. It is a little stuffy in here." Her words were quick and there was a note of panic in her voice.

"You are right. Let us go outside," he replied.

She lifted her horrified gaze up at him. "No . . . no, please. I need to go alone."

"But you can't . . ."

"Yes. Yes. Leave me, please," she said breathlessly, glancing back over her shoulder once more. "I need to get away."

With these words, she brushed past Thomas, almost breaking out into a run as she headed toward the exit. The young doctor followed her as far as the door, but just as he was about to step outside, he heard someone call his name. He turned to see Lady Marchant, the old harridan he had met at the cane shop.

"Ah, Dr. Silkstone. How fortunate to see you here."

Thomas managed a polite smile, but before he could make his excuses, the woman launched forth. "I mean to ask you about an ache I suffer in my left arm that is putting me in a very sour humor."

"I am sorry to hear that, your ladyship, but perhaps we could discuss the matter in my surgery," he replied, all the time glancing over her shoulder toward the door.

"I can see you are distracted," said the dowager, somewhat annoyed by the doctor's anxious manner. "I shall make an appointment."

Thomas smiled, bowed politely, then started off again, stepping out into the night. Of Lydia there was no sign. All he could see under the glow of the street lamps was a carriage pulling away and heading back toward Cockspur Street with Lovelock at the reins.

When he rejoined the count inside he was short of breath and deeply distracted.

"Ah, Dr. Silkstone," said the little man, standing beside two gentlemen who were familiar to him. "This is Dr. John Hunter and Mr. Giles Carrington."

Thomas gave a cursory bow. "Indeed, we have met before. How do you do, Dr. Hunter, Mr. Carrington?"

The Scot was looking customarily disheveled. There was mildew on the back of his frock coat and he smelled of preserving fluid.

"Och, yes, we met at Charlesworth's funeral. You're the man from the Colonies, yes?" He was every bit as brusque in his manner as before.

"I do come from America, yes, sir," replied Thomas wryly. He found himself in no mood for pleasantries.

The Scotsman raised a thick eyebrow and put a hand on his shoulder. Turning him away from the count, he confided: "I dunni care where ya come from, laddie, I'll wager you'd love to get your knife into that young singer." His hand fell hard on Thomas's back in a playful slap.

Carrington witnessed the bizarre incident and held Thomas's gaze knowingly. There was no suitable reply to such an inappropriate statement, Thomas told himself, so he let it pass.

"I am content to hear him sing, sir," he replied.

It seemed Carrington might be right. The accursed disease could already be affecting the anatomist's judgment, he thought. He turned back to face the others.

Sensing a natural enmity between the two men, Boruwlaski intervened, tugging at Thomas's coattails. He endeavored to change the subject. "Dr. Hunter has heard of Mr. Byrne and would very much like a private audience."

Once again Hunter's hand found its way onto Thomas's shoulder. "So what do you make of him, this Irish giant?" he asked, almost confidentially.

There was a derogatory tone in the question that irked the young doctor. "He is my patient, sir."

Hunter nudged him. "Yes, but speaking as an anatomist . . . Come, you must have thoughts, man?"

Thomas smelled his stale breath and pulled away without wishing to seem discourteous. "I am only an anatomist when I am dealing with a corpse, Dr. Hunter. To the living I am a surgeon and a physician," he replied, his eyebrow arched.

The Scot pulled away just as surely as if he had touched hot coals. "Then you are not the man I thought you were, Dr. Silkstone," he said coldly.

At that moment the master of ceremonies took to the stage to announce the concert would resume in three minutes.

"But where is Lady Lydia?" asked the count, his little head spinning around.

Thomas frowned. "I am afraid she is unwell and has returned to your lodgings, sir."

"Lady Lydia Farrell?" interjected Hunter. "The pretty young filly I saw you with earlier? Husband was a murderer, yes?"

Thomas stiffened, but he managed to keep his anger in check. "No murderer, sir, but *murdered*," he replied.

"Och, yes, but he died in jail, awaiting trial, I think you'll find," sneered the Scot.

Thomas resented his tone. Ignoring his last remark, he turned to the count and said: "I must see that her ladyship is safe."

"Of course," said the little man, giving a bow.

"Dr. Hunter, Mr. Carrington." Thomas nodded, taking his leave.

"No doubt our paths will cross again shortly," replied the anatomist.

Thomas feared they would, but for now, his main priority was to see what, or who, had so disconcerted Lydia.

Arriving back at Cockspur Street shortly before nine o'clock, Thomas was greeted by an anxious Mistress Goodbody.

"Oh, Dr. Silkstone! Thank the Lord you are here," she wailed. "Her ladyship is most agitated and will not let anyone into her room."

"I will go and see her now," he said, striding up the stairs. He knocked softly on Lydia's door. Mistress Goodbody and Eliza, Lydia's maid, followed.

"Your ladyship," he called. " 'Tis Dr. Silkstone."

They waited in silence, with their ears pinned to the door, until a few seconds later, Lydia's voice could be heard, soft and tremulous.

"Eliza may enter, but no one else. I do not wish to see anyone."

The lady's maid looked at Thomas. He nodded, sanctioning her entrance into the room, while he remained outside until Eliza reemerged a minute or so later.

Looking uneasy, she delivered Lydia's message to Thomas.

"Her ladyship says that she is sorry to cause you concern, Dr. Silkstone, but that the evening tired her so much that she feels she needs to rest."

Thomas eyed the maid skeptically. "I see." He nodded. "Please tell your mistress that if there is anything she needs, then she must not hesitate to call me."

Eliza curtsied. "Very good, sir."

Thomas hoped he would have more luck seeing his other patient. He found Charles Byrne sitting up in bed, with Emily fussing over his pillows.

"I see you are much restored."

"Indeed so, thank you, sir," replied the giant, his waxy complexion almost glowing.

"You have a good nurse," remarked Thomas.

Emily blushed and curtsied. "Will that be all, Mr. Byrne, sir?" she asked, not daring to look at her charge.

"Yes, thank you," he replied, and the young girl withdrew from the room.

"So you feel sufficiently restored to return to the cane shop tomorrow?" asked Thomas, sitting on the edge of the bed and feeling for the giant's pulse.

"That I d-do, sir," he replied.

Thomas put the heel of his hand to the giant's forehead. The raging fever had subsided and his eyes were no longer bloodshot.

"You have made a remarkable recovery." He suspected the efficacy of the tincture he had administered had little to do with it.

Knowing it would be at least another two hours before the count returned to his lodgings after the concert, Thomas decided to go home. He would be back early in the morning to check on both Lydia and the giant.

It was only a ten-minute walk to his rooms and the night was still quite young. He kept to the main thoroughfares where the lamps were lit and mercifully managed to avoid the attentions of the cutpurses.

Dr. Carruthers had already retired for the night and Thomas

climbed the stairs wearily, but sleep did not come easily. His head was filled with thoughts of Lydia. Why had she acted so strangely? He replayed the evening over and over in his mind, retracing every word, every gesture, and every nuance that had passed between them. He remembered their conversation about the lawyer Marchant. Perhaps he was the cause of her distress? Yet she had seemed well enough at the beginning of the evening.

The bell of St. James's struck three before Thomas finally fell into a deep sleep. In fact, his slumber was so deep that Mistress Finesilver could not wake him simply by knocking on his door several hours later. It was up to the count to enter the light-filled room and rouse his friend with a tug on his shoulder.

"Dr. Silkstone," he called anxiously. "Dr. Silkstone. You must come quickly. Something terrible has happened."

Chapter 16

The chamber had been left exactly the way the maid had found it, save for the bloody footprints. The young singer lay on his back on the mattress, his eyes closed and the coverlet pulled up under his chin. His head was tilted backward and his dark hair framed his soft, almost feminine features. His skin was as smooth as alabaster and his lips were fulsome, but colorless. It was only when she saw the splashes of blood that had collected on the rug by the bed that the girl went screaming to raise the alarm.

Thomas arrived at Smee's Hotel in Jermyn Street just after eleven o'clock that morning. Sir Peregrine Crisp, the Westminster coroner who had engaged his services, had already ordered that the room be secured until the young anatomist's arrival.

Signor Moreno, whose own room was only two doors away, had rushed to the scene as soon as he heard the maid's screams. So overcome with grief and horror had he been that his instinct, according to the hotel's proprietor, the eponymous Mr. Smee, had been to try to throw himself on the corpse, but he had been prevented from doing this. He had, however, stepped on the bloodied rug, and the footprints that led from the room and out into the corridor were his.

The count accompanied Thomas, and on their arrival they were met by a somber-looking Sir Peregrine and Mr. Smee. Understandably, the latter appeared most concerned that such a terrible event should have occurred in his establishment. He was a very rotund gentleman who sweated profusely.

"This will not look good. Indeed it will not," he muttered to Thomas as he led him up an uneven flight of stairs and along a narrow corridor to the soprano's room.

Sir Peregrine, a man of imposing stature who wore a periwig that had been in fashion at least twenty years before, led the way into the chamber, ducking at the lintel. Thomas scented the ferrous smell of blood in his nostrils as soon as he walked in.

"The door was apparently open, not forced, but nothing has been touched, Dr. Silkstone, although those are Signor Moreno's footprints," said Sir Peregrine, pointing to the crimson stains.

"And where is Signor Moreno?" asked Thomas.

Mr. Smee stepped forward. "He's in a very bad way, Doctor. My word, he is," he said, shaking his round head.

"I shall go and see him," the count announced, leaving the room.

The window shutters were still closed and Thomas asked for them to be opened so he could see more clearly the horror that lay in front of him. The maid obliged, pulling them back with trembling hands before curtsying and fleeing in tears. Light now flooded the small room. It was furnished comfortably, with a chest of drawers, an escritoire near the window, and a washstand, complete with pitcher and ewer. On the bedside table was a candle half-burned in its holder.

Thomas walked over to the burr-walnut chest of drawers and opened them one after the other. A coat and two shirts lay neatly in the first. Two pairs of shoes were ranged in the second. The third was empty. On the dressing table sat a looking glass in a fixed easel frame. Two brushes were positioned next to a circular leather case containing everything a gentleman might need for his toilet: eau de cologne, wig powder, toothpicks, and an alum block for shaving.

Following the young doctor's movements, Sir Peregrine became agitated. "May I ask what you are about, Dr. Silkstone? I asked you here to examine the body."

Deep in thought, Thomas looked at the coroner blankly at first and then realized he was being addressed. "Forgive me, sir," he said. "But do you notice anything odd, anything out of place in this room?"

The coroner looked about. "No. No, I do not," he said slowly.

"Precisely," replied Thomas.

Sir Peregrine rolled his eyes heavenward. "What on God's earth is your meaning, Dr. Silkstone?"

"My meaning, sir, is plain. There does not seem to have been a fight here. No violent struggle. It may mean that Signor Cappelli's attacker was known to him."

"That is all very well, but I'd be much obliged if you could turn your attention to the body, sir," charged Sir Peregrine, drumming his fingers on the dressing table.

Doing as he was bidden, Thomas studied the young man's face. There was slight bruising around the mouth. He parted the full lips. It was as he thought; there were incisions where the delicate inner skin of the lips had been pierced by his own teeth, and the front incisor was chipped. It looked as though he had been suffocated, but turning the coverlet back revealed much more.

Even Sir Peregrine, a man who had seen more corpses than the alleyways of St. Giles in his long career, was forced to look away in disgust. The source of the blood became immediately apparent. The young man's throat had been slit from ear to ear, but instead of a long, straight gash, the normal method of dispatch practiced by muggers and cutpurses, a large portion of his entire neck had been removed. A gaping black hole was left in the throat.

Sir Peregrine held his kerchief up to his mouth. Even Thomas felt slightly nauseous at the sight.

"What in God's name . . . ?" The coroner's horrified voice trailed off in disbelief.

"It seems the murderer has removed the trachea," said Thomas thoughtfully, bending over the victim's throat.

"But what . . . Why . . . ?" The coroner was so troubled his speech was becoming incoherent.

Thomas delved into his bag and pulled out a pair of forceps and a magnifying glass. Carefully prizing apart the two short flaps of skin that skirted the wound, he peered inside the gaping hole. To his utter amazement he found that the entire larynx had been removed, and with it the vocal cords.

"This is extraordinary," muttered Thomas, to himself as much as to anyone who would listen.

Suddenly, from down the corridor the two men heard a commotion. The shouting grew louder.

"Let me see him. I must see him." The distraught figure of Signor Moreno stood in the doorway, his face tearstained. The count was with him, tugging at his coat like a small dog.

"No, Moreno, you must not . . ."

The tall Tuscan merely brushed the little man aside and lunged forward into the room before dropping onto his knees at the sight of the young man's throat.

"You should not be here, Signor," Thomas reprimanded.

The coroner motioned to a fretful Mr. Smee to remove his guest and he duly obliged, putting his arm out to help the Tuscan steady himself.

"Carlo. Carlo," he wailed as he was led away.

"May I take custody of the body, sir?" asked Thomas, walking over to the washstand to clean his bloodied hands.

"You are not to dissect it, Dr. Silkstone," chided Sir Peregrine.

"I mean merely to examine it, sir," retorted Thomas.

"You have until first thing tomorrow," instructed the coroner. "After that the Tuscan consular officials will want the body back for burial."

"Thank you, Sir Peregrine," said Thomas, rolling up his sleeves and beginning to pour water from the pitcher into the large bowl to wash his hands. As he did so, however, he noticed something odd. The liquid was a deep pink color and smelled of something he could not quite place. Remembering Dr. Carruthers's words when faced with such a situation, he quickly poured a small quantity of the water into an ampule. "Ignore nothing, however insignificant it may seem at the time," his mentor had said when lecturing on the art of the postmortem. Although it seemed insignificant now, Thomas told himself, the liquid might be crucial later on.

The body was to be taken to Thomas's dissecting room in Hollen Street as soon as Sir Peregrine could arrange a cart and an escort. In the meantime the doctor decided to walk back alone. He felt he needed to clear his head. Although he said nothing incriminating at the time, he had a feeling that whoever carried out that ghastly murder was highly skilled. There had been precision and cold calculation in the incisions. He was convinced he was not dealing with a crime of passion, motivated by greed or lust or jealousy, but of something much more chilling than any of these venal sins. Whoever murdered this young man not only stole his life, but his voice as well.

A slow and steady rain began to fall, topping up puddles and potholes that were already full from a downpour in the early hours, as Thomas walked down Russell Street, his feet slapping in the mud. Passing carriages threw up spray as they progressed along the uneven thoroughfare of the Strand and he was beginning to regret declining the coroner's offer of a ride back to his laboratory. He did not want him to know that he intended to return via Cockspur Street.

He was approaching the junction of St. Martin's Lane when a small post chaise, drawn by four horses, swept past him, splashing his stockings and breeches as it did so. He looked up to curse the postilions and saw, staring down at him from the carriage window, the face of Lydia. He saw her lips part and her eyes widen as he held her gaze before the carriage turned out of sight around another corner. He assumed she was heading for the count's lodgings. He quickened his pace, no longer caring about his muddied breeches and wet topcoat.

Five minutes later Mistress Goodbody was opening the door to the bedraggled doctor.

"Why, Dr. Silkstone, but you are soaked! Come in, come in."

"Is Lady Lydia in?" he asked, wiping his muddy shoes on the boot scraper.

"Why, yes, she has just returned not five minutes past," she said, taking Thomas's wet hat, clucking like a concerned mother hen as she did so. "Please wait in the drawing room and I shall see if she is receiving visitors."

It was not long before she returned, looking slightly crestfallen. "I am afraid her ladyship says she is too tired to receive you today, Dr. Silkstone," she said sheepishly.

Unable to hide his frustration, Thomas sighed deeply. "Is Lady Lydia unwell?"

"Not unwell, sir." Charles Byrne's loud voice boomed from the doorway. He stood towering over Mistress Goodbody, dressed smartly, with his dark hair hidden under a powdered wig.

"Mr. Byrne. 'Tis good to see you looking so restored," greeted Thomas as the giant strode toward him.

"I am much better, in spirits at least, sir," he replied. "We have j-just returned from Lincoln's Inn to see the lawyer who says he can get my da a p-pardon. I made my mark on a paper."

Thomas's expression changed. The giant's words wiped the smile from his lips. He had suspected as much, but did not want to think of it. So Lydia had just returned from seeing that braggart Marchant and now would not entertain him.

"Perhaps you could convey my respects to her ladyship and tell her I am always at her disposal should she need me?" Thomas told him.

The giant nodded his large head, detecting the annoyance in the doctor's voice. "That I will, sir."

Chapter 17

Thomas returned home to find the coroner's men off-loading the makeshift wooden coffin into the side gate. They were accompanied by the count, who was directing proceedings. Mistress Finesilver was also watching, mindful of doors being scraped and windowpanes broken.

"Have a care, will you?" she called as the men carried the coffin on their shoulders through the narrow entrance to the laboratory and set it down on the floor.

By now the rain had stopped and pale sunlight drifted in through the high windows of Thomas's laboratory, making it easier for him to see. Even so, he knew he had to work quickly. He had only a few hours in which to determine the cause of death and, hopefully, to provide the coroner with some clues or pointers as to who might be responsible for this dastardly crime.

"I smell blood," said Dr. Carruthers, feeling his way into the laboratory. Since he'd gone blind, his other senses had become heightened to compensate for his lack of sight.

"Indeed you do, sir," said Thomas, preparing himself for the postmortem. He donned his large apron to shield his clothes from bodily fluids as he worked, and made sure his hair was secured tightly at the nape of his neck. "Sir Peregrine Crisp has engaged me to work on the body of a young man found dead in his bed this morning."

"And I am assuming there was foul play," said the old anatomist, easing himself into a nearby chair.

"Yes, unless he managed to slit his own throat from ear to ear himself," replied Thomas.

He pulled back the sheet in which the corpse had been transported. Already the body was beginning to turn, and rigor mortis had set in. He was glad that his mentor was sitting nearby. It was always good to bounce ideas and theories off one so knowledgeable.

"I shall examine the whole first, sir, before concentrating on the wound," he told Dr. Carruthers.

"Indeed so." The old man nodded.

Beginning at the young man's feet and legs Thomas noticed nothing unusual, save for the fact that they were completely hairless. Apart from slightly more developed thigh and calf muscles, and indeed their length, they could have belonged to a boy. His abdomen was insulated with a thick layer of fat and his breasts were budding 'round the nipples, like a pubescent girl's. Moving down to the genitals he noted that this was, indeed, a castrato.

"Moreno told Count Boruwlaski the boy had been involved in an unfortunate riding accident," said Thomas cynically, inspecting the area.

Carruthers let out a jaundiced laugh. "Yes, I've heard the horses around Bologna and Rome are particularly prone to throwing their young male riders," he quipped.

The operation to remove the testicles had obviously been carried out many years before by someone using crude instruments. The scar tissue was still rough and jagged. There was no seed, but there could still be pleasure at least. He had even heard of a castrato who was chased out of a European court for his philandering. At least that was some compensation for the agonies the boy must have suffered during the torturous procedure, thought Thomas.

"What devils do such things in the name of religion?" he muttered under his breath.

He moved up the body to the torso. "Interesting," he remarked.

"What have you found?" Dr. Carruthers tilted his head.

Thomas ran his hands over the smooth chest and thoracic cavity. "The rib cage is much bigger than one would expect on a youth of this size." He had often surmised that the physiology of a body could be adapted by its various uses, just as animals seemed to adapt to their natural habitats.

"Could it be the lungs are more developed than normal?" suggested the old anatomist.

"That is possibly the case." Thomas nodded, aware that a thorough and intrusive surgical examination of the chest was out of the question.

There were just two more areas to examine before Thomas reached the neck wound: the arms and hands. Again there was no sign of bruising. Opening the stiff, pale fingers, he also scrutinized under the nails. As far as he could see they were clear; no scraps of flesh or strands of hair lurked beneath the keratin to suggest there had been any form of struggle.

"The fingernails are clean, sir," he confirmed. "And now we proceed to the face."

Thomas inspected the mouth cavity once more, bounded at the sides by the maxillary bones. They were still intact, but he noticed now that there were more cuts on the tongue. These, together with the lacerations on the fleshy folds of the inner lips and the broken front tooth, merely confirmed his previous suspicions.

The nose, too, once elegant and pointed, now veered slightly to one side. Probing deeper he also found that the two palatine bones that form the roof of the mouth and the floor of the nose were crushed. A huge force must have been brought to bear on the face to produce such an effect.

"We have a classic case of suffocation here, Dr. Carruthers," he announced.

"So the poor devil was suffocated before he was sliced up," mused the old surgeon.

"Thankfully, it would seem so," replied Thomas. "So now we begin in earnest." He stood upright, stretching his tired back muscles before hunching over the corpse once more, a pair of forceps and a sharp knife in his hand.

"Tell me what you see," instructed the old surgeon.

Thomas took a deep breath. Now he was entering a realm that was familiar to him. Like a watchmaker, he knew what to expect to find in the internal workings of the human body. He understood the mechanisms of each organ, each shaft of bone and each cushion of muscle and its correlation to adjacent parts. He had come to comprehend the relationship between elements that made a hole and of corresponding functions and purposes. Yet how strange it was to be confronted with a clock case when most of its inner machineries had been removed.

"I am looking at the neck. About six inches in length from the mandible to the clavicle," he said.

"A long one," commented Carruthers.

"I see an incision has been made at the front of the neck just below the thyroid cartilage."

"Incision, you say?" repeated Carruthers. "Do not murderers usually slash, or cut or gash?"

Thomas paused and nodded slowly. "That is my experience, sir, but that is why this case is so unusual." He peered at the deep, gaping wound. The skin had been cut away in a neat and deliberate square as if it were surgical gauze. The tissues around the opening were swollen and a thin, brownish fluid had crusted around the edge, yet the cut was smooth. The blade used, he surmised, was sharp, clean, and concise.

"Go, go on," urged Carruthers.

Thomas delved deep into the wound and probed it using a scalpel.

"Well?" The old doctor was growing impatient.

"I need to be sure," Thomas told him, lighting a candle. "Can you hold this for me, sir? I need to be sure that my eyes are not playing tricks."

The old doctor began to move toward the table and Thomas took his hand before folding his fingers around the candleholder.

"If you stay there, then I will be able to confirm what I suspect," the young anatomist told him.

Now that the area was illuminated, Thomas could see much

more clearly. There was the muscular tube of the pharynx, extending from the base of the skull to its junction with the esophagus next to the ring of the cricoid cartilage. There, too, was the tip of the oropharynx, but of the larynx, which would normally lie in front of the lowest part of the pharynx, there was nothing. Between the pharynx and the level of the sixth cervical vertebra was just a dark void.

"It is as I thought, sir," said Thomas, snuffing out the candle with his finger and thumb. "The killer has cut out the larynx and with it the vocal cords."

"But who would do such a thing?" said Dr. Carruthers, shaking his head. "He would have to be mad."

"Or a genius," added Thomas under his breath as he began recovering the cadaver. It would remain in the laboratory overnight until the coroner's men came for it at first light.

The sun had disappeared behind dark clouds once again and the report for the coroner needed to be written. By now the stench of the corpse was too bad to remain in the laboratory, so Thomas suggested that he and Dr. Carruthers finish their discussion in the house. It would be up to Franklin, Thomas's white rat that lived in a cage in the corner of the room, to keep guard over the body until first light.

The young doctor was just locking the outer door to the laboratory when he heard footsteps on the gravel pathway.

"Who goes there?" asked the blind doctor.

" 'Tis Count Boruwlaski," replied Thomas, watching the little man bluster toward them.

"Count, what is the matter?" he asked, seeing the troubled look on the visitor's face.

"Ah, Dr. Silkstone, Dr. Silkstone. It is Signor Moreno," he cried, trying to catch his breath.

"What ails him?" frowned Thomas.

The dwarf shook his head and gulped. "They have arrested him for murder."

Chapter *18*

Sir Peregrine Crisp sat behind his lofty desk and frowned over the pince-nez perched on the end of his ample nose. Before him were Thomas and the count, whose short legs dangled helplessly from his chair.

"But, sir, you have yet to see my report," pleaded the young anatomist.

The coroner shook his bewigged head. "I have yet to convene a jury, Dr. Silkstone, but in the meantime do we want a madman we suspect of brutally slaying another to roam around our streets?"

Thomas was quiet for a moment. He knew he must not let his temper get the better of him. "On what evidence was Signor Moreno arrested, sir?"

The coroner huffed. "I have a witness," he replied assuredly.

Thomas was intrigued. Glancing at the count he said: "To the murder?"

The coroner threw up his hands in a show of exasperation. "Not exactly, but the proprietor saw the Tuscan leaving the boy's room in the early hours of the morning." Thomas and the count exchanged glances. "Does that satisfy you gentlemen?"

It clearly did not. "With respect, sir, that does not prove anything," ventured Thomas. He thought of the count's elegant friend in his stylish high-cut coat and his powdered coif and wondered how he would fare in amongst the rabble in Newgate Prison.

"That is why you will give me evidence in your report, Dr. Silkstone," replied the coroner through clenched teeth.

"And what motive would Signor Moreno have?" Now the count entered the fray to defend his friend.

Sir Peregrine sighed, signifying he was growing tired of this persistent questioning. "Jealousy, of course. He had lost his own voice and simply could not bear the adulation accorded to his protégé. I saw the boy perform, too, you know. All London was talking about him."

It was true that all the newssheets had proclaimed that a vocal genius was in their midst. Thomas was privately forced to concede that such a motive might have been possible, but certainly not probable.

"And now, gentlemen, if you'll excuse me," said the coroner, pointedly reaching for a heavy tome from a pile in front of him, "I have work to do, as I believe so have you, Dr. Silkstone." A cloud of dust billowed up from the desk.

"You will have my report first thing tomorrow morning, sir," said Thomas, bowing formally before he and the count took their unhappy leave.

Dr. William Hunter's house in Jermyn Street was a very grand affair, as befitted his status as physician to the queen. His erstwhile neighbors included the Duke of Marlborough and Sir Isaac Newton, and he was in no doubt that history would dictate that his own name should be spoken in the same breath as such men of stature in years to come.

When it came to his dining table, however, all pretensions to grandeur seemed to dissipate. Regular guests never expected more than two courses at dinner and, what was more, only one glass of wine was ever served.

On this particular evening, in the company of his brother John and Rupert Marchant, William did not need more than one glass of his regular claret to put him in a lively mood. His guest of honor was Sir Oliver De Vere, the lately appointed chief surgeon at St. George's Hospital, stepping into the shoes of the recently departed Sir Tobias Charlesworth.

"I propose a toast, gentlemen," said William, raising his glass to the sharp-eyed man who sat opposite him. "To Sir Oliver and to St. George's. May they both prosper."

All present raised their glasses to the surgeon, who acknowledged the toast with a measured nod of his stylish head. He had a reputation for being a traditionalist and upholding the ways of Galen. "I hope I shall continue to see that St. George's carries on its excellent work," he replied, pointedly looking at John. William's attentions also turned to his brother, who returned a sullen glare.

"So, John, I hear you are embroiled in yet more controversy," he chided.

His sibling looked thoughtful. He had no real love for his elder brother, thinking him more involved in pomp and show than in true study. He resented, too, the many years he had spent in his shadow, doing his bidding in his laboratory without any recognition for his invaluable work.

"Och, if you mean my submission to the Royal Society on my observations on fossil bones, then it has sparked debate, yes."

"Come, sir. Surely 'debate' is too mild a word. I have heard you may be asked to amend the paper or withdraw it," goaded Marchant.

"You are playing with fire again, brother, are you not?" warned William.

John shrugged. "Was not Galileo persecuted for his remarkable discoveries? Did not our own Newton fight the repeated attacks of a papist king on our universities?"

William nodded. "So you see yourself on some great scientific crusade, do you, brother?"

"I only speak of what I find, and my work has led me to believe that fossil decay requires many thousands of centuries."

"And what of Archbishop Ussher's hypothesis that the moment of creation occurred on October 3, 4004 B.C. at nine o'clock in the morning?" asked Marchant.

" 'Tis the common and decent Christian belief, yet my brother challenges it," interjected William, growing redder in the face.

John shook his head. "Gentlemen, the facts speak for themselves. A single deluge, such as described in Genesis, could not possibly account for the vast fossil strata that have built up on landmasses. I have seen the evidence with my own eyes and I know that the sea has made incursions onto the land not once, but hundreds of times since creation."

William sucked in his florid cheeks. " 'Tis dangerous talk."

John shook his head. "These are dangerous times," he replied. "Indeed, revolutionary times. The Colonies, Ireland, France; they are all breaking away from the past, the old ways, and looking to new futures. That is what we must strive for—a new world, based on science, not superstition, and I make no apology for that."

"A high ambition," said Marchant, his fingers playing on the stem of his claret glass.

Leaning forward, John became even more intent. "At this moment, all I can do is catalogue life in all its wonderful variety, but one day I firmly believe that man will possess the power of God in a living world." His companions looked at each other aghast. "One day we shall all worship at the temple of science," he cried.

"Enough, brother! I will not have blasphemy in my house," countered William, banging his hand on the table and rattling the cutlery and plates.

There was an awkward pause among the guests until their host composed himself. He filled their glasses in an uncustomary show of generosity. "Forgive our sibling squabbles." He smiled at Marchant and Sir Oliver, knowing that a change of subject was required to lighten the mood. "So, speaking of high ideals, have either of you seen this Irish Giant yet?" he inquired jovially.

"As a matter of fact, he engaged my services only this afternoon," said Marchant. "He wants a posthumous royal pardon for his father, no less." His voice was tinged with contempt.

William nearly choked on his claret. "Ha! Now, there's a *lofty* ambition if ever I heard of one." .

"I had a mind to turn him down, of course, but he came with

Lydia Farrell, and who am I to refuse such a fair damsel?" Marchant sneered.

John sat back in his chair, his agitation seemingly subsided. "Ah yes, the fair Lady Lydia. I saw her only the other night at a concert."

"She is indeed fair, and now a widow," said the lawyer, grinning.

"So while you have your sights on her," said William to Marchant, "I'm sure you have yours on the giant," he suggested, turning to John.

"You are right, brother," came the reply. "He would make an excellent addition to my collection." He paused, stroking his wiry whiskers. "And that is why I have arranged to see him tomorrow."

"You waste no time, sir," noted Sir Oliver, an eyebrow arched.

" 'Tis not mine to waste," retorted John. "He has tuberculosis and will be dead soon enough."

"And you would get your scalpel into this colossus?"

"Indeed so."

"Then let me propose a toast to both your ambitions, sirs," suggested William, urging his guests to charge their glasses once more. "Let us drink to Beauty and the Beast."

All four men raised their glasses. "To Beauty and the Beast," they cried.

Chapter 19

Thomas's quill hovered over the parchment. He was finding it much harder than usual to commit his thoughts in ink. His single candle cast a long shadow across the blank sheet as he sat at his desk in the study. Mistress Finesilver had urged him to come to dinner, but he had eschewed her braised pheasant and asked her to prepare a plate of cold cuts. Now even that lay untouched on a table in the corner. The taste of decomposing human flesh was trapped in the back of his throat, and the stench of it still lingered in his nostrils and on his skin and hair.

His report on the postmortem of the young singer was proving difficult to write. He kept thinking about Signor Moreno's reaction to the death of his protégé. He was sure those were not the anguished tears of a murderer, and yet now the Tuscan was languishing in Newgate, relying on his report to either release or condemn him.

All emotions must be swept aside. All hunches, all intuitions, all feelings must count as naught and be consigned to the realms of the fanciful, he told himself. Logicality must reign supreme. Fact was his master and he would be guided solely by what he had seen, not by what he felt. His quill started to scratch the parchment. He began with general observations: how the viscosity of the pool of blood suggested that the murder had been committed at least two hours before the body was discovered. How the corpse had been arranged, how pillows had been plumped behind its head, how the waters of the basin were already bloodied.

Next he moved on to his clinical observations. How the discoloration around the mouth, together with the lacerated inner lips and the chipped incisor, indicated suffocation. During the postmortem he had also discovered the victim's nose had been broken, indicating great force had been used. One of the castrato's pillows, he had noted, bore teeth marks. He suggested the young man had been asleep when the pillow had been held over his face for at least two minutes. Such an exercise, he observed, would require great strength. Cappelli would have struggled. He may have been asleep when he was attacked, but the body's involuntary responses would have reacted violently. He would have kicked and thrashed, of that there could be no doubt.

The victim was dead before any incision was made into the neck, he wrote. Hopefully, he thought, the young man would have been spared the terror of knowing what unspeakable horror was to befall him.

The incision was made from right to left, then down two inches and across and up, forming a square. He paused, picturing the assault in his mind. Right to left? Could it be the murderer was left-handed? To get a purchase, the victim must have been held from behind. Surely the downward angle of the cut was relevant. He mused on the possibility for a few seconds, but chose not to include it in the report.

He went on: *A sharp, possibly surgical instrument was used to achieve this precision. The larynx, containing the vocal cords, was then removed in its entirety. The wound was then left open, but an astringent was applied to stem the flow of blood.*

In summary, the person or persons who carried out the surgical procedure on the victim had a detailed anatomical knowledge and were skilled in the art of either butchery or surgery, Thomas concluded. He hoped his words would be enough to convince Sir Peregrine that he had arrested the wrong man.

Glancing at the timepiece on the wall, he was surprised to see it was past nine o'clock. He rubbed his tired eyes and rose from the desk. Dr. Carruthers would be in want of his company.

"There you are, young fellow," cried the old anatomist when he heard Thomas enter the drawing room. "So, you have finished your postmortem report?"

"Indeed, sir. A most disturbing case."

"Tut, tut. I detect emotion in that statement," he rebuked.

Thomas nodded as he collapsed into a chair. "You are right. I should have said 'a most *interesting* case.' "

Throughout his tutelage Thomas had always been taught to distance himself from the corpses he worked upon. To allow any emotional attachment or empathy was strictly forbidden in the discipline of anatomy. Perhaps that was why, he told himself, deprived of any professional emotion, he felt so passionately about Lydia. Outside his work, his father, Dr. Carruthers, and Franklin, of course, she was the only thing in the world that mattered to him. He recalled her expression the last time he had seen her and how she had rebuffed him. He wished he could understand why. If she had been suffering some form of ailment or injury, he could have dealt with it, but when it came to affairs of the heart, he was a complete and utter novice.

"Pour yourself a brandy and sit down," the old doctor told him. "Tomorrow is another day. Your head will be clearer in the morning."

Thomas walked over to the sideboard and helped himself to a large glassful in silence, any words of conversation choked by the maelstrom in his mind. Then, as if Dr. Carruthers could read his thoughts, the old man asked, "So, how is the lovely Lady Lydia?"

Thomas never ceased to be amazed by his mentor's perception, his ability to read his mind without the capacity to even observe his facial expressions.

"I am afraid I do not know," he sighed. "She has forbidden me to see her."

"Dear, oh dear," replied Carruthers, shaking his elderly head. "That will never do. How have you offended her?"

"I wish I knew. I don't even know if she is angry with me, or with someone else, but she is deeply troubled, that much I do know."

At that moment Mistress Finesilver entered the room in a fluster.

"Lady Lydia Farrell is here for Dr. Silkstone, sirs," she said, her hands smoothing her skirts.

"Well, well." Dr. Carruthers chuckled. "Let us hope you can sort affairs out between you, young fellow."

Thomas flushed. "Show her ladyship into the study, if you please," he instructed.

He found Lydia waiting there, pacing the room and looking every bit as fragile as she had the first time they had met, two years before. He saw no profit in standing on ceremony, and as soon as Mistress Finesilver was out of sight he rushed forward to embrace her, but instead of returning his warmth, she turned her head away. Thomas let his arms fall to his sides.

"Lydia, my love, what is it?" he pleaded. "Tell me, please, and we can put it right."

Still distancing herself from him, she shook her head. "I wish it were that simple," she replied, avoiding his direct gaze.

Thomas paused. "It's Marchant, isn't it? He's ensnared you? He has wealth and a title," he blurted. "I am a colonist and a humble anatomist, not fit to join the ranks of English nobility."

Lydia swung 'round. "How can you be so hurtful?" she cried. Color rose to her cheeks. "You dare suggest such a thing? How can you think so little of me?"

Thomas immediately regretted his outburst. He knew it was fueled by jealousy, but he could see no other reason for her irrational behavior. Emotional chaos was descending onto his ordered world again and he needed to grasp hold of logical explanations to escape being consumed by doubt and suspicion. Once again he walked toward her, arms outstretched, but once again she rebuffed him.

"I have come here to tell you something, Thomas," she said. Her tone was unfaltering; well-rehearsed, he guessed.

He grasped both her hands, and this time, she did not flinch. "Tell me anything, but please just put me out of this darkness. Not knowing what ails you is killing me."

She took a deep breath to compose herself. "I am breaking off our betrothal," she said, pulling her hands away. Thomas stared at her aghast. She caught his gaze for a split second. There was a look in her eyes he had not seen before. Was it embarrassment? Or was it guilt? Whatever it was, she did not wear it well, he thought, and she turned and made for the door.

"But, Lydia . . ." He grabbed her arm as she reached for the handle.

"There is no more to be said, Dr. Silkstone," she said with a cold finality, looking down at the arm he held so firmly. "Your housekeeper can show me out."

Chapter 20

Emily threw open the shutters, letting bright light flood into Charles Byrne's bedchamber. The giant stirred, his wiggling feet, like great sides of bacon, hanging out from the bottom of the bed. She giggled softly at the sight of them and watched as he raised his tousled black head above the covers and squinted against the sunlight.

"Good morning," she greeted him cheerfully. "The count told me I was to wake you so you would not be late for your visit this morning."

For a moment Emily's words were lost in the fog of his sleep, until he remembered with a shudder. "The surgeon?"

"Yes. You are to be washed and shaved and wearing your best clothes by ten o'clock sharp." She knew she was sounding more like a wife than a maid, but the newfound familiarity between them delighted her.

"I hate his s-sort," he growled, still under the covers. "Prod and p-poke. That's all they do. I'd like a guinea for every time I've been measured by one."

"They're not all like that," countered Emily, pouring hot water into the ewer. "Dr. Silkstone is a good man."

"Aye. He's the only one I trust, to be sure. The rest of them are a bunch of cutthroats," he grumbled.

Slowly lifting himself off the pillows, the giant sat on the edge of the bed. Even so, the exertion made him cough. Emily handed him a glass of water, boiled and cooled on Dr. Silkstone's instructions, that was always kept by his bedside. He drank it and it eased him.

"Thank you." He managed a smile.

"I shall leave you now to ready yourself," she said, turning, but he took hold of her hand.

"Will you help me?" he asked, looking down at her with sad eyes. Even when seated he was still taller than she.

Emily flushed. "Sir, I am not sure that is allowed."

"But there is no valet who can dress me here, and I needs look my best," he pleaded.

"Very well," she conceded. "But I can't stay long, mind, or Mistress Goodbody will come looking for me." She paused, thoughtfully. "Let's start with your hair, shall we? It needs a trim."

The giant rose and, still in his nightshirt, sat in front of his dressing table, his stubbly face reflected in the mirror. Finding scissors in a nearby drawer, Emily first combed his long black hair, taking care not to pull it. In silence she trimmed the ends by two or three inches, watched in the glass by Charles, the oval framing them both like a portrait. His thick locks fell to the floor, a gathering carpet of black, until Emily gave the hair a final comb.

"To your liking, sir?"

"Yes," said Charles. He smiled at her in the mirror.

"And now for the shave," she told him. Taking a folded white napkin that she had brought with her, Emily shook it out and tied it 'round his neck like a bib.

"I ain't never done this before." She giggled, lathering the shaving paste with a badger-hair brush. "But I see'd my dad do it lots."

Gently and carefully, she applied the white foamy lather to the giant's face in small circular motions. Charles luxuriated in the sensation. Her touch was as light as gossamer. Every stroke was a caress that thrilled him to the very bone. The paste was scented, too: a sweet smell that reminded him of lemons and wildflowers.

In the mirror he watched her work diligently until she became aware of his stare. She turned and caught sight of them together.

"We make a fine pair," he said, still gazing into the looking glass.

"I don't know what you mean," said Emily coyly. She picked up the razor from the dressing table and dipped it in the water to warm the blade. "Now hold still, if you please."

She did not feel comfortable handling the blade, but she began steadily enough at the left cheekbone and worked her way down in short, hesitant strokes. Next she moved to the right side and began with the same staccato scrapes, but applying just the right amount of pressure to the blade. When she arrived at the jawline, however, her grasp slipped a little. Her hand was growing tired, but she resumed the shave until two or three seconds later they both noticed a drop of blood budding like a red rose from a small nick on the bone.

"Oh dear," she whispered, leaning over to wipe the dark droplet with the corner of the napkin, but Charles stayed her hand. His expression had suddenly altered. His eyes widened and a look of fear was etched across his face.

"I am cut," he muttered. "I am cut," he repeated, only louder.

"I'm so sorry," said Emily. "But 'tis only a small nick."

"I cannot be cut," he cried, ripping the napkin from around his neck and springing up, knocking over the washstand as he did so.

"I must not be cut," he repeated. "Never! Never!"

With a wide sweep of his arms he sent everything flying from the dressing table; the pitcher, a brush, and a pot of powders went crashing to the floor as Emily watched in shock.

Outside on the landing, Mistress Goodbody was passing and heard the furor. Putting her ear to the door she listened to Charles's rantings and Emily repeating over and over again that she was sorry.

The housekeeper flung open the door. "What is the meaning of this?" she exclaimed. There were broken shards of china on the floor and pools of water.

Emily hung her head in shame. Charles, lather still covering his chin, was standing on the opposite side of the room. His breathing was labored and what could be seen of his skin above the shaving foam reddened. In the commotion he had torn his nightshirt and his bare chest was plain to see.

"Well, Emily?"

"I was only trying to help Mr. Byrne, mistress. I—"

"I asked her to help me shave," interrupted Charles. " 'Twas no fault of hers. She is not to blame, Mistress Goodbody."

The housekeeper flashed a look at the floor and the broken china and the bedclothes in disarray. "I will send someone else to clean up this mess, bless me, I will," she said, shaking her head. To Emily she ordered: "You better get downstairs, my girl. I will speak to you later."

By now Emily was in tears and she brushed past her mistress as quickly as she could, leaving Charles to face the house-keeper's disapproving gaze.

"I am s-sorry," stuttered Charles. "I will p-pay for the dam-age and tell the count what happened."

"So I am not to discipline the girl?"

"Please, no," exclaimed Charles, obviously upset by the very idea. "Emily did nothing wrong. Believe me, 'twas all my doing."

"Very well," said the housekeeper slowly. "If that is your wish, Mr. Byrne. . . ."

"That it is," he assured her and she left the giant alone, standing by his bed, trying hard to hold back the tears.

Thomas arrived at the count's Cockspur Street lodgings shortly after nine o'clock, as agreed. He had slept fitfully, his mind a battlefield after Lydia's unexpected outburst. On his way there he had delivered his postmortem report to Sir Peregrine Crisp.

"I am convinced Signor Moreno is not the murderer," he had told the coroner.

"I will be the judge of that," came the terse reply.

As his carriage pulled up outside the house, he looked up at the window in the vain hope that he might see Lydia's face. He did not, but he was determined not to give in. He would find out, sooner or later, what lay behind her decision to call off their betrothal. She owed him that much, at least, he told himself as he pulled the bell cord.

Mistress Goodbody answered the door. "I will tell the count you are here, Dr. Silkstone," she said, ushering him upstairs to the drawing room.

"Is her ladyship in?" he asked her, unable to curtail his curiosity.

The housekeeper turned to him, looking perplexed. "Lady Lydia left for Boughton Hall first thing this morning, sir."

Thomas's expression betrayed his disappointment, although he tried to show a brave face. "Of course she did." He nodded. "Her ladyship did tell me, but it slipped my mind."

Left to wait alone in the drawing room, he felt a wave of betrayal sweep over him. Shock shot through every nerve in his body and he suddenly felt nauseous. This was not the behavior of the woman he had come to know and love. Without warning she had made herself a stranger to him.

"My dear Dr. Silkstone, is anything wrong?" The count stood next to Thomas, staring up at his pale face. "You look most distressed."

The little man's concerned greeting shook Thomas out of his own malaise. Behind, towering over him, making him look like a child's poppet, stood Charles, seeming every inch a gentleman in fine new clothes made especially for him by the count's own tailor.

"I am a little tired," conceded Thomas. "I had to deliver the postmortem report to Sir Peregrine first thing this morning."

"Ah, yes." The count nodded. "And what, pray, did you conclude?"

Thomas did not feel it proper to divulge the contents of his report. He said simply: "My findings will, I am sure, lift all suspicion from Signor Moreno."

Chapter 21

The journey to Dr. Hunter's country retreat, about an hour's drive away from Covent Garden, in Earls Court, was a tense one. The count was haunted by the unfortunate predicament of his Tuscan friend in Newgate Prison, while Charles was in a morose mood, staring out of the carriage window. Thomas's thoughts were also elsewhere. With Lydia. She would be on the Bath road by now, maybe heading out of Slough, or maybe even as far as Aylesbury. Was she feeling as utterly dejected as he was? She had broken off their engagement and yet it seemed that she only did so out of a sense of duty, not because she wanted to. Something else was driving her, he told himself. There was some terrible compulsion behind her actions, and he had to discover what it was before the gnawing suspicions ate away his very soul.

After about half an hour, the bustling streets where hawkers vied for space with cattle drovers and their herds gave way to a more rural landscape. Soon four-story houses were replaced by thatched cottages. Thomas noted that the air was sweeter, too. Instead of the stench of decay and preserving fluid that hung over his laboratory, and the smell of piss and horse dung that pervaded many a London street, he detected hay and grass on the wind. He breathed in deeply and began to redirect his melancholy thoughts into more positive ones.

The young doctor had heard much talk about Dr. Hunter's new premises. His famous collections of species, from tapeworms and terrapins to fungi and fetuses, had grown far too big for his Leicester Fields home, so he had purchased this large plot in the country.

As the carriage progressed into the grounds, through high, spiked gates, a sense of unease settled upon Thomas. Spring-guns were mounted on the crenellated walls, presumably to discourage trespassers. They passed a fishpond bordered not by dancing dolphins or mermaids, as was the fashion, but by a neat row of small animal skulls. On the lawns, strange birds the height of small men roamed, their necks as long as their legs, while in the pastures beyond Thomas swore he could see bison graze, just as they did in his homeland.

As they approached the house, a newly built villa of brick, Thomas could make out a crocodile's head, its jaws agape, projecting over the main entrance. Four stone lions guarded the front door.

The count obviously shared his wonderment. "What manner of place is this?" he muttered.

But there was no wonder in Charles's eyes, only deep anxiety. "I do not like it," he confided.

Thomas was inclined to share his feelings. Even as a scientist himself, he found the use of specimens as architectural decoration distasteful, verging on the grotesque. There was an eerie sense that nature in all its glory was being in some way perverted and mutated into something frightening and unnatural. He had even heard talk in the coffeehouses that droves of human monsters could be found roaming the grounds, only to be anatomized on their deaths. Of course he did not believe the rumor, but he could understand how it had spread, and since Carrington had told him of the anatomist's self-mutilation in the cause of science, he could almost believe it.

"Come; the sooner you are examined, the sooner we can leave this ungodly place," urged Thomas, helping the giant down the carriage steps.

No sooner had he said these words, however, than an almighty roar shook the very ground on which they were standing.

"What in God's name was that?" cried the count, clutching his chest in fright.

"That, gentlemen, was a lion," came a voice behind them. John Hunter was smiling broadly, obviously amused by their reaction to the noise. "He is one of several beasts—tigers and leopards, too—which I keep in my underground dens. But there's no need to fear. They are quite secure."

"I am glad to hear it, sir," said Thomas, sighing with relief.

The anatomist, wigless and wearing a shabby topcoat, was pleasant enough in his greeting, but he reserved his most effusive welcome for Charles.

"By Jesu, what a specimen," he cried, tilting his head backward to take in the full extent of the giant's size.

"Dr. Hunter, this is Mr. Charles Byrne," introduced the count, clearly finding the anatomist's address verging on the offensive.

"Forgive me, Mr. Byrne, but, och! 'Tis not every day I meet a giant."

The three visitors followed Hunter along the path that snaked behind the villa toward a long wing that housed his laboratory. As they walked, they passed a large pen. Inside, what sounded like dogs began barking loudly as they heard the party approaching. The surrounding fence was high, but there were cutouts in the wooden panels for observation.

Curious, Thomas peered through one. "Surely those cannot be wolves?" he said out loud.

Hunter stopped in his tracks. "Wolves, jackals, and dogs," he concurred in a matter-of-fact way. "I have penned them all together to see what manner of hybrids might come out of them."

"And have they?" asked an incredulous count.

The Scotsman shrugged. "A jackal bitch gave me nine vulpine monsters."

Thomas glanced at Charles, who was now even paler than usual. His green eyes darted here and there, doubtless wondering what new horror would be revealed next.

"What have we done, bringing him to such a place?" whispered Thomas to the count as Hunter opened the door to his laboratory. Inside there were more curiosities, all manner of strange, large insects from foreign shores pinned flat to boards. Small creatures, too, like bats and voles were suspended in fluid in great jars on shelves.

Thomas saw the familiar figure of Giles Carrington sitting by a workbench, hunched over some specimens. The young student rose and bowed, regarding the visitors awkwardly.

"Mr. Carrington," Thomas acknowledged him.

"The lad helps me with my preparations from time to time," Hunter explained. By him on the workbench were three dead doves, their pure white plumage stained red with blood at the breasts. Thomas stopped to look at them.

"My latest discovery," said the anatomist, pointing to the carcasses. "Birds breathe partly through their wing bones. The air sacs in the cavities communicate with those in the lungs."

"Fascinating," said Thomas, marveling at the man's enquiring mind while at the same time being troubled by his ghoulish imagination.

As Hunter began to move on, Carrington darted a knowing look at Thomas before seating himself again at his workbench and picking up a brush once more. It was then that something registered with Thomas. He recalled his postmortem report, or rather an omission from his report. Carrington, he noted, was holding the brush in his left hand.

They walked on past various contraptions and strange-looking devices that Thomas had never before encountered, until they came to a small door.

"You'll have to duck right down," Hunter instructed the giant as he opened it. "This is where I examine my patients."

Charles glanced anxiously at the count and Thomas and, as if anticipating the next question, Hunter said: "I would appreciate some time with Mr. Byrne alone."

Boruwlaski paused. "Is that agreeable to you, Mr. Byrne?" he asked.

The giant nodded slowly, but anxiety was written all over his face.

"Please, take a turn around my grounds, gentlemen. I am

sure you will find plenty to interest you. I will call you when we are done," insisted the anatomist, his facial muscles flexing into a brief smile.

Bowing, Thomas and the count departed reluctantly, leaving Charles standing in the room with the anatomist, the top of his head cocked to one side so as not to touch the ceiling.

Charles Byrne surveyed the room with mistrustful eyes. An assortment of small animals that were unfamiliar to him, some with striped tails and even one that carried its babe in a sort of pouch, stood lifelike on shelves in various poses.

"You collect d-dead things, sir," he ventured nervously.

Hunter peered at him over a pair of spectacles, but ignored the observation.

"Where I c-come from we string up vermin," he continued.

"So do we," replied Hunter, adding under his breath, "of the human variety, too." He gestured to a large table. "Perhaps you would be more comfortable seated."

The giant obliged, the table creaking under his weight. He shivered and felt his chest tighten as his lungs went into a sudden spasm, forcing out a loud cough. Now the anatomist, too, was seated and poised with a pencil in his hand. He watched with interest as Charles's shoulders heaved for a few seconds, but offered no assistance.

"How long have you had the cough, Mr. Byrne?"

"A few months, sir," he replied, wiping the sputum from his chin with his kerchief. It was colorless, and for that he was grateful.

"Do you ever cough up blood?"

"No, sir," he lied.

"How is your health in general?"

"I'm as fit as the next man, sir."

Hunter threw down his pencil onto his desk, almost disdainfully. "Come, come, Mr. Byrne. Your height and weight put huge strains on your skeleton. You must suffer from aches and pains."

The giant nodded. "That I do, sir, but I cannot complain."

"Then you will not mind if I examine you?" The doctor was smiling now.

"If that is your wish, sir."

"It most certainly is. You may divest yourself over there," said Hunter, gesturing to a three-paneled screen painted with exotic birds.

Charles Byrne lumbered over to the screen, which barely came up to his waist. First he took off his topcoat and then his cravat and waistcoat before beginning to fumble with the buttons on his shirt.

"May I keep my breeches on, sir?" he asked, anxious to preserve what little dignity he had left.

"Och, very well," replied the anatomist reluctantly. It was his patient's upper torso, and in particular his lungs, that interested him most, so he conceded.

Thomas and Count Boruwlaski were now free to roam around the grounds as they wished. Nearby they could hear the crowing of cocks and other sundry fowl and decided to head for the barnyard.

"I would be happier if I had stayed with Mr. Byrne," said Thomas.

"Hunter will not hurt him," countered the little man. "Remember he is an old acquaintance; an odd one, true, but he means no harm."

All is well as long as the harm he does remains confined to his own personage, thought Thomas. He nodded to the count. "You are right. The man's genius renders him rather eccentric, but his work is for the good of us all."

The two of them walked on toward the barnyard, both savoring the country air after the relentless assault of the capital on the senses.

"I envy Lady Lydia's return to Boughton," said the count. "The air is so much fresher there and the countryside so pleasing."

"Yes," agreed Thomas thoughtfully.

The little man raised his gaze. "Do I detect a note of melancholy?"

The doctor stopped and turned to face him. Abandoning all formality he said: "How long does she intend to remain at Boughton?"

Boruwlaski was taken aback by the young surgeon's reaction. "I am not privy to her plans," he replied. "I know that she has seen to it that the lawyer works on behalf of Mr. Byrne to secure the royal pardon. She has asked me to oversee those affairs, but . . ." His voice trailed off as he shrugged his tiny shoulders before he added: "I think you will miss her ladyship."

The count was a wily judge of character and no stranger to affairs of the heart himself, but although he was well-meaning, he had no comprehension of the emotional torment Thomas was feeling. He simply smiled, masking his pain.

"Perhaps," he replied vaguely. His answer, however, was not heeded by the count, whose attention was already focused elsewhere. Thomas turned to follow the object of his morbid fascination.

"What goes on there?" Boruwlaski asked as both men watched a swarthy laborer wheel a barrow laden with wicker baskets down a ramp and into a tunnel behind the villa. High-pitched squeals and squawks emitted from the hampers. The man, with dark, matted hair under his large-brimmed hat, scowled at them momentarily before disappearing through a passage down below.

"Laboratory animals. Rats and mice," said Thomas, suddenly reminding himself of Franklin. He knew these rodents would not be so fortunate as to escape their unpleasant fates.

They looked uneasily at one another, as if reading each other's thoughts.

"We should return for Mr. Byrne," said Thomas.

The count nodded and they both started to make their way back to where they had left the giant in Hunter's care. Knocking on the laboratory door, the two men entered to find the anatomist measuring the giant's thighs.

"Och, Dr. Silkstone, what perfect timing. I need a willing assistant to hold the tape at one end for the final, but most important measurement. Would you oblige?" His tone was almost amiable.

Thomas smiled reassuringly at Charles, who, wearing his shirt once more, seemed happy enough to comply with the anatomist's request. Thomas uncoiled the tape, which was marked off in inch sections, and held it to the floor as Hunter mounted a stool and reached to the top of the giant's head.

"Ninety-nine inches. I make that eight feet and three inches," he announced, almost triumphantly, as if he had just reached the summit of a mountain. "You must be one of the tallest men in the world, Mr. Byrne."

Hunter walked over to his desk drawer and reached for a wallet. Opening it, he took out some coins. "Here's ten guineas, Mr. Byrne. Thank you for your time. Our meeting has been most informative."

"Thank you. I am most obliged to you, sir." Charles smiled, pocketing the money. He donned his topcoat once more and he and the count filed out of the room. As Thomas began to follow them, however, Hunter caught hold of his arm. The smile that had been on his lips only seconds before was nowhere to be seen.

"You know, do ye not?" His eyes were steely gray and piercing.

Thomas looked down at his arm. "I beg your pardon, sir?"

"You know the giant is dying."

Thomas felt his guts knot. "We are all dying, sir," he replied, holding the anatomist's cold stare. From the corner of his eye he could see Charles and Boruwlaski heading back through the laboratory.

"I give him a year at the most."

"Let go of my arm, if you please," Thomas insisted.

The anatomist relaxed his hold, then patted Thomas's shoulder in a friendly gesture, but there was no mistaking his meaning. "Forgive me. I am a little *intense* at times," he said, adding: "But the giant will be mine, Dr. Silkstone. I *will* have him."

Chapter 22

The rabble in Newgate Prison had not been kind to Signor Moreno. He had been in custody only three days and yet the count had been told on good authority that his topcoat had been stolen and his face bruised and bloodied, and he had not eaten since the night before the murder of which he was now accused.

The stench of ammonia made Thomas's eyes sting as he and the count accompanied a turnkey down the sunless passage. Decay and pestilence lurked in every nook and crevice. Water dripped down cold walls and cockroaches scurried about over filthy flagstones. The flaming torches on the walls provided what little light there was, but most of the time there was hardly any. From railings to the left and right of them spindly, dirt-encrusted arms reached out. Young and old were penned together, those in their youth at the mercy of ruffian rogues and brutish felons well-rehearsed in the ways of villainy.

One toothless old man pulled at the count's wig, but the jailer coshed his hand and sent him yelping back into the corner of the cell, like a wounded cur. There were curses and insults hurled and cruel laughter, too, at the sight of Boruwlaski. "Dance, dwarf, dance," they shouted before spitting at the little man.

Finally they reached Moreno's cell. He was lying on the bare stone flags, his shirt and breeches torn and bloodied. Manacles clenched both ankles and were fastened to the floor. There were two other men sharing the same damp, stinking space. They, too, were all chained fast, but their faces were hard and their expressions threatening. One looked as though he might have been a prizefighter, thought Thomas. His nose had been so badly broken, it veered to the right. The other, younger man was angular and sly.

"Wait here," instructed the turnkey as he entered the cell and quickly locked the grille behind him. "You, Moreno," he called, prodding the Tuscan's shoulder with his boot. He groaned and opened one eye. Thomas saw that the other eye was swollen so much that it was closed tight and purple as a plum.

"You are to be moved. These gents here have come to help you," said the jailer gruffly, as if talking to a wayward child.

Moreno lifted his head and tried to focus on the count, who stood anxiously on the other side of the bars. "Leonardo," he called. " 'Tis Josef. Josef Boruwlaski."

Slowly the prisoner managed to sit up. From his languid, deliberate movements and the involuntary winces of pain he made, Thomas suspected that at least one of his ribs was broken. Finally he heaved himself up, clutching onto the slimy outcrops of rock on the walls. The turnkey unlocked his chains and pulled him by the arm.

"Am I free?" Moreno asked pitifully.

"No," replied the count. "But we can make you much more comfortable." The little man had paid the head jailer twelve guineas for easement of irons and to transfer his friend to a single cell on an upper floor where there was at least ventilation from a window. A pallet and a blanket would be provided for his bed, together with a piss-pot, and he would be fed two meals a day.

Slowly they walked up the steps toward the lighter ground floor. Thomas held Moreno as they went, the latter's arm around the doctor's shoulders so that he could support a good deal of his weight.

The air, although still reeking, was a little fresher here, and the turnkey showed the men into a cell through a door with a rusty grille in it. Although the room was small and the window high, it was infinitely preferable to the airless hole below, thought Thomas. He led the Tuscan to his pallet and laid him down gently. Opening his medical bag, he btought out iodine and gauze and cleaned the wounds on his face.

"Who beat you?" asked Thomas softly.

"The men," Moreno replied weakly.

"Which men? The other prisoners?"

"Yes," he whispered, both eyes still closed.

"Why did they treat you so cruelly?" asked the count.

Thomas was now examining the Tuscan's torso. It was as he thought. At least two ribs had been cracked like the broken wooden staves of a wrecked ship. The accompanying bruising told him he had been kicked mercilessly. He took out a long length of bandage.

"I need to examine your back," he said. "I need to turn you on your side."

Thomas summoned all his strength so that the turn would be swift and clean, so as not to drag muscle and bone unnecessarily, but as soon as the Tuscan was laid on his side, a horrible truth revealed itself to Thomas and he froze as he realized what had happened. A crimson stain blotted the seat of Moreno's breeches. Now the count's eyes opened wide in horror, as he, too, realized the heinous crime that had been committed against his friend. He turned away, retching.

Thomas had never dealt with such an abomination before, but he knew his first duty was to remove any shame his patient might feel.

"Signor Moreno," he said softly. "Who"—he searched for a word—"violated you, sir? Who did this to you?"

The Tuscan's shoulders began to heave in small sobs, and gently, Thomas eased him onto his back once more. Tears were falling from Moreno's blackened cheeks. The count poured beer into a small cup and stood by his friend's head, lifting it gently so that he could take small sips. After a few moments, the castrato appeared more composed.

"The other prisoners, they did this," he said. He closed his one good eye as if reliving the whole ghastly incident.

"Why would they do such a thing?" asked Thomas.

"They could tell, you see." His voice was as thin as tissue.

Thomas and the count looked at each other, puzzled. "Tell what?" asked the doctor.

"They could tell from my dress and my voice and my manners, sir, that I am not like other men."

The count clenched his fists and beat against the cell wall. "Animals," he wailed, his face flushed with anger.

"You will be safe now," comforted Thomas. "I will see to your wounds and then you must rest." He motioned to the count to bid Moreno good-bye for the time being.

"I shall leave you now, my friend, but I will be back tomorrow. We know you did not murder the boy, and we shall have you out of here in no time." The count laid a sympathetic hand on Moreno's shoulder and the castrato managed a weak smile. Thomas only hoped the little man's words, although spoken from the heart, would prove to be true.

Both men were in a somber mood on their journey back from Newgate, distracted as they were by thoughts of the Tuscan castrato's unutterable humiliation, even though they did not speak of it between themselves.

Thomas broke the silence. "I do not believe that Signor Moreno murdered the boy."

"Of course he did not," replied the count indignantly. "But how do we prove it?"

"Whoever killed Cappelli used brute force to smother him. His facial injuries prove it. I do not believe your friend is that strong."

The count raised his eyes heavenward. "You know that judges never take note of your science."

Thomas sighed. He acknowledged Boruwlaski's words to be true. Even Sir Theodisius had reached his verdict in Captain Farrell's case without having heard the scientific proof of his innocence.

"You are saying that the boy was smothered by a huge monster who then set about removing his voice with all the delicacy of a Parisian pastry chef," huffed the little man, with a flourish of his hand. He turned his back on Thomas in anger.

The doctor paused for a moment, digesting what his companion had just said. It suddenly occurred to him that he might have a point. What if, he asked himself, there were actually two murderers? One who committed the actual suffocation, then a second who carried out the removal of the larynx. One with the brute force, the other with consummate skill. It would make perfect sense, he told himself, but he said nothing. For the time being at least, it would remain simply a theory. He would need much more evidence to turn it into proof.

The count, still in high dudgeon, remained leaning forward on the edge of his seat looking out of the window, his chin resting on the open ledge.

It was a Monday morning and the carriage was traveling toward Hyde Park Corner. A noisy crowd was just dispersing from the hangings at Tyburn. The tippling houses were spilling out their contents onto the street, men so drunk they could barely stand. There were swells, too, now climbing into their carriages after having enjoyed the best seats from which to watch what they called the "entertainment."

Thomas could see the unfortunate criminals, hanging like rag dolls in the wind. He counted three of them: two men and a woman.

A loud cheer went up from the crowd as the hangman and his men cut one of the bodies down and placed it unceremoniously into a waiting tumbrel. The sides were demounted to show the good denizens of London that justice had, indeed, been done. It was then driven off slowly, followed by the city marshal in full ceremonial attire on a gleaming white charger, much to the excitement of the throng.

A few relatives or friends had gathered around the one remaining man. Some were tugging at his legs to shorten his suffering. Another seemed to be lying on the scaffold under a dead man.

"What is that man doing?" asked the count incredulously.

"I believe he is trying to catch drops of the dead man's sweat," said Thomas. "They say it cures scrofula." Boruwlaski looked puzzled. "A type of tuberculosis," explained the doctor, suddenly reminded of the giant's affliction.

"Poor wretches," muttered the little man, his eyes still fixed on the grotesque scene. It was then that he saw a ruffian in a wide-brimmed hat climb onto the scaffold. He looked strangely familiar to him. There was something about his demeanor that struck a chord.

"You see that man, there on the scaffold?" The count pointed ahead.

"Yes," said Thomas, leaning forward even farther.

"Do you not recognize him?"

The young doctor studied the stained topcoat, the large hat, and the swarthy complexion.

"Indeed I do," he said as he watched him produce a knife from its sheath and sever the rope so that the hanged woman fell down into another's waiting arms like a bundle of crumpled rags. "Indeed I do."

Chapter 23

Emily's head whipped 'round at the sound of footsteps. It was shortly before midday and she was tending the fire in the dining room. She was not expecting anyone. Charles Byrne stood nervously at the doorway, like a child waiting to be punished. He was to leave shortly for the cane shop for another day of public exhibition and was dressed smartly. "May we t-talk?" he said, wringing his hands.

Emily rocked back on her heels and stood up. "Of course, sir." She nodded warily and gave a little curtsy.

The giant walked forward slowly. His expression was serious and Emily could not hide her apprehension as he approached. If he were to lash out as he did before when she cut him accidentally, then he could kill her with one blow. Her body was stiff with anxiety.

Seeing the look of trepidation on her face, Charles smiled at her. "Please, do not be afeared. I'll not harm you, that I won't." He stretched out his huge hand, his fingers spreading to grasp hers, but she avoided his touch. "I want you to know what made me act like a m-madman. Please, Emily." He said her name gently and slowly, as if he were learning it, saying it for the first time. "Emily," he repeated.

Now she allowed a smile to flicker across her lips. He moved closer and then knelt down so that his face was level with hers. He was looking at her in the eye; their faces were so close they could feel each other's warm breath.

"When the razor cut me . . . ," he began.

" 'Twas an accident, sir," exclaimed Emily, pulling away. He took her hand and pulled her back toward him gently.

"I know that. For sure I know that, but when I saw the blood, it reminded me of my da."

Emily frowned. "How so?"

Charles took a deep breath. "You know that he was scragged for a murder he did not commit?" She knew the talk, that the giant wanted a royal pardon for his father. She nodded.

" 'Twas worse. They took him down and delivered him to be c-cut up." His eyes suddenly filled with angry tears. "The surgeons took their knives to him."

Emily's hands flew up to her mouth to stifle a horrified gasp. She had seen the Corporation of Surgeons process with a body through the streets from Tyburn, like crows 'round carrion, ready to pick over the bones.

" 'Tis a terrible fate," she whispered.

"Aye. Then they denied him a Christian burial, so now he lingers in purgatory. God rest his soul." Charles crossed himself.

"So he cannot go to heaven?"

"They took him. . . . They took his remains t-to the s-slaughter-house," he choked out.

Emily lifted her forefinger to his cheek and lightly but deliberately wiped away a tear. He took her hand as she did so and kissed her soft palm, sending a thrill through every sinew of her body.

"Now do you understand?"

She searched his sorrowful face. "I do," she whispered. She put her arms around his neck and his black head nestled into her shoulder and, eyes closed, they held each other tight.

It was this tender scene that greeted Mistress Goodbody as she walked past the half-open door.

"Emily, enough!" cried the housekeeper. The maid immediately broke free from Charles's embrace. "Again I find you! Be gone downstairs!"

Emily fled, not daring to look at her mistress, leaving Charles to face the housekeeper's wrath once more.

"This cannot continue, Mr. Byrne," she warned him.

Remaining on his knees, like some religious supplicant, the giant looked humble. "I am sorry, Mistress Goodbody. 'Twill not happen again."

"I will see that it does not," retorted the housekeeper, her face set hard below her large cap. "Bless me, I will," she said to emphasize her point before shutting the door behind her.

Thomas Silkstone sat at his desk in his laboratory and rubbed his gritty eyes. The light was fading and he had been reading over the notes he had made during the postmortem on the young castrato. He was hoping he might find a spark of information that he had previously overlooked. Perhaps, he told himself, it might ignite a new line of enquiry; shed light on a certain aspect of the gruesome affair; illuminate a motive. He thought, too, of the count's remarks; the idea that there were two murderers working in conjunction had taken root in his mind and was now flourishing. The more he considered it, the more plausible he found it: one a brute, the other a craftsman. But there were no witnesses. Surely if two men had entered the hostelry they were more likely to have been seen. He resolved to return to the hotel to question Mr. Smee.

In the corner, Franklin, his rat, was scratching about in his cage. Seeing him reminded Thomas of the barrow full of squealing mammals at Hunter's laboratory and of the anatomist's chilling words. "The giant will be mine," he had warned. He remembered his eyes, too, cold and ruthless, and he suddenly shivered. Charles would be horrified at the very notion of being dissected. He must never know of Hunter's designs on his corpse.

So lost in his own thoughts was Thomas that he did not hear Dr. Carruthers shuffle into the room until he was standing close by.

"Ah, young fellow, how goes it?" he asked jovially.

Thomas smiled and turned to see his elderly master, dressed for dinner.

"You will be joining me tonight?"

Thomas had not dined with the old man since before the

night Lydia had announced she was breaking off their betrothal. His appetite had completely deserted him, but he knew that in order for his brain to function, let alone his body, he needed to take some nourishment, even if it was only a little.

"I will come with you now, sir," he replied, standing up and tidying his papers.

Thomas took Carruthers's arm and walked with him to the dining room. Unbeknownst to him, Mistress Finesilver had been instructed to serve his favorite dishes, boiled plovers' eggs and stewed carp. But even her finest offerings went barely touched. Conversation at the table was also difficult, despite the old anatomist's best efforts.

Finally, after trying to engage his protégé all evening, Carruthers could take Thomas's taciturn replies no longer. "I am not sure what passed between you and Lady Lydia the other night, but whatever it was, it has put you in a sour humor, young fellow," he said, pointing an accusatory fork in Thomas's direction.

The young doctor nodded. "I am aware that I am not my usual self," he acknowledged.

"Your usual self?" mocked Carruthers. "You are like a bear with a sore head."

Thomas felt obliged to give some form of explanation, while not revealing the full truth about the nature of his relationship with Lydia. "Her ladyship has left for Boughton and I am not sure when, or indeed if, she is to return."

"I thought as much." Carruthers nodded sagely. "So what do you plan to do about it?"

Thomas frowned. "I plan nothing, sir. She has told me in no uncertain terms that she no longer wishes to see me."

The old doctor let out a laugh. "Pah!" he cried, pushing his empty plate away from him. "You, one of the best anatomists in all London, nay, the world, are prepared to do as you are told by a young woman who is clearly unhappy?"

Once again, his master's intuition was correct. He must have sensed Lydia's troubled disposition on the night she visited the house.

"I have never known you to settle for the obvious, Thomas. Have you learned nothing from me? You may be an excellent surgeon, but of the heart you have very little experience. Look under the surface. Probe deeper, young fellow. Only then will you find the truth."

Thomas toyed with the stem of his wineglass. It remained full of claret. "You are right," he conceded. "But I cannot go to Boughton. An innocent man is behind bars for a murder he did not commit, the real killer or killers are still at large, and the giant needs my protection."

"So much weight on such young shoulders!" said Carruthers, wiping his chin with his napkin. "Then you must apply your surgeon's skills to more romantic affairs."

Thomas looked puzzled. "I am not sure I follow, sir."

The old man chuckled. "You may be good at wielding a scalpel, but try wielding your quill for something other than a postmortem report."

Thomas remained uncertain.

"Zounds! Write to her, young fellow. Tell her how you feel in a letter. Then you can be as logical in your arguments as you like."

"Yes," Thomas said slowly. The idea of making a reasoned argument greatly appealed to him. "You are right, sir."

"Logical, but tender, mind," warned Carruthers, raising a stern finger. "That way you have a much better chance of winning her back."

His old master was rarely wrong, thought Thomas. Even so, he knew this letter would require more of him than any postmortem report he had ever written.

Chapter 24

Lydia's unexpected arrival at Boughton Hall sent the household into a flurry. Her ladyship was not expected back from London for at least a month, and Mistress Firebrace, the housekeeper, had ordered the shutters in all the main reception rooms to be closed and dust sheets to be laid over the furniture. In fact, the first anyone knew of their mistress's return was when Will, the stable lad, came running into the kitchen with the news that her carriage had just driven through the main gates.

Mistress Claddingbowl went wailing into the larder, complaining that she had let provisions run low, and Howard the butler sent Hannah Lovelock and the other maids off 'round the house to pull up the downstairs blinds.

The servants only managed to assemble on the front steps of the hall, as was customary on her ladyship's homecoming, as her carriage swept 'round the circular drive and came to a halt. The diminutive Lydia alighted, looking even more fragile than when she had left. Her face was pale and drawn and she did not even manage to smile at the servants as she usually did.

"Welcome home, your ladyship," greeted Howard as she passed him on the steps.

"Thank you, Howard. I will go straight to my room," was all she replied as she headed inside and up the sweeping staircase.

Howard shot the housekeeper a worried look. He had not seen his mistress so forlorn since her sick and elderly mother had passed away almost six months ago. Prior to that had been the death of her husband and, of course, the murder of James Lavington and the subsequent execution of her cousin Francis. The whole sorry episode had taken its toll on her, yet, with Dr. Silkstone's help, she seemed to have recovered well. Her spirits had been once more restored and the air of gloom and depression that had hung over Boughton Hall for the past few months had apparently been lifted.

The arrival of her father's old friend Count Boruwlaski had been a welcome relief for her, and her help for the Irish giant had given her a whole new focus, or so he had thought. Her sojourn in London was to be a welcome diversion and a chance to catch up with old acquaintances. With the count and Dr. Silkstone to take care of her, she would be in safe hands, or so he had imagined.

Now he believed otherwise. Some terrible fate must have befallen her in London, he told himself. He watched from the steps as Eliza, her ladyship's maid, supervised the unloading of the numerous cases and boxes. He would question her closely. Perhaps she could shed light on what was causing his mistress such evident pain. In the meantime he would do all he could to see that she was comfortable, in body if not in spirit.

In the fading light of his laboratory, Thomas took up his quill with more anxiety than he had ever held a surgeon's knife and began to write. . . .

> *My Dearest Lydia,*
>
> *As I write, I imagine you reading this at Boughton Hall, perched on the window seat in the morning room or even in the gardens, looking out over the view. I expect the spring flowers will be blooming now and the air will be fresh and sweet. I can see your face, the curve of your neck, your chestnut hair worn high, then falling in curls. I will always carry your gentle beauty with me.*
>
> *The reality is, however, that our last meeting was a painful one. I know you have your reasons for want-*

ing me out of your life, but I need you to know that whatever your trials and problems, we can face them together. I beg you, let me share in your burden so that we can shoulder it as one and overcome any difficulties. I know there is something that troubles you deeply and is eating away at your soul. Let me be the one to heal you.

For me, being without you is like a body trying to function without its heart. All my senses are numbed. I have no feeling. Without you by my side, my life holds no meaning.

Forgive my outpourings of emotion, but I needed you to know that whatever has happened, or whatever I have said or done to alienate myself from you, I hope you will remember me fondly as a healer and as a devoted lover.

I am now, and always will be, your loving and faithful servant,
Thomas

As he held the sealing stick to the lighted candle, blobs of wax, like red droplets of blood, fell onto the folded letter. If Lydia was in any danger, he hoped to God she would tell him.

Entering her darkened bedchamber, Lydia Farrell felt safe for the first time in days. The curtains were drawn but bars of light still broke through. She traced her hand over familiar objects: her dressing table, her washstand, her looking glass. She glimpsed herself in the mirror. Her own eyes stared back at her from behind a mask, colorless and expressionless, almost unrecognizable. Would even Thomas know her? She hardly knew herself. How different she was now. Life had dealt her so many cruel blows in the last year, and just when she saw happiness on the horizon with Thomas, the past had come back to haunt her. She had been another person when it had happened: young, gullible, guileless, and so very much in love. She would have done anything Captain Michael Farrell told her to do for fear of risking a life without him: walk through fire, throw herself off a cliff, submit herself to a stranger. Even if it meant harming another, she allowed it. She trusted him implicitly and never imagined that he would put her through such an ordeal. Could she have run away? It was a question that tortured her so often. In the event, she'd let it happen so that they could remain together, forever, she thought. Even if it meant murder.

Chapter 25

Robert Smee was a busy man. "My word, I have an establishment to run, sir," he said when Thomas asked for a word in private.

"Sir, a man lies in prison, falsely accused. All I ask is five minutes of your time," Thomas urged.

Tut-tutting, Smee led the doctor into a dingy room lined with ledgers, piled high with boxes, and festooned with cobwebs. A half-eaten pie lay on the desk.

"I need to ask you, sir, about the murder of Signor Cappelli."

The little man bridled and took out his kerchief to wipe away the beads of sweat on his forehead. "I already told the coroner all I know."

"I would very much appreciate it if you could tell me, too," said Thomas.

"And why would I do that?" he huffed.

Thomas looked at the decaying pie and picked up the platter on which it sat. "Because, sir, I have reason to believe that you have rats in your guests' rooms, and you would not want such a story to be spread about town," he replied.

Mr. Smee's eyes bulged out of his fat face. "My word, sir! That would not be good for business."

"Indeed not, so . . ." agreed Thomas.

"What do you want to know, sir?" The hotelier motioned to a chair and Thomas sat down.

"Did you see anyone or hear anything unusual on the night of the murder?"

"I told the coroner. The only person I saw coming out of the young man's room was the foreign gentleman."

Thomas looked confused. "You are sure it was Signor Moreno?"

"Most sure," said the little man, wiping the back of his neck with his kerchief. "He is, well, a most striking gentleman, if I may say so." Thomas had to agree.

"And do you know what time this was?"

"I was just about to lock up. It was two o'clock, sir, just as I heard the watchman call the hour." He was unequivocal in his recollection. "I was coming 'round the corner when I heard the latch on the young man's door, and I stopped. It can sometimes be a little awkward if I meets guests in the corridor at night, sir, you understand."

Thomas nodded. Discretion was an important quality for an hotelier to possess. "And I sees him, the gentleman, pop his head out of the door, look right and left, then quickly go to his own room. Shifty, he was." He puckered his mouth. "How could he do a thing like that, then cry like a babe over it when 'tis discovered? He's a great actor, my word, he is. Would've given Mr. Garrick a run for his money."

"And then what happened?"

"I locked up as usual, hung the keys on the hook, and went to bed. 'Tis a sorry tale, my word, it is."

"And who else was staying that night?"

The little man shook his round head so that his wig slipped forward a little. "I am ashamed to say that the two gentlemen were my only guests, sir."

"I see," said Thomas.

"Times is hard, sir, and my business, well . . . You won't spread word about the rats, sir?"

"I will not, Mr. Smee," he replied. "As long as you do not leave moldy victuals around to attract the vermin."

"No, sir, you are right. Marie, Marie," he called. A flustered servant girl with a long strand of coal-black hair spilling out from under her cap came running. Thomas recognized her from his previous visit. She had been deeply distressed by the gruesome discovery of the young castrato. "You are not to leave old food lying around, you hear," he scolded. She curtsied and took hold of the offending plate.

"Wait," said Thomas as she turned to leave. "Did you see or hear anything unusual on the night of the murder, Marie?" Her eyes widened, and like a frightened rabbit, she froze.

Mr. Smee stepped in. "She is French. Her English is not good," he explained.

The girl answered nervously. "*Moi,* sir? *Non,* sir. I see nussing."

Smee shooed her away with his plump hand. "Get on with you, girl. We have a hotel to run," he chided.

"Of course." Thomas nodded. "And I have calls to make, so I will leave you to your business, Mr. Smee."

"Much obliged to you, sir," replied the little man, dabbing his forehead once more.

Thomas did, indeed, have calls to make. His next stop was Newgate Prison.

The turnkey led Thomas down the windowless corridor to Moreno's cell. Although a terrible stench still hung in the stagnant air, this part of the prison was a considerable improvement on the other godless area he had seen the day before. At least here he hoped Moreno would be able to regain his strength, if not his full health.

He found his patient just as he had left him, lying supine on his pallet, eyes closed. A flagon of small beer lay on the stone floor, together with a loaf of bread, touched only by the shiny black weevils that were feasting on it.

"Signor Moreno," greeted Thomas gently.

The Tuscan opened his eyes. The swelling on the left side of his face, Thomas noted, had gone down considerably. His elegant features were better defined.

"How fare you today?"

His patient eased himself up on his right arm, wincing as he did so. "My body is a little better, I thank you, sir."

"But your mind?" Thomas studied the pain-racked face that once must have been so handsome and knew that it was not only Moreno's physical injuries that would have to heal before he was well again.

From his bag he took out a pad of gauze and a bottle of arnica and knelt down to dab the bruising on his patient's cheek.

"Do you bring news, Dr. Silkstone?" Moreno asked meekly.

Thomas paused for a moment. "I have been talking with Mr. Smee," he said.

"The hotelier?"

"Yes." Thomas felt uneasy, but he decided he must confront the castrato. "He says he saw you leaving Signor Cappelli's room at two o'clock that morning."

Instantly, Thomas saw Moreno's body tense. For a moment he was silent, then he swallowed hard. "So that is why I am here," he whispered, staring blankly at the opposite wall of his cell.

The young doctor nodded. "But I do not believe you did commit the crime."

The Tuscan switched his gaze and fixed it on Thomas. "I swear to God I did not."

"So Signor Cappelli was alive when you last left him?"

Tears now welled up in the Tuscan's eyes, as if remembering the final encounter with his friend was too much to bear, and he began to sob, clutching his ribs as he did so. Thomas tried to still his heaving body.

"Signor, please. Calm yourself," he urged.

After a few moments, the sobs subsided and the young doctor thought that perhaps now would be the right time to divulge that the postmortem had revealed more than the cause of the young castrato's death. He had discovered evidence of recent sexual activity. Perhaps now he should tell him he had uncovered his secret.

"I know, Signor Moreno."

The Tuscan looked up at him, uncertain.

"I know that you and Carlo Cappelli were lovers."

Moreno closed his eyes momentarily. Thomas was not sure if he was relieved or anxious, but his swollen lips mouthed, "You are right."

Thomas sat on the edge of the pallet. "Do you want to unburden yourself, Signor Moreno? I am not here to judge you."

"But I am a sodomite. They can still hang me," he muttered.

Thomas knew what he said to be true, although he also knew that many a molly house would be closed down were it not for the patronage of the nobility and politicians. "If we can find the real murderer, there will be no need to incriminate you," he ventured. "Surely you do not want the brute who killed Signor Cappelli to go unpunished?"

"No, but . . ."

Thomas sensed the Tuscan was hiding something. "What do you know?" he urged. Silence. "You will hang, Signor Moreno. If you know the killer . . ."

"He made me swear. . . ."

"Who made you? Who?"

Moreno caught his breath. "The man who attacked me."

Thomas bent down to look his patient straight in the eye. "Tell me the truth, I beg of you, or it'll be the rope."

The Tuscan eased himself up slowly, putting much of his weight on Thomas, until he sat upright. "It was after the concert. We went back to the hotel. Carlo went up to his room and I stayed behind a while. That was when I saw him."

"Who?"

"The same brute," he replied, pointing to his bruised face. "He was talking with the maid. She was smiling at him."

"Marie, the French girl?"

He nodded. "I did not see him again until . . ."

"When did you see him again?" urged Thomas.

"When they threw me in that stinking cell. I recognized him immediately and he knew I did. He saw it in my eyes, and that's when he and his friend started to beat me. They said if I talked they would expose me as a sodomite, and then the big one . . . He . . .”

Thomas held up his hand. He did not need the Tuscan to relive his horrific ordeal.

“And you think this man may have had something to do with the murder?” asked Thomas.

“I do.”

“How so?” entreated Thomas.

Tears rose in the Tuscan’s eyes. “Because he said, ‘Your boy will sing no more.’ ”

The doctor put a comforting hand on his patient’s shoulder as the tears rolled down his cheeks once more. His revelation was not proof, but it was a start. “Then I must go now and see that he is not released. The coroner needs to speak with him. What was he arrested for?” asked the doctor.

Moreno shook his bare head. “I do not know.”

Thomas handed his patient a small bottle of physick. “A draft for the pain,” he said. He knew there was no time to waste, so he quickly packed his bag. “Fear not, we will have you out of here soon,” he reassured Moreno before looking through the grille in the cell door to call for a turnkey. But he did not need to. One was standing outside, jangling his keys. Thomas heard one turn in the lock and stood back as the door opened. Yet instead of the jailer come to let him out, he was confronted by the sight of Rupert Marchant, accompanied by a clerk.

“Well, well,” said the lawyer. “If it isn’t our friend from the Colonies.”

Thomas bowed low, hiding the look of disdain on his face. “Mr. Marchant. What a surprise.”

“Likewise. Dr. Silkstone, isn’t it?” came the contemptuous reply.

There was an awkward pause. “I have been attending to Signor Moreno’s wounds,” Thomas explained.

“Wounds?” he queried disingenuously. “Oh dear, have his fellow inmates been unkind?”

Thomas tensed, but bit his tongue. "I am afraid so, but I have given him something to ease the pain."

"Ah, good," replied Marchant. "Then he will feel strong enough to hear the formal charge I am about to put to him."

Thomas was bewildered.

"I am the prosecuting attorney in this case, Dr. Silkstone," the lawyer explained. "And I am about to charge Signor Moreno with murder."

The young doctor tried unsuccessfully to hide his shock. He replied politely: "Then I best leave you to your task," and bowed once more. Another turnkey was waiting to escort him from the jail, but Thomas was not yet ready to leave.

"Take me to the other wing," he ordered.

They walked out across the great expanse of courtyard that divided the richer prisoners from the poorer wretches. To Thomas's relief it was empty. He had no wish to run the gamut of inmates, even if most of them were too sick or too starved to hit out. Once again he was led into the bowels of the stinking building and endured the insults and gobs of spittle that rained out of the grilles on his way until he reached the cell where Signor Moreno had been imprisoned. But of the other two inmates there was no sign.

"Where have these men gone?" asked Thomas of the turnkey, who was also looking bewildered.

"They were here not an hour ago," he replied, scratching his lice-ridden head.

"I let them out," said the head jailer, sidling up to them. He was an ugly man with a cruel mouth. "They was only in for stealing a shawl from a stiff down Spitalfields way, and this gent came with all the right papers and said they was to be let go."

"A gentleman, you say?" repeated Thomas, not wholly familiar with rough speech.

"A clerk of the court, sir," replied the jailer, adding: "Good riddance to them, I say. Caused nothing but trouble in 'ere."

Chapter 26

Sir Montagu Malthus descended on Boughton Hall like a great black raven, sending the household into a flurry for the second time in a week. Now the remaining dust sheets were dispatched and shutters thrown wide open, restoring natural light to the house. Mistress Claddingbowl brought out a plum cake and baked a batch of biscuits, and fresh flowers from the gardens were arranged in the hallway.

Lydia had not been told the purpose of the visit by her late brother's godfather. The widowed lawyer rarely made a purely social call from his home near Banbury. His brief letter warned of a "pressing matter" that needed her urgent attention. She had a terrible suspicion as to what that might be.

Nonetheless, the news of Sir Montagu's imminent arrival had shaken Lydia from the torpor she had experienced since her return from London. She had simply drifted from room to room, running her fingers over mantelpieces and bookshelves, eating nothing and saying little.

"So, Lydia," Sir Montagu began, settling himself down on the sofa opposite her. "It must be difficult for you here alone." His hawkish eyes were glancing around the room, hovering over paintings and pieces of porcelain. He placed particular weight on the word "alone."

She poured tea and handed him a cup. "I manage well enough, sir. I have engaged an estate manager to deal with affairs and I carry on tending to domestic duties as before."

"How long is it now?" His head was tilting sensitively.

"Eleven months, three weeks, and four days." She suspected the timing of his visit did not simply happen to almost coincide with the first anniversary of her husband's murder.

"Yes. I thought so. Almost a year, my dear. And you have been so brave, what with Lavington and Crick and then your dear mama." His hooded eyes fixed on her.

"It has not been easy," she conceded, sipping her tea.

"Indeed, no, but I would put it to you that perhaps it is time to look to the future."

Now he was cutting to the chase, thought Lydia. "Oh, but I do think of the future, sir. I have plans for the estate."

He nodded his head and waved a dismissive hand. "Yes, my dear. I am sure you have, but I am talking about the distant future. You are, after all, the last of the Crick line."

Of course Lydia was painfully aware of the fact. She folded her hands on her lap. In the awkward silence that ensued she could hear the mantel clock ticking away the seconds. "Yes, sir," she said.

"Have you considered who will inherit the estate from you?"

She looked blankly at him as he reached inside his black satchel. He did not wait for a reply. "Can you imagine all this falling into decay, or worse still, being sold?" There was a note of terrible foreboding in his voice.

"Indeed not, sir." Lydia shook her head obligingly.

"That is why I have taken the liberty of drawing up a list of suitable candidates for you," he said in a matter-of-fact way.

"Candidates?" echoed Lydia.

"Suitable husbands, my dear." His emphasis was on the word "suitable."

Without saying a word she took the list that he passed over to her and scanned the names: the Earl of Wedmore, the Lord Belmont, Sir Humphrey Lupton—all eligible peers of the realm, all of the right lineage. One was widowed, the others were bachelors, but bachelors for good reason; either old, ugly or, in one case, insane. Most of them would do anything to lay their hands on Boughton Hall and its large estate, albeit they both were in need of some attention. She looked again. There was the Right Honorable Rupert Marchant, too. She thought of his smug lawyer's face, sneering at her lecherously. She knew of all of these would-be suitors, but her thoughts were of Thomas. Sir Montagu would, of course, disapprove of her union with a colonist and a commoner to boot. The doctor was her inferior in every way, in his eyes, but she was not strong enough to start a fight.

"It is a kind thought and I will consider the gentlemen, sir," she told him, smiling politely.

Sir Montagu's brows, which had knitted themselves together as she studied the list, now parted.

"Excellent," he said. "Perhaps you will permit me to arrange some introductions?"

He was being too hasty, thought Lydia. "In due course, sir," she replied. "It is still a little too soon."

Sir Montagu nodded and drained his teacup. "Just remember, dear Lydia, that an heir, preferably a male, of course, is essential to the future of Boughton, and it would be most desirable to have one sooner rather than later."

Again she smiled politely at him. After Edward's death he no longer had any official authority, but she knew that he was the man her late father had tasked with her well-being and he still held sway over her. She would play along with his conniving and interfering ways for as long as she needed to, and he would return to his country seat happy in the knowledge that his old friend's daughter would comply with his requests and that the future of the beloved estate would be secure, as her father would have wished. The right blood would course through her progeny's veins and Boughton would be saved for posterity. She was not prepared, however, for what came next.

"I do not detect any enthusiasm from you, my dear," said Sir Montagu, placing his cup and saucer on a side table.

Lydia apologized. "I am a little tired, sir, that is all," she replied meekly.

"Come, come. I can tell that none of these suitors appeal." His candor surprised her.

"As I said, Sir Montagu, it is just a little too soon to consider marrying again." She was polite but firm. Yet he persisted, fixing his gaze on her with a new determination.

"There is, of course, one name that is missing from that list, my dear." His tone suddenly became more intimate.

Lydia frowned. Did he know about her affair with Thomas? She swallowed hard. "And who might that be?" she enquired nonchalantly, trying to hide her fear of detection.

"My own." If Sir Montagu saw the momentary look of horror that darted across Lydia's face, he chose not to show it. "We would make the perfect match," he continued. "I am from an excellent line, as you know."

A feeling of nausea rose in Lydia's gullet. The very thought of this man, at least forty years her senior and a friend of her late father's, begetting a child with her was repulsive. She looked at his clawlike hands and imagined his cold grasp on her skin and she shuddered.

"You are most thoughtful," was all she could manage in reply.

He bent his head slightly to one side. The fleshy hoods of skin that hung from his brow seemed to retract slightly, showing more of his old man's eyes than usual. "So you will consider my offer?"

Lydia nodded. "I will, sir," she replied softly, all the while knowing that neither he nor anyone else had any idea that in all probability she had been rendered unable to bear children. In all likelihood there would be no heir. Ever.

Charles Byrne slumped into the chair and slipped off his shoes. His feet ached. It had been another hard afternoon in the cane shop. Every day more and more came to see him, each paying their half crown to gasp and gawp and point and stare. Touching was not permitted, although many tried.

The count poured him a large gin and handed it to him. "You are doing well, my friend. You have nearly fifty pounds."

"Fifty?" he repeated with derision. "That lawyer wants two hundred from me."

The count knew it to be true from the papers he had seen.

This royal pardon would come neither cheaply nor quickly, but he remained ebullient. "But all of London adores you. Look what it says in the newssheet," he cried excitedly, prodding the print with a podgy forefinger.

Charles's weary look reminded his friend that he could not read. "Listen to this, then," exclaimed Boruwlaski. "The *Morning Herald* says that you are 'beyond what is set forth in ancient or modern history.' " The little man lifted his shoulders gleefully. "It goes on: 'In short, the sight is more than the mind can conceive, the tongue express, or the pencil delineate, and stands without parallel in this or any other country.' What say you to that, Charles?"

The giant actually said very little and appeared distinctly indifferent to such plaudits. He took a large gulp of gin.

"I say I could eat a horse," came the dry reply.

Boruwlaski mused that such a feat was very probable, when a stony-faced Mistress Goodbody entered the room.

"Is there anything you require before dinner, gentlemen?" she asked, shooting a disdainful glance at the giant's stockinged feet. "Slippers, perhaps, Mr. Byrne?"

The giant eyed her suspiciously. "Emily. Where is Emily?"

The housekeeper shifted uncomfortably. "Emily is not here."

"Then where is she, pray?" intervened Boruwlaski.

"She has left the household."

"Left?" repeated Charles Byrne, pulling himself forward in the chair.

"And can you tell us why?" asked the count.

Again the housekeeper looked uneasy. "I dismissed her, sir."

Charles heaved himself up now, towering over the woman, scowling at her.

"On what grounds?" continued Boruwlaski.

Mistress Goodbody flashed a reproachful look at the giant. "She had ideas above her station."

The count remained calm but asked coolly: "Am I not master in my own house, Mistress Goodbody?"

She flushed. "Of course, sir."

"Then should I not sanction the dismissal of staff?"

"Yes, sir, but—"

"Where has she gone?" asked Charles, his anger mounting.

"Back to her parents, I suspect, in St. Giles," she replied, not daring to look up at the giant.

"Then you must send word that she is to return here," the count instructed.

"But, sir . . ." Mistress Goodbody began, but Charles Byrne had heard enough and stormed out of the room, brushing past the housekeeper as he did so, causing her to step backward. She opened her mouth to protest, but the count gave her short shrift.

"Do you not realize that that girl was the only person who could make him smile?" The count rarely showed his anger, but on this occasion he was truly riled. "She gave him hope."

"But I caught them . . ."

The count waved his small hand dismissively in the air. "Everyone is entitled to a little happiness in their lives. I want the girl found, and quickly."

John Hunter sat surrounded by his creatures captured in their glass jars and floating in preserving fluid and mused on the nature of the human brain. His candle was burning low, but he was too occupied to think of lighting another one just yet. He was contemplating the spongy gray tissue that lay in the dish before him, like some coral found in warm seas. The brain in question had once been housed in the cranium of his friend, the botanist Daniel Solander. At the postmortem he had found two ounces of coagulated blood in the right ventricle. He had not asked Solander if he could keep his brain, but he was an enlightened young man and would probably have agreed. Either way, his untimely demise had reinforced his own theory about apoplexy, and that could only be for the common good, he told himself. A knock at his laboratory door interrupted his train of thought and he rose and looked through the grille. Howison usually vetted his visitors at this time of night, as they were more often than not of the unsavory variety.

Straining his eyes in the darkness, he could see the scarred and battered face that was so familiar to him.

"Och, Crouch," he greeted, opening the door only slightly ajar and making sure their encounter was not witnessed. "Come in, man."

The ruffian took off his hat and strode in carrying a small bundle.

"So, you have something for me?" Hunter went over to his workbench and Crouch followed, laying the stinking rags down. They were streaked with dried blood. Taking a scalpel, the anatomist cut the string that held the frayed kersey bands together.

"Stillborn?" he said, lifting the child out of its filthy cocoon.

"Aye."

"A boy," he said, lifting the tiny body up to inspect its genitals. "I'll give you a shilling for it."

The ruffian's face dropped. " 'Tis worth two," he protested, but Hunter was not to be deterred.

"I heard you were detained at His Majesty's pleasure overnight at Newgate Prison," he said, his tongue as caustic as acid.

Crouch could not deny it. "Nicking from a stiff in the street." He tried to laugh off his misdemeanor, but the anatomist was clearly not amused.

He shook his head. "You must not let your petty thievery jeopardize my work, Mr. Crouch," he warned. "Nor your whoring."

"Whoring?"

"I heard you've taken up with a French tart in Haymarket. Don't lose your edge, Mr. Crouch."

"It won't happen again, Dr. Hunter, sir," said the ruffian, suddenly changing his tune.

"Och!" The anatomist gathered an odd laugh. "You make sure it doesn't." There was a smile on his lips, but his scalpel was still clasped in his hand and he added: "Or there'll be more than one scar on that ugly face of yours."

The grave robber licked his dry lips. "I see your meaning, Dr. Hunter."

The anatomist put down the scalpel. "Good. Now we understand each other, let's talk about another wee job I'd like you to do for me, shall we? There's a doctor from the Colonies who needs to be taught a lesson."

Chapter 27

Francois Dubois studied the pitted face of his most famous client in the looking glass as he mixed his shaving paste. Joseph Haydn sat in the chair. It was evident to the barber's trained eye that his right cheek was decidedly larger than his left and his nose was inflamed. The illustrious composer had already undergone surgery to remove the painful polyps, but they had reoccurred with a vengeance and on that particular morning were giving him much grief.

"You are ze only barber I trust wiz my poor, swollen visage," he pronounced as the Frenchman draped a hot, moist towel over his jowls.

Dubois smiled graciously. "I am honored, sir," he replied, but all the time he was thinking about how he would remove the troublesome growths. If he could only persuade Herr Haydn that he could tie a thread around the base of the growth and ligature it for several days until the offending polypus fell out of the nose. But he was a mere barber. Such chirurgical procedures were no longer allowed, not since the barbers and surgeons were forced to go their separate ways and barbers were relegated to mere mechanics, without art or intelligence. But soon, if all went to plan . . .

"Go steady. Go steady," warned Haydn as Dubois began to lather, his brush nudging against the swollen areas. The barber nodded, but he did not smile. He was mourning his lost profession. What satisfaction he would gain to be able to rid Herr

Haydn of those irksome nodules that so interfered with the compositions of his wonderful symphonies and librettos. Nowadays he was reduced to merely shaving those who could afford his services, but hopefully not for too much longer. He took his razor, and brandishing it like a conductor's baton, he got to work on Herr Haydn's face, sweeping and arcing and swishing with alacrity, until his cheeks and chin were as smooth as the buttocks of a babe.

"Excellent," pronounced Haydn as he examined his clean-shaven face in the mirror.

Dubois studied his own craftsmanship and gave a self-satisfied nod. "I am glad to be of service, sir," he said as his client handed over the appropriate monies.

Jean-Paul had just been called upon to fetch the customer's frock coat when the bell over the door rang and in walked a familiar face.

The composer eyed Giles Carrington as he approached. The student also recognized him. "Herr Haydn, good day to you," he greeted him, bowing low.

The Austrian looked at him slightly suspiciously, as if trying to place the young man.

"Giles Carrington, at your service, sir. I work for Dr. Hunter," he said.

Haydn snapped his fingers. "Ah yes, I remember now," he said, nodding. "You came to my aid ze ozer night." The composer turned to Dubois. "Zere was a misunderstanding about my nose," he told him. "Mr. Carrington here helped me escape Dr. Hunter's scalpel!" He was smiling as he recounted the episode, even though at the time it was clear to the student he had found it far from amusing. "My thanks to you once more, sir," he said as he was helped into his coat and left the shop.

Dubois smiled at Giles Carrington. "And how can I help you today, sir?" he asked as Jean-Paul looked on. The barber gestured to the boy to leave.

"I wish to buy one of your pomades," Carrington told him, sidling up to the counter.

Dubois nodded. "I have just the thing for you, sir," he said, bending low and emerging with a tall box. "I think sir will find this a most interesting scent." He opened the lid and Carrington peered inside.

"Indeed. I will take it," he instructed, and delving into his pocket, he brought out a fifty-pound bank note. "For your pains," he said to Dubois. And the Frenchman grinned from ear to ear.

Charles's day in the cane shop seemed to him even more arduous than usual. He was tired and in a poor humor, and even the smile that he had managed to cultivate over the past few days at the behest of the count seemed to have deserted him. "They will pay even more if you are congenial," the little man had advised. Smiling had come more easily to him before. All he had to do was ignore the curious hordes that paid to stare at him and think of Emily, waiting back in Cockspur Street, waiting with his slippers and his gin and her sweet look. Now that she was gone, there was nothing for him to smile about.

He sat down, letting the chair take his weight, to the enormous disappointment of those further back in the queue. Pulling out his kerchief from his pocket, he wiped the spittle from his chin. The count had also advised him to close his mouth when he was on show, but the size of his tongue made it difficult for him and the saliva collected quickly.

Surveying the crowd from his raised dais, he managed to nod now and again by way of greeting. Few nodded in return, rarely meeting his gaze. They were more interested in his physique than in his persona, regarding him more like a circus creature than a human being. Yet there was one man he saw, toward the end of the afternoon's queue, who seemed to engage with him more, to look him in the eye. No, stare, more than just look. But he did not fix upon his long legs, nor his massive shoulders, nor his mighty torso, but upon his eyes.

As he drew closer, Charles could see that he did not appear like the other spectators. He was not dressed finely. He did not even wear a wig. His complexion was swarthy and his dark hair was matted.

"I am come from Dr. Hunter," mumbled the stranger in a coarse whisper when he finally came level with the giant. "My master would like to see you again this evening. There will be a carriage waiting for you outside. You are to come alone and tell no one."

Charles was puzzled. "Why does he want to see me?"

The messenger looked warily around as the party behind him grew more agitated. "My master says he has a cure for your ills."

Charles's eyes opened wide in surprise. Dr. Hunter could cure him of his bloody cough, of his fever, of the surges of tiredness? "I will come," he assured him, and the man disappeared from view, leaving the giant with a smile on his face for the first time that day.

Emily O'Shea did not receive a warm welcome when she arrived home. She had picked her way through the potholes and animal entrails that littered the streets to the dwelling in St. Giles-in-the-Fields back into the bosom of her family, only to be shunned by her own father, and for good reason.

"And how are we expected to feed another mouth?" he shouted above the din of her screaming baby brother.

"I will find another place," she told him.

"Without good words from the housekeeper? That's rich," butted in her mother, who was trying to hush the child.

In a cot in the corner of the dingy room, Grandmother Tooley stirred.

"Emily. Emily, is that you?" she croaked.

The girl walked over to her. The old soothsayer seemed even more fragile than when she had last seen her. Her wiry gray hair had grown, making her face shrink into its silvery tangle, but she was now wide awake.

"Yes, 'tis me, Gran," said Emily, taking her cold hand.

The old crone's rheumy eyes were alert. "Did you see him?" she asked eagerly. "The tall man, did you see him?"

"Will ya shut up, you mad cow?" shouted O'Shea, taking off a boot and throwing it at her cot. It struck the corner, causing the old woman, and Emily, to flinch.

"Well?" said her mother, ignoring her husband and walking over to the old woman. " 'Tis true there's a giant in town, is it not?"

Emily nodded slowly. "Yes, 'tis so."

"You see. I told you Ma was a prophet," shouted her mother to O'Shea, a smug look settling on her thin face. He simply shook his head and swigged from his bottle.

"Bullshit," he cursed.

"So have you seen him?" pressed her mother. "I've heard tell he lights his pipe from the street lamp."

"Yes, I have seen him, Mother," replied Emily coyly.

"So," her mother sidled up to her and nudged her suggestively, "is he as big as they say?"

Emily nodded. "Yes, he is as tall as a haystack."

"And handsome?"

Emily thought for a moment. "He has a good face."

"I heard tell he scowls and spits and slobbers. Is that so?"

Before she could answer, O'Shea began to kick the bundle of belongings on the floor that she had brought with her from Cockspur Street. He was totally disinterested in the women's talk, but eager to see what his daughter had managed to pilfer from her erstwhile employer.

"What did ya manage to get, then?"

"There's only a change of clothes in there," she told him as he tugged at the string around the packet. He pulled out a dress, a cap, and a hairbrush and flung them all down in disgust. Finally there came a woolen shawl and from out of its coarse fibers fell a small tobacco tin. O'Shea seized on it.

Holding it up to the single candle that burned in the room, he opened the lid. "I could do with a smoke," he said. But instead of strands of aromatic tobacco, he found hair—thick locks of black hair held together with a thin blue ribbon.

"What be the meaning of this?" he cried indignantly, as if feeling cheated of a smoke.

Emily looked away, feeling the color rise in her usually pallid cheeks.

Her mother walked over to take a look. " 'Tis not your hair, and that's for sure."

O'Shea eyed his daughter suspiciously. "You got a sweetheart, han't ya?"

"No, sir," she snapped. But her eager denial betrayed her, to her mother, at least, who raised a skeptical eyebrow.

O'Shea sneered and threw the tin across the room so that the hair flew out on the floor and landed near Grandmother Tooley's cot. The old woman's head turned when she heard the commotion. Emily rushed to retrieve the locks from among the dirty rushes, but as she did so, her grandmother stilled her hand and opened her fingers. Her watery gaze settled on the strands of thick black hair, and their eyes met. Emily knew her secret was out.

The staff at Boughton Hall were in a subdued mood that evening as they sat around the table belowstairs. Their mistress was causing them great anxiety. Shortly after Sir Montagu's visit, Lady Lydia had retired to her bedchamber. Even Eliza, her own maid, was not allowed to attend to her.

The following morning a messenger came from London with a letter from Dr. Silkstone. It was delivered to her ladyship in her room, but she had not reappeared since. That was two days ago. Eliza had heard her mistress's sobs, and trays of food had not been touched, but nothing could tempt her from her bed.

"I wonder what Sir Montagu said that so vexed her," ventured Hannah Lovelock.

"That man's enough to vex anyone," jibed her husband Jacob. "He spreads trouble wherever he goes. 'E was the one who caused a lot of that business with the captain, remember? And now he's got it in for her ladyship." He ripped into a hunk of bread and began eating it.

"I reckon 'twas to do with her marrying again," said Eliza knowledgeably.

Hannah and the other maids leaned forward on the table.

" 'Tis almost a year," mused Mistress Claddingbowl, setting down a large pot of stew.

"And that letter yesterday, from Dr. Silkstone," said Hannah.

"Where is he? He should be here, looking after her," said Eliza, almost indignantly.

"They make a fine couple," said Mistress Claddingbowl.

"To you and me they do, but the doctor is not of the right rank," said Eliza.

"And he's a colonist," said Hannah, adding: "Maybe they can elope, like she did before with the captain."

"Sir Montagu has other plans," countered Eliza, taking out a piece of paper from her apron pocket. Unfolding it underneath the kitchen table so that only Hannah could see, she revealed the list of suitors that Malthus deemed suitable.

"This is what he showed her," she whispered. " 'Tis a list of husbands for her."

"Bless my soul," gasped Mistress Claddingbowl, seeing the script. "But that is not for your eyes, my girl!"

Undeterred, Eliza read out some names: "Lord Wedmore, the Right Honorable Rupert Marchant. All gentlemen of noble rank," she said, waving the piece of paper flirtatiously.

Jacob served himself with a large ladleful of stew. "Aye. Her ladyship needs help. 'Tis not a time for talk. We need action."

"What do you mean?" asked Hannah, frowning.

"Jacob is right. Her ladyship is sick. Talk of wedding again is making her ill. 'Tis clear to me she needs to see Dr. Silkstone," said Eliza.

The women nodded thoughtfully.

"But how to get word to him?" asked Hannah.

"What's this?" Howard walked in and saw the huddle, detecting gossip. He would have none of it. He strode over to where the women and Lovelock were sitting at one end of the long table. "You know I do not allow tittle-tattle about her ladyship."

Eliza, always bold, lifted her face to the butler, and stood up. "We are all concerned, sir, about her ladyship," she told him. A chorus of accord rippled around the table. Such an outburst clearly shocked Howard. He had never, in all his forty years of service, come across such rank insubordination, and yet perhaps the staff were correct to express concern.

"We are afraid that her ladyship might . . . ," began Hannah.

"Might be ill," Eliza finished the sentence for her, even though it was not what Hannah nor any of the others were thinking. None of them dared say the fears that they harbored for their mistress.

"Her ladyship has not requested to see Dr. Fairweather," he said, stiffening his back.

" 'Tis not Dr. Fairweather she needs to see," blurted Eliza. " 'Tis Dr. Silkstone."

"How dare you say such things, Eliza!" Howard was bristling with anger.

Mistress Firebrace had followed the butler and witnessed the gist of the conversation. "Really, Eliza. That is enough. It is not your place, nor anyone else's here, to pry into the affairs of the mistress," she scolded. But Eliza stood her ground.

"My mistress is not in her right mind at the moment. What if she does something to harm herself?"

Mistress Firebrace gasped at the insinuation that Lady Lydia might take her own life. "Enough. Go to your room," she ordered the maid. "Such insolence will not be tolerated." Her eyes darted to each and every one of the staff seated at the table by way of warning as Eliza walked out of the kitchen, defeated but unbowed.

Thomas picked his way along Dean Street that evening, heading for Smee's Hotel. He wanted to question the servant girl, Marie, more closely, convinced that she was hiding something. When he arrived there were four or five customers seated at tables in the barroom, most of them huddled around a struggling fire. Business did not seem to be booming for poor Mr. Smee, thought Thomas.

The girl was behind the bar. She recognized Thomas instantly and froze.

"A pint of ale," he ordered, cheerfully. "Marie, isn't it?"

She did not return his smile. "Per'aps," she replied, busying herself with the tankards.

Thomas settled himself on a stool by the counter. "You remember me, don't you?" he said.

She would not look him in the eye, but set the foaming pot of ale on the bar.

"Tuppence," she mumbled.

"I'll give you four, if you help me."

"I am working, sir. I cannot 'elp no one." There was an agitated spark in her voice.

Another man came up to the bar requiring service. Marie tended to him eagerly as Thomas watched her, but he saw that her hands were shaking. She was afraid. Of whom? Of Smee? He doubted it, but he did not have long to wait for the answer.

"I need to talk to you, Marie, about the murder," he said softly as soon as the man returned to his seat. "I believe you know something."

"I do not know anysing," she said, a strand of her black hair falling down from beneath her cap.

"But you were the one who found the body," insisted Thomas.

"Look, I don't know nussing. *S'il vous plaît, monsieur.*"

"An innocent man will be hanged, Marie, and I believe you know the truth."

For the first time the girl looked the doctor in the eye. "Please. Just leave me alone. *Je vous en pris,*" she pleaded.

"This man causing you trouble?" came a gruff voice from behind. Thomas turned to see a ruffian towering over him as he sat. He stood up, drawing himself to the same height, and looked into the man's face. There was the same scarred cheek with the same battered nose that he had seen with Signor Moreno at Newgate Prison. He suddenly felt sick at the sight of him, knowing what he had done to the castrato. He also knew he should not be trifled with.

"I was just about to leave," said Thomas, still unsure as to whether or not he had been recognized by the brute. He turned and left by the front entrance, his heart racing. He wanted to break into a run, but knew he must not, so he began at a steady pace, retracing his steps along Dean Street.

Over in the corner of the room, away from the fire, and

swathed in a sheath of scent that fended off the sickly-sweet smell of spilled ale and gritty tobacco smoke sat Francois Dubois. Unbeknownst to his daughter, he had been watching her. He did not like what he saw. There was a lull at the bar and Marie came to collect tankards left on one or two of the tables. She saw the lone man huddled in the corner, but did not recognize him from the back. Walking up to him, she asked: "What will it be, sir?" Dubois turned and she gasped. "Papa!"

"*Oui, c'est moi,*" he said warmly.

"I did not expect you," she smiled nervously.

"No, I am sure you did not, *ma petite,*" he replied, stroking his long, clean-shaven chin.

Marie looked at her father, wondering how long he had been spying on her with his weasel eyes that gave away so little. He spoke in his native tongue. "You are a fine young woman, Marie, so like your dear mother, God rest her soul. You have that ruffian under your thumb."

"*Oui, Papa,*" she bleated.

Her father took her hand in his and began to stroke it lightly. "I know his sort, Marie, but you must humor him, for my sake. *Tu comprends?*" His hand suddenly grabbed her wrist.

There was an awkward pause as Marie looked about her, hoping Mr. Smee had not witnessed the episode. Thankfully, he was nowhere to be seen. "I must go, Papa," she said quickly, but her father lifted her hand to his lips and kissed it softly.

"Not so fast," he told her. His voice was still measured. "That gentleman at the bar talking with you." Marie's olive skin flushed. "I believe he is a surgeon. He wasn't asking about the murder, was he?" he asked.

The girl swallowed hard and dared not look her father in the eye. "*Oui,*" she muttered.

"*Comment?*" urged Dubois, cupping his hand around his ear, even though he had heard her reply perfectly clearly the first time.

"*Oui,*" reiterated his daughter, only louder this time.

"And you told him nothing?" He tightened his grip, but the smile remained on his lips.

"*Rien de tout,* Papa. Nothing." She was growing tearful and more agitated by the second, like a fish dancing on the end of an angler's hook.

"*Bon,*" he said, finally letting go of his daughter's hand. "Make sure it stays that way. Your life could depend upon it, *ma cherie,* and I could not bear it if anything happened to you."

Thomas had made good progress down Dean Street and had just reached the junction with St. Anne's Court when he heard footsteps close behind him. He spun 'round instinctively to see two men in the shadows heading toward him, but he did not have time to escape. In less than a second they were upon him, dragging him into the alley. Over their faces they wore scarves that covered their noses and mouths. Only their eyes flashed at him in the darkness. One rained punches onto his face while the other kicked him in the ribs. Their grunts of exertion mingled with his cries for help, which soon turned to pleas for them to stop.

When they eventually did, after what seemed an age, Thomas was left bloodied and dazed. The sharp, stabbing pain in his side told him that at least one of his ribs might be broken, and the trickle of blood that flowed from above his left eye was evidence he had suffered either a superficial cut just above his brow or a more serious wound to his head. He managed to ease himself into a sitting position and felt his arms and hands, then his legs. On first examination he seemed in one piece. Then he felt his pockets. His purse was still there. At least he would have enough money to pay for a ride home.

He staggered into the main street, blood still gushing from his head, and with great difficulty held out his battered arm in the hope of hailing a carriage. One passed almost immediately, but it did not stop. It was already occupied. In the darkness he did not see that at the reins was Dr. Hunter's nut-skinned servant. He was transporting Charles Byrne to see his master at his Earls Court country retreat.

Chapter 28

The rows of skulls around the pond and the gaping crocodile jaws over the door pediment seemed even more terrifying to Charles Byrne as the carriage drew up outside Hunter's house in the moonlight. Holding a lantern aloft, Howison led the way down the path to the laboratory and past the anatomist's collection of strange and exotic specimens to the small room where Charles had been examined before.

Hunter was at his desk. He rose when he saw the giant. "Och, Mr. Byrne. Come in, come in. Sit ye down." He pointed to the table once more before sitting down himself and leaning back in his chair.

"You have caused quite a stir, Mr. Byrne." His manner was affable, but Charles remained anxious, darting glances here and there as if looking out for some new monstrosity on display. He coughed, too, although Hunter suspected that this was a nervous affectation rather than a symptom of phthisis.

"And you look well, sir," he said, adding, "given the circumstances."

Charles's black head swiveled 'round. "I am as well as a man in my condition can be, sir."

Hunter's eyes opened wide. "And in what sort of condition might that be?" he asked disingenuously.

"I think you know, sir, that I am not well and I was told that you have a c-cure. That is why I am here." His face was earnest. " 'Tis in the hope you can h-heal me."

Hunter's mouth flickered in a faint smile. He rose from his desk and walked over to a shelf upon which lay a large log.

"You see this?" he said, retrieving it and laying it down on his desk. "This comes from a horse chestnut tree, probably about one hundred and fifty years old."

Charles looked puzzled as Hunter turned the wood sideways to reveal a hollow interior. "Inside there is nothing, Mr. Byrne. Nothing. The wood has been eaten away by a parasite."

"I do not follow you, sir."

"This fine chestnut went into decline and within a few months withered and died. Outwardly its ailment was indiscernible, but inside . . . That tree is you, Mr. Byrne."

"You mean . . ." Charles's brows knitted themselves into a frown.

"I mean, sir, that you have consumption, as I am sure you know, and that the disease is eating away at you from within. At a generous estimate, I'd say you have no more than six months to live."

Charles sat impassively. "I know that the cough and the fever and the tiredness might kill me in time, sir, but you have a cure. Yes?" His eyes were wide with childish anticipation.

Hunter let out a cruel laugh. "Och, I have something much better than a cure, Mr. Byrne," said the Scot, patting the giant on the arm. Again Charles frowned, searching for meaning in the anatomist's words. "I can offer you immortality."

Trapped in a prison of her own making, Lady Lydia Farrell wrote the fifth and final draft of a letter from the confinement of her darkened bedchamber.

> *My Beloved Thomas,*
>   *As God is my witness, I truly never wanted to write this letter, nor did I wish you to receive it. You are the only person who has shown true devotion and compassion toward me during the past difficult year, and my behavior toward you in London was deplorable. I want you to know, however, that you*

were entirely blameless and in no way caused my petulant reaction to a chance encounter with someone from my past. This person was the instrument of my torture many years ago and I still bear the scars, both mental and physical, he inflicted. As long as he is alive, I cannot bear to live with myself.

Your last letter confirmed to me that I am taking the only course of action available to me. I cannot live with you, and Sir Montagu will put every obstacle in the way of our union. His visit earlier this week was to urge me to find a "suitable" husband so that I could produce an heir and save Boughton for future generations of my line. The thought of being sentenced, once more, to years of unhappiness and a loveless marriage bed is unbearable. While Sir Montagu cannot stop us legally, he will do everything he possibly can to thwart our marriage.

I have loved you from the moment I set eyes on you in your rooms in London, and always will. One day we will be together, forever, but it cannot be in this world, my beloved.

I shall always be with you.
Your ever-loving Lydia

Just before Hannah and Jacob were about to snuff out their candle for the night, there came a tapping on their door. Jacob rose, took the candle and, still in his nightgown, went to see who called at this late hour. It was Howard, wearing a pained expression on his face.

"Lovelock, I need a word." There was an awkward pause, as the head groom processed his words. "May I come in?"

The last time Howard had called on them it was to offer his condolences for the death of Rebecca, the daughter who had drowned two years before. He looked awkward and rubbed his hands together.

"May I?" he said, glancing at one of the simple chairs.

"Yes, sir." Jacob nodded.

"I am come on a very"—Howard searched for the right word—"delicate matter."

"Oh?"

"Her ladyship."

"Ah, I see," said Jacob.

"I know I may have appeared harsh to Eliza this evening, but I do share her concerns."

Hannah, who had been listening at the door, now entered the room. "Oh, sir," she blurted. "We are so worried, too, but what can we do?"

Howard's eyes were now more adjusted to the dark. The anxious faces of the husband and wife stared back at him from the gloom. He perched on the wooden chair, his small hands with their manicured nails splayed on his knees.

"Ordinarily I would not dream of interfering in her ladyship's affairs, of course, but I feel that in the absence of anyone else, I would be doing her a great disservice if I took no action at all to ease her current plight." The butler's glance darted back and forth from each of them, looking for some acknowledgment or sympathy.

Hannah was the first to offer her support. "Indeed, sir. But what can we do?"

Howard leaned forward, almost conspiratorially, toward Jacob. "Lovelock, can I trust you with an important mission?"

Jacob took a great gulp of air. "Anything for her ladyship," he replied.

"Good. Then I want you to ride to London at first light and ask Dr. Silkstone to make his way here with the greatest of haste. Say we are concerned for her ladyship's well-being, both in mind and body. He is sure to answer our plea."

Jacob nodded and Hannah clasped her husband's hand. "If any man can do that, Jacob Lovelock is your man, sir," she assured her master.

With a lantern held aloft, John Hunter led Charles Byrne outside to the entrance of his underground laboratory. Down five stone steps they went until they came to a door, which Hunter opened with a large key that hung from a belt around his waist. Once inside, there was a wall-mounted sconce, which the doctor lit so that Charles could see the room beyond more clearly. It was large and high-ceilinged and contained all manner of strange contraptions: long glass tubes and wheels and pulleys. A huge bricked-up cauldron with iron doors and a chimney vent above it took up one whole corner. Hunter led Charles past these strange contrivances and apparatus to a grille across the entrance to what seemed to be a small chamber carved out of the rock. It reminded him of the paintings of sacred grottos he had seen, where the Blessed Virgin herself had appeared to those of great faith. Inside he could make out more shelves that stored even more jars and flasks.

Hunter held the lantern aloft once more so that Charles could get a better view. He leaned down to look inside the glass containers. Each was labeled and each seemed to contain the disembodied remains of a human body part or organ: a bloated black liver, a row of yellowed teeth, the spongy hemisphere of a brain.

Charles looked at them suspiciously, not comprehending what he was seeing until, that is, the rays from Hunter's lantern picked out a solitary finger, long and delicate, floating upright in a jar. A human finger. The giant let out a gasp of revulsion when he realized what he was beholding.

"Come, come now, Mr. Byrne. Why so squeamish? You have seen my other specimens; my fetuses, my exotic creatures." Hunter smiled, seeing Charles's troubled expression. "Their owners were all dead when I deprived them of their parts."

The giant's eyes opened wide as his fear mounted. "Sir, I do not like this place," he said. "I would ask that we leave."

"Och, leave? But I wanted to show you how I can make you live forever, Mr. Byrne." There was a time, not so long ago, when he had conducted experiments to freeze animals—dormice, fish, and toads—in the hope that they could be brought back to life when thawed. He had dreamed that one day men would give up the last ten years of their lives to a kind of frozen oblivion and be resurrected every one hundred years. Now that his efforts had proved futile, he had decided to try another tack. He picked up one of the jars from a rack on a shelf. Inside, the deep red cushion of a solitary human heart was suspended in preserving fluid.

"Do you know what this is?"

What little color there was in Charles's face drained away. " 'Tis a heart, sir, and a human one at that. Can we go now?"

Hunter shook his head. "Not just any human heart, Mr. Byrne. This extraordinary organ once beat in the chest of our prime minister, the Marquis of Rockingham."

Suddenly the giant turned away and retched, his large shoulders heaving in a great convulsion. "I would leave now, sir," he cried as he barged past Hunter and headed back into the cavernous room, crashing into any obstacles that lay in his path. The anatomist hurriedly put back his jar on the shelf, locked the grille once more, and followed Charles into the eerie shadows, fearing the havoc he might wreak as he lurched through the darkness. Soon he could hear the door rattling.

"I am coming, Mr. Byrne," shouted Hunter, rushing toward the entrance.

"Let me out of here. Let me out!" cried the giant, shaking the lock.

"Calm yourself, sir!"

"I'll not be cut. I'll not be cut," shouted Charles as Hunter opened the door, allowing him to bound back up the steps, where Howison waited with the carriage. Without hesitating, the giant opened the door himself.

"Take him back to London," ordered the anatomist.

"I'll not be cut, you hear me?" called Charles out of the carriage window as he headed off back toward the city, cussing and cursing in his native Irish tongue.

"Och! I hear you," shouted Hunter, adding under his breath, "But you'll have no say in the matter, Mr. Byrne. You'll be long gone, like all the others."

Chapter 29

On the fourth day of her self-imposed exile, Lady Lydia Farrell called for her maid Eliza.

"I wish you to see that this is delivered to Dr. Silkstone in London," she instructed, handing over a letter.

Eliza curtsied and studied her mistress's face. She had not seen her for three days now and she noted that her cheeks were pale and sunken, so that her doleful eyes were even more prominent. There was something in her manner, too, that appeared odd. She would not raise her gaze, but kept it either firmly on the floor or toward the window, even though the blinds were still down.

"Would you like a tray, m'lady?" asked Eliza.

"No," she replied abruptly, then softening her tone, she added: "Thank you, Eliza. But I would ask that the dogcart be made ready."

Eliza smiled. "Yes, m'lady. 'Tis a lovely morning."

Lydia did not return her servant's smile and was not the slightest bit interested in the weather. Her silence dampened Eliza's enthusiasm.

"Have it ready by eleven," she instructed.

"Yes, m'lady." Eliza curtsied and left to inform the rest of the concerned household of their mistress's plans for the day. No doubt everyone would be delighted that her ladyship was in better spirits.

"That is good news," said Mistress Claddingbowl, rolling

out a batch of pastry. "Perhaps I could even tempt her with one of my pies."

"All in good time," replied Howard, taking the letter from Eliza's hands. "Whatever is in this letter, Lady Lydia will be able to tell the doctor in person, tomorrow," he said, waving it around before putting it his pocket for safekeeping. "I am sure he will come straight away."

Mistress Finesilver's knocks at his door woke Thomas from what had been a deeply disturbed night's sleep. Every turn, every movement he made, no matter how slight, had been accompanied by a stab of pain. The housekeeper entered at Thomas's bidding to find her master lying bloodied and bruised on the bed, still fully dressed. At the sight of him, her hands flew up to her face.

"What has become of you, Dr. Silkstone?" she cried.

Thomas tried to raise his head, but the exertion was too much for him. "I was set upon last night," he replied, sounding as if his mouth were full of pebbles. "I am hurt, but I will live."

Mistress Finesilver's maternal instincts, which usually lay well-hidden, now came into play and she sprang into action, pouring water and bathing Thomas's battered face. "But we must get you out of these clothes, sir," she exclaimed, looking at his blood-caked waistcoat with horror. "Ruth, Ruth," she called for the maid.

The notion of being undressed by two fussing women did not appeal to Thomas in the slightest, but he had not the energy to argue. Together they eased him into an upright position on the bed, slipped off his topcoat with great difficulty, and then tackled his waistcoat and shirt.

"Bring me a looking glass," he instructed so that he could inspect his own injuries. There was severe discoloration to his torso, especially below his rib cage, but the blood had flowed from only minor lacerations. Running his fingers along each shaft of rib, the ones he feared might have been cracked seemed to be smooth to the touch. He was heartily thankful that although his discomfort was great, a good application of arnica to bring out the bruising was probably all the treatment that was required. That, together with two or three days' rest.

Within the half hour Dr. Carruthers was at his protégé's side, displaying great concern for his welfare.

"But, young fellow, do you have any broken bones? A fever, what about a fever? A headache?" The blind anatomist seemed to have abandoned all professional decorum in his anxiety for the doctor.

If he had been able to, Thomas would have smiled. As it was, he was prevented from doing so by the stiffness of his mandible and its associated muscles. He said simply: " 'Tis merely bruising, sir."

Dr. Carruthers felt for the edge of the bed before seating himself upon it. "I'd like to get my hands on the blaggard that did this to you, young fellow."

"There were two of them," retorted Thomas.

"Did you see their faces?"

The doctor recalled the incident in his mind's eye; how he was walking along the ill-lit street when he saw the men approach.

"Their faces were hidden," he said, but then he remembered that he had seen a scarf slip slightly. Although it was pulled up again swiftly, he distinctly recalled the face now: the scar and the broken nose.

"The prizefighter," he muttered to himself as much as to Dr. Carruthers.

"Prizefighter," repeated the blind anatomist. "Prizefighter, you say." He stroked his chin in contemplation. "The only man I know of who answers to that description is no prizefighter at all, but a common criminal; a sack 'em up man."

Thomas managed to heave himself up on his elbows, his eyes opened as wide as his bruises permitted. "Go on, Doctor," he urged.

"Name's Ben Crouch. He has a sidekick called Jack Hartnett. No corpse in London is safe from those two. There's many a dissecting table that would remain empty without their evil trade."

Despite his discomfort, Thomas was now fitting the pieces of the puzzle together. His mind flashed back to the squalor of the jail. "They were the men in Newgate with Signor Moreno, too. They have something to do with the murder of the castrato. I just know it."

Carruthers nodded. "Maybe, but someone will have put them up to it. Those sort of scoundrels only do their despicable deeds to order."

Thomas looked at his blind mentor, whose unseeing eyes were as always closed, but in the ensuing silence their thoughts seemed to make themselves known to each other without words. At the exact same moment they both spoke the exact same name: "John Hunter."

Charles Byrne awoke with a start, cold and stiff on the slab of a mortsafe in the graveyard of St. Giles-in-the-Fields. He had just suffered a nightmare. In his dream he was on Dr. Hunter's dissecting table, tied down and unable to move. The doctor approached him, a glinting scalpel held aloft in his hand, like some pagan priest about to make a sacrifice. As he brought down the knife, Charles sat up, his heart pounding like a drum in his chest and the noise of it filling his ears. He looked around, shaking the fog of sleep from his large head. He was surrounded by gravestones, some worn, some new, some grand, some simple, some moss-covered as if growing out of the very ground itself. All were in higgledy-piggledy rows, layer upon layer of corpses consigned by plague and disease and time to their earthy resting place. What had brought him to this unsettling site he now tried to recall. He shivered as he cast his mind back to Dr. Hunter's underground cave where he had seen strange things, evil things; men's body parts preserved in jars and phials, instead of being where they should be, wrapped in shrouds and given decent burials in consecrated ground. What monster would deny a man a burial, he asked himself.

The last thing he remembered was wandering through the streets at a late hour. He had asked Howison to drop him off in St. Giles, where Emily's family lived. Emily. Now he recalled. He was looking for Emily, but it was dark and only the devil and his sort were out at that time of night, so he had lain on a tomb-stone and rested.

Now, in the cold light of day, surrounded by the memorials and trappings of death, fear began to take hold. He sensed he was being watched. He turned to see that he was, indeed, being gazed upon in awe by a curious urchin. As soon as he saw Charles's face, the child let out a loud scream. "A giant! A giant!" he cried and leapt up from the long grass where he had been crouching and ran off through the graveyard toward the gates.

Charles rose, aware that the boy's cries would alert the whole neighborhood. He followed quickly, past the charnel house, toward the gates. He knew his very presence in the streets would cause mayhem. He knew, too, that word would spread quickly and that, hopefully, wherever Emily was, she would hear of his arrival and come to greet him. She would look after him; she would keep him safe from Dr. Hunter and his evil plan. She would see to it that he did not end up like his father, as a piece of meat to be cut and sliced on a dissecting table, then dragged to the slaughterhouse.

He lumbered over the green tussocks of the graveyard to the gates and turned down an alley. At the end of it he could see people and carts plying along what seemed like a busy thorough-fare, so he turned off down another deserted side street. Shelter-ing in a doorway at the end of the lane, he spied a square where a crowd of twenty, maybe thirty people was gathered. They were listening to a man who was standing on some steps in front of a building, shouting, not in an angry way, but so that he might be heard by all. A crying baby held by a woman next to him also vied for the crowd's attention and next to her, seated on the steps, was an old crone. The man held something dark in his hand. Charles could not make out what it was. It appeared as though he was selling his wares.

A large cart was parked nearby, so, getting down on all fours, he crawled over to it. Then he crouched between it and the wall to gain a better view and to put himself within earshot of the hawker.

"Come on now. Don't be shy of Mad Sam," he called. "Work your own miracles with this hair from the amazing Irish Giant. Guaranteed to cure all your ills, as foretold by Grandmother Tooley. Only tuppence a lock."

Wives, young girls, and men on crutches came forward, some with limps, others with sores; some with coughs, others with toothache; all clamoring for a lock. The woman with the baby took their pennies, while the man put the strands of hair, held together by small lengths of ribbon, into their eager hands.

"Hold the hair where it ails and you'll be rid of your troubles," he shouted above the general fracas.

From behind the cart Charles looked on in shock. Who was this man? Where did he get his hair, if indeed it was his hair? Why would he say that it could work miracles? There were so many questions he wanted to ask and so much indignation that he felt, that he decided to abandon the cover of the cart and confront the hawker. Straightening himself to his full height, he strode toward him.

The first woman to notice him let out a scream.

"The giant!" she cried.

"The giant!" many echoed.

The crowd around Mad Sam parted. Some fled; others remained transfixed, compelled to watch the giant's reaction to the hawker.

Grandmother Tooley could not contain her wonderment and seemed to enter into some sort of trance. "The tall man," she screeched, pointing her gnarled finger at the giant. "The tall man from across the water, as I foretold."

Seeing Charles approach, instead of fleeing like many of his customers, Mad Sam stood his ground and smiled. "Well, well, ladies and gents, if it isn't the miracle worker himself," he cried, gesturing to Charles. "What an honor it is to meet you, sir, and a fellow Irishman, too." He beamed.

Those who had scurried off and hidden behind barrels and carts and crates now peered from behind them, anxious to see the next act of the drama play out in front of them.

Charles scowled at the hawker, who seemed totally unfazed. "Why look so sad, Giant? Your powers are helping all these good people."

There was a tense silence as Charles surveyed the faces that now cowered below him. Silence. The woman with the screaming baby looked at Mad Sam. The child had managed to get hold of a lock of the giant's hair and was now sucking it, peacefully and without a noise.

"The babe. He's stopped crying," she said to her husband. "He's stopped crying!"

Mad Sam's eyes opened wide with delight as he looked at the peaceful child. " 'Tis a miracle. The giant has wrought another miracle!" he exclaimed.

A collective cheer went up from the crowd, and now more people than ever rushed forward toward Charles, wanting to touch him. He soon became surrounded by hordes of citizens, tugging at his breeches and prodding at his legs.

Mad Sam climbed up to the top of the steps and held out his hand to Charles. "Here," he called and the giant strode up to join him, but the crowd followed him, pushing and shoving, so that some of the children and the cripples fell or were crushed in the melee. Word spread quickly in the back streets and alleyways of St. Giles-in-the-Fields, like a contagion. The cry went up: "The Irish Giant. The giant is here!" It soon reached Emily, who had been tasked with sweeping the floor at home. She ran to the window and looked down below to see a stream of people flowing toward the market square.

Hurrying downstairs, she joined the feverish throng and was carried along on their tide. Soon she saw Charles, standing at the top of the steps, his large head and broad shoulders towering above the baying crowds; bodies pressed against each other, trying to surge forward, as they so often did for a hanging. Their cries and shouts were deafening, but these were no jeers for injustices done. They called for Charles to look upon them as Christ would himself have laid his hands upon the poor and the sick, or simply to touch them.

Emily called his name, but her voice was lost in the caco-
phony of pleas and beseechings that came from all those milling
around her. "Charles," she cried again, but to no avail.

Another ten minutes of mayhem passed before the constables
finally came to break up the crowd with sticks. The unfortu-
nates scattered down side streets, disappearing back into their
hovels just as soon as they had come, like an army of ants. Only
Charles, Mad Sam, his wife and babe and Grandmother Tooley
were left on the market steps.

"We should charge you with breach of the peace," said one
of the constables, adding to Charles: "But we will not, just as
long as you, sir, leave the neighborhood straight away, before
you cause any more trouble."

The giant nodded. "I will go, sir," he replied with all the art-
less guile of a child. He had not wanted to cause such chaos. He
had only wanted to find Emily, but there was one other thing he
had to know before he returned to Cockspur Street.

"Is that really my hair?" he asked Mad Sam.

The hawker grinned. "Why, you wouldn't be doubting me
now?"

"Then how did you come by it?"

"Yes, how did you come by it?" came a voice from below.
Both men looked down to see Emily standing indignantly at the
foot of the steps. Charles's face broke into a broad smile and he
strode down to greet her. Enfolding her in his arms, he held her
tightly.

"Oh, dear Emily," he whispered. "I came to find you," he
told her, grasping both her arms. He looked at her intently, his
eyes moist with tears. "You are to return to Cockspur Street, on
the count's orders," he said.

She smiled and held his hand close to her cheek. "Then I shall
go back with you." She nodded. "But first, I need the answer to
your question. How did he come to possess locks of your hair?"
she cried, pointing a finger at her wayward father.

Mad Sam's face broke into another broad grin. "Why, my
dear daughter, I borrowed them from that tin of yours, of

course," he told her unashamedly, adding: "A man's got to earn a living any ways he can."

Charles shook his head sadly. "So this man is your father?"

Emily nodded. "It pains me to say so."

The giant's look was pitiful. "It seems that everyone wants to profit from my misfortune," he told her.

"Not everyone," she replied, kissing his hand sweetly. "Come, let's return."

Instead of allowing himself to be guided by her hand, however, Charles remained on the spot. "What is it?" asked Emily, puzzled.

A troubled look settled on his face. " 'Tis that doctor."

"The one you saw before at Earls Court?"

"Yes. He wants to cut me up when I die." His voice cracked as he spoke.

Emily looked at her father, then at Charles. "Do not fear," she soothed. "I will not let him do that. You will be safe back with the count." And patting the giant tenderly on the arm, she led him away by the hand.

By first light Jacob Lovelock had saddled the stable's fittest mount and headed off on the long journey to London. The sun had not yet risen over the Chiltern Hills, and the dawn was gray and chill. It had not rained for a few days now and the ground was dry, making the journey less treacherous underfoot. His progress toward the capital had been good. Stopping at Beaconsfield he had changed his horse, downed a pint of small beer, and bought a pie, which he ate in the saddle. By one o'clock he had entered the city by Newgate and was in Piccadilly less than a half hour later.

Mistress Finesilver answered the door to him with a look of surprise. "I am come with a message for Dr. Silkstone, ma'am," he said, black smuts marking his pitted face. "I have ridden hard from Boughton Hall."

The housekeeper arched an eyebrow. "I can see you have come from far," she said, staring at Lovelock's dust-covered jacket, "but Dr. Silkstone is indisposed." Her master was asleep, and she knew he needed all the rest he could muster. She told the messenger to come back on the morrow and was just about to close the door on her visitor when Dr. Carruthers happened to be walking by.

"Who goes there?" he asked.

Mistress Finesilver raised her eyes heavenward in annoyance. " 'Tis a messenger from Boughton Hall for Dr. Silkstone, sir, but I have told him he is not available," she replied curtly.

The old anatomist stopped by the open door, sniffing the stale air of the street. "I am sure that Dr. Silkstone is always disposed to receive a message from Lady Lydia, if that is the case," he said playfully.

"Not exactly, sir," replied Lovelock awkwardly. " 'Tis a message that *concerns* her ladyship, though, sir."

Dr. Carruthers tilted his head and puckered his mouth. "In that case, please come in. Dr. Silkstone met with an accident last night, but I am sure he is keen to hear any news about her ladyship," he told him, adding: "I only hope it is not bad."

Mistress Finesilver grudgingly led Lovelock up the stairs to Thomas's room and knocked on the door. Thomas bade her enter and assured her that he was well enough to receive a visitor, although he was shocked to see the head groom.

"Bring this man some food and ale, and water to wash," he told a surly Mistress Finesilver. "What is it, Jacob?" he asked anxiously as soon as they were alone.

"I am come with the knowledge of Mr. Howard, sir, but without the permission of her ladyship," he said, nervously fingering his dusty hat.

Thomas, who was now sitting up in bed with a cold compress at his cheek to relieve the swelling, frowned and bade Lovelock sit on a chair.

"Is Lady Lydia unwell, or in danger?" he asked, looking intently at the groom.

"Maybe," replied Lovelock.

"Unwell, or in danger, or both?" pressed Thomas.

Lovelock shrugged. "She's not been herself since she came

back from London. She shut herself in her room and then Sir Montagu came to talk to her of making a marriage and now she hasn't eaten for days. We are all concerned, sir."

Thomas began to sigh deeply, but was quickly reminded of his bruised ribs when he tried to do so. He should have guessed that Sir Montagu would soon be wanting to make a match for her. "Has Dr. Fairweather been called?" he asked.

Lovelock shook his head. "Eliza asked her if she would see him and she said no. We are worried, Dr. Silkstone, worried that she may do something terrible. She is in such a bad state."

Thomas closed his eyes momentarily. The servants were putting him in a difficult position. They had no idea that he and Lydia had been betrothed and that she had ended their engagement. They had no idea that he had been told that he must never see her again and yet he was the obvious person for them to turn to when they sensed their mistress was in grave danger. Their loyalty was unquestionable, albeit somewhat unorthodox.

"And there's this," said Lovelock, flourishing the list of suitors that Eliza had smuggled to him before he set off. "We thought you should see this."

Thomas scanned the list of highborn men thought worthy or desirable by Sir Montagu, but one name toward the bottom of the list rankled more than any other. It was the Right Honorable Rupert Marchant.

"Your mistress would be touched by your concern, as I am," he said finally. "As you can see, I am somewhat incapacitated at the moment," he lifted a bruised hand, "but from your tone, I feel I am needed sooner rather than later."

Lovelock nodded. "You are the only person who can help her ladyship, sir. We are sure of that," he pleaded.

"I must stress that I go only as a physician," said Thomas, "but go I will and right away."

The groom breathed a sigh of relief and his face burst into a smile. "Thank you, sir. Thank you," he said and he left the room to wait for the doctor to make ready for his long, and no doubt painful, journey to Boughton.

*   *   *

In a tavern just off Fleet Street, Dr. Hunter sat in his usual dingy corner, cradling a tankard of ale. This was where he did many of his dealings. His associates appreciated the anonymous surroundings, where they could blend in with the rest of the rogues and whores and general detritus of a city. It was his custom to keep his back to the wall and his eyes on the door so that he could see all the comings and goings.

A persistent fly was buzzing around his head and he kept trying to waft it away with a rolled-up newssheet. He had just been reading a report about an incident in St. Giles where the presence of the Irish Giant had caused a small riot. As he continued to battle with the fly, he saw Howison enter the inn and signaled him over. "It must be able to smell death on me," he said, still waving away the fly, as the servant sat down. "I have a job for you," he continued. "The giant."

Howison grinned, exposing a bottom row of rotting teeth. "Yes, sir," he replied.

"I want him, but he is not cooperating."

The fly landed on the table and started to sip some spilled ale. Seizing the opportunity, Hunter took an empty tankard, upturned it, and slammed it down, imprisoning the insect.

"You're to follow him everywhere. Watch his every move. Make him squirm. He is dying. There is no doubt of that, but we may have to devise a way of hastening his exit"—he broke off to lift the tankard slightly, so that, sensing freedom, the fly crawled to the edge of its prison and poked its head out—"so that I can get to work on him at once." He banged the tankard down suddenly, decapitating the fly.

Howison nodded. "I understand, sir."

Lydia drove the cart up to the pavilion just before noon. It was a sunny spring day. The trees were covered in a bright green haze of buds, and the fields were a subtle patchwork of soil and shoots. She was glad that she took in her last view of Boughton on such a day. This was how she wanted to remember it, bathed in warm sunshine. She walked over to the simple wooden cross on the ridge that marked her husband's grave. She had thought to have him reinterred in the family vault, but had not been able to face the thought of disturbing him again. Laying a posy of violets and celandine on the grassy mound, she said a short prayer before turning to enter the pavilion itself.

The once-white planks were now a dull, weather-stained gray. A pane of glass was cracked. An aura of neglect and decay surrounded it. It had been more than a year now since her last visit to this place. She remembered she had been shocked at its condition and had vowed to ask Amos Kidd, the gardener, to clean and repair the fabric of the building. Yet events had overtaken her and still nothing had been done, but at least it served her purpose.

The door creaked open. A large spider dropped down on a thread in front of her eyes. She swept it away with her hand and surveyed the space. More floorboards had been chewed by vermin, which had left more droppings in their wake. She walked to the far side, treading warily. Her eyes scanned the corner, and a smile flickered across her lips when she saw it. It was still where she had left it more than a year ago. The stone jar, about the size of a pitcher, with its narrow neck plugged by a cork, remained untouched. She bent down and picked it up. It still contained liquid, admittedly not as much as before. Francis had drained a gill or two off to take to Thomas for his scientific tests, but enough was left for her purpose. She did not bother to remove the stopper to remind herself of the familiar, nauseating smell. She would reserve that doubtful pleasure for nearer the appointed time.

Returning to the door, she took one last look around the room before climbing back onto the dogcart, the stone jar sitting securely at her side. She hid it under a shawl she had brought with her for that very purpose. No one would know. No one would suspect—until it was too late.

Chapter 30

Thomas knew there was no time to lose. Experience told him that Jacob Lovelock was not a man prone to exaggeration, and his concern for his mistress was very acute. Despite protestations from Dr. Carruthers and, surprisingly, from Mistress Finesilver, the young doctor slowly and painfully managed to mount a horse and, together with the head groom, he set off from London at around four o'clock that afternoon.

"We still have five hours of daylight," he said. "We can make it up to Beaconsfield before dark and stay the night at an inn."

Thomas's injuries still caused him great discomfort. His horse's every stride sent a jab of pain searing through his ribs. He was thankful that he had brought a phial of laudanum with him. After a couple of swigs of the bitter liquid had taken hold, his agony subsided and he was even able to urge his mount to gallop for some of the way. When the pain returned, even more violently than before, he would remind himself of his purpose. Lydia needed him, and for her he would endure his very own Calvary if it meant her own happiness and well-being could be restored.

That night, as he lay in his bed at the Saracens Head at Beaconsfield, a thousand red-hot pokers thrusting into his rib cage and back, he imagined that this was what was hell must be like. He closed his eyes and saw a raging pit of fire, and in the center, where the flames burned white, he saw Lydia's anguished face calling to him. It reminded him of that same look when he had broken it to her that her husband was dead. He recalled the day in Oxford when he had seen Captain Farrell hanging from the ceiling in the stinking jail. His expression had been calm, his eyes and lips closed as if asleep, and yet the crooked angle of his head as it swung from the silken curtain cord would remain with him forever. He was only glad she was spared the sight, but he knew the memory of that day still haunted her. That day. That date. It was April 30. Exactly a year tomorrow. It would be the first anniversary of Lydia's husband's death. The sudden realization of it made him shudder. Was this the reason for her obvious distress? Was this why she had shut herself away in belated mourning? Had some delayed reaction seized her mental faculties in a cruel vise? He could not arrive at Boughton too soon.

Safely returned to his lodgings in Cockspur Street, Charles Byrne's spirits were much restored. Knowing that Emily had been reemployed made him feel more confident. She was his rock, while all around lay a sea of torment and turmoil, and yet the Scotsman's words still haunted him.

"We were worried about you," said the count, handing his friend a glass of gin.

The giant took it, swigged it back, then held out the glass for more. Boruwlaski obliged. "I saw Dr. Hunter," Charles said, gazing into the fire.

The little man nodded. "Ah, really? And why was that?"

"He asked to see me." Charles took another gulp of gin. "I thought he wanted to help me, to cure my ills."

"And . . . ," urged the count, filling the glass once more.

The giant's eyes moistened and his jaw was set tight to stop his lips from trembling. When he finally spoke his voice was taut with emotion. "He told me that I will die soon and that when I am g-gone"—he broke off suddenly to take a deep breath—"when I am gone he wants to cut me up and put me in his museum of death." He drained another glass.

The dwarf paused for a moment, as if in shock, then put a hand on the giant's arm and filled his glass once more. "But, dear friend, you are not dying."

Charles looked down at him. "I am. I know I am," he said, nodding. "This cough. The tiredness. I have the white death and I know my days are numbered." The count knew it to be true, too, but he had always tried to ignore his friend's obvious symptoms. After a few moments, Charles continued: " 'Tis not the dying that worries me." His features were set hard in a scowl. " 'Tis being butchered afterward, like meat on a slab, like they did to my da."

Boruwlaski let out a sigh and tilted his tiny head. "That is Dr. Hunter for you. He collects things. You do not have to consent to this. It is your body. Do not concern yourself about it," he said, trying to make light of the giant's fears, but his seeming indifference only agitated Charles.

"That man would deny me my place in heaven, sir," he cried, suddenly trying to stand up. He failed, and slumped down again into his chair. The count could see he had touched a raw nerve.

"Even if you do die soon, my friend, which you will not, I can assure you that your body will remain in safe hands," soothed the count. "I will see to it personally."

His assurances seemed to calm Charles, and a smile flickered across his flaccid lips. "Thank you, Count," he said. "You are a true friend."

The little man returned his smile. "So, you are the talk of the newssheets," he said, lightening the mood of conversation. "This is what you are about when I am not at your side." He waved a copy of a newssheet before smoothing it to read an excerpt from an article. "A parson has expressed concern that a number of his parishioners claim they have been cured of various ills by Mr. Charles Byrne, the amazing Irish Giant, currently resident in London. You have wrought miracles!"

"I am no miracle worker. 'Tis a load of shite." Charles spat out his words contemptuously.

"But do you not see?" Boruwlaski could hardly contain himself with excitement. "We could charge even more, and still people will flock to see you."

" 'Tis true I need the money," conceded Charles.

"Indeed you do, my friend," replied the count, his expression suddenly altering to one of concern.

"You have heard more from the lawyer?" asked the giant warily.

The count nodded. "He says he is progressing, but that he needs more time to get the papers in order. And," he opened his hands in a gesture of resignation, "more time means more money to lawyers."

"Very well. I will return to the cane shop, but as soon as I make enough money to pay this lawyer for a pardon, I go back home," he said, adding ruefully, "afore 'tis too late."

Chapter 31

O n the morning of her carefully planned death, Lady Lydia Farrell rose to the chimes of St. Swithin's church bells as they called the faithful to Sunday worship. The sound traveled across the fields from Brandwick and filled her with a sweet sadness. Would God forgive her for what she was about to do? Parsons and priests would say no, that she was about to take a life that was not hers to take. She had neither the strength nor the theological intellect to argue with them. All she knew was that the only way out of her indescribable torment was to end her own life in this world and pray that the Lord would look favorably on her sins in the next.

The stone jar sat on the top of her chest of drawers. A large tumbler was next to it, waiting to receive its liquid at the appointed hour. Lydia traced the cork and the neck of the jar with her slender fingers, then held up the empty glass to the light before setting it down again carefully. Next she took out her prayer book from a drawer. She was just about to open it when there was a knock on her door. She knew it would be Eliza, as it had been at the same time every day for the past week.

"Ma'am," the maid called through the door. "I have left you a tray. Is there anything else I can get you?" Her mistress had not touched the cook's offerings over the past few days, yet Eliza persisted in bringing the food in a vain hope that her ladyship's spirits might be restored, if only slightly.

"No thank you, Eliza," Lydia called. The maid sighed and

turned to go back to the kitchen, but just as she did so, the door opened slightly. Lydia stood on the threshold, her face thin and wan.

"Thank you, Eliza," she said, gazing intently at the girl. "You have been a good servant."

Eliza appeared puzzled, but curtsied. "I hope I shall remain so, your ladyship," she replied, walking forward toward Lydia, but the door was shut in her face again and the maid went back to the kitchen, even more concerned than before.

Returning to her prayer book, Lydia opened it at a psalm she had already marked. She sat down at the window and read: *There is no health in my flesh because of thy displeasure; neither is there any rest in my bones, by reason of my sin. For my wickednesses are gone over my head; and are like a sore burden, too heavy for me to bear. My wounds stink and are corrupt through my own foolishness. I am brought into so great trouble and misery; that I go mourning all the day long.* Such words brought her comfort in her hour of need. Her Maker was the only person she could turn to. Even Thomas, her true love, would never understand what she had done. He would reproach her, blame her, and despise her if he ever discovered what happened. She would take her secret with her to the grave. That way only one man would know the truth, and even if he did, out of his own malicious, twisted spite, tell Thomas all, then she would not be alive to feel the righteous recriminations that would follow.

Surely the next life would be better than this? She would be free from the burden of guilt that she had been carrying 'round with her for the past five years. Surely God in his goodness would not judge her too harshly. Turning to the prayer book once more, she read the final verse of the psalm: *Forsake me not, O Lord my God; be not thou far from me. Haste thee to help me; O Lord God of my salvation.*

Thomas had wakened Lovelock before first light, unable to sleep because of his pain and his fears for Lydia. His anxiety had grown and multiplied like so many bacteria on a corpse.

"We cannot wait any longer. We must leave," he had told the groom, rousing him from his bed.

By six o'clock they were on the road again, and by ten Thomas finally spotted the spire of the chapel at Boughton. The bells of St. Swithin's were tolling the half hour as he dismounted and dragged himself, exhausted, up the steps of the hall.

Will had warned the household of his arrival, and Howard and Mistress Firebrace were there to greet him.

"Her ladyship remains in her room, sir," said the butler, obviously relieved to see the doctor.

"I shall go to her immediately," replied Thomas, clutching his medical bag.

All thoughts of his pain were banished as he strode up the stairs followed by the butler, the housekeeper, and Eliza, but as soon as he reached the landing he stopped dead in his tracks and doubled over.

"Get back, for God's sake, get back," he screamed, reaching for his kerchief and tying it over his nose and mouth. Running toward Lydia's room, he found it locked, so he stood back, took a deep breath, and then shouldered the door with all his strength until it flew open.

Lydia was lying prostrate on the floor, her skin as pink as rose petals. Thomas felt for a pulse but could find none. He looked around. On the dresser he saw the stone jug on its side, its contents spilled onto the rug below. The poisonous vapor was already in the air. Lydia's sleeve was soaked, too. He tore it off and flung it to the floor.

Howard appeared at the door, a scarf held over his face. "Help me get her out of here," Thomas cried, lifting Lydia under her head and arms. The butler tied the scarf behind his head and took his mistress's feet. They carried her to the landing and laid her down. Thomas shut the door as quickly as he could.

"Bring me blankets, sheets, anything to seal off this door," he called down the stairs to the anxious servants who waited below. By now some of them were beginning to choke or experience shortness of breath.

"Open all the windows, and then leave the house. Leave now," he called between coughs. He himself was choking, gasping for air. He threw a blanket up against the bedchamber door and lifted up Lydia in his arms, not knowing if she was alive or dead. All he knew was that he had to get her away from the deadly smell of cyanide before he could hope to save her.

Rushing downstairs with Lydia over his shoulder, he took her into the drawing room and laid her motionless on the sofa. The pink bloom of her skin told him that the poison had taken hold, invading her respiratory system, paralyzing her thoracic muscles. She was icy to the touch. Again he tried her pulse. Again he could not find one. Putting his ear to her breast he listened for her heartbeat. It was there, like a faint tapping on a drum, but that was all he needed to hear. He knelt down and parted her lips, opening her mouth with his deft fingers before taking a deep breath and placing his own lips on hers.

Howard and Mistress Firebrace watched anxiously from the doorway. When the housekeeper saw what Thomas was doing, she stifled a cry and looked away. The doctor took another gulp of air and once again blew into Lydia's mouth. This time her body shuddered. Thomas repeated the procedure and Lydia stirred again. Now her breaths came in short, sharp pants. Her back arched and finally her eyes opened wide with terror. She turned her head toward Thomas, still struggling for air.

"Lydia, Lydia. You're safe," he told her, trying to steady her shuddering body, clasping her face in his hands. But she could not answer. Her cold hands reached for her throat. Her tongue protruded and a strangled cry came forth, but still she could not breathe. Her body lurched upward in one last gasp of desperation before she fell back down again, her eyes closed.

The doctor felt for her pulse. It was barely discernible. Holding her face in his hands, he slapped her cheek lightly, looking for a response; there was none. She was now unconscious again, or worse still, thought Thomas, she might even have fallen into a coma.

Chapter 32

With the count's encouragement, Charles returned to the cane shop as before. He smiled as instructed and was courteous enough if anyone spoke to him. His companion remained at his side throughout the day, exchanging pleasantries and generally charming the spectators, helping them feel that their half crown was well spent.

It was toward two o'clock, when Charles was feeling at a low ebb, that he spotted an unwelcome face in the queue. Bending almost double, he whispered in the count's ear: "That man." The dwarf followed Charles's gaze. He knew instantly who he meant. "He is Hunter's man."

The count recognized the swarthy features and rough gait of the servant as he drew closer. "What can he want again?" he asked, puzzled.

Howison merely stared at the giant. Neither a word nor a gesture was forthcoming. He paused for three or four seconds, letting his gaze begin at Charles's feet and travel upward to his head. He then moved on.

"How strange," commented the little man.

"I like him not." Charles scowled.

"Smile, dear friend, smile," urged the count when he saw the giant's brows knit in a frown. "These good people would much rather see a happy giant than a sad one!"

Charles tried to oblige his ally, but found it increasingly difficult and was glad when the last spectator of the day left. He walked toward the door with the count, but when he looked out of the window, much to his consternation, he saw Howison standing watching him, propped up against a tree on the opposite side of the street.

The giant cursed and shot back from the window.

"What is it, my friend?" asked the count.

"Hunter's servant. He be here again."

The count peered through the window. "I cannot see him."

The giant peered cautiously, too. This time there was no one by the tree. "I swear he was there not a second ago," he said, shaking his head.

The little man smiled. "You are tired, my friend. Let us go home." He reached up and patted the giant on his thigh. It had been a long day for them both.

Thomas was sitting by Lydia's bedside, watching her for any signs of consciousness. There were none. They had moved her into another bedchamber and opened the windows so that she breathed nothing but the purest air. They had covered her in the lightest sheets so that even the effort of inhaling and exhaling should have been made easier, but still there was no response.

Coma. It was a word that Thomas feared, but he believed Lydia had now fallen into one. The great Hippocrates had first coined the phrase. It meant "state of sleep." It sounded so benign, but Thomas knew it was anything but. It was the condition of the body just before death. The cold, harsh truth was that Lydia was in a deep, deep sleep from which she might never awake. He had seen patients in such a situation as this before. Through his studies with Dr. Carruthers he had learned that there are different levels of consciousness. Normally the mind was alert, sharp, and quick to respond to various external stimuli, but when the brain became progressively less responsive it reached, at the lowest level of function, the state of coma. Like a watch that was wound up and working normally, the brain ticked along until some terrible trauma occurred and then the watch slowed down and almost stopped.

As he sat, keeping vigil over Lydia, Howard entered the room.

"How fares her ladyship, Dr. Silkstone?" he asked anxiously. He knew he spoke out of turn, but he felt he could talk to Thomas.

"She is stable now," he replied.

"And she will live, sir?" He sought a reassurance that could not be given.

"We can but pray, Howard."

The butler then took out of his pocket the letter that Lydia had written the previous day.

"Sir, you must see this," he said, handing it to Thomas.

The doctor looked at him, puzzled.

"Her ladyship gave it to me yesterday to give to you, sir."

"Thank you, Howard," he said, opening the seal with a scalpel from his bag. "You may go."

Perhaps here lay the answer to the nagging questions that were now plaguing him. His first and only thoughts had been for Lydia's health. He had needed to stabilize her condition. He knew how she had arrived in this comatose state, but not why. The harsh reality of the situation appeared that she had tried to take her own life. He remembered the overturned stone jar full of laurel water and the glass next to it. It was the same laurel water containing cyanide that needed to be drunk in large quantities to kill a human. He had already proved that in Farrell's court case. To him it seemed that she had been about to pour the poisonous liquid from the jar into the glass, but before she could drink it, the noxious vapors had overcome her. They were much more deadly than the poison itself. Did Lydia mean to take her own life, and if so, why? The young anatomist began to read the letter, and as he did so, a terrible feeling of bewildered despair began to engulf him. He had guessed that Sir Montagu was pressuring her to find a suitable match, but with whom was this "chance encounter" and "the instrument of my (her) torture for many years"? Thomas's stomach lurched as he read the words "and I still bear the scars, both mental and physical, he inflicted." Who on earth was this beast? Why had she not spoken of him before? They were to be married, yet she purposely withheld this terrible secret from him. He gazed at her as she lay there, deep in her own consciousness. Even in this comatose state, she was still so very beautiful. "Why, Lydia? Why did you not tell me?" he whispered.

He read the letter a second time. Whoever this monster was, she had seen him in London. This "chance encounter," as she called it, had triggered her violent response, thought Thomas. He cast his mind back to the night of the concert. It was there that she must have seen this man. He remembered Lady Marchant and Giles Carrington. The only other person he could recall seeing was Dr. Hunter. He had no liking for the man. He was rough and rude, no matter how skilled he was in his art. Yet despite his ill-educated manner, the Scot struck him, in relation to the fairer sex at least, to be a man who would never dishonor a lady of rank. No, whoever this evil fiend was, his actions had driven his beloved Lydia to attempt suicide. That she had failed was by sheer luck, not judgment. And even now it was by no means certain that she would not succeed in her ultimate purpose. He had to discover the truth, no matter how awful, and he prayed to God that he would be able to hear it from Lydia's own lips.

He looked toward the open windows and shivered. The drapes rustled in the cooling chill as night began to fall. Since his arrival at Boughton Hall, all his injuries, his bruised and battered ribs and his cut face, had been dissipated by his anxiety for Lydia. Now that he knew there was no more he could do to ease her suffering, his own pain seemed to return. He felt it gnawing into his abdomen like a dull ache, punctuated by stabs of pain every time he moved. It was growing dark and he craved sleep. It was approaching nine o'clock when downstairs Thomas heard voices. A few seconds later Sir Theodisius Pettigrew blustered in, his face red and agitated.

"Oh my Lord, Silkstone, what has befallen her?" he wailed, looking at the changed young woman who lay before him.

Thomas did not know how to frame his reply. He could not bring himself to tell the coroner about the letter; that Lydia had wanted to kill herself. He could not say that. He would not say that. "There was a terrible accident. Her ladyship was trying to dispose of some laurel water she found and mistakenly inhaled a large quantity of it," he told him.

"Laurel water?" The coroner looked askance. The very mention of the poison triggered memories of the inquest and trial of Captain Farrell.

"The very same." Thomas nodded, reading Sir Theodisius's thoughts. "But she did not drink it. The vapors have done this. They can be more harmful than the poison itself," he explained.

The corpulent coroner eased himself onto the edge of the bed. "How long will it be until she is restored?"

Thomas wished he knew. "I cannot say, sir. A day, a week, a month, a year . . ." His wan voice trailed off before he could bring himself to say "never."

The color in Sir Theodisius's face now drained away. "So what can we do, Dr. Silkstone?" he asked, his expression pleading with the young anatomist for some shred of hope.

Thomas could give none. "All we can do is wait," he replied.

Chapter 33

"He is there again," said Charles Byrne, peering through the drawn curtains of the upper reception room back in Cockspur Street.

The count, reading a book by candlelight, raised his tiny head. "Who, dear friend?" he enquired nonchalantly.

"Hunter's man. He is standing under the street lamp." He coughed.

The count tut-tutted. "Surely not again?" He climbed down from his chair and waddled over to the window, tiptoeing over to the sill to look out at the darkened street beyond. "I see him," he said.

"He has been following me these past three days," said Charles. "He's out to get me like Corny Magrath."

"What happened to him, pray tell?"

A shiver ran down Charles's long spine. "He was a giant afore me. At his wake they put sleeping medicine in the d-drink, then dragged him out over all the mourners and c-cut him up. Then they hung him up in one of their fancy colleges in Dublin for all to see."

The count paused, looking thoughtful. "Dr. Hunter is playing a game with you." The little man winked. "But we know you will never give in."

"Never." The giant nodded. "I may as well sell my soul to the devil as give my dead body to that m-monster."

"Because of what happened to your father?"

"Aye. I'll not be butchered like a piece of meat," replied the giant, lugging his frame across the room to his chair.

The count poured him a gin. "Tell me about him, Charles," he said, helping himself to a brandy and climbing back into his own chair.

"He was a good man. He never h-hurt no one. 'Twas Con Donovan that did it," he began, staring into the fire as it crackled in the grate.

"How do you know?"

After a reflective pause Charles turned to the count, wearing a glazed expression, as if he had just relived an unforgettable moment. "Because I was there."

"You saw the murder?"

He nodded. "Con was foolin' with Mary O'Malley in the b-barn. I came to see what was happening when I heard them laughing. They was rollin' in the hay. I saw them kissing, but then Con, he . . . well, he wanted m-more."

Boruwlaski drew closer, intrigued. "Did they know you were watching?"

"Only when Mary started calling for him to stop and he wouldn't. He put his h-hand over her mouth and I told him to let her go."

"And did he?"

"He started shouting at m-me, calling me names. Called me dirty. Said I only wanted to w-watch." The giant's eyes were now filling with tears. "He picked up a shovel and told me to get lost or he'd bash me. He said he wasn't afraid of m-me."

"And then?" urged the count.

"And then my da came to see what all the noise was about. And he saw Con and he saw Mary crying and he saw him turn and h-hit her with the shovel. 'Hush ya mouth, will ya?' he said, and he hit her and she fell back. B-blood everywhere."

"So you and your father saw all this?"

"Yes, but they believed Con over me and my da. They said I was s-simple. Couldn't be trusted to tell the truth. Said my da was foolin' with Mary and that he did it. They believed Con because his uncle was the p-parish constable." Tears now flowed down the giant's cheeks. "So they strung my da up by the neck, then took him to the local slaughterhouse to c-cut him, those butchers." Anger flashed across his face. "What right had they to do that? 'Twas the Lord's body, not theirs. It did not belong to them, and now the fires of purgatory will be licking at his heels. How can he rise on Judgment Day?"

The count shook his head. "God knows that he was a just man. He will be in heaven," he consoled.

"You think?" asked Charles innocently. He tried to stifle a cough.

"I am sure of it," comforted the little man, reaching over to touch Charles's hand. "And now this Con has confessed?"

The giant gulped down more gin. "He did when another girl came before the court and said she'd seen the whole thing. I saw her, too, but I thought she'd left the barn before the kissing. But she stayed to look out for her friend. She saw him strike Mary but was afeared to say so before because he told her he would kill her, too."

"So now he will hang, too?"

"He ought to, but my ma has pleaded that he be sent far away. Says she doesn't want no more killing."

"Your mother is a generous woman."

Charles turned to the little man, wiping away his tears with his shirt sleeve. "Will I see her again, Count? Will I ever get home?"

"How goes it with the giant?" asked Dr. Hunter when Howison returned later that evening. In his servant's absence he had begun feeding some of the living specimens.

Howison took off his hat and scratched his matted hair. "I do as you bid, sir," he replied.

"So you went to the cane shop and he saw you there?"

"Yes, sir."

"And you followed him home and waited outside and he saw you there?"

"Yes sir. Just like I did yesterday and the day before." There was a certain insolence in Howison's voice.

"Och, I don't know what is wrong with the wretched creature. I only told him he'd not long to live and offered him twenty guineas to dissect his corpse. It was only his cadaver I was asking him to sell, not his soul," said Hunter, clearly annoyed. He was standing beside a large glass tank that contained a bright red frog. "I think we will have to make contingency plans, Howison," he reflected as he took a live mouse and held it squealing above the tank.

"Yes, sir," replied Howison, grinning broadly.

"Have you seen any deterioration in the giant's health?"

"Sir?" Howison did not understand his master's question.

"Does the giant seem worse?"

The servant rubbed his nut brown forehead. "I cannot rightly say so, sir," he replied. To him the giant seemed no better or no worse. He coughed now and again and looked weary at the end of the day, but no more than most men who have plied their trade for eight hours straight. He added: " 'Tis early days yet."

The mouse let out a shrill squeak and squirmed wildly the moment the frog's poison dart pierced its fur. Both men looked at each other and smiled as within a second or two, the struggling stopped.

"There is only one problem with that," said Hunter finally, dropping the mouse in front of its waiting predator. "I am not a patient man."

Count Josef Boruwlaski felt a tiny pang of guilt as he entered the cell of his old friend Leonardo Moreno the next morning. It had been well over a week since his last visit. He had seen the castrato shortly after Dr. Silkstone's call, and his physical state had been most distressing to him, so he did what any right-minded man in his position would do—he stayed away. He was therefore exceedingly glad to see the castrato had enough strength to pace up and down in his cell, even though his face was thin and waxen.

"How fare you, Leonardo?" he greeted him in Latin, a language they both spoke fluently.

Moreno managed to bend down to embrace him. "All the better for seeing you, dear Josef," he said.

"I am glad my visit brings you some cheer," said the little man as the jailer locked the door behind him.

The Tuscan looked grave and spoke in hushed tones. "I am told that my trial will be within the week, but I have not yet seen a lawyer to prepare my case."

The count shook his head. "In England they say you do not need a lawyer to defend you. All you need to do is speak the truth plainly if you are innocent. You have seen a lawyer for the prosecution?"

"Yes, a man by the name of Rupert Marchant, I think his name was."

The count's eyes opened wide. "But I know him!"

"You do?"

"He is acting on Mr. Byrne's behalf to obtain a pardon for his father," said the little man excitedly.

Moreno's frown turned to a smile. "Then perhaps you can vouch for my character, Josef. Perhaps he will be kinder to me in court."

"I shall indeed be happy to be a witness as to your good character, Leonardo," said the little man. "And, of course Dr. Silkstone's report points the finger of blame away from you. All will be well," he assured his friend. "All will be well."

The hours hung heavily at Boughton Hall. Thomas took it in turns to watch over Lydia with Sir Theodisius and his wife, and either Eliza or Hannah Lovelock was always in attendance, too. Parson Lightfoot also called, offering his well-worn platitudes to anyone who would listen. Yet there was no alteration in the patient's condition, not a flicker of an eyelid nor a change in the light rhythm of her breathing.

Thomas had spent the time both resting and reflecting. His bruised body was now repairing, but his mental state was still in turmoil. He must have reread Lydia's letter a dozen times, and the only conclusion that he could draw was that she must have seen someone in the audience at the concert that night who had resurrected a long-buried memory that so disturbed and horrified her as to make her suicidal.

Thankfully word had spread that Lady Lydia had suffered a terrible accident. This had, in part, been put about by the servants as they went to market in Brandwick. Whether or not they believed their own rumormongering was another matter, thought Thomas, but their loyalty to their mistress appeared steadfast.

Three days had passed, three days and three very long nights since Lydia had fallen into her coma, and there was no way of telling how long she would remain in this state. He knew he could not stay by her side indefinitely, even though he wished to. He had duties and obligations to fulfill, not least to Signor Moreno and to Charles Byrne. With this in mind he had sent for a nurse from London, a good woman he knew personally, who could be trusted to be diligent in her care of Lydia. She would be able to monitor her pulse, turn her to prevent sores, wash her, and moisten her lips with water.

On the morning of the fourth day Sir Montagu Malthus arrived unannounced from Banbury. He swept into Lydia's bedchamber to find Thomas seated in a chair by the bed. He was staring at the locket she had asked young Will to give to him as a token of her love before they parted for the winter and which he always kept with him.

"Ah, Dr. Silkstone. I heard you were here," he greeted Thomas haughtily.

The young doctor leapt to his feet. "Sir Montagu, how good of you to come," he replied, although he did not mean it.

"A terrible accident, I believe?" he said, looking at Lydia, lying senseless on the bed.

"It appears so," replied Thomas, not wishing to elucidate.

"That cursed laurel water?"

Thomas nodded. "The vapor from it, sir."

He frowned. "I should've made certain there was no more of it on the estate." He added pointedly: "It needs a man to take charge."

Thomas felt himself flush with anger. "I believe her ladyship is capable of running her own affairs," he replied hastily.

Sir Montagu's brows knitted together. "You think so, do you?" He smirked, looking the doctor straight in the eye. His face was so close Thomas could smell his rancid breath. "Then who shall inherit the estate if there is no heir?"

Thomas remained looking straight ahead as Sir Montagu circled him. "Surely that is for Lady Lydia to decide, sir," he replied.

The man let out a disdainful laugh. "And you are hoping that she chooses you," he said, pointing an accusing finger at Thomas.

The young doctor clenched his fists at his sides. Anger was welling up inside him, yet he knew he must keep it in check. "I do not feel it is seemly to talk of such matters, sir, while her ladyship lies in a coma."

His words registered almost immediately with the lawyer. "You are right, Silkstone," he acknowledged. "It is a discussion for another time perhaps. But be assured, as long as I draw breath, Lady Lydia Farrell will not be marrying an upstart from the Colonies." He spat out these last few words with a tone of utter derision in his voice.

Thomas was thankful when Howard knocked on the door, interrupting Sir Montagu's tirade. "Begging your pardon, sirs, but I have an urgent message for Dr. Silkstone." He handed over a letter to Thomas.

"It seems I am needed back in London immediately," he said, looking at Sir Montagu. "A nurse will be arriving later today to keep watch over her ladyship."

Malthus's head jerked in acknowledgment. "Then we shall have to continue our conversation at a later date, Dr. Silkstone," he replied acerbically. Thomas nodded, even though he dared not think about the future.

Chapter 34

To the morbidly fascinated and the sexually adventurous who sat in the public gallery of the Old Bailey that day, Signor Leonardo Moreno, the famous foreign castrato, was so much more than a curiosity. True, they had paid their half crowns to see midgets and giants and brothers joined at the hips and women with beards, but this was an altogether better class of monstrosity. Not only did he not possess any testicles, he was a murderer, too, and one who had taken obvious pleasure in executing the most macabre of acts on his victim.

This Tuscan so-called "gentleman" bore himself admirably, they observed, as he lined up with the seven other felons charged with various offences at the same session. They had heard he was a sodomite, that he and the young man he killed so brutally were lovers. But how could a man with no balls perform? How could he wap a man, woman, or beast, for that matter? So much to see and so many tantalizing questions! What an exciting day in court it would be, they all said.

The count had brought his friend a fine silk coat to wear, and his powdered wig covered the last few remaining scabs and bruises on his forehead from his earlier beatings. Yet he still looked a shadow of his former self to Boruwlaski. He seemed to have shrunk, both in weight and height.

Thomas was shocked at the change in his appearance, too. True, the last time he saw him, the Tuscan had been in a dire state, but prior to his imprisonment he had been proud and handsome with an enigmatic air about him. His incarceration had robbed him of much of his exotic glamor. Now he simply looked drained and resigned to his fate.

Thomas had only arrived at the Old Bailey just in time. He had taken the coach from Oxford the previous morning, but torrential rain had forced him to stop at Windsor for a few hours before he could continue onward to London. He was tired from his journey and still suffering from being flung around mercilessly in a springless coach. Nevertheless, he was eager to do his duty and speak about his postmortem findings on Signor Cappelli's body as and when he was called.

The court rose for Judge William Ferrers, a stern-looking man who would clearly not suffer fools gladly. The jurors sat near the lawyers' semicircular table, twelve of them, all together, followed by the prosecutor. Thomas shot a look of disgust at Rupert Marchant as, exuding his usual air of arrogance, he took to the courtroom floor to begin the day's business. He studied his gait, his sleek manner, his slack mouth. He was as slippery as a dish of eels, thought Thomas. How could such a man be considered worthy of Lydia? Then again, he mused, had not Lydia insisted on seeing him by herself in relation to the giant's affairs? Could it be that he was the cause of her flight from London? Was it he she saw at the concert that night?

One by one the other defendants appeared before Judge Ferrers: a horse thief, a highwayman, and a young moon-cursor, no more than twelve years old. There were two women, as well, both charged with theft, although they both pleaded their bellies and their cases were referred to a female jury. Justice was swift. Most of the defendants were in the dock for no more than ten minutes, and in all of their cases the judge ruled they were guilty.

Finally, toward an hour later, Moreno took to the stand. A large glass mirror had been positioned to reflect daylight onto the accused, and at that moment a ray of bright sunlight struck it, illuminating the Tuscan's anxious face, forcing him to shield his eyes. There were murmurings in the gallery. Was this a signal of divine displeasure? A sign that the wicked would find no hiding place in the house of the Lord?

"I understand you are a foreigner, Signor Moreno," said the judge slowly, enunciating his words to avoid any confusion. "Can you understand the court proceedings?"

The accused looked a little uncertain, but nodded. "Yes, Your Honor," he replied. The charge was put to Moreno in English and he pleaded not guilty.

"The court calls Count Josef Boruwlaski," cried the clerk.

There was a shuffling near the lawyers' table and in two or three seconds, the count emerged to an eruption of laughter from the public gallery.

"Order, order," cried Judge Ferrers, bringing down his gavel hard.

With difficulty the little man, dressed in a smart red coat and breeches, climbed into the witness box, but there was more laughter when his head could not be seen. Becoming increasingly irritated, the judge called for a stool for the count and warned that if there were any more outbursts he would clear the public gallery.

"Count Boruwlaski, how long have you known the defendant?" asked Marchant once order was restored.

"For almost forty years, sir," replied the count. "We met at the court of the Empress Maria Theresa and came across each other many times in our travels."

The prosecutor nodded. "And you were aware that Signor Moreno was what is known as a musico, or better described as a castrato?"

A ripple of laughter ran through the gallery.

"Please explain, sir, for those members of the jury who are not familiar with the term what exactly this means, Count," asked the judge.

The little man looked slightly uncomfortable. He cleared his throat. "A castrato is a man who is castrated as a child so his voice does not deepen in adulthood. Instead he may become a soprano or a mezzo soprano," informed the court.

"And Signor Moreno was one of the most famous in Europe?" questioned Marchant, pacing backward and forward, his fingers clutching his black robe.

"Indeed." The little man nodded. "He had *la voce di un angelo*—the voice of an angel—and would reduce many a crowned head to tears," he reflected.

"Indeed, but his singing days were over, I understand," pressed Marchant. The count nodded. "And a younger musico, shall we say, was superseding Signor Moreno, which naturally made him jealous."

The count frowned and Moreno bristled, gripping the stand. Boruwlaski fumbled for a reply, adding to his friend's anxiety, and before he refuted the allegation, the Tuscan protested out loud. Shaking a fist at Marchant he cried: "That is untrue. He was my protégé. I loved Carlo."

Thomas closed his eyes in shock. Moreno may as well have just placed the noose around his own neck. Marchant smiled and seized the opportunity like a lion on its prey. "You loved him, Signor Moreno?" he quizzed, an eyebrow raised in a cynical arch.

The courtroom erupted and Thomas leapt to his feet in a moment of frustration, looking toward the terrified Tuscan, who now realized, too late, that he had spoken out of turn and to his great discredit.

"Order! Order!" called the judge once more.

The prosecutor walked toward the table and picked up a bundle of letters. He held them up to the court. "These *billets-doux,* gentlemen of the jury, are proof, sickening proof, that the relationship between Leonardo Moreno and Carlo Cappelli was anything but brotherly. It was sexual and depraved in its nature."

Now the spectators began to bay. Thomas looked at their faces; their features were changing, brows knitting together, teeth clenching and baring. They were turning ugly.

"Did you know of this, Count Boruwlaski? Were you privy to this behavior?" pressed Marchant, suddenly turning on the little man. "Indeed, perhaps you were tempted to indulge in such an accursed abomination yourself?"

Even the judge was outraged at this unwarranted slur. "Out

of order, Mr. Marchant. May I remind you that this gentleman is a character witness, not the accused?" he reprimanded.

Marchant acknowledged his misdemeanor with a bow. "Forgive me, Your Honor. I was merely trying to familiarize the court with the devious and twisted nature of homosexual relationships. But I digress. Tell us more about Signor Moreno's good character."

The count tugged at his waistcoat as if he had just emerged from a fracas and began once more. "Over the years, Signor Moreno has traveled widely and has never been the cause of any scandal or gossip," he began. "His conversation has always been witty and affable and his bearing impeccable. Indeed, I believe he was a favorite with the Duke of Saxony."

Marchant interrupted. "Note the use of the past tense, gentlemen," he said to the jury, then to the count: "Pray continue."

Clearly affronted, Boruwlaski nevertheless complied. "Signor Moreno performed on the duke's request at many concerts and in several operas. Indeed, the great Mozart even wrote an aria specifically for his unique voice," said the little man.

"But is it not true that about five years ago, Signor Moreno's voice began to falter and he could no longer sing that particular piece?"

The count nodded. "That is so, sir."

"In fact, Signor Moreno's voice deteriorated to such an extent that he had to give up singing altogether two years ago."

"Where is all this leading us, Mr. Marchant?" queried Judge Ferrers, becoming impatient.

"It demonstrates my argument, sir, that advancing years had robbed Signor Moreno of his extraordinary voice, that he chose his protégé to service his own sexual appetites, and when his protégé began to enjoy the adulation that had once been accorded him, he decided enough was enough and he cut short his life in the most brutal way."

"Conjecture, Mr. Marchant," said the weary judge, holding up his hand to halt the lawyer's diatribe.

Marchant conceded with another bow and dismissed the count, who waddled down from the witness stand in a most vexed state.

The dwarf glanced over at his friend, whose appearance seemed even more fragile than before.

Robert Smee followed, perspiration dripping from his brow. He comported himself in his usual nervous manner and his testimony was almost identical to the version of events he had told Thomas. "He looked shifty, sir; my word, he did, turning this way and that, to see if anyone was around."

Next a cry went up from the clerk: "The court calls Marie Dubois."

Dubois, thought Thomas. Could she be related to the barber? He studied her as she walked to the stand; her hair and skin were dark, just like her father's would have been in his prime.

The timorous girl made a reluctant witness. On the verge of tears for most of her testimony, she kept her face to the floor and mumbled her words so that Justice Ferrers had to ask her to repeat herself on numerous occasions. "I 'eard noises in se gentleman's room."

"What sort of noises?" asked the judge.

"First I 'eard talking, sen I 'eard shouting." The girl shot a glance at Marchant. "Sen I 'eard a cry."

"A cry?"

The prosecutor intervened. "What sort of cry, Mademoiselle Dubois? A cry of pleasure or of pain?" He turned smugly to face the gallery as a ripple of laughter pulsed through the onlookers.

"Of pain, monsieur," she replied.

"What time was this?" asked the judge.

"After two o'clock."

There were murmurings of disapproval throughout the courtroom, and the reluctant servant was allowed to step down from the stand, her work done.

Finally Thomas was called as an expert witness. He did not relish the position. This was the second time he had found himself in a witness box instead of his dissecting rooms. Outcomes in court seemed to him to be based more on conjecture and hearsay than on solid evidence.

"Tell us what conclusions you came to in your postmortem report, Dr. Silkstone," ordered Judge Ferrers.

Thomas knew his evidence needed to be clear and comprehensive. His language would not be technical and he would lay out his findings and conclusions as clearly as possible. "I believe the pressure marks and injuries around the victim's mouth and face show that he was first suffocated, probably with a pillow in his sleep, and that afterward his larynx . . ."

The judge interrupted. "Larynx?" he repeated.

Thomas realized his mistake. "His voice box," he continued, "was removed surgically by a person who knew precisely what they were about," he told the court.

The judge reflected. "So a surgeon or anatomist?" asked the judge.

Thomas nodded. "Yes, Your Honor. Certainly someone well versed in the ways of human anatomy."

At this point Rupert Marchant leapt to his feet. "Sir, if I may?" he asked the judge.

"You may cross-examine the witness," came the reply.

"So you are saying that someone suffocated Signor Cappelli, obviously using brute force, then performed an operation on him?" asked the lawyer. There was a note of derision in his voice.

Thomas would not be bullied. "I venture, sir, that two assailants were at work; one to suffocate, the other to operate."

At this assertion, the public gallery erupted once more until Mr. Justice Ferrers brought down his gavel and called "order."

"An interesting hypothesis, Dr. Silkstone," remarked the judge. "Have you any other facts with which to support this assertion?"

Thomas felt uneasy. "I am afraid I do not at this moment in time, sir," he replied, glancing across at Moreno, whose hopeful expression collapsed as he spoke. "But there are certain lines of enquiry, sir, that I believe need to be followed."

The judge shook his head. "Please confine yourself to your dissecting rooms, Dr. Silkstone. The coroner and I will decide the rest. That will be all."

Thomas felt duly humbled, but his humility soon turned to anger, especially when he caught Marchant's victorious sneer as he left the witness stand. His disputations carried little weight with the entrenched legal profession. It seemed to him that they were as set in their ways as those of his own, blind to new ideas and new ways of thinking.

Moreno's case was the final one of the day. Soon the jurymen would huddle together to give their verdict before delivering it to the judge. They would seal the fate of a man in only a few short seconds of whisperings and suppositions, thought Thomas.

There was a hushed silence as the court waited for the judge's direction, so it came as a shock to everyone, not least to Thomas, that Mr. Justice Ferrers chose another course of action, and a rare one, instead.

"I call for a respite," he cried.

A look of shock darted across Marchant's hitherto smug face, while Thomas breathed a sigh of relief.

"I am not convinced by the arguments for or against the defendant, and I order that he return to the court at the end of the month, by which time I trust I will be better satisfied as to his innocence or guilt," said the judge, bringing down his gavel.

Thomas rose to signal to the Tuscan, showing him his support, and then turned to find the count. As he did so, however, he caught sight of a burly man in the public gallery who was making his way out of the courtroom. It was the prizefighter, Crouch.

The count approached Thomas. "We could not have hoped for more in the circumstances." He smiled, but the young anatomist did not reply. His eyes were following Crouch as he reached the exit.

"Forgive me, Count. I must go," he said, brushing past the little man and hurrying out of the courtroom, his gaze fixed on Crouch as he pushed his way through the crowd and out onto the street.

A carriage was waiting for the prizefighter outside and he climbed in hurriedly and was off in a flash, heading north, out of the city. Thomas was only a few paces behind, but he was not quick enough to stop the coach. His horse was tethered in stables at the rear of the court. Nevertheless, he managed to mount and set off on the same road shortly afterward. Riding almost at a trot, he wove his way around handcarts and wagons, until at last, along High Holborn, he saw Crouch's carriage.

He followed it at a steady pace for another twenty minutes up Oxford Street. It was as he suspected. He needed to prove his theory that not one man, but two, were instrumental in the brutal killing of Carlo Cappelli. Up until now he had no proof to link the prizefighter with Dr. Hunter. Convinced that all that was about to change, he rounded the bend and Earls Court came into view. As Thomas suspected, the drawbridge was down and in drove the carriage, carrying the villain. Crouch was the murderer. Marie Dubois had given him free access to Cappelli's room. He had suffocated the young castrato, there was little doubt in Thomas's mind, and John Hunter had worked on the warm corpse with such cold precision with his scalpel and tweezers to satisfy his morbidly insatiable curiosity. The brute was about to impart to his master the day's proceedings in court. No doubt Hunter would be deeply disturbed by the fact that Moreno had not been found guilty—for the time being, at least. Thomas knew that this brief respite would mean the Scotsman would only redouble his efforts to see that the Tuscan was taken to the rope at the end of the month. Satisfied of the link between Crouch and Hunter, Thomas turned his horse and headed for home. Now he would need to find hard evidence—evidence he was sure lay within the walls of the anatomist's macabre fortress. He was convinced that Cappelli's larynx was being stored in a preserving jar, somewhere in Hunter's laboratory, but he had no idea how he would gain access to the premises in order to prove his hunch without being detected. It was then that he thought of Carrington, the young student who was so keen to assist him and who had, for a while, been concerned about his master's mental state. While he only worked for Hunter in his laboratory very occasionally, he nonetheless had access to his specimens. On the morrow Thomas resolved to go to St. George's and enlist the young man's help.

Chapter 35

The light was starting to fade as Thomas made his way back to Hollen Street. Even so, he decided to call in on the count and Charles. He had not seen his patient for almost a week now and he wondered how he was faring. The groom took his horse and he was just climbing the steps to the front door when he caught sight from the corner of his eye of someone staring at him. He turned to see the dark figure of Howison, leaning brazenly on a tree trunk, simply watching him. Thomas felt slightly unnerved, but did not acknowledge the servant.

Inside, he found the giant by the window in the upstairs drawing room, gazing down onto the street below. He was in a melancholy mood, clutching a glass of gin in his enormous hand. Boruwlaski sat nearby.

"What is Hunter's man doing there?" asked Thomas.

"He follows Charles everywhere," said the count, handing the doctor a brandy. "You know that madman wants to dissect him."

Thomas felt he could not feign ignorance. "I had heard," he said, turning to the giant. "But he cannot without your permission, Charles. And you have friends who will see to it that your wishes are carried out." His voice trailed off. There was no longer any point in denying that he would die sooner rather than later.

The giant turned. "I want to d-die at home, in Ireland, Dr. Silkstone."

Thomas felt awkward. He dealt with death on a daily basis, yet it was always hard for him to make plans with one who was still living. "The count and I will do everything to assist you," he replied, looking at Boruwlaski for reassurance.

"I do not trust that doctor," said Charles, dragging his weary body over to a chair. Thomas noticed that even walking was becoming a struggle for him now. "H-Hunter by name and hunter by nature," he mused, easing himself down.

"But his man dared not follow you to the palace," chimed in the count, settling himself opposite Thomas.

"What's this?" asked the doctor, intrigued.

"The king and queen asked to see Charles at Kew Palace. They were most impressed!" The little man beamed.

Thomas smiled. "That is indeed good news!" he said, and Charles suddenly lifted his head.

"Even better, my friend," continued the count, hardly able to contain himself, "the king says that he will look into the case of Charles's father. He will personally deal with it!"

"I am delighted for you," said Thomas, turning to Charles, but while the giant managed a smile, it was a weak one, and he winced with pain.

Noting this, the count changed the subject. "Tell me, Thomas, what happened today, after court?" he enquired.

The young doctor told him that Crouch's trail had led him to Hunter's laboratory, as he had suspected. "Hunter is up to something. I'm convinced he had a hand in young Cappelli's murder," he said.

Boruwlaski looked quite shocked. "Surely not?" he exclaimed. "I have known him for a while now. He is a genius, ahead of his time, yes, and he sails close to the wind when he consorts with grave robbers, but a murderer? I cannot believe it!"

Charles raised his large head. "I can, to be sure," he said. "The way he looked at me with those c-cold eyes of his. The way he has set that filthy dog on my tail." He motioned to Howison at the window. "I s-say he would do anything for a c-corpse."

Thomas nodded. "It seems we are all agreed that Dr. Hunter

has scant regard for the law when he deals with the dead, but whether he would commit murder is another matter." He recalled the pus-filled syringe that Carrington had shown him. Was the self-administered syphilitic poison turning Hunter's mental faculties as it did with so many of its victims? He feared as much, and a shiver ran down his spine. "I shall find out, gentlemen," he declared, rising from his seat.

"You are not leaving us so soon?" asked Boruwlaski, surprised by the doctor's intention. Thomas was, however, mindful of the late hour and unwilling to risk the lawless streets once more. He also knew he must rise early the following day.

"I am afraid I must," he replied. "I shall go to St. George's first thing tomorrow to make enquiries."

"But you have not told us about your visit to Boughton Hall. How is her ladyship? Well, I trust?" enquired the count innocently.

Thomas's face dropped. He could not bear the thought of having to explain what a nightmare the past week had been and how the ordeal continued. He looked solemn. "I am afraid to say Lady Lydia is unwell."

Boruwlaski frowned. "I am sorry to hear that" he said, but, detecting the young doctor's unease, he did not press him any further. "Let us hope she is soon restored."

Thomas nodded, forcing his features into a half smile. "Let us hope," he echoed.

Yet another candle had almost burned to its wick in Lady Lydia Farrell's bedchamber. Sir Theodisius Pettigrew had lost count of the number he had seen flare and splutter in a pool of hot tallow. Either he or Nurse Pring had always lit another before the light was extinguished, of course, but each taper marked the passage of yet more time without the merest flicker of hope.

Three days had now passed since Dr. Silkstone had left Boughton; seven since Lydia had fallen into this state of deep slumber. The hour was late and the coroner, too, felt like sleeping. For the last few days he had only dozed in fits and starts, waking every two or three hours. Nurse Pring kept vigil at night, but his own presence not only reassured her during the long, dark hours, but made him feel a little better, too. His own sense of helplessness was slightly assuaged knowing that should Lydia awake, then his would be the first face she would see, and not some stranger's.

During the hours of daylight, when the house was awake, his vigil was less of a burden. Downstairs he would hear the natural domestic rhythms of the hall: the maids' shoes on the marble tiles, the sound of doors being shut or opened. Outside there would be the occasional shouts from the gardener or the groom, the barking of dogs and the calling of doves. His own dear Hetty would take her turn at Lydia's bedside, too, and the servants would look in every hour to see if anything was needed. But nothing was.

Not even food had offered him comfort. Mistress Claddingbowl had tried to tempt him with her tarts and pies and roasted joints, but, strangely enough, none of her victuals held any appeal. The coroner's usually voracious appetite had deserted him, along with his good humor.

And what would his old friend the fifth earl make of all this, he asked himself. He was glad Richard had been spared the sight of his beautiful daughter thus indisposed. He had known before his death that he was not leaving his beloved Boughton in safe hands. He despaired of his only son Edward's wastrel ways and had confided as much on his deathbed. But Lydia, his dear, sweet Lydia, with her angelic looks and her gentle disposition; she was the light of his life, and now that light was dim and flickering and could expire at any moment.

Sir Theodisius wiped a tear away from his flaccid cheek. He and his beloved wife had not been blessed with their own children, and Lydia had always held a special place in their affections. They had watched her grow into a fine young woman. They had fretted, along with her mother, the dowager, when she married the ne'er-do-well Farrell, and mourned with her when he and Lady Felicity were taken from them. The young woman had suffered so much over the past twelve months, but just as it seemed that she had finally found happiness with Dr. Silkstone, this terrible accident had occurred.

Not in all his threescore years and ten had he observed two people so in love. He had seen their stolen kisses when they thought no one was looking and he was sure that both had marriage in their sights, although nothing had been said. With this in mind, however, he had taken it upon himself, in loco parentis, to make some enquiries of his nephew, who lived in Philadelphia. He knew that this was Dr. Silkstone's hometown, so he had written to ask if anything could be ascertained regarding his parentage. The reply had arrived only two days ago. He had read it to himself in Lydia's bedchamber, then out loud again, so that if, by some strange happenstance, she might be able to hear his voice, then she could listen to its contents.

Sir Theodisius's nephew, a wealthy merchant, spoke very highly of the Silkstone family. Dr. Thomas Silkstone Senior was, indeed, the very pillar of the community, counting among his patients several politicians, including George Washington and Benjamin Franklin. As Presbyterians, originally from Yorkshire, they also owned estates in New Jersey and Maryland and did many charitable works, establishing a school and a hospital for the relief of the sick poor.

"Your Dr. Silkstone may not be titled, my dear, but he comes from an excellent family," assured Sir Theodisius, patting the coverlet on Lydia's bed as if she could hear him. Sir Montagu would find it very hard to raise objections to such a union, if it was ever proposed, when, or if, Lydia ever regained consciousness, he told himself. The thought of this beautiful young woman trapped indefinitely in a silent prison was suddenly too much for him to bear and he began to weep freely this time, his flabby jowls wobbling with every sob.

Chapter 36

Thomas took a coach out to St. George's Hospital, on Hyde Park Corner, first thing the next morning. The air was no longer as fresh as the institution's founding fathers would have wished it, and the once-quiet countryside was being swallowed up by the city's voracious appetite so that traffic and noise swirled around the building day and night.

Climbing three shallow steps, Thomas entered via a narrow blue door and found himself in a large, stone-flagged hallway. The place was bustling with physicians and surgeons as well as patients in various states of distress. He gave his name to a porter who sat at a desk behind a wooden screen.

"Dr. Thomas Silkstone to see Mr. Giles Carrington," he said.

A young man standing nearby looked up and regarded Thomas with a strange expression.

"I will send word to Mr. Carrington," said the porter. "Please wait here, sir."

Thomas did as he was bidden, pacing up and down past the dispensary and other offices that led off the reception area, but he was suddenly aware that he was becoming the object of some curiosity. Huddles of young men were gathering nearby, looking at him, whispering and smiling. Giles Carrington arrived not a moment too soon for Thomas's comfort.

"Mr. Carrington," he greeted the young student courteously. "I am come to see you on a most urgent matter. Is there somewhere we can talk privately?"

Carrington looked puzzled. "Yes, indeed, Dr. Silkstone," he said. "We can walk in the grounds. We will not be overheard," he assured him, leading Thomas outside to a flower garden.

Thomas began earnestly. "I am speaking to you in the utmost confidence," he said. "It concerns the murder of Signor Carlo Cappelli."

"The castrato?" replied Carrington. "I have read about the case in the newssheets. The case is the talk of taverns and dinner tables throughout the capital."

Thomas nodded and took a deep breath. "I carried out a postmortem on his body and found that his larynx had been surgically removed, with great skill."

"Yes, I read that, too," replied Carrington, looking serious. "A terrible affair, but they have charged a fellow countryman, yes?"

Thomas nodded. "Yes, but I believe the man is innocent." He went on: "I also believe that the murder was the work of two men; one to smother the victim and the other to carry out the surgery."

Carrington stopped walking, contemplating the hypothesis. He turned to face the doctor. "And you think Dr. Hunter may be responsible?"

Thomas was slightly taken aback by the student's forthrightness, but he welcomed it. "In light of what you told me about him, I wondered if the disease might be turning his mind."

Carrington closed his eyes. "I feared something like this might happen," he said, shaking his head. He leaned closer to Thomas. "He has a secret store."

"A secret store?" echoed Thomas, frowning.

" 'Tis where he keeps all his special specimens. He will not let me see it and he keeps it under lock and key. I'll wager that is where you will find this poor unfortunate's larynx and many more body parts besides."

The young student spoke with a confidence that shocked Thomas. "So you believe that your master is capable of such an act?"

Carrington looked Thomas straight in the eye. "I fear so, sir."

The doctor nodded. "Then we must find a way of entering this store and searching it to try to obtain evidence. How can this be done?"

Carrington thought for a moment, then said: "I will be working at the laboratory tomorrow. I know where he keeps the key. I shall look for the larynx, and that will be our proof." There was a note of excitement in his voice that unsettled Thomas. He feared that such enthusiasm for the task would be the young man's undoing. If Hunter were to find that his pupil had betrayed him, God alone knew what he might do.

"Be careful, Mr. Carrington," he warned. "Dr. Hunter is clearly unstable."

The student nodded. "Have no fear, Dr. Silkstone. I am up to the task," he said gravely, any trace of his boyish enthusiasm now dissipated.

Just as they were about to bid each other farewell as they walked back toward the gateway, Thomas saw another young student smile at him on the path and remembered the curious looks of the others as he waited in the hallway earlier.

"Mr. Carrington, I have noticed that some students are regarding me very oddly here. Do you know why that might be?" he asked.

Carrington let out a spontaneous laugh. "Why, yes, sir. All of London's anatomists know that you are the Irish Giant's physician and that you are the man to beat to dissect him when he dies!"

Thomas looked askance. "In God's name!" he exclaimed. "You jest?!"

The student shook his head. "Why, no, sir. Dr. Hunter is not the only one with designs on the giant. His brother, William, is another who would love to get his hands on the carcass, to name but one."

A sense of repulsion suddenly filled Thomas. Members of his profession were, at times, no better than a pack of baying wolves or conniving vultures intent on scavenging, with scant regard for human dignity. He would personally see to it that they would all be disappointed in their quest to dissect Charles Byrne.

Arriving back in Hollen Street before noon, Thomas went immediately to his laboratory. Franklin, his pet rat, was gnawing away at the bars of his iron cage and he opened the door and let him roam freely. Walking over to his desk, he picked up the sheaf of notes he had made on Carlo Cappelli's postmortem. Somewhere, he told himself, within those pages, lay some vital clue as to the murderer. For the moment, however, he had to trust in the investigations of a guileless but enthusiastic youth, and he felt most uncomfortable with it.

Was Dr. Hunter really capable of such a gruesome crime, he asked himself. He had already proved himself to be totally irrational in his behavior toward Charles. Setting his man on him to shadow the giant day and night was a cruel and heinous act. He was playing games of the mind, taunting him, just as a childish bully would in a schoolroom.

The dividing line between genius and madness was a thin one, he knew, but could such a man turn from a committed anatomist to a scheming murderer? He was inclined to think not, but then he was reminded of the vile syringe that Carrington had discovered. Who in his right mind would infect himself willingly with such a scourge? The answer was, surely, no one in his *right* mind.

He was reminded, too, of the episode involving Mr. Haydn that was reported by Carrington. That he should ever countenance manhandling a close acquaintance against his will in order to perform a potentially life-threatening surgery would also be inconceivable to any sane man.

Thomas sat down at his desk and ran his fingers through his hair in a gesture of despair, and his thoughts turned to his beloved Lydia. Since his return from Boughton four days ago, he had heard nothing. He would go back as soon as he was able, but he needed news from Carrington before he could leave London, even it was only for a few meager days, to be by Lydia's side.

His beloved had now been in a coma for seven days, and he knew that with each passing day, hope of her full recovery faded. Yet he refused to give up. He watched Franklin shuffle across his desk, nudging papers and sniffing the air, oblivious to the fact that his master's world was so chaotic and traumatic. A copy of the *Morning Herald* lay on his desk. Mistress Finesilver must have put it there while he was at St. George's. Feeling in need of a diversion, Thomas opened the newspaper and scanned it. In amongst news of the war in his homeland and the domestic squabbles of Whigs and Tories, he came across several advertisements that vied for the attention of Londoners. In Piccadilly, a Mr. Katterfelto offered punters the chance to see insects in all manner of liquids through his greatly improved solar microscope, and in Spring Gardens, a few doors away from where Charles was exhibiting his mighty physiognomy, spectators could be treated to an extraordinary mind reader. Mr. Breslaw declared he could command a fresh egg to dance on a stick by itself to the accompaniment of a violin and mandolin. Such weird and wonderful claims managed to bring a smile to Thomas's lips. But a little farther down, his attention was caught by a much larger advertisement. Another giant, by the name of Patrick Cotter O'Brien, was coming to town. He was, according to the newspaper, a direct descendant of Brian Boru, the ancient king of Ireland. To view this unique spectacle, the esteemed public need only pay one shilling. Worse still, it was claimed he was a full four inches taller than Charles Byrne.

Chapter 37

Like an artist surrounded by all the paraphernalia of his craft, Giles Carrington sat at a table in Dr. Hunter's laboratory, encircled by all the tools of anatomical preservation. There were pipes and pipettes, brass wires and bristles, and there were reeds and syringes for the delicate task of injecting blood vessels, highlighting them in different colors to expose their diverse routes around the specimen.

His master had given him the job of preparing a coil of human intestine that sat like a sleeping snake in front of him. He did not know how the specimen had been obtained, but he could guess. Nevertheless, he did not question. He simply injected the vessels with warm water to flush out the blood and dispel any air. Into the open end of the coil he inserted a pipe and held it securely with pins before reaching for his syringe and injecting the wax he had colored earlier. Vermilion, blue verditer, and king's yellow were hues on his artist's palette.

With the utmost care and precision, on the depression of his syringe, miraculous pathways would appear before him in color, routes taken by blood and bile not visible to the naked eye. Lacy lanes of blues and reds would dart hither and thither, reaching to the farthest edges of the tissue—the wonder of the human body played out before his very eyes.

He was sitting back admiring his artistry when he heard the door latch click and in walked Dr. Hunter. His shoulders were hunched and he looked to be in a sour mood, as usual, before a sudden twinge of pain seemed to stop him in his tracks and he doubled over, steadying himself on a nearby chair. Carrington had seen this happen before. He wondered if it was the burning of the pox.

Righting himself, Hunter walked toward his pupil and stopped to hook a pair of spectacles onto his nose. He peered at the specimen over Carrington's shoulder.

"Did ya not use rhinoceros hair?" he snarled, prodding the intestine.

"Goose quill, sir," replied Carrington nervously.

"Sloppy work, young man. Sloppy. Ya'll need to do better than that," he remarked before moving toward a cupboard. Opening the door, he paused, selected a flint glass jar containing a lizard with a double tail, then exited the room without another word.

Carrington watched him go, loathing the old man with every fiber of his being. Nothing was ever good enough for him. No wonder he was so hated at St. George's, with his brusque manner and crude tongue. Now was his chance. Reaching down to the drawer in the desk, he took out a key and went to the door in the wall. Opening it with ease, he was immediately hit by the stench of rancid fluids. Recovering himself, he adjusted his eyes to the darkness. Inside, ranged on two shelves, were at least a twoscore of sample jars. There were organs: bulbous hearts, livers, kidneys, and spongy brains that floated serenely in yellow preserving fluid. There were digits, too, disembodied fingers and toes. He had seen Hunter enter this secret lair before, carrying glass flasks and cylinders, but he had no idea as to the extent of the collection.

He moved closer, leaving the door slightly ajar so that a shard of light illuminated the shelves. There were more organs, eyes and even teeth, but what really distinguished this array of samples from the others was the labeling. In large, clear script each jar carried not only a number and a Latin name, it carried the name of a human, too. There was the brain of Daniel Solander, a coiled length of artery from Sir Tobias Charlesworth, and the heart of the Marquis of Rockingham. Like some great Papist reliquary, John Hunter had taken it upon himself to preserve the organs and body parts of the great and the noble in his own private shrine. Whether or not the deceased or their loved ones had given permission for such unorthodox practices, Carrington could not tell. All he knew was that if the constables were to find a jar containing the larynx of the young Carlo Cappelli, then this crazed surgeon would not only be an anatomist to the dead, but a murderer of the living.

He scanned the shelves once more to find the perfect place, then reached ahead of him. And now there it was. Not so clearly visible as to attract immediate attention and half-hidden by a jar. It was not injected with colored dyes like the other samples, suggesting haste. Nor was it labeled with a name. That would have been far too incriminating. Yet, it was the only larynx, as far as he could see, in the collection, and someone of Dr. Silkstone's forensic ability would be able to say, with scientific certainty, that the parts had once belonged to the young castrato because of their unique characteristics.

Now all that remained was to show Dr. Silkstone this remarkable and damning discovery and Dr. John Hunter, the maverick anatomist, the enemy of St. George's, and the scourge of the establishment, would be charged with murder. In all probability, his body would be dissected by that august body of men, the Corporation of Surgeons. They would relish every slice of the scalpel, every probe of their forceps. How very ironic. How very fitting, he thought to himself, as he locked the door behind him and returned the key to the drawer.

Chapter 38

Charles Byrne sat forlornly in a chair by the window, looking out onto the square and, more precisely, onto Dr. Hunter's man below, still propped up against a tree as he had been for so many days now. At the giant's side was a bottle of gin and on his lap was a small sketchbook. In his large hand he wielded a pencil with great difficulty, his thumb and forefinger struggling to grip the delicate drawing instrument.

He looked up when Emily entered the room. On the count's instructions, Mistress Goodbody had been much more lenient toward the girl. If the giant wished her company, then that was perfectly acceptable, her master had said. Charles's health was fast fading and his melancholy mood needed to be lifted if possible. The arrival of the new giant meant that his own audience had dwindled, and he had even been forced to move premises and reduce his admission fee.

"You are drawing, Charles," said Emily, delight and surprise mingling in her voice. She peered 'round his shoulder. "What is it?" But she frowned as soon as she could make out the image.

" 'Tis my coffin," he replied taciturnly.

"But, Charles," she chided him, "you must not think of death."

He shook his large, sleek head and sighed. " 'Twill be knocking at my door soon," he said. "And when it does, I don't want that devil, Hunter, to have my body."

Emily's expression was tinged with sadness. She reached out

and put her hand on his arm. "You know we will not let that happen."

He nodded. "That is why I am making plans." His voice was suddenly more purposeful as he looked at his sketch pad. "I am to be buried at sea," he told her. "My coffin is to be of lead. It must be taken to the mouth of the Thames and sunk so that no one, not Hunter nor any of those baying dogs that call themselves surgeons, can get their filthy hands on my corpse."

Emily regarded Charles, teary-eyed. " 'Tis a good plan. Have you told Dr. Silkstone and the count?"

"They will know soon enough," he said softly, reaching for her hand. "My time is near, Emily."

Somewhere from within the deep labyrinth of Lydia's mind, light began to filter. It was almost imperceptible at first; the blackness changed to dark blue. Still there was nothing. No sight, no sound, but an altered state, then slowly, very slowly, the brightness began to creep, its probing fingers searching for any rocky ledges, any fragments of being it could find to cling on to.

The colors gradually changed from blue to green to yellow, until finally she could see shapes. They were blurred at first, their outlines melding into the background, but soon they became confident in their own forms, defined and sharp and real.

Now she entered her own personal reality. She could see herself in a small, unfamiliar room. Her husband was with her. She was anxious, crying, but she did not know why. He gave her a gill of brandy. She sipped it and her throat burned, but he urged her to drink more, tilting her head back with his hands. She drank, and as she did so, she became less aware of her body, her legs seeming almost weightless. She felt him unfastening her clothes, loosening her stays, but she let him, because she was becoming powerless, senseless.

He carried her into another room. She felt the cold on her bare arms and smelled a harsh, metallic smell in her nostrils. There was an old man and, behind him, a fat woman. The old man, his hair tawny and flecked with gray, said something in a strange accent before Michael laid her on the table. The woman placed a black veil over her face so that the colors left her, obscured by the dark mesh. Now she saw only shapes. She was frightened and she called out for her husband, but he had gone.

The fat woman forced some black, foul-tasting liquid down her throat that made her head spin. She heard her own cries grow feebler as rough hands pulled up her petticoat, exposing her lower abdomen. She wanted to lash out and to sit up, but they had strapped her down, fastening leather thongs with metal buckles that cut into her skin around her wrists and ankles if she tried to move.

She saw the man come to her with cupped hands. He put them over her lower belly as if searching for something; a sound, a movement, then after a few moments he made a mark with ink. She let out a faint cry, but try as she might, she could not move.

" 'Twill all be over soon," said a voice. "Just a wee prick."

And still he came toward her with a long, hollow needle clasped in his hands. She saw it hover over her and she saw him plunge it down, piercing the mound of her rounding belly.

"Lydia! Oh, my dearest Lydia!" Sir Theodisius detected movement. He saw her eyelids flicker and her lips part and the look of horror on her face. He grasped her hand in his. "Lydia. Lydia. 'Tis your Uncle Theo," he soothed.

Heaving himself up from his chair as fast as his corpulent frame would allow, he shambled over to the door and called down the hallway to anyone who would listen. "She wakes. Her ladyship wakes!"

Nurse Pring was in the next room, taking a well-earned nap, but on hearing the cries she rushed to Lydia's side. She found her patient in an agitated state, her head rolling from side to side on her pillow, her face set in a frown, and her thin voice calling out through parched lips.

Dipping a sponge in water, the nurse let droplets fall onto her mouth. Lydia licked her lips. "More," she croaked.

"We need to call for Dr. Fairweather, sir," Nurse Pring told Sir Theodisius, who duly obeyed the implicit order.

In the meantime, Lydia had opened her eyes fully. Her expression was less pained, but she still looked apprehensive.

"Who are you?" she enquired of Nurse Pring.

"I am your nurse, your ladyship. You have been very unwell, but please God, you will soon be restored," she said, smiling.

Lydia's eyes darted 'round the room. "Where is this place?"

"Why, 'tis your home. Boughton Hall, my lady."

"Boughton Hall," she repeated, as if the name were unfamiliar to her.

"And what day is it?"

"Why, it is a Tuesday and you have been in a deep sleep for these past ten days," replied the nurse.

At that moment Sir Theodisius returned to the room, a wide grin stretching his fat cheeks. "I have summoned Dr. Fairweather," he said, walking toward the bed once more.

"Thank you, sir," said Nurse Pring, measuring out a draft that Thomas had left for Lydia when, or if, she awoke.

"And I have sent word to Dr. Silkstone. I am sure he will be here just as soon as he can, my dear," he said to Lydia, easing himself once more into his bedside chair. But Lydia did not return his smile. She simply looked blankly at him.

"Dr. Silkstone? Who is Dr. Silkstone?" she said.

Chapter 39

Folded carefully inside the pocket of Charles Byrne's topcoat was a very special piece of paper. It was white and measured half the size of an average pocket kerchief, but it bore the moniker of the Bank of England. It was worth more than seven hundred pounds.

That evening, when all was quiet and the count was dining with his society friends, the giant took a carriage and headed toward Haymarket. He did not feel strong. He had endured several bouts of coughing that day and he knew his condition was worsening. He had given up all hope of the lawyer, Marchant, being able to obtain a posthumous pardon for his father, so he had grudgingly paid him the money he owed him. His hope, although admittedly a slim one, was that His Majesty King George would keep to his word and take up the matter with his Minister of Justice.

At around nine o'clock he arrived at the Cock Tavern. Naturally when he walked in, the drinkers and the hussies all stopped what they were about to stare at him. Even the fiddle player fell silent. He was used to such behavior, and while it always made him feel uncomfortable, he knew straight away where he was heading.

Mad Sam O'Shea sat in a corner with four or five other men, all of them jug-bitten. There were women with them, too, sitting on their laps or seats nearby. One had her bubbies out. They were laughing and carousing, but when Charles caught the other Irishman's eye, the merriment melted away.

"Be gone, now, I say," cried the wayward hawker to a trollop who had draped herself 'round his shoulders. The other women followed suit. Tugging at his topcoat in a businesslike manner, O'Shea gestured to the settle next to him that had been occupied by two of the doxies.

"Charles, my dear friend, I got your message, sure I did." He smiled.

The giant was surprised to be received in such a familiar way, but he returned the smile to his fellow countryman. He sat down on the settle, stretching his mighty legs out in front of him.

"You need my help, is that so?" asked Mad Sam, his eyes as bright as gemstones. Emily had sent word to her father that Charles was in need of a great favor, but that he would make it worth his while.

"I am not sure if Emily told you, s-sir, but I am not long for this world."

Mad Sam shrugged and crossed himself. "None of us are, Lord bless us," he slurred.

Charles continued: "There are those surgeons that would c-cut up my body when I am dead, sir, and put it on p-public show, like some common criminal. They would deny me entry into heaven, sir, so they would."

"I have heard the talk, Giant. You are a wanted man, 'tis true." He nodded sympathetically. "So tell me, what do you propose?"

Thomas was at work in his study, assiduously going through his notes on Carlo Cappelli's postmortem, as Franklin scurried about in the corner. He wondered how Carrington was faring, if he had managed to gain access to Hunter's secret store. Then, as if someone were reading his thoughts, Mistress Finesilver appeared at the door and announced there was a young gentleman to see him. It was Giles Carrington. He walked in looking nervous and worried, fingering the brim of his tricorn hat as he sat down.

"You have news?" asked Thomas eagerly.

"I am afraid I do, sir," came the reply. "I went into the storeroom and I found it was full of more samples; human samples."

"Go on," urged Thomas.

"It is as we feared, sir," said Carrington, looking grave. "There was a jar containing a larynx."

"Were there any markings on the jar?"

"No, sir. Nothing, but it is possible to prove it belonged to the castrato, yes?"

Thomas nodded slowly. It would be possible to identify it from its unique physical characteristics. He sighed deeply. "Yes. Yes, I can," he replied. "I must confront Hunter." His expression was grave.

Carrington frowned. "Will you not tell the coroner first, sir, so that he can call the constables?"

"This jar," said Thomas abruptly, "it was not labeled, you say?"

"No, sir. The larynx did not seem to have been prepared in any way—just dropped into the preserving fluid, as if in haste."

Thomas nodded. " 'Tis a serious business to accuse a man, and particularly one of such standing, of being complicit in a murder, Mr. Carrington, but it is becoming apparent that Dr. Hunter has many questions to answer. I have seen a convicted criminal enter his premises, and now this . . ." His voice trailed off.

The student nodded. "It would be the right and proper thing to do to go to Sir Peregrine. Hunter is clearly a danger to himself and others. The infection has turned his mind, as well as his body." Thomas detected a note of frustration in Carrington's voice.

"You have no love for your master, do you, Carrington?"

The young man looked uncomfortable. "I have no love for a murderer," he replied.

Nor had Thomas, and he feared that unless he acted quickly,

young Cappelli would not be the only victim. Dr. Hunter had another, altogether bigger prize in his sights.

Charles was as pleased as he could be with the evening's transactions. O'Shea had vouched for the loyalty of his friends, and it would be their job to keep watch over his sealed coffin. He would remain under their charge until such time as a wagon would transport it to Margate in Kent. The mad Irishman and his friends would accompany it. From there it would be lifted onto a barge and taken out to sea to be sunk into the depths of the English Channel, where no thieving anatomist could reach it. For their pains the guardians would be paid a handsome five pounds each. And to prove he could pay them the money, Charles had flourished his seven-hundred-pound note before their very eyes. It was a fine plan, thought the giant as he walked out into the night air and headed back to the comfort of his bed.

It had begun to rain quite heavily and, as he rounded the corner into Cockspur Street, his eyes half-closed against the stinging drops, he did not see the three gin-soaked scoundrels lying in wait for him in the shadows. They had been drinking in the Cock Tavern, as they did most nights, and spotted his bank note. They were never known to miss such an opportunity. One hit him on the head with a pickax handle and as he went reeling from the blow, another pulled him down to the ground while the other felt inside his coat.

"Here it is," cried the villain with the nimble fingers, waving the precious piece of paper in the air.

The other men stopped kicking the giant then, although one of them did boot him once more in the head, just for luck, and the thin trickle of blood from above his eye mingled with the rainwater and joined the general filth that ran down the street.

Dr. Carruthers delivered the longed-for news. It was a late hour, but Thomas made preparations to be on the road to Boughton at first light. The message from Sir Theodisius said only that Lydia was awake. It was a blessing, indeed, but the Oxfordshire coroner had neglected to give any further details. Thomas did not know what to expect. Inhalation of cyanide vapors could lead to a whole multitude of complications including vertigo, a weak pulse, and even short-term memory loss.

He was about to retire to snatch a few precious hours of sleep when there was a furious knocking on the door downstairs. He hurried to answer it, not wishing to alarm Mistress Finesilver. Standing breathless on the doorstep he recognized the house boy from Cockspur Street.

"Sir, I am come from the count. He says Mr. Byrne is hurt and needs your help right away," he panted.

Thomas grabbed his coat and his medical bag, which was already packed in the hallway, and followed the servant to a waiting carriage. Arriving at Cockspur Street a few minutes later, he was greeted by Boruwlaski, worry etched all over his small face.

"What has happened? The boy said Charles was hurt," said Thomas, rushing into the hallway.

"He was beaten senseless by a bunch of hoodlums," replied the count, leading the way upstairs. "They stole all his money."

The giant was lying on his bed, fully clothed, but barely conscious. Blood stained his waistcoat and breeches. Emily sat by his head, sponging a wound. She moved away as Thomas approached. Opening his bag, he took out a bottle of tincture of iodine and began dabbing the cut on Charles's forehead. It was not as deep as he had first feared and did not, in his opinion, require stitches.

Thomas administered laudanum for the giant's pain and told Emily to apply arnica to his bruises. "If his condition worsens, then you must call for Dr. Carruthers, who will know what to do," he instructed the maid. "I am needed elsewhere, but I intend to be back as soon as I can," he told her, secretly praying that Lydia would be in a fit enough state to return with him to London.

Chapter 40

Time was not on Thomas's side. He was yet to confront Dr. Hunter. Signor Moreno languished in jail; Charles's injuries, although not life-threatening, could worsen his chronic condition; and Lydia, although conscious, would need many days, if not weeks, to recover from breathing in the toxic cyanide vapors. Sleep was out of the question that night. Instead he went straight from the giant's bedside to stables in Fleet Street, hired a good mount, and rode out of London as dawn was breaking over the city.

Before ten o'clock he had a fresh horse, and he finally arrived at Boughton shortly after three that afternoon. Sir Theodisius, alerted to his arrival a few moments before, was in the hall to greet him, a relieved look on his round face.

"Oh, Dr. Silkstone, how glad I am to see you," he cried.

Thomas was equally glad to be at Boughton and to see that the coroner was in an ebullient mood.

"How fares Lady Lydia?" he asked anxiously.

"Why don't you see for yourself?" said Sir Theodisius, pointing the way up toward the bedchamber.

Thomas nodded and bounded up the stairs. The exhaustion from riding since dawn disappeared as he made his way to the room. To his delight, he found Lydia sitting up in bed, finishing off a bowl of broth held by Nurse Pring. As soon as she saw the young doctor, the nurse rose and curtsied.

"Dr. Silkstone!" Looks of surprise and delight mingled on her face, but on her patient's there was nothing. Lydia looked at Thomas and registered no emotion, no flicker of recognition.

"Your ladyship, 'tis Dr. Silkstone, come to see how you fare," the nurse said gently.

The color had returned to normal in Lydia's cheeks and her eyes were bright, but Thomas could see that her breathing was labored.

"Thank you, Nurse Pring. I shall examine her ladyship now," he said, and the nurse left the room, leaving Thomas alone with his patient. His instinct was to rush toward her, sweep her up in his arms, and hold her tightly. He had feared that this moment might never come and had rehearsed it in his own mind so many times. But now that it had arrived, that they were together, alone, there seemed to be a strange distance between them. He sat on the bed. He wanted to take her hand in his and kiss it, but he did not. The enigmatic look in her eyes prevented him from doing so.

"Lydia. Your ladyship, 'tis I, Dr. Silkstone. Thomas," he said softly.

"Thomas," she echoed, tilting her head slightly as she studied his face. "Thomas," she repeated, only this time with more conviction in her voice.

"Yes," he said gently. He laid his hand flat on the bed coverlet, but still did not dare to touch her. He knew that cyanide poisoning could sometimes cause temporary amnesia in its victims. He feared he might find her in a confused state, but this was worse than he had imagined.

"You have been very ill, my lady. You have been asleep for almost two weeks. I am here to take care of you. To see that you recover," he told her. "May I examine you?"

Again she looked at him strangely, as if her mind was in another place, trying to recall faces, names, places. "Yes," she replied.

Gently he took her wrist and tried to find her pulse. He saw her take a deep breath and close her eyes for a moment, as if his touch thrilled her, and when she opened them again after two or three seconds, she looked at him again.

"Thomas," she said, only this time, there was meaning in her voice. "Thomas," she repeated, smiling. She put her hand on his on the coverlet and he felt a surge of joy.

"Oh, my love," he said, leaning forward and putting both arms around her. He felt tears welling up in his eyes.

"I remember," she said. "Yes, yes, I do."

Wiping away a tear, he studied her face once more. Even though she could remember his features, he suspected the fog of the coma still shrouded many of her memories. There would be questions from her and the answers would be painful, but for the time being he rejoiced in her emergence back into reality.

"I am here to help you get well," he told her. "Tell me how you feel?"

"I am a little short of breath," she replied. "And a little giddy."

"You have been out of bed?"

"Nurse Pring bade me walk to the window to see if I could. I was unsteady on my feet."

" 'Tis to be expected," said Thomas as he resumed feeling for her pulse. When he did feel the beat, it was weak, as he suspected it would be.

"Thomas," she said. "Tell me what happened? They said it was an accident, that I breathed in poisonous vapors, but I do not understand how." She paused thoughtfully. "I do not believe they are telling me the whole truth."

Thomas felt his own heart miss a beat. Her memory was worse affected than he feared, yet her faculties and her perception remained sharp. He took a deep breath and held her hand. "There is so much to tell you, my love, but it should wait until you are stronger."

She frowned. "But why should you keep anything from me?" she asked. "Is my past so terrible? Have I done something so dreadful that I must be shielded from it?" Her voice was becoming agitated, and with it, her breathing came in shorter, sharper pants.

Thomas knew he needed to calm her. "I will tell you the

truth, I promise, just as soon as you are feeling a little better. But now you must rest."

He made her lay her head back on her pillows and her breathing eased. "You have to trust me, my Lydia," he said, gently stroking her forehead. Her eyes closed. "I will not let anyone hurt you ever again," he told her. "You are safe now."

Back in London, Emily was also doing her best to reassure Charles Byrne that his wounds would soon heal and that all would be well. She had been at his side all night and was with him when he woke around noon. He had cried out in pain when he tried to sit up, and she had given him laudanum from the phial Dr. Silkstone had left. It seemed to ease him and he slept some more until late afternoon.

"I am a dead man," he groaned as she tried to make him drink a little chicken broth later that evening. "I have lost everything."

Emily's eyes played on his head and face. The skin was black and purple, like a pulped plum. "How could they do this to you?" she lamented.

"They took my money. They took it all," reflected the giant mournfully. "Now I'll never get back home."

"Do not give up all hope, Charles," she soothed, trying to coax another spoonful of broth through his swollen lips. "Do not forget the king can still grant your da a pardon." She tried to sound cheerful, but in reality, she knew there was little hope left. She had seen from an upper window that not only Howison waited for him outside. Hunter's surly lackey had been joined by more men now, envoys of other anatomists eager to get their scalpels into such a prize. For all she knew, they could even have beaten up her beloved to hasten his death. They scented blood in their nostrils. Soon they would come in for the kill. She knew that Charles had asked her father and his friends to keep watch over his remains and sink his coffin into the sea once he was gone, safe from the surgeons' knives, but she feared strong liquor might mean they did not keep to their word.

She put the half-empty bowl of soup down when she saw he would drink no more. "You need to rest now," she told him.

"Emily," he said, as he watched her smooth his coverlet.

"Yes, Charles," she replied, looking at him with a gentle smile.

He held out his huge hand and took hers, enveloping it as petals close around a bud. She gazed down, and the sight of it brought tears to her eyes. "Whatever h-happens to me," he said, fixed intently on her, "I want you to know that I love you."

She smiled tenderly. "Here, I have something for you," she said, delving into her apron pocket and taking out a lock of her own hair, tied with a white ribbon. "I kept some of yours, so 'tis only fair that you should have some of mine."

The giant's enormous fingers closed 'round the lock and he held it to his lips to kiss it before holding it to his breast.

At that moment the count burst into the chamber, unaware of the scene of tender intimacy that he had just interrupted.

"I have great news," he cried excitedly. He climbed up onto a chair by the giant's bedside, clutching a sheet of parchment. " 'Tis from His Majesty's court. They have granted your father a posthumous pardon, Charles!" Forgetting the extent of the giant's injuries, he leaned over and planted a kiss on his friend's cheek in the continental manner. Despite his discomfort, Charles managed a smile. Even Emily abandoned all decorum in front of the count.

"I'm so happy for you," she cried, squeezing Charles's hand.

The little man was so caught up in the moment that he jumped down from the chair and started dancing a jig, flourishing the parchment in his tiny hand. "A pardon, a pardon, a very royal pardon," he sang, making Emily laugh. Even Charles began to chuckle, but his exertions caused him to cough, making his bruised ribs doubly painful.

"We must leave you now. You must rest," said the little man, bringing his moment of madness to a sudden halt. "I am sorry."

Emily sketched a curtsy and left the room, but the giant beckoned his small friend over to him. Turning his large black head, he whispered into the little man's ear: "Thank you, Count. At least now I can die a happy man."

Chapter 41

Memories, mused Thomas, *are what make us what we are. Without them we cannot be ourselves. They shape our characters and our actions. All that we do and all that we are comes from our own experiences and the recollection of them.* Stored deep within the secret labyrinths of the brain, they could be selected and recalled at will, like books in the Ancient Library of Alexandria. He was watching Lydia as she slept opposite him in the carriage on the journey to London and he knew that she was still not herself. Until she recalled all that had gone before, until she could once again open those books of memories, she could not move on with her life.

He did not know how long her memory loss would last. He had heard of cases where the patient never recovered from the amnesia. He took comfort in the fact that hers was only a partial loss of recollection at the moment. She had recalled Sir Theodisius and snatched fragments of her childhood, like playing with her brother, although she had not remembered that he was dead. Naturally she had been devastated when Thomas had told her, but then the realization had triggered other memories, too, and she spoke of her cousin Francis and of her late husband. Thomas feared that such a torrent of terrible memories might push her into a deep depression, and he had reluctantly sedated her.

He had carried her into the carriage while she slept and her head rested on his shoulder. She was well covered with a blanket and a shawl, although the spring weather was fine and warm. Now and again, her breathing came in short gasps, but Thomas had seen such symptoms before and knew that they should pass in a few days.

Lovelock was at the reins, with Will as footman. The ground was dry and hard, so that they were making good progress when Thomas saw the milepost for Beaconsfield. They were now more than forty miles into the journey, and Lydia began to stir. She rubbed her eyes, opened them, and to Thomas's delight, smiled when she saw his face.

"Where are we?" she asked, sitting up and straightening her back.

"Near Beaconsfield. Another three hours and we should be in London," he told her.

She seemed satisfied with his answer and turned to look out of the carriage window.

"How are you feeling?" he asked.

After a moment she turned to look at him. "Very strange," she replied. "In myself I feel weak and tired, but I also feel"— she paused, searching for the right word—"empty."

"Because you cannot remember?"

"Yes." She nodded. "Although I do remember more now."

"Go on," Thomas urged.

"I remember Michael and what happened, and Mama. I seem to be able to recall things that happened a long time ago, and yet . . ."

"And yet you cannot remember what happened just before you were poisoned."

"Is that what usually happens?"

Thomas nodded. "Your long-term memory does not seem to have been so badly affected. But your short-term memory will return. Have no fear," Thomas assured her.

She smiled and slipped her hand in his. "I remember us," she said. "I remember how very much in love we were."

"And are," he said, kissing her hand.

She held his gaze. "Can you love someone who tried to take their own life?"

Thomas froze. She was staring at him with trusting eyes. Did she really recall what happened or was she testing him?

"You were not well and I was not with you," he replied. "You would not let me help you, but I am here now."

"I cannot remember why, Thomas." She shook her head and withdrew her hand from his. "If only I could remember why," she cried through clenched teeth. Thomas felt her frustration.

"Something happened," he said slowly, recalling the night of the concert.

"What do you mean?" She frowned.

"You saw someone, or someone said something to you that changed you. You were so agitated. You returned to Cockspur Street and then the next day you came and told me you wished to end our betrothal."

She turned and looked unseeing out of the window. "The concert. The concert with the young castrato," she said slowly.

"Yes. Yes. That's right!" In his excitement Thomas took both her hands in his. They had just begun the steep descent of White Hill from Holtspur Heath. There was dense woodland on either side and the leaves were already out, creating thick green canopies on either side. But before Lydia could say any more, there was a loud cry and a horseman came thundering past the carriage window. A second later Lovelock was pulling up the horses and they came to an abrupt halt, almost throwing the passengers onto the other side of the carriage.

"What is it?" asked Lydia nervously.

Thomas put his head out of the carriage window. The horseman wore a black mask and was pointing a pistol at Lovelock, and when he saw Thomas, he turned the barrel on him.

"So, who have we here?" sneered the man.

"I am a surgeon and a physician, sir," replied Thomas.

The highwayman pulled on the reins to make his horse backtrack to give him a better view inside the carriage. Lydia put her head down, not wishing to meet his leering gaze, but it was too late. He had seen her.

"Well, well, and this is your patient, I presume." His manner was snide and cocksure. "A fair one, and that's for sure. Let's be havin' you, then." He leaned over and opened the carriage door. "Out you come. Both of you," he barked.

Thomas resisted. "Can you not see this lady is sick?" he cried. But the highwayman simply cocked his pistol and pointed it at the doctor's head.

"Get out or I'll blow your brains out," he ordered.

"No! No, please!" screamed Lydia, tugging on Thomas's coat as he rose.

" 'Twill be all right," he told her.

"And you," shouted the thug to Lydia.

"Leave her, will you. She is sick, I tell you," shouted Thomas. Once again, he found himself staring down the barrel of a pistol.

"She looks well enough to me." He smirked, watching Lydia cautiously make her way out of the carriage, clinging on to the door to steady herself. His eyes alighted on a jeweled clasp that Lydia wore on the front of her bodice. "And that looks good to me, too," he said, lurching forward and ripping off the ornament in one fell swoop.

Lydia screamed and hid her face in Thomas's shoulder. He knew there was no point in fighting back. Every week some poor unfortunate traveler ended up dead at the hands of a highwayman. Instead, he comforted her. She was now crying almost uncontrollably. He feared for her breathing. He could hear her gasping for breath in between sobs.

"You've got what you wanted, now go," cried Thomas. But the highwayman started to laugh.

"That's rich, that!" He was doubling over, clutching his sides mockingly, but then he stopped suddenly, dismounted, and walked over to Thomas. Grabbing him by the throat, he hissed menacingly: "I haven't even started."

Thomas swallowed hard, feeling the man's grip tighten, but then it suddenly loosened as the sound of hooves approached.

"Constables!" cried Will Lovelock.

Two men on horseback were galloping down the hill toward

them. The highwayman ran to his horse, mounted, and rode off, firing a single shot in the air as he did so. Thomas rushed to comfort Lydia, who was now shaking and struggling to breathe.

The constables pulled up their horses. "The lady is not hurt, sir?" one asked.

"No, but in shock," replied Thomas, helping Lydia toward the carriage.

"We needs be after 'im," shouted the other and they jabbed their horses' sides and were off in hot pursuit of the highwayman, leaving Thomas, Lydia, Lovelock, and Will to compose themselves.

They settled Lydia back in the carriage and covered her with blankets to keep her warm. She was still shaking violently and looked dazed, but Thomas thought it best to continue their journey. From out of his bag he took smelling salts and tried to revive her. They eased her stupor a little, but it was a while before her condition stabilized and Thomas gave the order to move on.

He held her close in the carriage, stroking her hair, but her tears still fell. "You are safe now, my love," he comforted her.

Lovelock made good progress through Beaconsfield and on beyond Windsor until they reached Newgate. The landscape was now more familiar to him. Trees gave way to tall buildings, and the smell of dung and filth wafted into the carriage. It was growing late, and darkness was closing in. Lydia had not spoken since they had moved off again, sleeping for most of the journey, but now that they were in the city and the rhythm of the carriage changed, stopping and starting to allow flocks of sheep or carts to pass, she awoke and sat up.

"My brooch," she whispered, suddenly feeling her dress. Thomas thought of the garnet and enamel clasp that the highwayman had ripped so cruelly from her bodice.

"The constables will retrieve it for you," Thomas assured her, but she lifted her head from his shoulder and looked at him.

"No, you don't understand," she said, looking intently at him. "The brooch, it made me remember."

"Remember what?"

She swallowed hard and took a deep breath. "When I had the long sleep, I had a dream. Only it wasn't a dream. It was a memory, a memory that I had tried so hard to forget. When the man touched me and pulled at me, then I remembered." She shuddered and turned to Thomas. "You must promise me that what I am about to tell you will be our secret."

The young doctor looked at her earnestly. Her expression was pained and frightened. "I swear, on my life."

"I pray to God you will not think less of me, but I understand if you do." Her voice was cracking with emotion.

"There is nothing in the world that you could do that would make me love you less," Thomas cried, taking both her hands in his. "You are the kindest, noblest, and most dutiful person I have ever met."

"If that were only so," she muttered, her head dropping in shame. "I was young and foolish. I didn't understand—" She broke off.

"Whatever has happened, whatever you have done, your burden will feel less if you share it with one who loves you beyond all else," he told her, pulling her toward him again.

"I remember now why I tried to kill myself, and I wish I had succeeded," she sobbed.

"You must not speak so, my love," scolded Thomas.

"I am a wicked woman."

"How could you do anything wicked? Tell me what it is that so distresses you."

Once more she took a deep breath, as if preparing herself for her confession, and then began: "You know we eloped, Michael and I?"

That much Thomas knew. He nodded.

She went on: "We lived in Bath, as man and wife. I loved him so much, but I knew that Mama would never consent to our union unless Michael renounced any claim to the Boughton estate. After about six months I feared I was with child—I had been feeling unwell for some time—and I told him so. He changed toward me. He said we could not have a child out of wedlock. I knew he was right, but I thought perhaps he would marry me and we could survive on my modest income. I thought that all would be well." There was a note of pleading in her voice. She went on, "About a week later, he said we were to go on a journey, to London. I thought perhaps he had arranged a marriage service there. How wrong I was." The tears returned, flowing freely. "He took me to a house, I cannot recall where, and he started to ply me with brandy, which I did not want. Then he led me through into a room." She paused once more. "I cannot speak of it, Thomas. I cannot speak of the horror. They lifted me onto a table."

"They?" Thomas interrupted.

"This other man, he fastened me down. I tried to cry out, Thomas, but I couldn't move. He had a needle. A hollow needle," she sobbed. "And he did it. He did it! He plunged it into me and poured in some poison to kill the child in my womb." She hid her face in his shoulder, her whole body convulsed with sobs.

"And you saw that man again?"

She nodded, her head still buried in his coat.

"He was the one you saw at the concert, and you remembered." He paused. "John Hunter."

Thomas felt the tears well up in his own eyes. The enormity and the gravity of what he had just heard left him numb. He recalled the fetuses he had delivered before their time; at five months there was hair on the head, there were nails on toes and fingertips; at six months a babe could cry and suckle and kick. Eyelids could open, fists could punch, the grip was strong. In his mind's eye he pictured the inside of the uterus, dark and red and safe, a mother's crimson cushion protecting the unborn. The child was curled, with knees flexed and its head on its chest, soothed by the distant rhythm of its maternal heartbeat. All was peaceful and secure until . . .

The carriage rounded Whitcomb Street and came to an abrupt halt. Thomas put his head out. They had stopped far short of the count's lodgings.

"What is it, Lovelock?" he called.

"Up ahead, sir," said the groom, pointing to the street that was blocked by a sea of people, some carrying torches aloft.

"In God's name! Charles," muttered Thomas. "Take us 'round the back entrance," he shouted.

Lovelock turned the horses at speed and they entered the mews via a gate at the rear of the property.

"What is it, Thomas?" asked Lydia, anxiously.

"I fear that word has spread about Mr. Byrne."

"So they are the anatomists' men?"

"Yes. They are waiting for him to die."

He helped Lydia out of the carriage, and together they made their way into the house. Leaving her in the capable hands of Mistress Goodbody, Thomas made his way upstairs, where he found Charles sitting in a chair by the window, the count and Emily at his side, watching the commotion in the street below.

"What is going on?" panted Thomas, rushing over. He gazed in disgust at the men below. They were shouting, jabbing fists triumphantly in the air, but he could not make out their words. "Vultures," he snarled.

"Vultures?" repeated the count. "No. No," he said, waving his small hand. "Tell Dr. Silkstone, Emily."

The maidservant, who had been looking down on the crowd below, turned and, much to Thomas's surprise, smiled. "They are not vultures, sir," she said. " 'Tis my father and his band of Irishmen."

Puzzled, Thomas surveyed the mob once more. Flaming torches illuminated faces that looked up eagerly out of the gloom. "Look, there he is." Emily pointed. "There is my da." O'Shea stood at the head of the crowd, his eyes wild with excitement.

"Mad Sam." The count chuckled. "And there is the crook-backed boy who was with Charles before, when he showed himself at fairs," he cried, pointing into the mob.

For a split second Emily was taken aback. She did not know that the count knew of her father, but she was nevertheless proud of him and his band of men. "They are here to guard

Charles against Dr. Hunter and anyone else who would take him." She beamed.

Relieved, Thomas nodded. "You have loyal friends," he said, turning back to Charles, who was looking pale after his exertions. Yet he wore a strangely serene look on his face.

"They'll look after me well, Dr. Silkstone," he wheezed. "They've promised me that." But just as he spoke these words, he began to cough again, as if the very effort of speech was too much for him, and this time he could not hide the blood in his kerchief.

Thomas shepherded the giant back into his bed. His pulse was now weak and his breathing labored. He was running a fever, too, and his black hair was plastered to his head with sweat. His whole body juddered every time he coughed, and his face contorted in pain. Thomas feared the worst and gave him more laudanum to dull his suffering. The count and Emily joined him at the bedside.

"I fear the time draws near," said the little man, reaching up and touching the giant's hand. "We must put the plans in place."

"Plans?" asked Thomas.

Emily stepped forward. "Mr. Byrne asked to be buried at sea."

Thomas nodded. "So that Hunter cannot get his hands on him?"

"Exactly," replied the count. "I have engaged an undertaker who has made a coffin for him. When the time comes, we will lay him in it and arrange for it to be taken to Margate, where it will be lowered into the sea."

"My father and his friends will keep watch over him all the time," said Emily, moving closer to the bed. Her eyes were glassy. "Hunter'll not have him, Dr. Silkstone. We have made our promise."

As the night wore on, they watched as Charles began to toss and turn more violently. Delirium took hold. He began to cry out, and his arms flailed, as if he was fighting off some unseen foe. Emily sponged his forehead with vinegar, but still he writhed and shouted.

The count paced the room anxiously, his little arms locked together behind his back, deep in thought, feeling helpless. Finally he said: "Those men out there are guarding Charles's body, but I shall help protect his soul. I shall send for a priest."

Thomas acknowledged the gesture. "Yes, I think it is time," he conceded.

It was just before midnight when Mistress Goodbody entered the room. "There is a young man downstairs to see you, Dr. Silkstone," she said.

"Did he give his name?" asked Thomas.

" 'Tis Mr. Carrington, sir," she replied. "Shall I tell him to go away?"

"Carrington," echoed Thomas, thoughtfully. "No, send him up, if you please."

The student appeared at the doorway looking grave. "I heard the giant's condition is worsening," he said.

Thomas arched an eyebrow. "Bad news travels fast," he remarked.

"All of London's surgeons are in a flurry, Dr. Silkstone. They all want to dissect his corpse."

"I know, and we must see to it that they do not have their way," replied Thomas. "That would be against Mr. Byrne's express wishes."

Carrington glanced at the window. "Those men outside?" he said, motioning to the mob below.

"They are also here to protect Mr. Byrne," explained Thomas. "Hunter will have to get past them if his plan is to succeed."

"So the giant really is near the end?" queried Carrington.

Thomas sighed. "I am afraid so," he replied, glancing over to the bed. The fever had broken, but Charles seemed to have slipped into unconsciousness. "All we can do is watch and wait."

Chapter 42

In his laboratory at Earls Court, Dr. John Hunter was making his final preparations. Earlier in the evening, Howison had brought word of the giant's condition. He was not expected to last through the night, and Hunter found himself relieved that he would not have to call upon his henchman to do anything more than watch and wait. Howison would, no doubt, have relished the opportunity to hasten the giant's demise personally, but now there would be no call. Even so, everything needed to be in place.

The anatomist had spent the day sharpening his instruments. On his workbench he laid out his curved amputation knife, his saw, and his bone shears. There were buckets for the entrails and kidney dishes for the organs, if there was time to retrieve any, which he strongly doubted. Everything was neat and in order, arranged like the sacred paraphernalia of priesthood in preparation for a great sacrifice. Next he would lay kindling under his copper vat, which was already filled with water. He hoped to light the fire soon, but he had one more call to make.

Mr. Pertwee had been engaged as the undertaker. He had done business with him on many occasions. With his beady eyes and thin lips, he drove a hard bargain, and he would certainly want to make a meal of his latest commission.

Discretion, nay, secrecy was paramount. One of the news-sheets had dubbed his fellow anatomists "Greenland harpooners" out to kill a gigantic whale. How William Cruikshank and

Matthew Baillie at the Great Windmill Street anatomy school would love to get their bloody hands on the corpse of the colossus. Or John Sheldon in Great Queen Street. He'd lived with the embalmed naked body of a beautiful woman in a glass case in his bedroom for the last ten years. The Irish Giant would have been a fitting companion for her. But despite Byrne's constant rebuffs—he still did not understand why—Goliath's corpse would soon be his. Of that he was sure.

Under cover of darkness, he drove himself to Mr. Pertwee's funeral parlor. He had known the undertaker for three years now and done deals with him more than once. Working with Crouch and Hartnett, he always had an eye to the main chance and never shied away from a good business proposal.

The anatomist found the undertaker hard at work on the giant's coffin.

"Ah, Dr. Hunter. I've been expecting you," said the wily man, a hammer in his sinewy hand. He was putting the finishing touches to the casket's handles.

"So this is it," said Hunter admiringly. "A fine piece of craftsmanship," he observed, running his hand along the smooth grain of the lid.

"That it is," agreed Pertwee, standing back to consider his own work. "But plain, mind. I could've made so much money if I'd but made an extra niche to hide one of your fellow knife men in there, I can tell you."

Hunter had heard the rumor that one of his number planned to hide himself inside the giant's box so as to be ready for the sack 'em up men when they came to collect their quarry at the witching hour. His plan, however, was much simpler.

"I have a proposition for you, Mr. Pertwee."

"I was wondering what was taking you so long, Dr. Hunter."

A man with ideas and an attitude above his lowly station, thought the anatomist, but he persevered. "I will give you thirty pounds if you bring the giant's body to me."

The undertaker shook his head and laughed. "You'll have to do better than that," he said, resuming his carpentry.

"Forty, then."

No response.

"Fifty?" A note of desperation sounded in Hunter's voice.

Pertwee stopped hammering. "Come now, Dr. Hunter. I've been offered one hundred already." He smiled, his small eyes opening wider with excitement.

Hunter shook his head. "Och! You drive a hard bargain. A hundred, you say." He paused for a moment, then said rashly: "I'll double it."

Pertwee looked satisfied. "I want to see the note first, mind," he stipulated.

"I shall return very soon," said Hunter purposefully. Secretly he wondered how on earth he could lay his hands on such funds at such short notice.

Thomas found Lydia lying in her bed, but awake. She had not yet snuffed out her candle, despite the late hour.

"How are you feeling, my love?" he asked.

"I would feel better if I knew you could forgive me," she said.

He suddenly remembered his shock in the carriage after her revelation had left him speechless. They had then been confronted by the crowd in Cockspur Street. He had not told her his feelings. He had not offered her the comfort she so desperately craved. Walking over to the bed and sitting on the edge, he put an arm around her shoulders. In his duty to care for Charles, he had neglected her, and she needed him every bit as much as the giant.

"There is absolutely nothing to forgive. You did nothing wrong, my dearest Lydia. You are the victim in all of this. Hunter is the one with blood on his hands." He hesitated. "And now, if he has his way, he will soon be having even more."

"How is dear Mr. Byrne?" she asked forlornly.

Thomas sighed deeply. "He has taken a turn for the worse, I fear. The count has sent for the priest."

"I must go to him," she said softly. "To say good-bye."

Thomas did not try to dissuade her. He knew it could be her last chance.

* * *

Father Finnan arrived just as dawn was breaking. He stepped over the few stalwart guardians who were sleeping in the street. Huddled in blankets and shawls that Mistress Goodbody had managed to find, there were about six of them who remained throughout the night. But they seemed oblivious to the priest's presence as he picked his way over their slumbering bodies and into the lodgings. Only one man was watching, propped up against a tree, his hat slouched over his face. As soon as he saw the cleric he left.

Mistress Goodbody, who had herself endured a near-sleepless night, showed the priest up to Charles's bedchamber, where Thomas was keeping his vigil. The others had joined him a few moments before: the count, Carrington, Emily, and, of course, Lydia, who sat in a chair close by the giant's bed.

From out of his small case, the wigless priest took out his Bible and prayer book, his holy water and a phial of sacred oil. Thomas watched him in silence, contemplating how the cleric's actions and his sacred objects reminded him so very much of himself and his own instruments. He watched him don his purple surplice, just as he himself would put on his surgical apron, and then approach Charles as he wheezed and struggled to hold on to each breath.

All was now set for the performance of the last rites. Anointing the giant's forehead with sanctified oils, the priest recited a prayer in Latin and made the sign of the cross. *"In nomine Patris et Filii et Spiritus Sancti,"* he intoned. From Charles's swollen lips came a feeble "Amen." It was the first word he had spoken for several hours. It was also his last.

As they all lowered their heads in a final prayer, Emily stepped forward and held the giant's hand. She prayed for the repose of not only his soul, but his body, too.

The end, when it came about two hours later, was over in an instant. Charles had slept since the priest's departure, but he opened his eyes very briefly to see Emily at his side.

"I am here," she said softly, and he smiled before coughing and turning his head so that she did not see the crimson thread of blood that spilled onto the pillow.

Chapter 43

In the opinion of the undertaker, Dr. Hunter was obviously not quick enough to return with his bank note. Time was money. The anatomist had decided the most likely person to give him a loan was his associate Pidcock, who kept a menagerie off the Strand and who usually provided him with animal carcasses. Pidcock hemmed and hawed, but finally agreed to a transaction. By the time the anatomist arrived back with the two-hundred-pound note, however, there had been other approaches. Several, in fact. Naturally, because of such demand, the price for the undertaker's duplicity had risen. It was now five hundred pounds.

Back went Hunter to Pidcock. There was more procrastination. What guarantees of repayment would he have and, more importantly, what assurances could he give him, knowing his old friend as he did, that his entrails would not end up in a glass jar for all to see? Those delicate matters dealt with, the menagerie keeper went ahead and lent Hunter the money.

Now all was in place. Howison had brought word that the priest had visited Cockspur Street. All he could do was sit and wait for news from the undertaker. There might only be hours left before the giant was in his grasp.

Mad Sam O'Shea heaved himself up from the roadway outside Cockspur Street where he had spent the previous night. He was cold and stiff and his head felt as if it had been kicked around by apprentice boys like a pig's bladder. Grabbing hold of the railings, he tried to remember where he was and why he was there. Four or five of his friends were still lying in the gutter. The morning traffic was beginning and there was cursing and cussing from occasional drivers as they zigzagged their carts through the bodies that still lay motionless on the edge of the road.

As the haze of strong liquor wore off, he recalled the night before. He remembered they had word that the giant, their fellow countryman, was in trouble. The knife men were after him. He was wounded and sick and he needed their protection. So he had gathered together a bunch of brave Irish lads and marched to his rescue. "To Cockspur Street!" he had roared. On the way they had stopped off at the Lamb and Flag for a few tipples. After all, they knew they would be in need of fortification afore any fight. Then they bought a couple of flagons of gin to sustain them through the dark hours. But the night had been long and chill, and one by one they had fallen, like brave warriors on a battlefield.

Now what of the giant, he asked himself. Had Hunter come in the night? Surely not. They would have known. One of them would have woken, to be sure. He took his easement in the street, then knocked on the front door. An indignant Mistress Goodbody answered it. "No hawkers," she said, looking at the dirty wastrel who now stood before her.

"We are here to help the giant," he pleaded as she began to shut the door in his face.

"The giant?" she repeated, putting her head around the door once more. Recognizing the shawls she had lent the men, she relented. "Yes, of course."

"Me and my men was guarding the place last night, so we were. Remember?"

The housekeeper raised a skeptical eyebrow. "Indeed I do now," she conceded. "But you are to come 'round the back. We can't have the likes of you using the front door."

The Irishman did as she bade and waited belowstairs to see whether or not Dr. Silkstone and the count would receive him. They said they would, much to Mistress Goodbody's surprise, and Mad Sam O'Shea entered a drawing room for the first time in his life.

"Mr. O'Shea," greeted Boruwlaski. "Please, have a seat," he said, even though he knew Mistress Goodbody would be displeased by the thought of such a dirty rump on her pristine furniture.

The Irishman was taken aback by the count's size and his jaw fell open in surprise. The little man merely brushed off his reaction. "So, you are, or rather were, a friend of Charles?"

O'Shea looked shocked. "He is gone?"

Thomas nodded. "Just an hour ago. He passed peacefully."

The Irishman crossed himself. "May his soul rest in peace."

"It is his body we are more concerned with at the moment," interjected the count.

"Indeed it is, to be sure, sir," replied O'Shea. "And that is why I am here."

"It is?" Thomas was perplexed.

"We made this deal, see," began the Irishman, turning toward Thomas. "Me and the lads are to guard him until we find a barge at Margate, then we shall take him and throw his coffin in the sea."

"And you agreed all this with Mr. Byrne?" pressed the count.

"Word of honor," he replied, crossing himself once more. "As God should strike me down if I be tellin' a lie. 'Tis not safe here, so we keep watch over his coffin in a room at an inn, or some such place, and then take it to the coast. He gave us a fiver each."

Thomas shot a look at Boruwlaski. "What say you, Count?"

The little man nodded his head. "It makes sense to me. We can send a messenger on to arrange for a barge, then a cart can carry the coffin to the coast."

"And we will go with it to see that no harm comes to our beloved countryman," added O'Shea.

"And where do you propose to hide the body in the meantime?" enquired the count.

"Somewhere safe, where we can trust the landlord," replied the Irishman.

Thomas thought for a moment. "I know the very place," he said.

Downstairs, Giles Carrington was tucking into a hearty breakfast in the morning room. He looked up when he heard Thomas. The doctor had not slept for almost forty-eight hours and he was looking, and feeling, exhausted.

"Ah, Carrington," he said. "I am glad you are here. We have work to do."

The student rose from the table and bowed. "I am glad you think I can be of service, sir."

Thomas looked grave. "We must all rally 'round now, for Mr. Byrne's sake," he said.

Carrington nodded. "He is a great loss, sir."

"Indeed. He will be sorely missed," answered Thomas. "But now we have promises to keep. Will you come with me?"

The young student looked confused. "But I thought we needed to stay here to guard the body until the undertaker came, sir?"

Thomas smiled. "Mr. Byrne will be safe in the hands of his fellow Irishmen," he told him, walking to the window. He pulled open the shutters to reveal the ragtag crowd, whose numbers had now swelled to about a dozen, waiting outside in the street. "There are more at the rear entrance, too," he said.

"Mr. Byrne will, indeed, be safe." Carrington smiled.

Together they walked out onto the street and hailed a carriage. On the way Thomas revealed the plans about the giant's sea burial that had been made without his prior knowledge. They were not to his liking, but they were what had been agreed to by Charles.

"The coffin is to stay here overnight until plans are made to take it to Margate," explained Thomas as they came to Smee's Hotel.

"Here?" Carrington suddenly looked uneasy when the carriage stopped outside.

"Yes," replied Thomas. "The landlord owes me a favor. I can trust him not to let me down for fear of jeopardizing his business."

The young student appeared to grow more agitated. "I have

just remembered an appointment," he said. "I am needed at St. George's."

Thomas thought his behavior very odd. "But you will return?" he said, knowing that he would need the young man's help in the execution of the plan to bury the giant at sea.

He nodded. "Indeed I will. I shall return to Cockspur Street later on today," he promised, and with that he hurried off in the direction of Hyde Park and disappeared from view.

In an upper room, Mr. Smee was watching the carriage that had just drawn up outside his establishment. The two gentlemen who alighted looked of a proper sort, he told himself. They would not cause trouble. They would be good for his business. He was just about to go downstairs and welcome them himself—Marie was prone to Gallic surliness and could not be trusted—when he saw the face of one of them and recognized it. It was that doctor from the Colonies who asked so many questions about the murder. And the other gentleman with him; he had seen him before, too, but he could not quite place him. Perhaps he had seen him in the bar, talking to Marie. Oh, but he could not be dawdling. He had a business to run, but what could this gentleman, this doctor who had so upbraided him about the cleanliness of his hostelry, want now?

"Ah, Mr. Smee," Thomas greeted the innkeeper, who appeared, flustered, at the bottom of the stairs.

"Dr. Silkstone," he said, bowing low.

"Good day, Mr. Smee," replied Thomas.

"How may I help you, sir? Do you require a room?"

"Indeed I do."

Smee was taken aback. He thought this doctor might wish to pry further; ask more questions; bother Marie again.

"I have a proposition for you. One that will require discretion and propriety on your behalf, sir," Thomas told him.

The landlord straightened himself and puffed out his chest. "Then you have come to the right place, sir," he replied. "I run a very respectable establishment, as you know."

Chapter 44

Mr. Pertwee delivered the coffin to Cockspur Street later on that day. Because of its size, it was decided to bring the giant's body down from his bedchamber rather than try to maneuver the huge casket upstairs.

Emily had dressed the body. She had washed Charles in lavender water and combed his hair and seen to it that his shroud was neat. In his grasp he held the lock of her hair, tied with the white ribbon. "Good-bye, my love," she whispered, stroking his hand for the last time.

Thomas returned to assist the count in supervising the transfer of the coffin to Smee's Hotel. The omnipresent figure of Howison had not been seen since yesterday. Neither man took it as a good sign. It merely signified that news of the giant's death was out.

It took eight of O'Shea's strongest men to shoulder the casket out of the house as evening drew down and onto a waiting cart at the rear. On top of it they loaded crates of cabbages and rhubarb to disguise the real cargo. It was then driven to the inn, escorted by two Irishmen and Crookback in a cart at the front and two on horseback behind. Thomas and the count followed on.

By now the light was fading and the strange cortege arrived at the hostelry at dusk. Smee was waiting at the back and guided the coffin inside. "Take care," he called as a corner of the casket hit a door lintel. "Not that way! Oh, my word!"

He showed them into a large room at the rear. He did not

possess a table big enough to take the weight, so they laid the coffin on the floor and the men sat 'round it, as if it were some ancient altar.

"Ale all 'round," called O'Shea, wiping the sweat from his brow with his neck scarf.

"Aye," they all chorused, settling themselves down on the rush-strewn floor.

"Let us drink to Charles Byrne. The tallest man that ever lived!" cried Crookback.

Smee looked nervously at Thomas and the count. As if reading his troubled mind, Thomas assured him: "We will see to it that they settle their bills before they leave. Have no fear on that score."

Giles Carrington was waiting for Thomas when he arrived back at Cockspur Street with the count. He apologized for absenting himself so hastily earlier in the day. "I remembered I had to prepare some specimens for a lecture," he ventured by way of an excuse.

" 'Tis no matter. Just as long as you are here now," said Thomas, settling himself by the fire in the drawing room. He was tired and every bone in his body ached. He had been away from home and from Dr. Carruthers for four days now, and he longed for his own bed and, he dared say, Mistress Finesilver's food.

They had felt like the longest four days in his life, too. So much had happened. Lydia's dreadful revelations and Charles's death, coming as they did in such quick succession, had shocked him to his very core. But he could not allow himself the luxury of mourning. Not yet. Not until Charles's dying wishes were carried out and he was laid to rest far beyond the reach of John Hunter.

"We have arranged for the coffin to travel on a barge out to sea. O'Shea and his men will escort it. Lady Lydia wishes to travel with it, too, and Emily will go with her as her maid," Thomas told Carrington.

"And the count and yourself, sir?" he asked.

"I am afraid I will not be accompanying the cortege," inter-rupted the little man. It was clear that he had taken the death of his friend, albeit expected, very badly. He sat, cradling a glass of brandy, in a very morose mood. "I have already said my fare-well."

Thomas addressed Carrington. "You are to accompany Lady Lydia in my absence. I still have unfinished business to which I must attend."

"The murder case?"

"Yes. I shall confront Hunter and see if he confesses."

"And if he does not?"

"Unless he has a credible explanation for storing the larynx, I shall go to the coroner, who will have him arrested."

The young student nodded. "He is the murderer, of that there is no doubt. Him and that thug Crouch."

Thomas could not hide his surprise at this confident asser-tion. "You know more?" he said, leaning forward in his chair. This was the first he had heard of Carrington's suspicion that Crouch was involved. If that was the case, then it confirmed his own theory that not one but two men were responsible for the gruesome murder.

"I think Crouch killed the castrato as he slept, then Hunter moved in with his scalpel," said the young man, displaying a confidence that surprised Thomas.

"But what makes you think Crouch was involved? How do you know of him?"

Carrington shrugged and his mouth curled. His expression was bitter. "I saw him at the laboratory once or twice. That twisted face of his! Then I saw him again at Smee's."

"Smee's?" repeated Thomas. "Does this have something to do with your reluctance to accompany me this afternoon?"

Carrington nodded. "I've seen Crouch there, too." He paused, adding the French girl.

Thomas nodded, recalling the feeling of the hoodlum's boot in his ribs after he, too, had seen him at the hotel with Marie Dubois. "And you would testify to this in court?"

Carrington's expression was set hard. "As if my life depended on it. I know that he and that butcher are in league, sir," he said, his voice tinged with loathing. "I would do anything to see them put behind bars, or better still, swinging from the end of a rope."

Thomas frowned. It was strange for him to see such hatred in a person's eyes. But it was there, burning as intensely as the coals in the grate. The onus was now on him to go and confront the object of that hatred before Hunter could commit any more crimes and prevent him from sticking his knife into Charles's cadaver. He felt weighed down by the responsibility of his task. He needed sleep, he told himself. He would feel better after a good night's rest, but before he left for his own home, there was one more thing he had to do.

Lydia sat up in bed as soon as she heard the door open. She looked anxious and held out both arms to Thomas.

"I was afraid you wouldn't come," she gasped.

He said nothing at first, but simply held her. "I have neglected you," he told her, stroking one of her soft, thin arms. "How do you feel, my love?"

"Better for seeing you," she replied, but her voice was tinged with sadness.

"Are you sure you are strong enough for the journey tomorrow?" He started to feel for her pulse. It remained weak.

She nodded. "I must go and say good-bye. I brought Charles to London. If I hadn't . . ." Her voice dissolved.

Thomas shook his head. "You must not blame yourself for everything bad that has happened," he told her, wiping a tear from her cheek. "Charles suffered from the white death. He would have died whether here or in Ireland."

"I still feel . . . ," she began, but stopped herself in midsentence. "But you will be with me, and that will make me stronger," she said, looking up at him with a childlike innocence. A pang of guilt now stabbed his own conscience.

"I will follow on," he told her. "I will join you in Margate, but first I have some unfinished business."

Lydia's face dropped and she sat back on her pillows. "Hunter?"

Thomas nodded. "I have to confront him about the castrato's death."

"Then your mission is a vital one." There was a look of resolve on her face.

"Giles Carrington and Emily will accompany you. Carrington is a medical student and will be able to attend to you if necessary." It was reassuring for Thomas to know that if Lydia's health should relapse, then the student would be able to treat her. "I will be following on horseback, right behind you," he explained.

Lydia smiled. She seemed satisfied with arrangements. He only hoped her faith in his plans was not misplaced. So far everything had gone smoothly, almost too smoothly. Charles's coffin was heavily guarded in a secret location and would soon be out of reach to all in Neptune's kingdom, but he could not help but think that Hunter would not give up so easily. The doctor imagined him plotting and planning with Howison, Crouch, and any other shady villain in his pay. His prey remained within his grasp and the scent of blood was still in his nostrils. There was yet a chance that he would make a move, but before he could do that, Thomas needed to uncover the truth about what really happened the night of the murder.

Meanwhile, in Earls Court, a frustrated Dr. Hunter had summoned the undertaker.

"Where is my giant, Pertwee?" he stormed. His clenched fist thudded on the table, causing the mortician to flinch. Pertwee knew this old Scot was hard to please and had a short fuse, but he had never seen him so angry before.

"I have a plan, dear Doctor, that will deliver the goods in the next twenty-four hours," he said assuredly, but Hunter was not impressed.

"Och! Do not patronize me, Pertwee. I am not your 'dear' Doctor. I am dear to no one, save my wife and children. I have paid you money and I want my goods," he thundered. His face was now red and sweat had broken out on his temples. He became unsteady on his feet and slumped into a nearby chair.

"Sir, but you are unwell," said Pertwee, rushing forward.

"I will be in a better humor when I have got what I've paid for," he told the undertaker, breathing hard.

"I am glad of it, sir," said Pertwee.

"Good, now go get me my giant," cried Hunter, watching the undertaker leave while trying to still his shaking body.

Chapter 45

O nce they had passed the boundary stone, the motley crew of mourners was seized by the need for refreshment. Perhaps it was because they were now out of the City of London's authority and on the road to Kent that they felt safer, mused Mad Sam O'Shea. Or was it simply that they had been up at the crack of dawn, heaving the monstrous casket onto the cart and lugging it for a good few miles already? Either way, the refreshments at the Thomas a Becket beckoned. The watering hole of many a good pilgrim over the years, it would certainly provide well-deserved respite for him and his men this morning, he told himself.

The bizarre cortege pulled up outside the inn. O'Shea and Crookback were in the front seats while the other men—there were four of them—sat on what were by now foul-smelling cabbages and rhubarb that covered the coffin on the wagon. They all climbed down, and two remained to guard their precious cargo while the others piled into the hostelry.

A few moments later a carriage pulled up. Lovelock was driving with young Will at his side.

"What are they doing?" asked Lydia anxiously, looking out of the window, seeing the cart with its odd load. "Surely they should not have stopped?"

Carrington shook his head. "These Irishmen are a law unto themselves," he said reprovingly.

"Begging your pardon, my lady," interjected Emily. "But my father will take good care of Mr. Byrne. I know he will."

Lydia nodded. "Yes. Yes, of course he will," she replied. "Let us take this opportunity to take refreshment, too, shall we?" she suggested.

Thomas felt a great nausea in the pit of his stomach as he rode out to Earls Court. He loathed and detested Hunter for what he had done to Lydia and, no doubt, other women in her situation, yet did not relish his task. It was a terrible thing to accuse a man of murder when all he had was hearsay evidence and no witnesses to the actual act itself.

Howison was at the gate. He recognized Thomas and sneered. "Welcome, Dr. Silkstone," he said, his weather-beaten face stretched into a broad grin. The doctor did not return the greeting. All he could recall was that menacing face as he leaned against a tree in Cockspur Street, day and night, shadowing poor Charles.

"I am come to see Dr. Hunter," he told him.

He was led past the neat row of small skulls, through the great hall lined with pickled animals from moles to monkeys and into the laboratory, where he found Hunter leaning over some vast tome and making notes, spectacles hooked over his nose. The anatomist looked up when he heard Thomas approach.

"Ah, Dr. Silkstone, what a pleasant surprise," he greeted him, removing his glasses. Thomas was surprised at his affability, and more than a little suspicious. Here was a man whose most cherished ambition, nay, obsession, had been thwarted, despite weeks of careful planning. The giant had slipped out of his grasp and his body would be halfway to the coast by now, and yet the anatomist seemed almost cheerful. Thomas was about to shatter his mood.

"I am come on a most serious matter, Dr. Hunter," he told him.

"Then you better sit down, Dr. Silkstone," he said, gesturing to a chair.

"It concerns the murder of the young castrato, Signor Carlo Cappelli."

Hunter nodded. "I have read of the case. A most unpleasant murder, by all accounts."

"Indeed so, sir. I was tasked to carry out a postmortem on his body," said Thomas.

The anatomist leaned forward gleefully. "Och! How fortunate you were. Fascinating, I shouldn't wonder. I have always wanted to dissect a castrato, as you know." His expression was one of delight, and Thomas recalled the night of the concert and his interest in Cappelli's physiology then. He went on: "As their body grows, their lack of testosterone means their epiphyses do not harden in the normal manner, you know. That is why they are often so tall and with unusually long ribs. Did you note that, Silkstone?"

Thomas was taken aback by this enthusiastic reaction to his original question. "I was trying to ascertain how Signor Cappelli died, sir, not studying the physiology of a castrato."

Hunter reflected for a moment. "Pity, that," he lamented. "A wasted opportunity. But what about the vocal cords? Were they small? 'Tis the extraordinary power of their lungs forcing air through those tiny cords that makes their voices so high, you know. I'd love to get my hands on such a larynx."

Shocked by such a reaction to his questioning, Thomas decided to plunge in. "But I believe you have, sir," he blurted.

Hunter stiffened and looked puzzled. "What did ya say?"

Thomas took a deep breath and repeated himself. "I believe that Signor Cappelli's larynx is in a preserving jar in a store cupboard in this very room, sir," he said unequivocally.

The anatomist paused for a moment, his gnarled fingers stroking his chin in thought. "And I assume Giles Carrington told you this," he said finally.

Thomas felt the blood pounding through his ears. "Yes sir, he did."

"Then let us see if he is right," said Hunter, calmly reaching down to his desk drawer and bringing out a key. Lighting a lantern, he walked over to the door in the wall and unlocked it. Opening the grille wide, so that Thomas could see everything, he revealed his store of human organs, all floating weightlessly like exotic fruits in brandy.

The young doctor could not hide his amazement. There was row upon row of jars and ampules, each neatly labeled and each bearing the name of the organ within, together with its previous owner's.

"So, this is my collection of human body parts, Dr. Silkstone," he said proudly, walking into the storeroom. "Each organ is here for a reason, a purpose. You see this one," he said, pointing to a cylinder containing what appeared to Thomas to be a section of a small intestine with a hole in it. " 'Tis a duelist's jejunum. That is the bullet hole, right through the middle. And this, this is the Marquis of Rockingham's heart," he announced proudly. "He gave me permission to have it afore he died."

"So you keep these for study, sir?" asked Thomas.

Hunter nodded. "For study and for posterity," he replied. "One day, not in my lifetime, but maybe in the next century, or the one after that, men might be able to learn from these samples. It might help them in the curation of so many diseases that blight mankind."

Thomas was stunned by such a momentous revelation. Here was a man ahead of his time, he thought; a true disciple of science and imagination. He felt almost humbled by such breadth of vision and momentarily forgot the purpose of his visit, his eyes playing on the endless possibilities of future discoveries encapsulated within the jars before him.

Forcing himself to be pulled back into the moment, he remembered his purpose. "Sir, are Signor Cappelli's vocal cords here?" he asked earnestly.

Hunter shook his head. "If they are, Dr. Silkstone, I have not put them there."

Together they scanned the shelves. It was Thomas who spotted the jar first, slightly hidden by another vessel.

"Could these be they?" he asked, taking the jar off the shelf.

"I have not seen those before," replied Hunter, "and I do not have any other such specimens." It was clear to Thomas that he was telling the truth.

"So someone else must have put them there?"

The anatomist nodded and the men exchanged knowing looks. In an instant Thomas knew. "Why would Giles Carrington want to have you arrested for murder?"

Hunter walked out of the storeroom and Thomas followed. " 'Tis a long story," said the old anatomist, easing himself onto the chair once more. "His father died under my knife. He was a wealthy banker and he suffered an aneurysm in his leg. I operated on it, but it was before I had perfected my technique and he died a few days later."

"I see," said Thomas quietly, trying to digest the implications of such a revelation.

"I thought no more of it. Och, my patients die every day, but then last year, the lad came to me, telling me he was the son of this man and he wanted to be a great surgeon. I thought it a noble ideal and I felt obliged to him as well. I had, after all, deprived him of his father, albeit unintentionally."

"So you took him under your wing, and all the time he was plotting your downfall," said Thomas.

Hunter nodded. "It certainly seems that way, Dr. Silkstone," he replied. "But you will have to ask him yourself. Could it be that Giles Carrington is your murderer, Dr. Silkstone?" he asked calmly.

It was only then that the horror of the situation struck Thomas. "But he is with Lydia," he exclaimed, suddenly remembering the giant's funeral procession eastward to Kent.

"Then you must go to her at once, Dr. Silkstone, afore he murders anyone else!" cried Hunter, a hand held aloft melodramatically.

Thomas did not appreciate being mocked so cruelly, but he knew the anatomist was right, and the sick feeling in his stomach that had seized him before now gave way to rising panic. He had to catch up with the funeral cortege, and quickly.

John Hunter watched the young doctor race to his waiting horse and gallop off down his drive. He smiled to himself. In his eagerness to save his beloved Lydia from the clutches of a suspected murderer, he would surely be distracted. It would make Pertwee's mission so much easier. The giant would soon be his.

Chapter 46

Despite numerous stops along the way, the bizarre funeral procession made good progress. They arrived at their appointed inn shortly before nightfall. Lovelock had gone on ahead previously and arranged for Charles's casket to be stored overnight in the tavern's barn.

Lydia, Carrington, and Emily had followed on behind, driven by Will, ensuring O'Shea and his crew did not become too distracted by the pleasures of hostelries along the route. The road was being well used. There were parties of pilgrims heading for Canterbury and cartloads of fruit coming to the city from the orchards of Kent. Lydia had intended to keep a weather eye open, but she was still tired from her ordeal and left it to Carrington to watch for any suspicious signs. There was still a danger of them being followed, and the newssheets carried several warnings about the unscrupulous nature of those who would seek to anatomize their precious cargo. Lydia shivered. She, too, had experienced firsthand Hunter's ruthlessness and knew that he never gave up easily, although with each mile away from London, she told herself, the risk lessened.

The inn was adequate in its provisions and Emily was on hand to see to her needs. Over dinner in an upper room Carrington spoke to Lydia of his work at St. George's Hospital. He seemed a pleasant enough young man to her, if a little intense at times. It was only when the talk turned to the pursuit of the giant's corpse and the name of Hunter passed his lips that his expression altered. Lydia noticed that he shifted uncomfortably on his chair and that he diverted his eyes away from her face.

"That man is evil," he said through clenched teeth. Lydia did not contradict him. She believed, from her own experience, that what he said was true, but she could see that there was some deeper substance to his hatred of the anatomist.

"He has wronged you, Mr. Carrington?" she asked.

He looked at her straight. "He murdered my father," he hissed.

Startled, Lydia leaned back from the table. "That is a grave accusation, sir. How so?" she asked, wide-eyed.

"He operated on his leg. My father suffered an aneurysm, a large swelling that threatened to kill him. He was in agony and most of the surgeons he saw recommended amputation." Carrington touched the blade of the knife that rested on the table before them. "But my father would do anything to avoid losing his leg, so when he heard of John Hunter and his newfangled operation to tie off the artery, he asked to be his patient."

"But the operation failed?" suggested Lydia.

Carrington nodded. "He died in unspeakable anguish a week later." The student's eyes filled with tears at the recollection.

Lydia felt his pain. She recalled her own agony at the hands of Dr. Hunter. "I am sorry for your loss," she murmured, placing her hand over his on the table in a spontaneous gesture of empathy.

Instantly he lifted his gaze, and she realized what she had done was inappropriate. "Forgive me, Mr. Carrington," she said, withdrawing her hand quickly, as if she had just touched hot embers. "I am tired. I must abed," she told him, rising from the table. "Tomorrow will be a long day."

Downstairs the Irishmen and Crookback sipped their tepid ale and reminisced with tales of the giant Byrne around a roaring fire. While not all their recollections were accurate, blurred as they were by liquor, they were all fond.

"I recall the time he gave me locks of his hair to sell, and when a cripple held on to his legs he could walk again," said Mad Sam O'Shea, looking deep into the embers of the fire.

"And I recall he patted me on the 'ead," chirped up one of the younger members of the group. They raised their cups to that memory, too.

Crookback had his stories, as well. "There was a time the showman would give us no supper and Charles, God rest his soul, stood up to him and picked him from the ground. Lifted him clean three feet in the air," he recalled. " 'Give us our bread,' he growled at him, and sure enough we shared not a loaf but a leg of mutton an hour later!"

There was a general chorus of approval and another toast was drunk. "To the finest Irishman that ever lived," they cried, their sentimentality growing with each pot of ale. And so the night went on.

Outside, across a small courtyard, in a barn not ten yards away, lay the object of their adulation and the subject of their numerous toasts. Charles Byrne's body was safe. No one could enter the barn without first passing the back windows of the inn, where they all sat, keeping guard over the remains of their friend in their own very special way.

About ten miles to the west, Thomas had been forced to stop for the night in an inn at Gravesend. He was making good progress when his horse went lame and he had to walk the last five miles into the port. He reluctantly ate some bread and cheese, even though he had no appetite for it, and retired early so that he could leave at first light. With a good night's rest and a fresh horse, he reckoned he could easily catch up with Lydia and the funeral cortege before they reached Margate, where Charles was to be consigned to the sea. He prayed the giant's hapless friends would keep true to their word. Now that he knew Giles Carrington could not be trusted, the band of Irish reprobates was his only hope.

*   *   *

The next morning the sunlight seemed brighter than usual to the Irishmen. The clatter of horses' hooves and the shouts of the pot boys and scullery maids were louder too. And how stiff they were! What sort of mattresses were these that they were as hard as wood? It was only a few moments after their waking that they realized they had, indeed, slept on wood. They had not taken to their beds that night, nor even dozed by Charles's coffin as planned. The liquor had got the worst of them, and one by one they had fallen into a drunken stupor by the hearth.

As soon as he realized what had happened Mad Sam scrambled up and rushed out of the door, shouting.

"The giant. The giant!" he cried, hurtling toward the barn. His motley crew followed in hot pursuit, hollering and shouting as if the very world were coming to an end. But they need not have worried. The gigantic coffin was still there, resting peacefully on the flagstones. O'Shea ran a careful hand over the lid. It was all intact. The nails were as secure as the teeth in his head. He patted the box like a horse, then bent down and whispered: "Are you well in there, Charles, me old *cara?*" Satisfied that he had received a reply in the affirmative, Mad Sam nodded vigorously. "All's well," he told his men, and they breathed a collective sigh of relief.

Alerted to the commotion below as she dressed, Lydia told Emily to look out of the window. The maid watched anxiously as the men emerged from the barn, but her expression changed when she saw they were smiling.

"Mr. Byrne is safe," she told her mistress.

"We must thank God for that," replied Lydia. It was certainly no thanks to the Irishmen, she thought.

Chapter 47

Howison, Pertwee, Crouch, and Hartnett traveled through the night. They reached Castle Street just before dawn. John Hunter was there to receive them. Without ceremony they brushed away the few stinking cabbages that had covered the coffin during the journey from Kent and prized open the lid.

There it lay. The most sought-after corpse in London, nay, in England, and now it belonged to John Hunter. But they must make haste. It was turning. The other men gagged on the familiar stench. Besides, there was no time to gloat over those who so desperately wanted to get their knives into this precious flesh. It would soon be light and the news, once uncovered, would travel fast.

They hauled the carcass, wearing only its funeral shroud, onto a smaller wagon that waited, already harnessed to three water buffalo. Howison climbed on board.

"Thank you, gentlemen," called Hunter to Pertwee, Crouch, and Hartnett as he cracked the whip. They did not wave back. They were too busy counting their money.

Westward they drove, to Earls Court, all the time looking over their shoulder. Were they being followed? What was that in the shadows? A horse? Who was the rider? Would they take word to others of his kind? Would they say "John Hunter is on the move! John Hunter has the giant! Ambush him! Steal the corpse!" But no. They reached their destination just as the sun was rising behind them and made sure the great drawbridge was lifted to make them secure.

Together they heaved the gigantic corpse off the wagon and put it ignominiously into a handcart, trundling it with great difficulty along the path and into the laboratory underground.

The anatomist had lit the fire under the copper vat before he had left for Castle Street, and the room was now filled with steam from the boiling water.

"You want him on the table?" asked Howison.

Hunter nodded and together they lugged the great carcass up onto the dissecting slab. Rigor mortis had set in, but that did not bother the doctor. There was no time for his usual practices: Meticulous anatomization was out of the question.

"Guard the door," he barked to Howison. Aware that his fellow anatomists would be capable of scaling even high walls to steal his booty, he was afraid they would be besieged at any moment.

Quickly he unwrapped the shroud and allowed himself the luxury of marveling at his prize. Charles Byrne's great hulk was as extraordinary in death as it had been in life. "You are wondrous," he muttered to himself before reaching for a cleaver.

Taking a deep breath, he let the blade first fall on Charles's left leg. The blow sprayed his topcoat with fluids and, evidently irked by the inconvenience of this, he flung it off to the ground and carried on in his shirtsleeves. Next he sliced through the bone with a saw, drawing it across like the bow of a cello. He repeated the procedure with the right leg as Howison looked on from the doorway in admiration. There was sweat on his forehead, and he wiped it away with the bloodied sleeve of his shirt. More sawing. He was playing arpeggio: up and down, across, backward and forward. His muscles ached from the pressure.

Out of breath from his considerable exertions, and wet with the steam, Hunter next chopped off the arms. They put up less resistance, the bones of the humerus capitulating sooner than the femurs. Gathering the limbs together he tossed them, one by one, and without the slightest ceremony, into the boiling vat.

How he would have loved to explore those muscles and tease out those sinews. But there was no time.

Returning to the corpse, he was left with the torso and the head. Ah, the head, he said to himself, gazing at the giant's face, framed by his flowing black hair. Eyes, thankfully, closed. What mysteries did this skull hold? What explanation could it give for this Goliath of a man? Just why had he grown so tall? Sadly, he would never know. There was no room for sentimentality. The cranium had to be severed. He called over to Howison. "Help me pull the corpse." Together they heaved the giant up the table so that while his body was supported, his head dropped down over the side, exposing his neck and throat. "Put a basket down there," he ordered and Howison obliged. And now Hunter stood, both anatomist and executioner, and taking a deep breath, he lifted the cleaver above his own head and brought it down again deftly. There was a splintery, cracking sound that lasted only a split second. With one fell swoop Charles Byrne's head was off, dropping into the waiting basket like a rotten cabbage, and without hesitation John Hunter picked it up and flung it into the seething copper to be boiled away with the rest of the large chunks of human meat.

Chapter 48

Lydia put her head out of the carriage and breathed in the salty air. She had never seen the sea before, and now it stretched out before her like a great azure carpet, fringed by the cream and gold shingle of the shore. A dozen or so fishing boats bobbed on choppy waters a few hundred feet out as seagulls whooped and called above. In the distance great cliffs of chalk rose from the beach, while up ahead the twin towers of a church poked over the horizon.

"Reculver," said Carrington, following Lydia's gaze. "We shall soon be in Margate."

"Yes." Lydia nodded and slipped her gloved hand into Emily's. The maid was sitting beside her and had remained silent throughout the journey. "We shall watch from the cliff top," she said. "Mr. O'Shea has made all the arrangements with the fishermen."

Less than two hours later they were in Margate and had stopped by the wooden pier. Lydia surveyed the scene, scanning for Thomas. Her efforts were in vain. A few fishing boats were in port, but most were out at sea. There were hoys, too, loading and unloading cargo. Donkeys waited patiently with great panniers on their backs, flicking troublesome flies from their eyes with jerks of their heads. Horses pulled carts and wagons laden with barrels of fish to take to London. There was noise, shouts from the fishermen and the dockers, and gulls, circling overhead. But of Dr. Silkstone there was no sign.

O'Shea halted the cart by one of the hoys and climbed down to talk to a stocky man on board. Lydia saw him nod and call some of his men over. They lowered a gangplank so that O'Shea could board. He gestured over to his gang. There were nods and handshakes and the others returned to the coffin.

"This be the vessel, your ladyship," said O'Shea to Lydia.

"But Dr. Silkstone is not here yet. Can we wait?" She was growing increasingly anxious.

"The tide waits for no one, ma'am. The skipper says we need to leave port in the next hour, or we'll lose another day."

"Very well," she said reluctantly. "We shall drive up to the headland and watch you discharge the coffin from there."

Lovelock drove them east up a steep track that led to the cliffs that stood sentinel over the vast sweep of the bay. All the time Lydia was looking out of the window, watching for Thomas, but as the road rose, the people below became as small as black pebbles on the seashore. Even if he had been there, she would not have been able to distinguish him from the others below. She could, however, discern the hoy as it left the port, making its slow and solemn progress with its precious cargo. She wrapped her shawl around her. The sea breeze was stronger the higher they rose. She saw Emily shiver, not from cold, she suspected, but with the thought of seeing Charles's body consigned to the depths.

" 'Tis what he dearly wanted," comforted Lydia.

"Aye," replied the maid. "But 'tis a sad thing that it had to come to this."

Lydia knew exactly what she meant.

When they reached the crest of the hill, all three of them alighted. Lydia had brought her prayer book with her, the same one that she had consulted in her darkest hour at Boughton. She had chosen a few words of commendation and had hoped that Thomas would be able to read them as Charles was lowered into the sea. In his absence, she would have to ask Carrington, she told herself.

As they stood on the cliff top, the wind whipping around their faces, they could still make out the hoy, struggling to leave the shelter of the port. Although the tide was with it, the wind was blowing onshore, pushing against the vessel as it attempted to make headway, like some great, unseen hand. Lydia had brought a telescope with her and was watching the mariners on board trim the sail to the prevailing wind.

After a few minutes, however, they began to make progress and were soon rounding the foreland and heading out to sea. So preoccupied were Lydia, Carrington, and Emily with the spectacle that they did not notice a lone horseman galloping up the track until he came to an abrupt stop just a few feet away.

"Dr. Silkstone!" cried Lydia as she saw the doctor dismount and hurry over to her.

"Thank goodness I have found you," he panted. He was relieved to see that Carrington did not seem to have done anything untoward in his absence. His accusations would have to wait until after the interment. "I am in time?" he said.

"Yes. The vessel will be in the right position soon," replied an unsuspecting Carrington.

"Twenty fathoms out," said Thomas, repeating Charles's instructions. He had even heard a rumor on his travels that there were those with diving bells who would seek to haul the giant's coffin to the surface.

Lydia handed Emily the telescope. "Here," she said. The servant had never held such an instrument before, but with help, she put it to her eye and was able to focus. "Tell us when it is time," she instructed.

Next she handed Thomas the prayer book. "Could you read a psalm for Mr. Byrne, please?"

The doctor took the psalter and opened it at a marked page. Through the telescope Emily could see the men were heaving the coffin into position on thick linen straps.

"It is time," she said.

Thomas turned his face to the sea and read: *Thou shalt not be afraid for the terror by night; nor for the arrow that flieth by day; Nor for the pestilence that walketh in darkness; nor for the destruction that wasteth at noonday. A thousand shall fall at thy side, and ten thousand at thy right hand; but it shall not come nigh thee.*

They stood in silence for a few more moments, saying their wordless farewells, as they watched the great coffin plunge into the sea, safe from the clawing hands and sharp knives that had hounded Charles ever since he had come to London.

"He is safe now," said Lydia to Emily. The maid crossed herself and nodded, wiping away the tears that streamed from her eyes. As the two women began to walk back to the carriage, Thomas took the opportunity to confront Carrington.

"I have spoken with Hunter," he said. His expression gave nothing away.

The young student looked uncomfortable and let out a nervous laugh. "And he denied any wrongdoing, of course."

"Not only did he deny murder, he accused you of the killing as a way of revenge for the death of your father. You wanted Hunter disgraced, did you not?" Thomas's voice remained calm, but his thrust was cutting.

Carrington's expression changed. "Of course I want him disgraced. Any surgeon, any physician, any anatomist worth an iota of respect wants him disgraced, Dr. Silkstone."

"So you do not deny putting the castrato's larynx in the storeroom to implicate Hunter?"

The student stiffened, as if proud of himself. "I do not deny it, but I did not commit the murder."

Thomas was stunned, but he did not show it. He thought he could be confident in his accusation. He persisted.

"So how did you come by this?" he asked, walking over to his horse and pulling out the jar containing the larynx from a pannier. "You, of all people, know I can prove if it is Cappelli's or not."

An insolent look settled on Carrington's face. "Save your science, Dr. Silkstone," he sneered. "It is Cappelli's sure enough and, yes, I put it in Hunter's store, but I did not commit murder."

"But you know who did?"

Carrington raised a contemptuous eyebrow. "Perhaps," he tormented.

Thomas grew impatient. "Constables are waiting below in the port," he said, pointing below. "They are waiting for my signal."

Carrington let out another nervous laugh. "That was a foolish move to make, Dr. Silkstone," he shouted, the gathering wind muffling his words. Suddenly his eyes darted to his right and he rushed forward, grabbing hold of Lydia as she was about to climb back into the carriage. Emily screamed as she watched the student take her mistress by the throat, then put his hand over her mouth. "Let me leave on my own, Dr. Silkstone, or I will take her with me."

Thomas rushed forward, too, but Carrington only tightened his grip on Lydia's neck. "Let her go, Carrington. It's over. You know you cannot escape," the doctor told him, walking slowly toward him.

"Oh, but I can," he countered, and flinging Lydia to the ground, he jumped up onto Thomas's horse and began kicking it violently and tugging at its rein. The crop had been left on the saddle and now he used that, too, lashing the animal ferociously. But instead of galloping off, the terrified horse reared up on its hind legs and let out a loud whinny before bolting off along the cliff top toward the town.

Thomas ran to Lydia. "Leave me, you must get after him," she said as Emily comforted her.

"The constables are waiting for him. They will arrest him," replied Thomas. But just as he said this, there was another whinny in the distance from the horse. Running over to the crest of the hill he could see the beast rearing up halfway down the track. It was up on its hind legs, neighing loudly as it had before. Only this time Carrington was not in the saddle.

Chapter 49

The journey back to London was spent in sober reflection. Naturally the constables had questions about Carrington's death. Witnesses said that the horse had thrown him and that he had rolled over the cliff edge, plunging sixty feet to the beach below. Their accounts were accepted and his body transported for burial.

Lydia was still in shock from the assault and had accepted a draft from Thomas. Much of her journey was spent asleep. The only person who could take comfort from the trip to Margate was Emily, believing that her beloved giant's wishes had been fulfilled.

Count Boruwlaski was waiting for them on their return to Cockspur Street. Once Thomas had settled Lydia in her room and said farewell to O'Shea and his gang, who had escorted their carriage, he joined the little man in the drawing room. He seemed delighted to see them return safely from their sad mission and relieved that Charles's dying wish had been granted.

"I was most concerned that Hunter's men, or some such other villains, would get their hands on him," he told Thomas over a brandy.

"Indeed we all were," agreed Thomas. "There was one very unfortunate incident, however," Thomas began. He told him how Carrington had hidden the jar with the castrato's larynx in Hunter's storeroom.

"Naturally, after that, I assumed he had murdered Signor

Cappelli, but he denied it, saying he only wanted to implicate Hunter in the murder."

"And you believed him?" asked the little man.

Thomas paused for a moment. "Yes, I did. I do not believe he would have denied it. He seemed almost proud of his hatred toward Hunter and would have admitted the act if it were true."

"And meanwhile Moreno remains in Newgate Prison." Boruwlaski looked grave.

"You have visited him?"

"Yes. He grows weaker and thinner each day."

"And we have less than two weeks to find the real killer," said Thomas to himself as much as to the count.

Mr. Smee broke out into a sweat the moment he saw Thomas standing in the hallway. "Dr. Silkstone," he greeted him nervously. "What a surprise! My word, it is."

"Not an unpleasant one, I hope," said Thomas graciously.

"Why, not at all." The little man giggled. "May we fetch you some refreshment?" Thomas would have enjoyed nothing more than a tankard of cool ale, but he could not allow himself to be distracted. He wanted to revisit the scene of Cappelli's murder. Sir Peregrine had given him no time at all in which to investigate the area properly. There could have been clues, vital ones, on the rug, in the drawers, under the bed, that held the key to the murderer. And he had a hunch.

"No, thank you," he replied. He wanted to see if he was right.

"I trust the giant gentleman was delivered safely to his grave," said Smee in a reverent tone.

Thomas nodded. "Yes. May he rest in peace," he said, adding quickly: "But I am here on another matter, I am afraid, Mr. Smee."

The little man tensed visibly and brought out his large kerchief from his pocket.

"What sort of matter, pray tell, sir?"

"I have been tasked to see that there are no vermin on your premises," Thomas told him, managing to keep a solemn face.

Smee blushed, recalling the embarrassing episode of the vict-uals in a downstairs room. "I run a respectable establishment here, my word, I do, sir," he blurted indignantly.

"I know that your standards have improved much since my previous remarks, Mr. Smee, but nonetheless I need to satisfy His Majesty's minister in charge of public health," replied Thomas, inventing the grand title on the spot.

His words, nevertheless, had the desired effect. Smee swal-lowed hard. "Then by all means, feel free to inspect all the rooms, sir. I will do anything I can to assist. My word, I will." He mopped his shiny brow as he pictured being hauled in front of King George himself and admonished.

Thomas was businesslike. "Then I shall start with your kitchen," he said. The little man bowed and led the young doc-tor down a narrow flight of stairs to the kitchen and scullery. A fat woman sat mixing dough in a large bowl while a young boy peeled potatoes nearby. The stone flags were covered in dis-carded peelings and the occasional crust, and a dog lay chewing intently on a bone.

"The floor needs sweeping regularly if rats are to be discour-aged, Mr. Smee," he said, shaking his head. He took out a note-book from his bag and, using a pencil, wrote a few words.

"My word, indeed it does," tutted the little man; then ad-dressing the fat woman he chided: "You heard the good doctor, Cook."

The tour next progressed upstairs. Thomas was shown into the room where Moreno stayed. He gave it a cursory inspection. "You have let this room since the murder?" he asked.

Smee shook his head. "No sir. Murders are not good for busi-ness. My word, they are not." Thomas felt a twinge of guilt at leading this sad little man a merry dance, but he would be kind. "It is in order?"

"Yes, Mr. Smee," he said, again taking out his book and making notes. The proprietor craned his neck in a vain attempt to see what was being written.

Thomas looked up. "Shall we move on?"

Smee nodded and once again led the way along the narrow

landing, but instead of stopping outside the room where the murder had been committed he walked on, heading for the stairs.

"Mr. Smee," called Thomas. "We have not seen this room."

The little man turned. A bead of sweat was running down his nose. "Forgive me, Dr. Silkstone, but no one has been in that room since . . ."

"Since Signor Cappelli's death?" said Thomas obligingly. It was just as he had hoped, and suspected, although he kept his glee in check.

"Marie could not bring herself to enter and clean, and no one wants to sleep in a bed where a man has had his throat slit," bemoaned the little man. "The door's been locked these past two weeks."

That was music to Thomas's ears, but he did not let his guard slip. "Dirty, unused rooms become palaces to rats, Mr. Smee," he scolded. "I should not have to tell you that. Pray, let me enter."

With a trembling hand, Smee turned the key in the lock and opened the door. The room smelled loamy and damp, with the ferrous hint of congealed blood that only an anatomist would recognize. Specks of dust danced like mad midges in the thin lines of light that forced their way through cracks in the shutters.

"Open the window," instructed Thomas. Smee obliged.

The bed was just as it had been left, with the counterpane turned back to reveal a small patch of dried blood. There were clues here, lying in front of him. Of that he was certain. He wanted to inspect everything thoroughly, to take samples, swabs, but he knew he had no authority. He was chancing his luck as it was.

"Do you have a small brush?" he asked an anxious Mr. Smee.

The little man balked, as if requiring some explanation.

"If I am to check for rats, I need to sweep under the bed, sir," explained Thomas, adding pointedly: "Droppings."

Seemingly satisfied, Mr. Smee turned tail and headed downstairs, giving the young doctor valuable time. He examined the sheets more closely, looking for blood, for stains, for anything. And there was something. A long, black hair. He moved swiftly, opening his bag and taking out a pair of tweezers. Carefully, he lifted the hair and put it in a glass phial, which he returned to his bag.

Kneeling down he inspected the floor. The bloody footprints were still there, made by large, tapered feet—Moreno's, he knew. But what was this? There were other outlines, broader, squatter, not made by shoes, but by boots perhaps. There were two such outlines, broken and faint, but distinguishable nevertheless. Someone else had mistakenly trodden in the viscous blood that was spilled on the rug. Another man other than Moreno, Smee, Sir Peregrine, and Thomas himself had been in the room since the murder.

Hearing Smee's footsteps coming up the stairs, he switched his attention to under the bed.

"Here we are, sir," said the tubby man, out of breath after climbing the stairs. He handed Thomas the brush and the doctor began to sweep the floor underneath the bed. As luck would have it, there was plenty to sweep. He had guessed it would be an area that was rarely cleaned, and he was right. By the time he had finished, he had two or three spoonfuls of dirt, which he carefully scooped up onto a piece of parchment and decanted into a glass jar. Although there was plenty for Thomas to analyze, he could not see any telltale rat droppings. But he would not give the landlord his verdict just yet.

Mr. Smee watched him anxiously. "I'll have to scold that Marie. My word, I will, sir," he wailed.

"Indeed you will, Mr. Smee," replied Thomas, securing the lid of his glass jar and returning it to his bag. He suspected that the sullen girl would not take chastisement well. But that was not his concern. His work was done and he could not wait to return to his laboratory to analyze the contents of his jar, but he forced himself to remain professional.

"If I find anything untoward, I shall contact you immediately," he told Mr. Smee, who was wringing his chubby hands. "But I am sure I shall not," he added with a smile.

*   *   *

Emily climbed the sagging stairs up to the room in St. Giles with a heavy heart. Her ladyship had given her leave to spend a few hours with her family on her return from Margate. She was grateful to her. There was a strange emptiness inside her now that Charles was dead. She had only known him for a few weeks and loved him for even less, but his absence left a void that only time would fill.

How she hated this vile place: the dripping walls that closed 'round her, the smell of piss that choked her, the ceaseless voices, punctuated by cries when a woman was beaten or a child kicked. She had been lucky to escape the rookeries and she could not wait to return to Cockspur Street, but she needed to see her family first.

As she made her way through the maze of corridors up to the top landing, she noticed something odd. It was still dark and damp and the dogs still barked and the men still scowled, but there was something else. A delicious smell was wafting down the stairs. Hot food. Not the usual crusts or maggoty cheese. She sniffed once more. Meat. Real meat. Not offal. Not potatoes. Meat.

Not bothering to knock, she found her mother at the table. She was bending over a roasted joint. The woman looked up, surprised. She did not smile.

"I heard the giant died," was all she said.

She was slicing the meat thickly, the bloody juices dribbling onto a tin plate. Her sharp knife made light work of the muscle. Emily suddenly thought of Charles. At least now he would be spared such an indignity. She nodded slowly, sniffing the steam that spooled from the joint. Her mouth began to salivate. She remembered she had not eaten all day.

"Is it mutton?" she asked.

"Yes," came the terse reply.

"And Da is not back yet?"

"He's back, all right, but he's gone out drinking again."

In the corner, seated in a chair, sat her grandmother. The baby sat placidly on her knee as she fed him small slices of meat.

Emily had barely seen her brother when he was not bawling. Grandmother Tooley smiled broadly, showing her toothless gums. Her small, gray head was lost inside a thick woolen shawl that Emily had not seen before. How would she manage to chew this new-gotten meat, Emily asked herself.

"Gran," she cried, rushing over to the old woman. "You look in good health."

The old woman nodded. "That I am, child," she croaked, but her voice was stronger than before. Emily blinked. She looked stronger, too. The life that seemed to be ebbing from her as she lay in her dirty cot seemed to have returned. The breathless urgency with which she warned her granddaughter that a tall man from across the water was coming was all but a distant memory, as faded as her complexion had been. Now there was color in the old woman's cheeks and a keen look in her eyes. She held out a hand to her granddaughter. It no longer shook like an autumn leaf. It was steady and the grasp, when Emily took it, was firm.

"So, your giant has gone, child," said the old woman.

Emily's eyes welled up at the memory of him. "Did you know he was going to die, Gran?"

The old woman shrugged. "We are all going to die," she answered, lifting the baby and returning him to the filthy floor.

Emily knelt down. "But did you not foresee that it would be so soon?" Her voice was plaintive.

"I could not foresee it, no," replied her grandmother, her response oddly reticent.

Emily cocked her head to one side. Something was amiss. She sensed it as surely as she sensed the smell of the hot mutton. "How did you know he was coming?" she asked. "Who told you about the giant?"

Her mother swung 'round, waving the carving knife in her hand. "You would question your grandmother's prophecies?" she scolded. "She is told by a higher power." Her eyes shot heavenward and she crossed her bony chest.

A higher power. Her mother's words resonated in her head as her mind took her back to Charles's last night on this earth. She recalled looking down on the crowd in the street below, Count Boruwlaski at her side. The men had gathered to protect him, brave and true. They saw to it that no knife man would plunge his scalpel into her Charles. There was great sadness, but there was joy, too; joy that her father, her drunken, ne'er-do-well father, had sprung to his fellow countryman's defense. And the count had known his name.

Emily scrambled suddenly to her feet. "Did the higher power tell you about a dwarf, too, Gran?"

The old woman's expression hardened. Her brow furrowed, turning the ridges on her face into deep ravines. A shocked silence sliced through the air as surely as the carving knife through the meat.

"I don't know what you can mean!" cried her outraged mother. "How dare you speak to your grandmother so?"

But the old woman did not shriek in indignation. She did not protest her powers. Her granddaughter was far too shrewd for that, she knew. There was no point in trying to hide her deception. "We have eaten well thanks to the dwarf," she said calmly.

Emily felt anger twisting her guts deep inside her. "And what did you do in return?"

Grandmother Tooley pulled the shawl tighter 'round her head, trying to take refuge in its warmth. "We did no harm." She darted a look at her daughter, as if asking for support.

"Your da was drinking all our money, so when the dwarf came and offered—"

Emily broke in. It all made sense now. "So Count Boruwlaski asked Gran to spread the word about the Amazing Irish Giant so that the crowds would come and pay their half crowns?"

Her mother's gaunt face hardened defensively and she rebuked her daughter. "Your brother cried all day and all night through hunger. There was no milk in my breasts. Now, thanks to the little man, I could go to the cook shop and buy meat. Real meat!" She pointed at her son. "He has food in his belly and is content."

"And did my father know of this?"

A sneer crossed her mother's thin lips. "He's in his cups most of the time. What need was there for him to know? No harm's been done."

"No harm," echoed Emily. "But I trusted you," she said, shaking her head and looking at her grandmother, who seemed to shrink once more before her eyes. "You lied to me."

The old woman shifted in her chair and pinned her grand-daughter with a knowing look. "A great hunger makes liars of us all," she said sagely.

Emily returned her gaze. How could she hate her? She knew what she said was true. Grandmother Tooley was no soothsayer, no prophetess, but her pearls of wisdom were worth more than a half leg of mutton. She could not be angry with her, or her mother. It was Count Boruwlaski who had betrayed her trust.

Back at Hollen Street Thomas found Dr. Carruthers seated in his study.

"Ah, Silkstone, young fellow. Welcome home. I was beginning to think you'd left us for good," greeted the old surgeon.

"I was beginning to feel that I had," he replied, smiling and dropping into a chair opposite his mentor.

"Still, the giant is buried at sea?"

"Yes. Yes, indeed." At least one thing had gone according to plan, Thomas told himself. "But I am afraid that Carrington, the student I told you about, is dead."

The old surgeon arched a brow. "How so?"

"He fell from his horse and down a cliff."

"That was careless," said Carruthers dryly.

"He was trying to escape from the constables. I had just ac-cused him of conspiring in Signor Cappelli's murder."

"Ah. I see. And did he?"

"I believe so, but I still have no clue as to who carried out the act itself."

"So you have discounted that scoundrel Hunter?"

"Carrington was trying to implicate him. He bore him a grudge."

"I see. Then perhaps you need to go back to Dr. Hunter and ask more questions, young fellow."

Thomas knew Carruthers was right. He would pay another visit to the anatomist first thing tomorrow to inform him of Carrington's death and to find out if he could suggest a possible motive for Cappelli's murder. He would also need to analyze the contents of the sample jar. Before that, however, he needed his bed. It had been a very long time since he had enjoyed eight decent hours of sleep. He resolved to return his medical bag to his laboratory instead of taking it up to his room.

Carrying a lighted candle, he opened the door. That same familiar sharp smell of preserving fluid greeted him. It evoked cleanliness and order and it made him smile. He had just deposited his bag on the workbench and was turning to leave when he heard a noise coming somewhere from the far corner of the room.

"Who's there?" he called. No reply. With his candle aloft he took three or four steps farther into the laboratory. He saw his table, his books, and his phials ranged just as he had left them. All seemed in order. His instrument box, too, lay untouched. Using his free hand, he flipped open the lid. A blade glinted in the candle glow and he grabbed it quickly. There was the noise again, a slight, scratching sound.

"Come out," he called, tension rising as he clutched the knife to strike.

It was then that he heard a squeak, a small, pathetic note, and he realized his mistake. It was Franklin, his rat, scuttling about in his cage. In his absence he had forgotten all about his furry white companion. He hoped Mistress Finesilver had not neglected him while he was away.

By the light of his candle Thomas could see he had scraps and water in his bowls, but the peevish housekeeper was no lover of rodents and had not changed his bedding for days. The familiar smell of ammonia stung his eyes. He opened the cage door and Franklin came up to him, his long whiskers twitching wildly at Thomas's familiar scent.

"Hello, boy." He smiled, holding out his palm. The rat approached and walked straight onto his hand. Thomas lifted him out of the cage and lowered him gently into his pocket. "Poor old boy. You shall stay with me tonight."

Wearily he climbed the stairs and opened the door to his room. It had been almost a week since he had slept in his own bed. Holding his candle aloft, he looked around the place that was so familiar and comforting to him. He guided the beam of light over his books, his papers, his brushes and creams and powders on his dressing table. All was just as he had left it. It reminded him of Signor Cappelli's room. He thought of his gentleman's cabinet, how elaborate it was, with its pomades and its pastilles and the alum block.

Reaching into his frock-coat pocket he retrieved Franklin and set him down on the dressing table. As he expected, the creature scurried from object to object sniffing, bringing a smile to Thomas's face. But when he came to the alum block his pink tongue suddenly appeared and he began to lick it. Thomas watched him for a moment. Was it the potassium in the block he craved? He had heard that animals with certain mineral deficiencies often sought them out in nature, so that cats with kidney problems might lick coal for its carbon. Could Franklin be doing something similar? He was just about to pick him up when he stopped dead in his tracks. An alum block, for shaving. He recalled the alum block in Cappelli's room. What would a castrato, without any body hair at all, want with an alum block? He had often recommended alum himself to treat canker sores, but that was in powder form. In a block, the alum was mixed with potassium and rubbed over the wet, freshly shaved face. The substance acted as an astringent to prevent bleeding from small shaving cuts.

His memory flashed to the gaping wound in the young man's throat and the lack of blood around the lip of the incision. "Franklin!" he cried, picking up the rat and dropping him back in his pocket. "Why did I not see this before?"

Taking the lantern he dashed downstairs and into his laboratory. He needed to find the phial of bloodied water he had taken from the pitcher in Cappelli's room. There it was, on the shelf, just as he had left it. Carefully he uncorked the ampule and dipped a litmus paper into the cloudy solution. In a few seconds he had the result he had suspected. The paper had reddened, denoting the presence of potassium alum in the water. Whoever had sliced the castrato's throat so meticulously and precisely could probably also give a gentleman a very good shave.

Next he delved into his bag and brought out the sample jar and the glass phial that held the long black hair. Using his tweezers he teased the strand out and held it up to the candle. It was straight and he guessed it was at least twenty inches long. It must belong to Marie, but it did not incriminate her. After all, she would have made Cappelli's bed. He put it to one side. The contents of the jar would be much more interesting. He lit a lantern, then emptied out the dust onto a large piece of parchment. Small fragments, their identities were too tiny to discern with the naked eye, presented themselves to him. There would be particles of dead skin, silk threads, cotton fibers, splinters of untreated wood, dead insects and . . . What was this? Another hair. Another black hair. Only this one was short. It measured no more than four inches in length. Thomas reached for a glass slide and placed the strand onto it. Moving the lantern next to his microscope, he looked through it. He could see the flat, overlapping tiles of the shaft clearly. He reached for the other strand of hair and placed it carefully on the same slide. They looked identical, until he came to the ends. Gently pulling at the longer strand, like a thread of cotton, he examined the cortex. He could see it had fallen out at the club-shaped root and the end was split longitudinally three ways. When he looked at the other strand, however, it was clear that it had been cut at one end with scissors. It was clean and sharp, not simply broken off at a weak point from the length. The horny cells from both strands appeared almost identical in nearly every respect apart from the fact that the shorter one had been sliced neatly at the end. The thought suddenly occurred to him. It was from a different head.

Returning to the pile of dust once more, he used the tweezers to search for any more hair. And yes. What was this? Another one. Very short and coarser than the others. Gently he lifted it onto another slide and examined it under the microscope. This one was also dark, but its physiological makeup was entirely different. The cortex had a much wider circumference. A whisker, perhaps?

Thomas rubbed his tired eyes and looked at the samples again. He had once read that a person lost up to one hundred head hairs a day. Could these two hold the key to a murder?

Chapter 50

Armed with what could be new, crucial evidence, Thomas rode out to Earls Court the following morning to question Dr. Hunter further. He arrived at the premises to find the drawbridge up, but just as he was about to ring the great bell for attention a cart pulled up. It was carrying crates of livestock, squawking chickens and ducks, and there was one containing a mangy mongrel. It regarded him dolefully. He knew its fate and it sickened him.

When the drawbridge was lowered and the cart passed through, Thomas followed on behind and took the path, unchallenged, to the underground laboratory. Holding his ear to the door, he could hear movement inside. He knocked and waited. There was no reply, so he opened it and entered. A sickly, cloying smell hung in the still air. He glanced over at the copper in the corner. The doors were open. Something had been recently boiled.

Down at the far end of the room, shrouded in the shadows, he saw Hunter busying himself, walking to and fro and chuntering, seemingly to himself.

"Dr. Hunter," Thomas called.

The anatomist stopped dead and peered ahead of him, shielding his eyes against the sunlight splaying out from the open door.

"Who's there?" he shouted.

"Dr. Silkstone. I need to talk with you."

There was a short pause. Thomas could see him fumbling for a moment in the shadows as he moved closer toward him.

"Stay there, Dr. Silkstone. I shall be with you shortly," he barked.

Thomas wondered what hapless specimen had fallen prey to his eager scalpel now. He ventured a little farther into the laboratory.

"I bring news, sir," began Thomas as the old anatomist started to walk toward him, wiping his hands on a cloth. He seemed a little out of breath.

"I was not expecting visitors, Dr. Silkstone," he said, drawing up alongside the doctor. "I have much work to do."

Thomas saw the spatters of dried blood on his shirt and felt duly chastised. "Forgive me, but what I have to tell you is of great importance."

"Well?"

"First of all, I regret to say that Giles Carrington is dead." To Thomas's surprise Hunter's expression did not change. He had expected to see some flicker of shock on the anatomist's face, but there was nothing, not even a question, so Thomas elucidated. "He died while trying to evade arrest. He confessed to planting the larynx in your storeroom."

"And second?"

Thomas noticed Hunter was wiping his hands with irrational fervor now.

"And second, I have found traces of potassium alum around the wound of the castrato. I believe whoever carried out the removal of the larynx could well have a connection with the barber's trade."

For the first time during the course of the conversation Hunter seemed to digest the information that Thomas had just relayed. "Then I'm sure you and Sir Peregrine will be able to track the culprit down and prove his guilt with your new methods, Dr. Silkstone," he said. "But I am afraid I really must get on. Please show yourself out." His lips lifted in a stilted smile and he turned quickly, heading back toward the gloom of the far corners of his laboratory.

Thomas, however, was not satisfied. There were so many questions he needed to ask him. He began walking quickly behind the anatomist. "Sir, please," he called, now in the farthest corner of the room where the light was at its weakest.

Realizing he was being followed, Hunter turned again quickly. "Be gone, sir," he snapped. "Go away." But it was too late. His eyes now adjusted to the murky gloom, Thomas could see what Hunter did not want him, or anyone else, to see. Hanging from a long rope suspended from the ceiling was a skeleton: a human skeleton measuring more than eight feet tall.

Thomas gasped in horror. Eyes wide, he stared at the grotesque image before him as the grim reality of what he could see dawned on him. "No!" he cried. "But . . ."

Hunter smiled nervously. "You and your cronies must admit defeat, Dr. Silkstone," he said.

"Then what was in the coffin?" asked Thomas, his head still reeling from the shock.

"Paving stones. The undertaker swapped the coffin when those Irish buffoons rested for the night."

Thomas steadied himself on a nearby table. "How could you have known? We planned it all so carefully," he said, shaking his head in disbelief.

Hunter let out a mocking laugh. "Och! 'Tis simple. You were betrayed, Dr. Silkstone."

Thomas eyed him incredulously. "Betrayed? By whom?"

"By me, my dear Thomas," came a familiar voice from out of the shadows.

Count Josef Boruwlaski stood looking up at the young doctor, his tiny face set in a characteristic smile.

"You! How could you?" cried Thomas.

"Och! I am sure the count found it rather easy," interjected Hunter. "I asked him some years ago if he would donate his body to me on his death. For some strange reason he declined, but he offered me a much more interesting proposition."

Thomas looked at the little man askance. "So you betrayed Charles Byrne to save your own skin?"

The count shrugged. "This way only my portrait and not my skeleton will be hung in Dr. Hunter's collection for all to see."

Every nerve ending in Thomas's body tingled with shock. Such unimaginable betrayal left him feeling sick, and his eyes began to fill with tears. He looked over to Charles's skeleton as it dangled helplessly in the air, like a criminal on the end of a rope. Just as his father had been wrongly executed and his body dissected, so, too, was his son being cruelly humiliated in death.

It was then that Thomas recalled the count's efforts to help Charles gain a posthumous pardon for his father. He turned to Boruwlaski. "And what of the pardon? The lawyer?"

The little man shook his head. "There was never any pardon, Thomas. Marchant was working for us." He paused, his squat finger pointing in the air. "But, of course, Charles did ask King George in person for one. So one never knows."

Thomas slumped into a nearby chair, his head in his hands, as if the past few months had all been a dream to him and now he was waking to a nightmare. He looked up, his eyes playing on the skeleton once more. He could see the steel pins at each joint where Hunter had pieced the limbs together after butchering the corpse. The bones were yellowed, too. Thomas could tell they had been bleached in a hurry, so desperate was Hunter to land his prey.

"How could you? How could you?" he muttered, not expecting and not hearing a reply.

Now in death, as in life, Charles Byrne would be an object of morbid curiosity: a freak of nature, a monstrous mutation. Deprived of a decent burial, his only legacy was to remain as an exhibit for all eternity, denied even the right for his own bones to return to dust without the intrusion of the knife and the boiling vat.

"I trust you will say nothing of what you have seen here," said Hunter.

Thomas regarded him with disdain. "So that you are not besieged by others of your kind who would steal the bones? Or because decent people would mob you?"

The anatomist nodded. "Both," he replied curtly.

"I will say nothing," sneered Thomas. "But not to protect you, or you, Count. I will say nothing to protect those who loved and cared for Mr. Byrne." He thought of Lydia and Emily and how such betrayal would be too much for them both to bear.

Slowly he rose and took one last, lingering look at Charles's skeleton. "Rest in peace, my friend," he whispered, and he turned and walked away, his own heart breaking with every step.

Chapter 51

It was no longer to the dead, but to the living that Thomas knew he must now turn his full attention. Time was fast running out if he was to save Leonardo Moreno from his undeserved appointment at the gallows.

It was shortly before noon when he reached Newgate Prison. The familiar stench, as vile as any dissecting room on a hot day, assailed his nostrils as soon as he entered the wealthier prisoners' wing. An ill-visaged jailer led him down the corridor to the small cell and let him inside. A shaft of sunlight had pierced the narrow window high up in the wall, and the Tuscan, hunched on his pallet, was watching dust motes dance like moths in the beam. *This is a good sign,* thought Thomas. *He is still trying to connect with the outside world. He has not given up all hope.* But his optimism was short-lived.

"Signor Moreno, how fare you?" he greeted him.

The prisoner tried to rise, wincing in agony as he pulled himself forward. But the effort seemed too much for him. The past month of incarceration had put twenty years on him. His joints were clearly stiff as starch and his muscles were wasting away.

"Please, stay where you are, sir," urged Thomas. He could not bear to watch such painful exertions. Although the count had kept him updated on the Tuscan's state of mind and body, the young doctor was still shocked by the prisoner's rapid deterioration. Moreno lifted his head. Even his once-lustrous lashes seemed scant and crusted with pus, and his eyes were glazed and listless. Worse still, Thomas could tell they were devoid of hope. The prisoner remained silent.

The young doctor took a chair from the corner of the cell and sat by his patient. "I am come to examine you, Signor Moreno," he said softly, taking him by the hand and feeling for his pulse. It was weak, but not worryingly so.

Next Thomas bade him lie down so that he could inspect his torso. Lifting the soiled shirt, he could see that the wounds were healing well. He ran his fingers over the rib cage. Moreno stifled a cry, but Thomas was satisfied the bones were knitting, although still tender to the touch.

The next area for examination was more delicate. "Will you permit me to look at your other wound, sir?" inquired Thomas tactfully.

Moreno nodded submissively and turned over slowly. The young doctor was swift and efficient in his examination and, mercifully, pronounced the wound completely healed. Although suffering from the deprivations of the cold and damp and a diet deficient in most nutrients, the Tuscan's bodily health was not as bad as Thomas had feared. It was his mind that was in need of healing.

The doctor sat back in his chair, leaving Moreno lying prone, staring up at the stone ceiling. "You are doing well, sir," he said encouragingly.

He saw the Tuscan's lips flicker in an ironic smile. "I do not see that as a reason for cheer," he replied.

"How so?" Thomas frowned.

"I would sooner have died of my wounds than suffer the public indignity of the gallows, Dr. Silkstone."

The young doctor shook his head and leaned nearer the pallet. "I am edging closer to finding the real killer, signor," he said.

The Tuscan turned his head. "You are?"

Thomas nodded. "Yes, but I need to ask you some personal questions."

"Go ahead. I have nothing to lose," he replied, raising his arm in a laconic wave. "You are already privy to my darkest secrets, Dr. Silkstone."

"Did you or Signor Cappelli ever have the need to shave, sir?"

Moreno raised an eyebrow. "No, sir. I have never grown facial hair and Cappelli's skin—" He broke off suddenly and swallowed hard at the sudden recollection of his dead lover. "His skin was as smooth as silk."

It was as Thomas thought. "So can you tell me if you have seen this before?" He bent down and produced the alum block from his bag.

Moreno frowned. "No, sir, I have not," he replied. "But I believe it is something barbers use."

Thomas nodded. "You are right, sir, but I found it in Signor Cappelli's room. Can you think why that should be?"

The Tuscan shook his head. "No, I cannot."

"And he did not visit a barber when he came to London?"

"Why would he? He had all his own powders and pomades. He took great pride in seeing to his own wig and—" Moreno suddenly stopped midsentence.

"What is it, sir?" pressed Thomas.

The Tuscan turned his head to face him. "I recall he complained of a toothache the day after we arrived in London." His features suddenly became animated. "We were rehearsing with Herr Haydn, but Signor Cappelli could not concentrate. He was in too much pain."

"And?"

"And Herr Haydn recommended his barber. He said he was good at pulling teeth and a great deal more besides."

Thomas felt his own heart hammering inside his chest. This could be the breakthrough he needed. Were his suspicions about to be confirmed? "Can you recall the name of the barber?"

Moreno closed his eyes, deep in thought. "He was French," he said finally. "Dubois. His name was Dubois."

Thomas found Smee's Hotel almost deserted. It was midafternoon and there was no one to greet guests. He wandered unheeded into the bar. It smelled of tobacco smoke and stale beer. From the taproom beyond he could hear the sound of a pump and he knew she must be there. There was only one other drinker, and he was distinctly the worse for wear. He was asleep, his matted head resting on the sticky table, a half-empty bottle of gin at his elbow. By the looks of him Thomas guessed he had been imbibing for many hours. He took a seat at a settle in the dingy corner and waited. A few moments later Marie Dubois came into view and headed toward him to take his order, but it was only when she was standing close to him as he sat that he lifted his gaze.

"Is there something you want to tell me?" he asked, fixing the girl straight in the eye.

Marie, her long black hair swept off her face and piled medusa-like on the top of her head, let out an involuntary bleat, like a sacrificial lamb. Quickly she turned to see if anyone had seen the encounter. They were alone, save for the slumbering drunkard.

"I do not understand you, sir," she replied breathlessly, picking up an empty pewter tankard from the next table.

"I think you do, Marie," insisted Thomas. "What was your brother doing in Signor Cappelli's room?"

An expression of panic flashed across her face and the tankard she was holding clattered to the floor. "How do you . . . ?" she blurted.

"Did he bring the alum block? Or was it your father?" pressed Thomas, still looking at her intently. "How much did Carrington pay him for the larynx?" He was bombarding her with accusations like grapeshot, but they were wounding her more than he dared hope. Her eyes darted hither and thither and her breath came in short, sharp rasps. "'Tis over, Marie. Carrington is dead. 'Tis over for you, your brother, your father. . . ."

She was shaking her head now and long strands of hair were breaking loose like writhing snakes. "No!" she hissed. "No!" And grabbing a half full pitcher from the table, she threw the contents at Thomas's face and scrambled toward the door.

Wiping the ale from his eyes, he ran after her and lunged for her just as she reached the threshold. He grabbed her arm. She turned once more to face him, tears now pouring down her cheeks. She was frightened and he suddenly felt sorry for her. "If you tell all you know, the court will be lenient, Marie," he told her. "I know you didn't want to . . . ," he began again, but he did not finish his sentence. Looming behind Marie in the doorway stood her brother, Jean-Paul, and behind him, Dubois himself.

"You were saying, Dr. Silkstone?" said the barber. His manner was oddly self-assured. There was a strange look in his eye and a smirk on his lips. There was no trace of the genteel mien with which he usually greeted his clients. He motioned to his brooding son, who barged past his sobbing sister and rammed Thomas's arms behind his back. The doctor let out a startled cry, but he knew he had to be calm. He did not wish to inflame the barber's passion even more. He had come across patients like him before. They suffered from delusions of grandeur. They needed to be treated with respect.

"You are a fine barber, Monsieur Dubois," said Thomas as Jean-Paul manhandled him onto a nearby settle. The brute forced his hands behind his back, securing them with thick twine that cut into his wrists, but he tried to remain composed.

The Frenchman eyed him, proudly thrusting out his hairless chin. "I am indeed a fine barber, Dr. Silkstone. But I would make an even better surgeon." He arched a brow as he gazed down imperiously at his helpless victim.

It was just as Thomas had suspected. He was suffering from a severe sense of inferiority that had lain festering within him for many years. He would flatter him rather than confront him with the brutal truth.

"But you are the finest in your field, sir. You provide a vital service to so many gentlemen," said Thomas, his words gathering pace. "Your skill is consummate. Your clients speak very highly of you. Why, Herr Haydn—"

"*Tessez-vous!*" cried the barber, clapping his hands. "You talk too much."

"Forgive me, I—"

"Enough, I said!" he barked once more. "I have heard enough from your kind," he sneered.

Thomas swallowed hard. "My kind?"

"You surgeons and anatomists. You think you are so superior. You close your ranks like a cabal. You look down on men like me."

The young doctor could sympathize with these sentiments. He did not care for the superciliousness displayed by his profession. "*I* do not look down on you, sir," he protested. "Neither of us is native here. I am away from my homeland, too. I am not one of those surgeons who puts his own interests above those of his patients. It takes many years of—"

But Dubois did not want to listen. He raised his hand and a tangy scent of lemons filled the air around him. "Enough, I said! You talk too much, Dr. Silkstone."

"I am only trying to—"

"Enough!" Dubois turned and opened a small case he had brought with him. Thomas watched him, sweat now breaking out on his own forehead.

"Do not tell me how many years it takes to become a surgeon. I have served my apprenticeship, Dr. Silkstone. I deserve to be accorded that status," he said, fumbling in his case.

"I do not doubt it, sir, but there—"

"Silence, Dr. Silkstone. You talk too much!" he barked once more before his hands emerged from the case. Thomas's eyes opened wide with terror when he saw what the barber was holding.

"I know a surgical procedure that will help you with your condition, Dr. Silkstone," he said coldly, glaring at Thomas with his weasel eyes. In his left hand he held a razor.

"No, Papa!" screamed Marie, but her father took no notice, walking slowly toward Thomas, the blade held aloft.

The young doctor shuffled on the settle, but Jean-Paul clamped his hands on his shoulders, forcing him down. The barber grabbed hold of Thomas's head and jammed a wodge of gauze between his jaws on either side of his face, wedging open his mouth.

"Normally I would give a patient strong liquor to dull the senses, but I will deny you that, just as I was denied entry into se

Company of Surgeons," he growled. He was bending low now; Thomas could smell his peppermint-scented breath and the lemon scent on his skin. All his senses were suddenly heightened. He could feel his heart beating faster in his chest and his breathing quicken. He could feel the hairs rise on the back of his neck and his guts heaving.

"Now, let me see your tongue, Dr. Silkstone," ordered Dubois, lifting the blade.

Thomas called out, but he could only grunt. His tongue was jammed under the gauze. His shoulders were still clamped hard by the brute as the razor hovered by his cheek. Suddenly he felt an extraordinary surge of energy, like a wave washing over him. The only sound he could hear was his heart pumping rapidly. Taking in great gulps of air and summoning all his might, he drew back his knees and kicked out with both his feet, hitting the barber in the shins and throwing him off balance. He jerked back, crashing into a table. Marie rushed forward and Jean-Paul released his grip on Thomas's shoulders.

Seizing the opportunity, the young doctor leapt up and began running for the door, his hands still bound.

"*Suivez-t'il!*" cried Dubois, steadying himself with a chair. "Don't let him get away!"

Jean-Paul lumbered after him, reaching Thomas just before he made it to the door. Grabbing him by the shoulders, he dragged him back into the room.

"Put him on a chair this time so we can tie his legs," ordered his father.

Once more, the brute pushed Thomas down onto the seat. From his pocket he again produced the twine and, thrusting the doctor's legs apart, he bound each one tightly to a chair leg. There was no way that he could kick out again.

Dubois approached him once more, the blade flashing in his hand. "You must hold still, Dr. Silkstone. I would hate for my blade to slip!" he sneered, bending over Thomas a second time.

The doctor braced himself, clenching his fists so tightly that he could feel his nails cut through the flesh on his palms. He tried to close his mouth, but the gauze was still jammed between his jaws, preventing movement. The blade came closer. He closed his eyes and felt Dubois's pincer fingers against his gums and teeth, probing for his tongue. He would wake soon from this nightmare, he told himself. Any moment now.

Suddenly there was a commotion outside. Shouts could be heard in the hallway. The barber retracted his hand and Thomas opened his eyes to see Dubois motioning to Marie to see what was happening. But she did not get far. Before she reached the threshold, the imposing form of Sir Peregrine Crisp appeared, accompanied by five constables.

"Francois Dubois, I arrest you in the name of His Majesty King George!" he cried. The constables surged forward, heading first for Jean-Paul. Releasing his grip from Thomas's shoulders, he lunged forward, but the constables' cudgels were more than a match for him and he was felled by a blow to the back of his head. Marie did not put up any resistance, but instead of relinquishing the blade, her father remained rooted to the spot, still hunched over Thomas.

"Come closer and I will give this man a shave he will never forget!" Dubois warned Sir Peregrine.

Thomas darted a look at the coroner, then back to Dubois, his eyes wide with terror as he saw the blade flash once more in the candlelight. Just at that moment, the drunkard, who had been sleeping throughout Thomas's ordeal, chose to stir. Dubois saw him from out of the corner of his eye and turned. The constables took their chance. One of them knocked the razor out of his hand with a cudgel while the other pinioned his arms behind his back. He struggled momentarily, cussing and oathing in his native tongue. But he was no match for the burly men who soon pushed him out to a waiting wagon.

Another constable came forward to release Thomas. As soon as his hands had been cut free, the doctor took the gauze out of his mouth. He rubbed his aching face as Sir Peregrine approached.

"I thought you were never going to come, sir," complained Thomas, still clutching his jaw.

"I was in court when I was handed your note, but a moment

longer and we would have been deprived of your dulcet tones forever!" replied the coroner, patting Thomas on the back.

"I am most grateful to you, sir," said Thomas; then, turning toward the drunkard in the corner whose stirrings had distracted Dubois, he called, "And thank you to you, sir, too."

The man, who still appeared stupefied by liquor and unaware of the dramatic scene just played out before him, raised his disheveled head and stared blankly into the distance, trying to focus. Thomas recognized him instantly. It was Mad Sam.

"O'Shea!" he exclaimed.

The Irishman eased himself back into his chair, shaking the fog of strong drink from his head. "Why, Dr. Silkstone!" he cried, his face splitting into a broad smile. "Will you not join me in a drink?"

Thomas paused for a moment. Seeing O'Shea, he was suddenly reminded of the tragic fate of Charles Byrne. He looked at Sir Peregrine. "Forgive me, sir, but I need to talk with this gentleman. I will come to your office later."

The coroner raised an eyebrow. "Very good, Silkstone," he said. "I am sure you could do with a stiff drink."

Thomas walked toward O'Shea, who was already pouring out gin into a tankard. He took out a chair and sat down beside the Irishman.

"I will join you in a drink, sir," said Thomas, who never usually touched gin. "And I would propose a toast."

The young doctor raised his tankard and clinked it against O'Shea's. "To our dear departed friend, Mr. Charles Byrne," he toasted. "May his soul rest in peace," he said, then quietly to himself he added, "even if his body does not." And with that, the two men gulped down their liquor.

Chapter 52

It was mid-June and the sun was high in the sky over Boughton Hall. The red kites soared overhead in the warm thermals and the scent of honeysuckle filled the air. The dissecting rooms of London were a world away and Thomas could at last find the peace he so craved after the past few tumultuous months.

Lydia walked by his side on a path of bleached stones in the gardens. She was fully restored to health and happy to be back at her beloved country home. Yet he noticed she was still quiet, as if something was troubling her. He had not pressed her. He had held off quizzing her since their arrival from London, but now, as they walked arm in arm, surrounded by clipped yew hedges and away from prying eyes and gossiping tongues, he resolved to ask her if anything else troubled her. As they sat on a seat under the shade of a large hornbeam, there was an awkward silence.

"There is something you wish to tell me, is there not?" he said, taking her hand in his.

She looked at him with her large, doleful eyes. "You know me so well." She smiled. "Yes. Yes, there is."

"So?" He lifted her hand and kissed it. "I am listening."

Sighing deeply, she turned her head away, looking into the distance. "You know I told you about Hunter—" She broke off, as if uttering his very name was too much for her. Thomas put his arm around her. "How he tried to kill my baby."

"Yes." Thomas nodded.

She turned abruptly, looking him in the eye. "He did not succeed."

The doctor swallowed hard in amazement. "Go on," he urged.

"Afterward my belly still grew, and four months later I gave birth to a boy."

Thomas looked at her in disbelief. "You have a son?"

She nodded. "He was beautiful. Perfect in every way, apart from his arm." Her voice was now choking with emotion. "It was withered." Thomas thought of Hunter's long needle piercing the uterus. Instead of penetrating the fetus's heart, brain, or lungs to kill it immediately, it must have gone straight through its arm, severing vital arteries. "We called him Richard, after my father, and all was well until the fifth day, when Michael came into the bedroom to tell me he was dead." She wiped away a tear from her cheek. "He said the nurse found him in his cradle. He would not let me hold him, but I could see no sign of life. He was so pale and limp. He called the undertaker and we buried him in Bath."

Thomas held her close. " 'Tis a terrible thing to lose a child," he comforted, but she pulled away. "Michael said nothing. 'Twas as if the babe was never born. I wasn't allowed to say his name. Then, a few weeks later, we made our peace with my mother. Michael renounced all claim to my inheritance and we were married."

The familiar look of hurt and pain had returned to her face once more. No wonder her soul was so tortured, thought Thomas.

She continued: "Nothing was ever said again about Richard, even though I remembered him in my thoughts and prayers every day and longed for another child. But although I was a dutiful wife, I did not conceive." Thomas feared that because of the attempted abortion, she might never be able to bear a child again. He was sure she was aware of that, but he suspected there was more.

She took a deep breath and carried on: "Then, one day, after

Michael's death, I was looking through some of his private papers and I came across some bills."

"What sort of bills?" urged Thomas.

"They were from a wet nurse, and they were for the care of Richard Michael Farrell."

Thomas did not try to hide his shock. "So you think the child lives?"

"I wrote a letter to her, but she replied saying that because no one had paid the bills for a while and letters to Michael had gone unanswered, she had given Richard's care over to a workhouse." Her tears were flowing freely now, but Thomas wiped them away and smiled. Finally he had found that source of the deep, terrible pain that had caused Lydia so much suffering. For a long time he had suspected that despite everything that she had endured since the death of her brother, there was something else, something more, that had been eating away like a cancer. Now he knew what it was he could try, like any good physician, to devise a remedy for it. The treatment might prove painful, but he would endeavor to heal her the only way he knew how. He slipped his hands in hers and held them tight. "I promise you," he told her, fully understanding her pain for the first time, "if your son lives, we shall find him, as God is my witness."

Back in London, five men met in an upper room. One of their number was absent. They were in a black humor as they sat 'round a large table.

"Gentlemen, I am afraid I have bad news to report," announced Sir Oliver De Vere. "Our plans seem to have received a setback."

They mumbled and murmured over their claret; Keate, Gunning, Walker, and Home. Their master explained: "You may have heard that Giles Carrington died in Margate; a most unfortunate accident."

"Or fortunate," piped up Keate.

"How so, sir?" pressed Walker.

"At least he could not reveal that he was on our mission."

General agreement was voiced at this remark, but Sir Oliver

continued: "As for Monsieur Dubois, the bitter and twisted Frenchman so anxious to join our ranks on completion of his task, he was arrested for the castrato's murder, and his son sent to Bedlam."

"I hear we have that colonist, Silkstone, with his newfangled science to thank for scuppering our plans," ventured Gunning.

At the mention of Thomas's name there was a collective jeer. "Yes, Silkstone is a thorn in our side."

"Was it not he who Charlesworth was about to consult over his reforms?" interrupted Gunning.

"Yes, he and Hunter," replied Sir Oliver.

"So how did Silkstone uncover our barber?" asked Keate.

"He traced the castrato's alum block back to the salon," revealed Sir Oliver. "There was a lock of the boy's hair at the murder scene, too. The daughter broke under questioning."

"The girl at the inn?" asked Home.

"The very same. She confessed to letting her father and brother into the room."

"And the prizefighter?" asked Gunning. "Was he not charged, as we planned?"

"No. The girl blabbed that she was put up to it by her father. There was no evidence against Crouch."

"Will the Frenchman talk?" asked Walker.

Sir Oliver smiled. "There is no fear of that, gentlemen." He smirked. "He slit his own throat before he said any more. Rather apt, don't you think?"

Gunning huffed. "I did not think he had the wit to do such a thing after what we saw. Eh, Keate?" He glanced over to his colleague. "Well, I hope his corpse ended up at St. George's."

"Like the carter's." His colleague chuckled.

Nervous laughter rippled 'round the room.

"And the sodomite has gone free?" queried Home.

"Sadly, yes. There is no justice, gentlemen," mocked Sir Oliver.

"So now we will renew our efforts to destroy Hunter's name?" asked Gunning.

"Indeed," replied Sir Oliver, stroking his chin enigmatically.

The other men leaned forward, elbows on the table, their interest piqued. "I have devised another, more subtle plan," he told them and, gesturing toward the door, he called out: "Mr. Foot."

At this bidding a dapper little gentleman with a haughty air entered the room, a bundle of papers under his arm. He bowed graciously.

The master introduced him. "Mr. Foot is known to you all, gentlemen, as a surgeon of impeccable integrity," he began. "He has been gathering evidence against the Scotch heathen for a number of years now and he plans to write the man's biography. I put it to you, sirs, that the quill is mightier than the sword. So, from now on, instead of the cutthroat razor, the pen will be our weapon with which to slay this scourge of our sacred profession." And with that the surgeons raised their glasses in a toast. "To Galen," they cried, "and the destruction of Dr. John Hunter, the most reviled anatomist that ever lived."

Postscript

D r. John Hunter waited two years to reveal the existence of Charles Byrne's skeleton, and then only to close associates. It can be seen to this day hanging at the Hunterian Museum at the Royal College of Surgeons in London. In 1909, a postmortem examination revealed Charles Byrne suffered from a tumor in his pituitary, the gland responsible for producing a growth hormone. In 2010 the results of tests carried out on his bones by Professor Márta Korbonits of Barts Hospital, London, were published in the *New England Journal of Medicine*. They revealed that Byrne and up to 300 living patients inherited their genetic variant from the same common ancestor and that this mutation is some 1,500 years old. The study of Charles Byrne's bones makes it possible to trace carriers of this gene and treat patients before they grow to be giants.

John Hunter died in 1793 after an attack of angina, brought on by a particularly heated meeting with the board of St. George's Hospital regarding various reforms he wished implemented. He was also betrayed by his brother-in-law, another surgeon, named Everard Home, who either plagiarized or destroyed much of his writing. Jesse Foot published his scurrilous biography in 1794.

Hunter's remains lay forgotten in the vaults of the church of St. Martin-in-the-Fields, off what is now Trafalgar Square, London, until a young army surgeon discovered them in 1859 and had them reinterred to the north nave of Westminster Abbey.

Three years later the Royal College of Surgeons affixed a plaque. Part of the inscription reads: *The Royal College of Surgeons of England has placed this tablet on the grave of Hunter to record admiration of his genius, as a gifted interpreter of the Divine power and wisdom at work in the laws of organic life and its grateful veneration for his services to mankind as the founder of scientific surgery.*

Glossary

Chapter 1

St. Bride's: The church itself was designed by Sir Christopher Wren. When in 1764 its steeple was struck by lightning, Benjamin Franklin was asked to design a lightning conductor for it, but there was a row between the inventor and King George III as to the shape of the ends of the rods. The king finally won the day, much to the delight of the British press, which praised their sovereign as "good blunt honest George" while Franklin was described as "a sharp-witted colonist."

sack 'em up men: The London anatomist Joshua Brookes refused to pay a retainer to a gang of resurrectionists and found a rotting corpse on his doorstep. His neighbors were so scandalized that they almost beat him to death.

grave-clothes: Thanks to a quirk of English law, to steal a shroud or a coffin was considered a crime against the property of a dead man's heirs and subject to stiff punishment, and even hanging, but a man did not own his own body.

Leicester Fields: John Hunter's premises spanned an area between what is now Leicester Square and what used to be Castle Street. The strange configuration of the premises, with two distinct entrances, one where polite society entered and the other where corpses were brought at night, is believed to have inspired Robert Louis Stevenson's *Dr. Jekyll and Mr. Hyde.*

Hunter moved there in 1783. He is also believed to have been the model for Mary Shelley's Victor Frankenstein.

measured the length: Anatomists would pay resurrectionists for a corpse by measurement. A child would be priced around a guinea while an adult might fetch four guineas. (A guinea was twenty-one shillings.)

Chapter 2

Count Josef Boruwlaski (1739–1837) was born in Poland. He measured only twenty-five inches. He toured Europe and ended up living in Durham, England, where there is a life-size statue of him. In England he enjoyed the patronage of the fashionable Duchess of Devonshire. It is not known how he came by his title.

showman: Joe Vance was also Charles Byrne's agent.

Giant Byrne: Charles Byrne sometimes used the stage name O'Brien to link him with a long line of giants descended from Brian Boru, the legendary nine-foot-tall Irish king.

The Phoenix: A lugger that was wrecked off Newquay, Cornwall, in 1781.

didicoys: Gypsies.

Chapter 3

The Gazetteer and New Daily Advertiser: Published from April 27, 1764, until November 1796.

St. George's Hospital: Originally where the Lanesborough Hotel stands today, it was at Hyde Park Corner. The location was chosen because it was in the countryside, where the air was cleaner.

Gunning, Keate, and Walker: John Gunning bore a grudge against John Hunter, believing he was better qualified for a post at St. George's Hospital. Thomas Keate was Gunning's assistant.

William Walker was one of Gunning's surgical colleagues.

St. James's Church: In Jermyn Street, just off Piccadilly, it was designed by Sir Christopher Wren and was once the most fashionable church in London.

Lord North: The first British prime minister forced out of office by a motion of no confidence. He resigned in March 1782 because of the British defeat at Yorktown the year before.

cock's comb: John Hunter conducted several experiments on living animals. Samuel Johnson was one of the few thinkers of the day who condemned such cruelty.

William Hunter: John Hunter's elder brother, he established himself as an anatomist in London years before.

addressed a skeleton: Although most of John Hunter's lectures were well attended, he sometimes struggled to attract an audience and reportedly addressed a skeleton.

Chapter 4

old Araby: An archaic reference to the Arabian Peninsula.

ring from Marie Antoinette: Count Boruwlaski relates the episode in his memoirs when one of Maria Theresa's children gave him a diamond ring. Legend has it that the child was the young Marie Antoinette (then called Maria Antonia). However, there is a discrepancy with the dates and, as all the daughters of the empress had the first name Maria, the count was probably confused.

Kings of Ireland: There was a great blurring of lines between Irish myth and fact when it came to tales of past leaders.

St. Giles: The area in London most associated with an Irish population during the eighteenth century, with many engaged in seasonal labor and street selling. It was also one of the most depraved areas of the city with regular murders, rapes, illegal gambling, and cockfighting.

rookeries: The slum houses were called "rookeries" because the name suggested people were packed into nests.

Chapter 5

coach from London to Oxford: From 1671 there was a daily coach service from London to Oxford during the summer. The coach left at six A.M. from Thomas More's house near All-Souls College in Oxford and arrived in London later the same day. In London it left from the Saracens Head on Snow Hill.

a Negro slave with a rare skin condition: In 1792 a freed black man named Henry Moss started to turn white and began exhibiting himself. He became a sensation. He suffered from vitiligo, a condition in which skin cells fail to produce melanin.

a white woman without arms or legs: The records of the Pennsylvania Academy of the Fine Arts show that Sarah Rogers exhibited a landscape painting in 1811.

Count Boruwlaski wrote an autobiography: *Memoirs Of Count Boruwlaski.*

St. Bartholomew's Fair: A charter fair that ran from 1133 to 1855, when it was suppressed because of the lewd behavior it encouraged.

lodgings: While Charles Byrne did lodge at Cockspur Street, near Trafalgar Square, the count had lodgings nearby at 55 Jermyn Street, just opposite Hunter's house at the time, courtesy of Georgiana the Duchess of Devonshire, who was his patron.

Spring Gardens: A short street 'round the corner from Cockspur Street.

Lincoln's Inn: One of four Inns of Court in London to which barristers of England and Wales belong.

Chapter 6

control nature itself: Hunter conducted several experiments on cross-breeding and successfully mated a cow with a buffalo belonging to the Marquis of Rockingham.

Anne Hunter: John Hunter's wife was a minor poet and librettist. Her social literary parties were renowned at the time.

Franz Joseph Haydn: The Austrian composer visited London twice, but not until the 1790s. He did work on librettos with Anne Hunter during this time.

Chapter 7

the white death: Many names were given to tuberculosis. Others included consumption and *phthisis* (Greek for "consumption").

Candlemas: A Christian feast day in February, marking the presentation of Jesus in the Temple.

Chapter 8

linkmen: Men who held lanterns to guide travelers through the streets.

footpads: Highway robbers who worked on foot rather than on horseback.

Ben Crouch: A former porter at Guy's Hospital, he was also a prizefighter. He was described as "a powerful, overbearing man with a pockmarked face and filthy temper." He had risen to command the notorious London Borough Gang "because he was of superior intelligence and did not get drunk as often as the others." (Cole, H., *Things for the Surgeon*. London: Heineman, 1964.)

Jack Hartnett: Crouch's accomplice who, on his death, left an estate of £6,000.

St. Martin-in-the-Fields: The church was opened on Christmas Day 1733 and remains very little altered by Trafalgar Square.

John Howison: A shadowy figure who conducted various nefarious duties for both William and John Hunter.

Chapter 9

Knipe brothers: Identical twins born in 1761 in Ireland, they both measured seven feet two inches. They exhibited themselves in London in April 1785.

knobbed whelk (Busycon carica gmelin): Designated by New Jersey as the official state shell in 1995.

ear horn: The first stethoscope was not invented until 1816 by René Laennec in France.

Galen: A Roman gladiatorial surgeon (130–200 A.D.), who was the first to recognize that pus from wounds inflicted by the gladiators heralded healing (*pus bonum et laudabile* ["good and commendable pus"]).

bloodletting: Many Georgians, whether ill or not, routinely asked to be bled. As much as thirty ounces of blood would be taken at a time.

Everard Home: John Hunter's brother-in-law and one of his pupils. He was quick to betray him after his death.

educated in the classics: John Hunter's brother William sent him to St. Mary Hall, within Oriel College, Oxford, but he left after only two months.

Chapter 10

Dr. James Graham (1745–1794): He was a charlatan and a pioneer in sex therapy. At his Temple of Health and Hymen, housed in a magnificent building at London's Adelphi, "maidens" would perform educative sex acts and his electrical apparatus supposedly encouraged fertility.

celestial bed: The huge, elaborate bed had a tilting inner frame that supposedly put couples in the best position to conceive. Dr. Graham gave Charles Byrne a personal invitation to try it out, although this was declined. One newspaper stated Byrne declared himself to be "a perfect stranger to the rites and mysteries of the Goddess Venus."

red and white striped pole: The modern barber pole originated in the days when bloodletting was one of the principal duties of the barber. The two spiral ribbons painted around the pole represent the two long bandages, one twisted around the arm before bleeding and the other used to bind it afterward.

giving clysters: To give an enema.

Act of Parliament: In 1745 the Company of Barber-Surgeons was dissolved when the surgeons split from the barbers to form the Company of Surgeons.

nasal polyps: Haydn suffered from nasal polyposis for much of his adult life; this was an agonizing and debilitating disease in the eighteenth century, and at times it prevented him from writing music.

white lead powder: By now many women were no longer wearing the heavy white-lead makeup used since Elizabethan times.

Hanover Square Rooms: Also known as the Queen's Concert Rooms and opened in 1741, these were London's main assembly rooms established principally for musical performances.

Chapter 11

a salty pearl: Bladder stones, although sometimes confused with kidney stones, were very common in the eighteenth century, especially among those with diets high in animal protein. Diarist Samuel Pepys underwent the operation to remove the stones, known as a lithotomy, in 1658. The surgeon at St. Thomas's Hospital removed a stone "the size of a tennis ball." Pepys, of course, survived.

Chapter 12

liable to swing: Up until 1832, stealing a corpse was only a misdemeanor at common law, not a felony, and was therefore only punishable with fine and imprisonment, rather than transportation or execution.

lain with a child virgin: It was a common belief that sex with a child cured venereal disease.

Covent Garden or Haymarket: These areas were particularly noted for prostitution. An estimated 63,000 prostitutes lived in London in the 1700s, making a staggering one in five women "whores."

syphilis: It is widely believed that the disease was first brought to Europe by the returning crewmen from Christopher Columbus's voyage to the Americas at the end of the fifteenth century.

mercury that poisoned the blood: The mercuric chloride used to treat syphilis was so toxic that it sometimes poisoned its users and the symptoms were confused with those of the disease it was supposed to treat.

study the disease in depth: Hunter wrongly believed syphilis and gonorrhea were manifestations of different symptoms of the same sexual illness. An entry in his copious notes implies that he did, indeed, infect himself.

lancet: Used to prick the skin, the word is derived from a lance once carried by knights in the fifteenth century.

Chapter 13

half crown: Two shillings and six pence.

Lincoln's Inn Archway: Built in 1697, it is one of three principal entrances to the Inn and leads to New Square.

a pantomime: Harlequin Teague; or, The Giant's Causeway ran for nearly a month at the Haymarket Theatre.

King's Bench: Around 60 percent of those sentenced to death in the eighteenth century were pardoned.

troubles over the years: The relationship between Irish Catholics and the ruling English Protestant government had long been difficult. Political power rested in the hands of Anglo-Irish settler-colonials, while Catholics were penalized.

Chapter 14

Haydn chased by Dr. Hunter: An account of the episode was given by Haydn himself. He wrote: "It seemed to me that he pitied me for not wanting to undergo the happy experience of enjoying his skill."

Italian states: Before 1851 the country of Italy did not exist. Instead the area was made up of several principalities.

Chapter 15

menagerie at the Tower of London: The first guidebook to the Tower was published in 1741. Animals listed included the lions Marco and Phillis and their son Nero.

Signor Carlo Cappelli: The most famous castrato of the day was Carlo Maria Broschi, known on the stage as Farinelli (1705–1782). He was one of the greatest singers in the history of opera.

your knife into that young singer: In 2006 the exhumation and examination of Farinelli's remains were carried out by the Centro Studi Farinelli, an independent society in Bologna, with the aim of learning more about the physique and physiology of a castrato.

Chapter 16

Westminster coroner: In Westminster, a district of London, the **coroner** was appointed by the Dean and Chapter of Westminster Abbey.

It was furnished comfortably: Wardrobes did not come into fashion until the nineteenth century. Clothes were usually laid flat in drawers.

an alum block: Used by barbers as an astringent after shaving, the block, which was usually mixed with potassium, also acted as a blood coagulant.

Chapter 17

Bologna and Rome: There were several communities of castrati living in and around Bologna, Rome, Naples, and Venice at the time.

philandering: The celebrated castrato Venanzio Rauzzini (1746–1810) was chased out of the courts of Europe for his sexual antics with noblewomen. He settled in Bath, England.

Chapter 18

physician to the queen: Although no man-midwife was allowed to attend Queen Charlotte, William Hunter examined several royal babies shortly after birth, as well as looking after the recovering mother.

The Royal Society: Founded in 1660, with King Charles II's approval, it was a group of eminent scientists and philosophers, including Sir Christopher Wren and Robert Hooke.

observations on fossil bones: John Hunter was at odds with the established thought, maintaining that fossils took "many thousand years" to form.

Galileo persecuted: In 1633 Galileo was found "vehemently suspect of heresy" for believing the sun and not the earth lay at the center of the universe, according to the Catholic Church. He lived under house arrest for the rest of his life.

Newton: The great scientist Isaac Newton opposed King James II, who wanted only Roman Catholics to be in positions of power in government and academia.

Archbishop Ussher: James Ussher (1581–1656) was Archbishop of Armagh, and his theory about the age of the world prevailed among many until the eighteenth century.

Beauty and the Beast: Originally a French fairy tale, the most popular version was translated into English in 1757.

Chapter 20

a child's poppet: A doll.

Chapter 21

Earls Court: The district was a quiet village in the 1780s, about two miles outside London.

famous collection of species: Much of John Hunter's collection was destroyed in the Blitz; however, thousands of specimens remain and are housed today in the Hunterian Museum, London.

villa of brick: John Hunter purchased farmland at Earls Court in 1765, but his house was not completed until 1783. Lightning conductors, invented by his friend Benjamin Franklin, were installed on the chimney stacks. The house was demolished in 1886.

a lion: John Hunter built three subterranean dens in which to house his collection of wild cats.

nine vulpine monsters: Wolves, jackals, and dogs were penned together. One litter produced nine hybrids out of a jackal bitch and a mastiff.

wing bones: Experimenting on birds from his own aviary, John Hunter proved that air sacs in their bone cavities communicate with the lungs.

affairs of the heart: Count Boruwlaski married a French noblewoman, Isalina Borboutin, of normal height.

Chapter 22

cur: Slang for a mixed-breed dog.

easement of irons: Everything had its price in Newgate. For a fee the leg irons, worn constantly by all prisoners, could be removed. Extra food, bedding, alcohol, and water could also be provided.

hangings at Tyburn: The gallows at Tyburn stood on the area known as Hyde Park today. Executions were held at eight A.M. on Monday mornings. A multiple hanging might attract around one hundred thousand people. The gallows were last used in November 1783.

scrofula: A type of tuberculosis affecting the lymphatic system around the neck. It was also known as King's Evil because it was widely held that a king's touch could cure it.

Chapter 23

scragged: Slang for "hanged."

Corporation of Surgeons: Each year six hanged criminals were dissected by members of the Corporation.

Chapter 25

Garrick: David Garrick was considered the finest actor of his day. He died in 1779.

small beer: Weak ale. Water was considered so dangerous to drink that even children drank beer. Some hospitals allowed patients three pints a day free of charge.

sodomite: The penalty for homosexuality was death.

molly house: A tavern or private room where homosexual men could meet.

Chapter 26

ancient or modern history: This quotation is from the *Morning Herald* newspaper, which sang Byrne's praises on more than one occasion.

Daniel Solander: A Swedish botanist who worked in the new British Museum, he died suddenly, aged forty-nine, from a stroke, and Hunter did not hesitate to dissect his friend.

Chapter 27

remove the painful polyps: Haydn underwent surgery several times to remove the polyps, but they kept reoccurring.

Chapter 28

cauldron: A sketch of this vat, housed in a brick casing, can be seen in the Hunterian Museum.

Marquis of Rockingham: John Hunter was one of the many surgeons who attended the British prime minister, who suffered terrible abdominal pain during his second term in office in 1782. On his death, Hunter performed a postmortem, but it proved inconclusive. He did, however, note that the valves to the arteries of the heart were partly furred.

Chapter 29

sack 'em up man: A resurrectionist. See Chapter 1.

mortsafe: A framework of iron bars used to protect graves from robbers.

Chapter 31

There is no health in my flesh: Psalm 38:3–6.

poisonous vapor: Laurel water is a poison whose chief toxic component is cyanide, which is distilled from laurel cherries. Diluted, it was used primarily for bronchial ailments.

pink bloom: A sign that is sometimes found when cyanide poisoning has occurred is a red or pink discoloration of the skin.

placing his own lips on hers: Dr. H. R. Silvester is said to have pioneered what was known as the Silvester Method. First appearing in the *British Medical Journal* in 1858, the position of the prostrate patient's arms was alternated between above the head and against the chest to help respiration. The practice is now obsolete.

Chapter 32

large quantities: Contemporary experiments on two ounces of undiluted laurel water showed it took a greyhound thirty seconds to die in convulsions. The Emperor Nero also used it to poison members of his family.

Chapter 33

Corny Magrath: A famous giant, Cornelius Magrath was born in 1736 in Ireland. When he died in 1760, mourners were drugged and his body was stolen for dissection by students at Trinity College, Dublin. His bones were preserved and put on show. They still remain at the college.

sent far away: Up until the American Revolution some British convicts were sent to North America; however, after 1776 this practice stopped and the British were forced to look elsewhere, to the newly discovered Australia.

Chapter 34

Old Bailey: The origins of the Central Criminal Court date back to the late sixteenth century, but the court was rebuilt in 1774.

sodomite: There were a number of homosexual castrati, as Casanova's accounts of eighteenth-century Italy testify.

wap: Slang for "to have sex with."

moon-cursor: A link boy or man (see chapter 8) who robs his clients or leads them into a gang of robbers in the dark.

pleaded their bellies: Pregnant women often asked for clemency. At the Old Bailey between 1674 and 1830, 268 women who were sentenced to death claimed pregnancy. However, the Murder Act of 1752, making hanging for murder mandatory within two days of sentence, made this far less likely.

a large glass mirror: A mirrored reflector was placed above the bar or dock in the courtroom so that light from the windows would illuminate the faces of the accused, so the jury could see their expressions. A sounding board over their heads also amplified their voices.

musico: A derogatory term for a castrato in the eighteenth century.

Chapter 35

Kew Palace: A royal palace on the banks of the Thames, favored by King George III before his madness.

Chapter 36

Whigs and Tories: The main political parties of the time.

Mr. Katterfelto: His solar microscope afforded views of insects.

Mr. Breslaw: A magician and mind reader.

Patrick Cotter O'Brien: An Irish giant who arrived in England in 1779 and exhibited himself in Bristol.

Chapter 37

rhinoceros hair: Bristles were sometimes used to show where blood vessels began or ended. Rhinoceros hair was considered ideal.

lizard with a double tail: Hunter captured this while serving in the army on an island off Brittany, France. It is preserved in the Hunterian Museum.

Chapter 38

move premises: John Howison even took rooms near Byrne. He was listed in the parish rates books at No. 12 Cockspur Street for a while in 1783. Byrne moved lodgings several times in order to avoid him.

piercing the mound of her rounding belly: While there is no written evidence that John Hunter performed abortions in this manner, he did assist in terminating the pregnancy of Mary, Countess of Strathmore, by giving her "a black inky kind of medicine" to drink.

abortions: These were not illegal in the United Kingdom until 1803 when "making an abortion after quickening" became a capital crime.

Chapter 39

a very special piece of paper: From 1725 the Bank of England issued partly printed banknotes for completion in manuscript. The £ sign and the first digit were printed but other details had to be written. By 1745 denominations ranged from £20 to £1,000.

English Channel: The term "English Channel" may have come from the Dutch *Engelse Kanaal,* used on Dutch maps since the sixteenth century.

Chapter 41

Ancient Library of Alexandria: Created in the third century B.C., in Alexandria, Egypt, this was the largest and most significant great library of the ancient world.

Chapter 42

Greenland harpooners: The *Morning Herald* described the anatomists as clamoring after the giant's body "just as Greenland harpooners would an enormous whale."

William Cruikshank and Matthew Baillie at the Great Windmill Street: The two anatomists succeeded William Hunter in the running of his famous anatomy school.

John Sheldon: The anatomist lived with the preserved body of a woman in a glass case in his bedroom for ten years.

hide himself in the giant's box: The *Morning Herald* reported that an anatomist had ordered a niche made for himself in the giant's coffin, so that he would be on hand at the "witching time of night, when church-yards yawn."

blood that spilled: Charles Byrne died on Sunday, June 1, 1783.

Chapter 43

Pidcock: An animal dealer who owned a menagerie in the Strand.

coffin in the sea: It is believed that it was Byrne's express wish that he be buried in a lead coffin at sea, although no direct evidence of his burial wishes survives.

Chapter 45

boundary stone: From 1550 the bridge along the route from London out to Southwark, toward Kent, was regarded as the limit of the City of London's authority. There is still a boundary stone stating this.

Thomas a Becket inn: St. Thomas-a-Watering was the first rest stop on the journey to Kent where travelers would traditionally water their horses. The history of the landmark pub near this site, called the Thomas a Becket, cannot, however, be traced back further than 150 years.

epiphyses: The ends of long bones, originally separated from the main bones by a layer of cartilage but later united to the main bones through ossification.

duelist's jejunum: The piece of intestine with a bullet hole in it belonged to Colonel Frederick Thomas, who was killed in an illegal duel in 1787. John Hunter attended the man, but there was nothing he could do to save him.

for study and posterity: John Hunter was a man of extraordinary vision. His preservation of Charles Byrne's skeleton led, in 2011, to the discovery of a gene that causes a certain form of giantism.

an aneurysm in his leg: Hunter pioneered a new technique in this field that went on to save countless lives.

Chapter 46

Gravesend: A major crossing point of the Thames since the fourteenth century. The Native American princess Pocahontas, who was married to an early Virginia settler, died here before returning to America. There is a statue of her in St. Giles's Churchyard.

cara: Irish for "friend."

Chapter 47

water buffaloes: John Hunter drove a cart pulled by three Asiatic water buffaloes.

What mysteries did this skull hold? Byrne's skull was opened in 1909 and traces of a pituitary tumor that caused a hormonal imbalance were discovered.

Chapter 48

Reculver: The twin towers of Reculver's ruined church, nicknamed the two sisters, are the main landmark along the stretch of coast from Herne Bay to Margate.

pier: Up until the end of the eighteenth century Margate Harbor was protected by a timber pier that ran from east to west in a crescent shape.

hoys: Small coastal sailing ships which carried goods and occasional passengers.

diving bells: A newspaper reported that some anatomists had "provided a pair of diving bells, with which they hope to weigh hulk gigantic from its watery grave."

Thou shalt not be afraid . . . : Psalm 91:5–7.

coffin plunge into the sea: Charles Byrne was supposedly buried at sea on June 5, 1783. The *Edinburgh Evening Courant* reported, "Yesterday morning the body of Byrne, the famous Irish Giant, who died a few days ago, was carried to Margate, in order to be thrown into the sea, agreeable to his own request, he having been apprehensive that the surgeons would anatomise him."

Chapter 49

carefully scooped up: The dustpan was not invented until the mid-nineteenth century.

in his cups: A phrase dating back to the Bible, meaning "to be drunk."

litmus paper: The lichen-based paper was brought into general use first in the 1600s by Robert Boyle (1627–1691).

a long, black hair: Dr. Edmond Locard (1877–1966) was a pioneer in forensic science. His exchange principle states that the culprit always leaves something behind.

Chapter 50

mangy mongrel: John Hunter performed a number of experiments on living dogs which involved shocking acts of cruelty. Three live sheep and an ass were also used to prove his theories.

measuring almost eight feet tall: While alive Byrne is said to have measured eight feet two inches. His skeleton measures seven feet and eight inches.

only my portrait: A portrait of Boruwlaski, painted in 1782 by Philip Reinagle, hung in Hunter's museum for many years. It is now on display at the Hunterian Museum.

an exhibit for all eternity: Byrne's skeleton remains on show at the Hunterian Museum at the Royal College of Surgeons, London.

decent people would mob you: It was not until 1787 that Hunter wrote to Sir Joseph Banks of the Royal Society to say: "I lately got a tall man. But at the time could make no particular observations. I hope next summer to be able to show him."

Chapter 52

Bedlam: Short for Bethlem Royal Hospital, this was an asylum in London for the insane.

THE DEAD SHALL NOT REST

Tessa Harris

ABOUT THIS GUIDE

The suggested questions are included
to enhance your group's reading of Tessa Harris's
The Dead Shall Not Rest.

Discussion Questions

1. What are the parallels between the powerful physicians in the novel and the multinational drug companies of today?

2. How does Thomas develop as a character in this, the second book in the series?

3. Does the course of the War of Independence affect any attitudes toward Thomas in this book?

4. Anatomists in the eighteenth century found corpses so hard to come by that they were forced to turn to grave robbers for a regular supply. Nowadays, more people donate their bodies to science. Would you?

5. Should organ donation be made compulsory?

6. Freak shows have long been considered an affront to human dignity, but in an age with little social welfare, what was the alternative for the severely disabled?

7. Charles Byrne and Count Boruwlaski both have major disabilities but are treated in very different ways. Why is this so, and how would they be treated today?

8. How far do revelations about Lydia's past go to explain her submissive character?

9. Was John Hunter a medical visionary or an evil obsessive?

10. Charles Byrne's skeleton remains on display in the Hunterian Museum in London to this day. Should he be given a proper burial?